The Hush

Books by Sara Foster

Come Back to Me
Beneath the Shadows
Shallow Breath
All That Is Lost between Us
The Hidden Hours
You Don't Know Me
The Hush

The Hush

SARA FOSTER

BLACK STONE
PUBLISHING

Copyright © 2021 by Sara Foster
Published in 2021 by Blackstone Publishing
Cover design by Darren Holt, HarperCollins Design Studio

The characters and events in this book are fictitious.
Any similarity to real persons, living or dead, is coincidental
and not intended by the author.

Printed in the United States of America

ISBN 978-1-6651-0685-6
Fiction / Thrillers / Suspense

Version 1

CIP data for this book is available
from the Library of Congress

Blackstone Publishing
31 Mistletoe Rd.
Ashland, OR 97520

www.BlackstonePublishing.com

For Marian
And in loving memory of Dorothy and Jill

When, lo, as they reached the mountain-side,
A wondrous portal opened wide,
As if a cavern was suddenly hollowed;
And the Piper advanced, and the children followed,
And when all were in to the very last,
The door in the mountain-side shut fast.

Robert Browning,
The Pied Piper of Hamelin: A Child's Story

PART I

first stage

[CLASSIFIED DOC]

SENT THROUGH PRIVATE SERVER,
FROM MI5 TO THE PRIME MINISTER'S OFFICE AT 10
DOWNING STREET

URGENT

The YouTube site hosted by PreacherGirl has been permanently taken down.

Total views: 4,065,341.

Police task force Delta will continue to look for the person behind the "PreacherGirl" pseudonym.

As agreed, all media inquiries will be dealt with by the Press Secretary's office.

Out of the twelve girls originally mentioned as missing, three have been located at home.

Out of the twenty-six girls mentioned in the comments by site viewers, eleven have been located at home.

This leaves a total of twenty-four girls, names appended, whose whereabouts are still unknown.

Possible link to Project 9.

We need to talk.

1.

A distant siren merges into the staccato shriek of an alarm clock, and Lainey's dream slips away. She comes to in her own bed, her body heavy on the sagging mattress, the weight of the blanket pressing her down. Rolling over, she gives the alarm clock a whack, hoping it hasn't woken her mother. From his basket nearby, Fergus lets out a low grunt. Beside the bed, there's fluttering and rustling.

She sits up and rubs her eyes. Her room is still dark, full of shadowy cubist shapes. Although the autumn temps have dropped already, she hasn't turned on her heater yet, and the morning air is chilly. It's raining outside, and the rush of water is a million murmuring voices, cajoling, soothing, warning, impatient. *Get moving*, they say. *Get this done.*

Lainey hesitates, thinking of her plans this morning. There's an icy lump in her belly. And she hasn't accounted for rain.

She tiptoes to the bathroom, alert for any other sound. All is quiet. She sits on the toilet with her head in her hands, staring at the scrappy fabric of her knickers caught at her knees. If she stays here and prays hard enough, something might change. Except she doesn't believe in miracles.

Finally, she gets up to wash her face and brush her teeth. Her hands

3

shake as she gulps water from the tap, and she sighs. If this is going to work, she needs to stay calm.

Back in her room, she moves stealthily, gathering what she needs. She gives Fergus a few treats then unclips her watch, attaching it to his front right paw. Fergus looks mournfully at it, then his trusting brown eyes turn toward hers.

"Sorry, buddy," she tells him, stroking the spaniel's ears and kissing the soft swatch of fur between his eyes. "I need you to cover for me. I won't be long." She still feels paranoid doing this, but now the watches are compulsory, day and night, and she can't risk being tracked for the next hour or so.

Before leaving, she pulls the pillowcase off a large container by her bedside. Three fluffy-feathered baby starlings begin to chirp, tiny beaks bursting open like bright-yellow petals. She's only had them for fourteen days, but they've changed so much already from the half-feathered scruffs she'd rescued from a nest, shielding them from the sight of their dead mother, who'd lain at the base of the sycamore tree, decapitated by a passing predator. It had been fortunate Lainey had seen the hollow and checked it, but then she is always looking out for animals in need.

She grabs the tub of mealworms and presoaked dry cat food, pulls off the cellophane, then dips tweezers into the gunk before offering tiny portions to each waiting mouth. The last two weeks of her holidays had been taken up by their feeding demands: every half an hour at first, then gradually eking out the time and encouraging them to start eating independently. They can manage for a few hours now, but still prefer being hand-fed.

After a few rounds of this, they settle. "I'll be back soon," she reassures them, and replaces the cover. "Take care of them, Fergus."

Fergus whines softly and rests his chin on his front paws, head leaning leftward, avoiding the watch.

Lainey surveys the room for a moment, checking all is okay, then hoists her bag over her shoulder. Time is ticking. She creeps down the dimly lit stairs, wincing at every creak. If she can just get outside, then her mother mightn't even realize she's gone.

At the bottom of the stairs, she unlatches the door. It opens to a gloom-struck scene: dark, dismal, wet. Beyond the low gate, ten paces away, a truck drives past the terraced houses, wheels spinning and whooshing in the puddles. Lainey turns and slowly, cautiously, closes the door behind her. There's the faintest of clicks. Seconds later, she is beyond the safe confines of home, head bowed, sprinting toward town.

6:55 a.m.

Emma listens to Lainey's slight footsteps; hears the soft shutting of the door. She jumps out of bed and hurries to the window, watching the silhouette of her daughter disappearing into the gloaming beyond the streetlamps. *Where the hell is she going? It's not even seven, for Christ's sake.*

But there's no time to speculate. She grabs the thermometer by the bedside and holds it close to her forehead until it beeps, indicating the wireless transfer of data to the hospital. Next she takes a swab from a packet in her top drawer and pops it into her mouth, sucking on it for a few seconds, trying to ignore its gritty dryness against her tongue. She removes it and sees the color is blue. Neutral. Next, she runs her watch over the tiny barcode at its base, until another beep tells her this data has also been delivered. After ten seconds, her watch lights up with one small word on the screen: *Negative.*

In other words: no virus detected. Time for work.

The day looms before her, its endless demands exhausting her before she's even moved. There's a ten-hour shift on the ward to contend with, and she's promised to meet Cathy for lunch. Cathy will be full of crises and concern, but Emma doesn't blame her, because all anyone can think about is the growing catastrophe at the hospital. At some point during the past few months, the days had turned into minefields. Every hour at work is uncharted territory that must be tiptoed through, hyperalert, preparing for the next inevitable explosion. And once a day is conquered, it doesn't drift away from Emma like it used to. It turns to stone and settles inside her. There's a cairn in the pit of her belly.

No doubt, as hospital management, Cathy is getting it in the neck from the powers that be. Of course everyone wants answers. And because

Emma is in the trenches, down on the wards, Cathy often questions her for small details, grilling her for anything they might have missed. "I don't know," Emma has insisted, over and over, trying not to picture the row of tight little faces in the morgue, those tiny stubborn mouths that had refused to open, to breathe. "I don't understand what's happening. I'm frightened too."

This time last year, a stillbirth had been an event. Rare and tragic. Usually, with answers delivered via an autopsy. Then rumors began five months ago—disturbing reports from hospitals in the north of England about births going wrong—but they were nothing compared to the shock of delivering a little girl, plump and perfect, who came easily into the world but refused to take a breath. Emma won't ever forget the stunned silence. The steady panting of the mother turning to howls of confusion; the father staggering and vomiting on the floor. The hasty efforts at resuscitation. The swift removal of the child for assessment. The parents' never-ending, agonizing questions, which no one could answer.

Emma had gone home that evening, taken a long, hot bath, and prayed to every god she could think of that she would never experience a day like that again. It hadn't worked. Instead, her days have become a lottery, the live births interspersed with the Intrapartum X babies—or the "doll babies," as the media calls them—the ones who twist and wiggle in the womb, showing no signs of anything amiss; who are perfectly alive during delivery, their steady heartbeats tracked as they descend into the birth canal, but who, once born, refuse to take a breath or open their eyes. No matter how much resuscitation they're given. No matter how much the adults implore them.

Within a few nightmarish months, almost every hospital across the country had experienced such an event. At first it was one in every ten births, then one in eight. Now the ratio is creeping closer to one in five. Cesareans don't help. It doesn't matter how rapidly a neonate is plucked from the womb—if it's an Intrapartum X baby, it will go limp the moment it's touched. The babies demonstrate no signs of pain and no will to stay in the world. They are pristine human specimens.

They just won't breathe.

In the beginning, Emma spent long hours awake at night going over each birth, searching for an answer to this nightmare. She'd read the latest research, obsessed about numerous theories and quizzed weary obstetricians and frazzled nurses. The only result was a week off work with sleeping tablets, and after that she'd taught herself not to dwell on her more disturbing thoughts. Now, as she heads to the kitchen to make a drink, she forces her thoughts away from work for a few minutes, her mind turning to Lainey's sudden flit. Her heart contracts. When was the last time she checked in with her daughter?

When Lainey was small, they'd talked about everything. Craig had left before Lainey could even walk, and in a family of two, all focus was on each other. Emma was the sun, and Lainey the flower in bud, leaning and unfolding toward her mother's light. But, as Lainey had blossomed, the shadow between them had grown too. Lately, they'd been little more than tenants sharing the same house, thanks to Emma's erratic shift pattern. Between the all-encompassing nightmares at the hospital and Lainey's unpredictable social life, it is hard enough to find themselves in the same place, never mind with enough energy to talk. And Lainey doesn't confide much in Emma anymore, which makes Emma want to weep, even though she knows it's to be expected. "We knew we'd have to let them go one day," Cathy had said on a recent night out, raising her glass of wine as if toasting their losses at a living wake. "It's just happened so bloody fast."

But no matter how sympathetic her friends are, Emma still hasn't completely got the hang of stepping back. Otherwise, she'd dismiss this horrible urge to run after Lainey to check she's all right. And she wouldn't have shrugged off all her better judgments about prying, and walked upstairs into Lainey's room to find Fergus fast asleep, wearing Lainey's watch.

7:10 a.m.

On Frederick Street, a shadowy figure emerges from a driveway and joins Lainey, their footsteps instantly in time with one another.

"I hope I don't look as knackered as you do," Sereena says. "Did you even brush your hair?"

Lainey laughs. "You look pretty average, I'm sorry to say. Did you get out okay?"

"No sweat." Sereena combs her fingers through her damp hair. "Mum's snoring like a walrus in there."

"What did you do with your watch?"

"Moodle's wearing it as a collar. She isn't happy, but I think she'll settle down. I hope she does, anyway, otherwise the government spies will think I'm a loony turning circles in my bedroom."

Lainey pictures Sereena's obese tabby prowling around with her new choker. She smiles, then remembers the reason they're here. "Do you think we're being too paranoid—about the watches, I mean?"

Sereena shrugs. "After what happened to Ellis and PreacherGirl, I think it'd be weird if we weren't paranoid. Why else is it illegal to remove them for more than five minutes?" She trails off, and Lainey knows she'll be stewing about the new rules. The watches have only been compulsory for the last twelve weeks; before that people could at least sleep without them. But these new waterproof versions are supposed to serve a whole host of functions: ID, credit payments, and making a continual record of health data. All under the auspices of keeping them safe, but Sereena's convinced it's really about surveillance and tracking. She'd suggested using their pets as decoys a few weeks ago, and Lainey had heard it was being copied all over school.

She thinks over Sereena's words. "Have you found out anything more . . . about Ellis?" she asks nervously.

"Nothing." Sereena bites her lip, and the space between them is filled with unspoken worries. Ellis Scott was the same age as them, and Sereena had gotten to know her at a camp a couple of years ago. Lainey had been jealous of their friendship at first, but that hadn't lasted long, because Ellis was so easy to warm to. Tall and willowy with long, dark hair, she was always sharing jelly sweets and talked incessantly about being a fashion designer. Her hobby was scouring charity shops and buying mismatched pieces of clothing that she'd turn into art pieces, cutting them up and splicing them back together, sewing on beads, buttons, and tassels. After she'd finished she would give them away to her friends.

To start with, only Sereena had known that Ellis had walked into a pharmacy and bought a pregnancy test, expecting them just to take her ID. Instead, she'd had to take the test inside the shop—with a security guard called to stand outside the toilet door. The pharmacist had insisted on seeing the sodden stick and recording the results. Soon after, Ellis had disappeared, along with her family, and no one had seen them since.

The girls had been confused and concerned when Ellis didn't pick up their calls, but the panic hadn't hit until a couple of weeks ago, when PreacherGirl dropped her song about twelve pregnant girls who'd purportedly vanished, accompanied by a scrolling video of their names and photos. Ellis wasn't listed, but the stories were all too familiar, and Sereena had added her friend's name to the missing in the comments. It had meant betraying Ellis's confidence, but she wasn't sure what else to do.

Since then, Ellis's absence has felt increasingly sinister. To begin with, the whole town was talking about it, but once PreacherGirl's site was taken down, many people felt it was too dangerous to continue whispering conspiracy theories in case their watches were recording all conversations. Nevertheless, a few of Lainey and Sereena's friends are still determined to find Ellis, so far with no success.

Lainey had watched this all unfold with growing horror. Four days ago, she'd broken down and told Sereena she feared she might be pregnant, too.

"So," Sereena says, interrupting Lainey's thoughts, "d'you reckon we'll pull this off? I keep wondering if we've missed anything, but it seems pretty easy to me."

Lainey shrugs. "Glad you're confident. The rain's making me nervous. Wet footsteps are a giveaway."

"Rain's good. Gives us more reason to keep our hoods up. Just wipe your feet when you get inside, and you'll be fine." She rubs her arms. "I wish it wasn't so bloody cold, though. The seasons are stuffed, aren't they? September's practically winter now."

Lainey eyes the dimly lit street ahead of them. She's shivering too, but she's not sure it's from the cold. "Thanks for coming."

"It's no problem—I should be thanking you. Any chance to mess with this screwed-up system, and you know I'm there. And depending on what happens, I'll help you decide what to do next."

Lainey nods, but in truth she can't think beyond the next hour. Sereena doesn't press it. As always, Sereena seems to understand. Ever since their first year at school, when they'd bonded over McVities cookies, practicing their cartwheels, and a Japanese cartoon series called *Power Girls*, they'd been fiercely loyal friends. In second grade, when Tyler Goldsmith began bullying Lainey, Sereena had smacked him in the face and got suspended. In fourth grade, when Sereena got appendicitis, Lainey had sat and read joke books to her in the hospital until she had to stop laughing because of the pain.

As they near the small row of shops on Glace Street, their pace slows. "Just wait," Lainey says, and they watch from a distance for a few minutes until they see the pharmacist unlock the shop doors. Lainey glances left and right. As they'd hoped, there's no one around yet. They'd picked this place because of its early opening time and its location: in a secluded spot, out of the way of traffic.

"Right, then," Lainey says. "Now or never." Her breath grows shallow. She makes a conscious effort to deepen it, thinking of Mrs. Allerton, who for years had insisted they meditate in health class, her nostrils flaring like a wild horse's as she demonstrated the inhale and exhale. Lainey tries it now and ends up snorting nervously instead. Her stride falters.

"Keep walking," Sereena hisses. "No backing out. Pull your hood up a bit and put your scarf over your face."

"Don't be so bossy," Lainey objects, but does it anyway. They're within a few feet of a small row of shops when Sereena whispers, "Ready?"

"Ready."

Sereena suddenly twists and falls heavily. Lainey doesn't mind this part, because they'd orchestrated it. But they hadn't planned for the back of Sereena's head to meet the glistening pavestones with a crack.

"Shit!" Lainey pauses automatically to crouch down and check on her friend.

Sereena puts her hand up to feel the injury. Her face is screwed up in pain, but she hisses, "Don't stop. Quick. Go."

There's a beat while Lainey hesitates, but then she's running into the pharmacy at the end of the row, ignoring the health-check station by the door, crying out, "Help, help!" as the pharmacist rushes around the counter to greet her. The woman is in her late thirties, hair in a high ponytail, thick lashings of makeup doing nothing to hide the deep circles under her eyes. Her face is full of concern.

"My friend, she just fainted outside, she's lying on the pavement," Lainey manages, close to hyperventilating. "Do you know first aid? Please, help us."

The pharmacist looks beyond Lainey and sees Sereena on the ground. As she runs across, Lainey makes as if to follow, then stops. She scans the shop, checking it's empty, then hurries across to the counter, pulling her hood and scarf up around her face, head down to evade the cyclops eyes of any security cameras. She lifts the counter hatch and slips through to the serving side, scanning the rows of cold and flu medication and allergy relief, until she sees, on the bottom shelf, a group of pink-and-white boxes. She grabs one of those, and then goes to another section and takes a little white box of tablets. She knows where to find them thanks to their scoping efforts over the last few days, and so it only takes seconds.

"What are you doing?"

The voice is tiny, a mouse-squeak. Lainey freezes, then turns.

Sitting on the floor, in the corner beneath the counter, is a small girl. Her back against the wall, a Disney princess coloring book on her lap and a yellow pencil in her hand. Her dark hair is glossy, held back by a hairband with a blue-and-red pattern that Lainey recognizes as St. Stephen's Primary School colors, with bright-yellow ribbons at the ends of her braids, and she wears the familiar blue-and-red uniform that Lainey had once worn herself. She stares up with dark, curious eyes.

"My friend needs these," Lainey says, showing her the small white packet of tablets. "She's fainted."

The girl doesn't reply, but her gaze travels to the box in Lainey's other hand. Lainey shoves it into her pocket. She would stay and beg the girl to keep her mouth shut, but there's no time and she sprints for the front door. The whole thing has taken less than a minute and the pharmacist is still leaning over Sereena, who is at least conscious and talking.

As Lainey approaches, the pharmacist frowns at her. Lainey holds up the little packet of glucose tablets. "Can I give her these? She's got diabetes. I think her blood sugar might be too low." This is the simplest cover story they'd thought of, but Lainey has never been a good liar, and she fears she's blushing.

The pharmacist frowns. "You can't just take those. You'll need to pay for them, you know."

"I . . ." Lainey stalls, briefly thinking of the watches at home. The pharmacist's attention flickers over Lainey's wrists, and Lainey's glad she can't see that underneath their coats their arms are bare.

"There's no money in my account. Do you take cash?" she asks, already knowing the answer.

"I can't," the pharmacist says, frowning. "You know that. You can only pay for medicines with a card or your watch—it's been like that for weeks."

Sereena sits up, rubbing her head. "It's okay, I just got faint for a second. Home isn't far, and I've got stuff there . . ."

The pharmacist is concerned. "Are you sure? I'd give you some myself if it were up to me, but I can't . . . the new rules . . . I'd be breaking the law. I could be put in jail," she reminds them, as though she can't quite believe it, her expression asking them to understand.

"Don't worry," Lainey says. "Thanks anyway." She hands the tablets to the pharmacist, then helps Sereena to her feet. "Can you walk?" she asks, putting her arm around her friend. "Let's get you home."

As soon as they're out of earshot, Lainey pulls Sereena closer. "Is your head okay?" she asks in an urgent whisper. "It made a horrible crack when you fell."

Sereena half laughs, half grimaces. "It'll be fine. Stings a bit—I think I've grazed it. I need to work on my dramatic falls. Still, at least it made the whole thing seem authentic. So, did it go as planned?"

Lainey groans. "Almost. There was a bloody kid behind the counter."

"What? Like, serving?"

"No, she was only little, five or six. She was sitting on the floor coloring."

"Shit, that must be her kid," Sereena hisses, then shrugs. "Oh well, too late now. But did you get it?"

Lainey touches the pink-and-white box in her pocket, her heart beginning to race. "Yes," she says, "I did."

7:50 a.m.

Emma will be late if she doesn't leave now. She'd taken her time getting ready for work, hoping Lainey would reappear, listening for the key in the lock. Disappointed, she stands in front of the mirror by the front door and studies herself solemnly: her clean, crisp blue shirt with white trim and the hospital logo, a lanyard with ID and hospital codes around her neck. The silver watch attached to her breast pocket is an antique compared to the newfangled watch strapped to her wrist. She tries out a smile. "I'm so sorry," she says to her tired, pale face. "I'm so sorry for your loss."

Does she look genuine? Can she still show compassion when, in truth, she's exhausted? When every day she thinks of quitting the job she's loved for fourteen years. Despite the many practicalities of tending to a laboring mother, she's never lost sight of the miracle of birth, in whatever form it took. Up until recently, with current world-class medical care, they rarely lost mother or child. If they did, the whole department would mourn. Now, it was a race to get the reports and procedures finished before the next stillbirth. And the United Kingdom is watched fearfully by a world still tormented by years of lockdowns and losses, after all the time it had taken to get back to some semblance of normality beyond the pandemic and food shortages.

It had been seven years since world tensions had risen sharply in the wake of the virus, the entire planet's population suffering from collective post-traumatic stress disorder as chaos bubbled just below the surface, breaking through as authoritarianism, terror attacks, fracking protests, drone strikes, tariffs and sanctions. But finally, there'd been a surge of people power: massive protests worldwide, followed by a global strike three years ago, which had brought new climate-change accords and a renewed sense of determination to safeguard the planet. A few years of grace had followed, shifting only when the babies in England began dying from an unknown cause.

The media had been largely responsible for the initial panic. They broke the news early and with enough hyperbole to create hysteria, speculating wildly and protractedly on every possible cause, from terrorism, to a new viral pandemic, to the will of God. Despite this, there are still no answers, not even with the finest medical scientists working around the clock. There are a few immediate areas of consensus—that the problem isn't contagion or infection, and it seems confined in origin to the UK—but otherwise the pathology of the disease remains unknown. In every conceivable way, this cohort of children is perfect. They should be alive, but instead they've become the newest threat to humanity, shunting terrorism, world unrest, climate change, and the problematic new virus vaccines from the headlines, topping even the perilous daily melt of the icebergs in the Arctic and Antarctic. As a result, women must now present their IDs for every pregnancy test purchased, then take the tests on-site, the results recorded and the health authorities notified. Antenatal clinics are emptying of patients. In Whitehaven Hospital, they have delivered so many of these babies that Emma often dreams of them, their perfect little faces impenetrable, guardians of a secret the world cannot yet fathom.

If she'd chosen her job just for the babies, she might already have quit in despair, even if it meant slipping toward the breadline. But it's the mothers who keep her returning to the hospital, day after day. The mothers need her more than ever. They're the ones who give Emma her courage and determination to do what she does right now: collect her bag, straighten her back, and walk toward her front door.

8:00 a.m.

Lainey crouches behind a low wall, watching her house amid the cramped row of Victorian terraces, as though she's a burglar scoping for entry. An occasional car glides down the street, while her head thrums like the distant beat of helicopter wings. Sereena has gone home to get ready for school, but Lainey needs to wait for her mother to leave, and of course Emma is taking her sweet time this morning. Lainey has a twinge of horror that Emma won't go at all; that she'll be waiting at the kitchen table, arms crossed, to demand that Lainey explain herself. The only thing

14

that's keeping Lainey from full-blown anxiety is that she knows her mother's shift pattern. Emma is conscientious about getting to work on time; she can't afford to lose her job.

Just as Lainey's legs are cramping and her neck is beginning to throb unbearably, Emma appears. Lainey watches her mother turn back to double lock the front door, then set off down the path. She is, as always, perfectly turned out: blond hair in a high ponytail, clips keeping back any loose strands. Her uniform is freshly washed and pressed, and her sensible black shoes are shiny.

As far as Lainey knows, her mother doesn't have big dreams: it's enough to go to work, cook a nice meal, drink a glass of wine with a friend, get a decent sleep. She's a good mother. She tries to help but doesn't overstep. She always listens but doesn't ask too many questions. So Lainey doesn't understand why, sometimes, when they sit across from one another, eating meals and making idle conversation, Lainey wants to lean over and shout into her mother's face. She's not sure what she wants to say, or what she's looking for. A reaction? An acknowledgment that Emma is capable of recognizing the tumult of feelings that maraud through Lainey? Or perhaps it's more than that: perhaps she wants a sign that her mother holds some deeper understanding of why all this is happening. That she cares about the bigger picture of their lives, beyond the ritual of work and home, and the exhaustion of each day.

When the street is empty, Lainey races across to the house. Once inside, she runs upstairs and into the bathroom, pulling the box out of her pocket. She puts it on the ledge of the sink for a moment and takes a few steadying breaths, catching sight of herself in the mirror. She sees a red-faced, puffing girl, hair unkempt now that her hood is pulled back. A girl way out of her depth with what she's about to do.

But this can't wait any longer.

Opening the packet, she reads the instructions, then sits down and awkwardly pees on the little stick. Setting it in the sink, she slumps to sit with her back against the door, then curls up in a protective ball, as though the testing stick might suddenly explode. She tries to count to a thousand this time, as slowly as she can, summoning her courage as the numbers get higher. When she reaches two hundred, she can't bear it any longer. She jumps up and looks into the sink.

Two little pink lines stare back at her. She moves to the packet, to triple-check what that means.

Pregnant.

Shit. Shit. Shit.

She staggers back, away from this crippling, undeniable knowledge. But she already knew, didn't she? She *knew*. She's felt nauseous for weeks. Her boobs are sore, and her sense of smell is hyperactive. She's checked the symptoms online, and perhaps she didn't really need proof, after all. It was the final, faint gasp of hope that had sent her on this morning's errand, and now that's gone.

Shit.

There's a sudden loud knocking at the front door, and it spurs her into action. She shoves the stick back into its box and grabs the whole lot, running through to her room and pushing it under her bed. The chicks burst into chorus, and Fergus jumps up from his slumber, as though trying to pretend he's been alert and guarding them this whole time.

She ruffles his fur and removes the watch as quickly as she can, as the knocking comes again. She straps it back onto her wrist as she races down the stairs and pulls open the door, already certain whom she'll find.

Liam grins. "You *are* there! What're you doing? I thought you must have gone already." He frowns as he registers her flustered expression. "You look spooked." He traces a line down her cheek with his fingertip and leans in like he might try to kiss her.

She ducks away. "I'm fine. I'll just get my bag."

Liam hovers in the hallway, messing with his phone, occasionally pushing the flop of his dark fringe away from his face. When she comes back, he grins. "I wish we could skip school and do something more interesting." He nods suggestively, and Lainey tries to smile. If someone had told her last year that Liam Whittaker would one day want to walk to school with her, that he'd imply he'd prefer to *stay home* with her, she would have been secretly thrilled. But it isn't like she'd thought it would be. *He* isn't at all as she'd imagined. He crosses small boundaries that are hard to explain, a petty thief stealing goods too meager to moan about. Some are physical: the way he plays with her hair as though he's trying to tidy her up, like she's an overgrown hedge that needs pruning. Others are less tangible. The long pause he leaves if he doesn't like her joke or observation, the way he changes the subject so that she feels judged and belittled without being sure why. The ease with which he races ahead when he meets a friend, so she ends up ten paces behind them, unsure if she's welcome in the conversation.

This is the fourth day in a row he's turned up to walk with her. She doesn't get why he's still hanging around, since she gives him little encouragement. Sereena thinks that's the problem. "You're a challenge for him now," she'd announced. "You'll have to spell it out for him, tell him to get lost, or he'll keep sniffing around, hoping you'll take pity on him and give him what he wants."

Sereena doesn't need to spell out what that is. Neither of them has any doubt about that.

Lainey thinks of telling him about the disaster hidden beneath her bed. Surely, he'd run then. *Probably straight to the authorities*, she thinks with a shudder. And since his dad is a high-ranking government minister, he's likely to be listened to.

"Come on," she says, pushing past him for the door, pretending not to notice his hand reaching out for her. "We'll be late."

Liam shrugs and follows her out.

2.

On the bus, Emma keeps her head down and her book open on her lap. She'd got on early enough to grab a seat, but now people are squashed together in the aisles. There are cheap nylon trousers ten inches from her face. The air is stuffy with so many people breathing and coughing and sniffing in the confined space. It's hard to relax after years of social distancing, even though you can't ride the bus anymore without first scanning your watch to prove you've had a clear health screen within the last twelve hours. And there are health stations everywhere: schools, shops, petrol stations—not to mention the hospital's remote staff-screening procedures at home. Really, the country is more protected from contagion than it's ever been. And yet . . . she shudders, thinking of the babies. Every day she hears a new theory, but nothing fits. This one feels primal, beyond human control.

She tries to distract herself and focuses on the page in front of her. The novel had won the Women's Prize for Fiction a few years ago, and Cathy had insisted Emma borrow it—but she can't get farther than a paragraph without her mind drifting. Still, at least it's something to hide behind, making it less likely that people will notice her or try to talk to her. She keeps her coat tightly buttoned, despite the fact she's sweating.

Her uniform tends to attract unwanted attention. Nowadays, many of the nurses get changed at work, and Emma had tried it for a while, but it felt too furtive, too chaotic. She needs to get ready at home, to look in the mirror and remind herself why she's doing this. *The mothers.* She needs to prepare her face to meet their beseeching eyes and their unspoken question: *Will you help, or are you the harbinger of our curse?*

The bus travels through the suburban streets, skirts the industrial estate, then heads across the traffic bridge toward the town center. At the library stop, there's a few minutes' delay for the heavy exchange of passengers. The woman next to Emma gets up, and Emma shuffles along so she's beside the window. Most of the people around her are hunched over tablets or phones, and an old man with a shiny bald head and a large paunch protruding over his burgundy cords gets on and sits beside her, clutching an old iPad. The bus jerks as it moves away from the curb, and Emma catches sight of the headline on the screen: MARY'S BIG GAMBLE PAYS OFF.

Beneath the large letters, there's an unflattering picture of the prime minister, stooped at a lectern. The picture's been taken in profile, backlit so that it highlights the outline of Mary's short gray hair: both the perfectly coiffed waves at the front and the tufts at the back that have refused to conform and protrude at odd angles. The photographer had captured her looking down as she read her notes, giving her a few extra rolls of chin and making her eyes appear closed. It's a pose of prayer. Or despair. A definitive portrait of the leader of a tired, beleaguered country.

Emma doesn't quite know what to make of Mary anymore. She'd swept to power on a tidal wave of popularity, thanks to her willingness to step outside her comfort zone and confront some of the immense problems of climate change head on. She'd restored the country's good standing across Europe and the wider world by joining a series of new global commitments to help the planet adapt to the inevitable changes wrought by increasing temperatures, and had taken time to explain the science in plain language across a series of dedicated documentaries, gathering the goodwill of the country behind her. She'd openly wept at a service commemorating the terrible storms and landslides of twelve months ago, which had cut off the north of England, leaving over a hundred people stranded on a highway with no hope of rescue, families freezing to death in their vehicles. Her grief-stricken face was iconic, even more so because she had gone on television the following night and promised her fellow citizens that she would do everything in her power to never let that happen again. And when the interviewer had asked what she would say about her tears being a weakness, she had fixed him with an icy stare and said, "I think you're confusing weakness with compassion."

And yet, the prime minister seemed to be drifting away from her centrist policies. She had never managed to shake herself free of the contenders for her throne: a group of middle-aged men known colloquially as the New Conservatives, whose popular support had been surging since the onset of stillbirths, as panic spread through the population. Despite belonging to the same political party, they had openly denounced her inclusivity and seemed determined to oust her before the next election. Grant Whittaker, the local MP for Whitehaven and rumored head of the pack, had only recently been promoted to health secretary in a move that had shocked many, since a decade ago his extramarital affair and associations with medical research companies profiteering from the pandemic had made him a pariah. It had appeared to Emma and her friends as a case of Mary choosing to keep her friends close and her enemies closer.

Emma turns to stare out the window, watching the pavement as the busy city streets recede, until the adults striding purposefully to work with glazed eyes are replaced by scattered groups of milling, jostling schoolchildren. She thinks again of Lainey, gets out her phone, and taps a message.

> Morning, sweetheart. Where'd you go so early?

She hesitates momentarily, imagining the clench of Lainey's jaw as she reads this, the presumption that Emma is prying rather than concerned. But still, Emma wants to know. So she grits her teeth and presses Send, then stares at the screen, thinking of all the time she's wasted watching her phone, waiting for replies that never came. She puts the device back in her bag before she can get sucked in again.

The bus lurches to a stop and Emma gets up with a polite, "Excuse me," shuffling past everyone, out of the suffocating warmth and into the chilly morning air.

Until a few months ago, there'd been a stop right outside the multi-level gray monolith that serves as the main hospital building, but not anymore. As Emma walks toward the police cordon, her attention shifts to the fourth-floor row of windows with their blackout blinds. Her floor. All light on that level is now artificial to prevent drones or telescopic cameras getting a glimpse inside.

At the cordon, Emma holds out her wrist so they can scan her watch. The security is only a gesture, really—by now most of the police stationed here can recognize her by sight—but in the current climate, procedures are followed to the letter.

"How're you doing today, Emma?" Jason Langford calls out to her, his phone at the ready in case she agrees to an interview. He's one of the seasoned journalists that have been stationed here for weeks, jostling for stories they can feed to the insatiable online news feeds. He and Emma once went to the same running club, a lifetime ago for her. He must know that the instant she talks to him, she'll be fired, but he tries every morning anyway.

She gives him a wry smile, and steps onto no-man's land. The worst part of the journey to work is the ghost walk, as Emma has come to think of it: the last few feet across an empty car park, which five months ago would have been bumper-to-bumper at this time of the morning. Over a narrow street and past a small general store on the corner, now permanently closed, its owners relocated a few blocks away. No need to look left and right for the unceasing traffic that had once frequented the area. There is no one, except for a few other lone wanderers converging, on the same shift. But as strange as it still feels, it's better than running the gauntlet of those chaotic weeks after the first Intrapartum X baby was born here. It's preferable to the hordes of journalists pressing around her, wanting to know her name, her ward and what she can tell them. It's silenced the religious groups praying loudly and warning of the End of Days with their harrowing wails of communal pain. It's even stopped the gawkers with nothing better to do than stare at hospital walls.

But the cordon is only the first step to keeping order, because the cordon is understaffed, thanks to the tight stretch on police resources, so the most determined people continue to find their way in. It doesn't help that sick people need visitors, and it's impossible to do thorough background checks on everyone. On at least three occasions, photos had been taken inside the maternity wards and posted online. One tabloid had labeled them the *wards of death*: three little words that, ever since she had read them, could induce instant queasiness in Emma.

When she reaches the double doors, she glances around, as she's been taught. People may only enter the building one at a time, and a couple of nurses hang back, waiting for their turn. Emma steps forward and taps her key card against the small black unit fixed to the wall.

The double doors slide slowly open. She only has seconds before they'll shut, so Emma slips inside, out of the gray light of morning, and the doors close again, swift and smooth, swallowing her whole.

8:45 a.m.

"Lainey, are you listening to me?"

No, she isn't. Her mind has been overrun by those two pink lines.

She still can't believe it. She'd bled, hadn't she? She'd thought it had been a late, light period. She'd been so relieved. When she'd not bled again, she'd waited for weeks, thinking she was just late. What did the blood mean, then? Was it a sign of something wrong?

Is it a doll baby?

She wants to be sick.

"Lainey?"

Liam's irritated voice is loud enough to finally draw her back to the moment. "What? Sorry . . ."

"I'm trying to warn you—Dad wants me to tell everyone that it's a bad idea to go to the women's protest tomorrow. Don't let Sereena push you into it."

Lainey tries to reorientate herself, to focus on his words. She registers Liam's solemn expression, and then their surroundings, surprised that they're almost at the school gates. "I can make my own decisions, thanks, and it's not a women's protest, it's a student march for women's rights."

"And the difference is?"

"Well, for starters, some men think it's worth turning up too. There are people going from most of the high schools and colleges around London, so I've heard. It should be massive—they're expecting the biggest turnout since the climate marches."

"It won't make any difference," Liam replies, shaking his head, his brow furrowing. "The new laws are there to stop the babies dying, so it doesn't matter how many people protest, they won't cave on this one. And I'm warning you, Dad says the police won't be messing around if there's any trouble. You can't graduate if you're in prison."

Lainey stops walking, absorbing his words. The last time she'd seen Grant Whittaker was when he'd turned up on school sports day a year ago, just prior to the last election, wearing a smart gray suit with a blue rosette on the lapel, shaking hands with parents like he was at his own personal rally. She'd heard some of the adults laughing about him, calling him a charmer, but her mum hadn't found it amusing. "Smarmer, more like," she'd muttered so only Lainey could hear.

As Lainey regards Liam now, she sees the resemblance to his father: the same patronizing, know-it-all smile, and it riles her. "I doubt they'll put us kids in jail for holding up a few signs. Anyway, I'm rapidly losing my enthusiasm for graduating when they don't even want us to get jobs. They want us all cleaning toilets and scrubbing floors and collecting rat carcasses out of floodwaters up north. Now that they've made the community service compulsory, we'll all be bussed up there as soon as we leave school."

"I doubt it. If anything, they'll want us sandbagging and building walls down here, ready for the sea rise. Dad thinks it's too late for some of the places up north. York can't recover fast enough before they're underwater again. And now Hull's in trouble, too, and Lancaster . . ."

Lainey waves him away. "Don't remind me, it's too depressing. Your dad seriously said that? You're telling me the government has already given up on entire cities?"

Liam blushes a deep, angry red. "Don't twist my words. They're doing all they can as part of the new International Climate Council accords, which is why we're all legally obliged to plant fucking trees every month. They're just getting things done carefully, without the panic that the protesters always stir up. York's always been flood prone."

Lainey sighs. "I can't be bothered to argue. Besides, tomorrow's not just about that."

"Really?" Liam stops walking and turns to face her. "What's it about, then?"

She bites her lip as she watches his mind working furiously, but it's too late to retract her words.

He looks skyward and then back at Lainey. "Please don't say Ellis."

She doesn't reply. Just raises her chin.

Liam's mouth drops open, and then he laughs. "Seriously? You're not buying into all the PreacherGirl bullshit, are you? God, Lainey, it's a complete hoax. Why do you think PreacherGirl stayed anonymous? So she can mess with your mind, make everyone paranoid, and then disappear when she's had her fun. PreacherGirl's a glorified troll, that's all."

Fury rises in Lainey. "Perhaps you should do some of your own research, rather than believing everything your dad tells you. He knows where Ellis is, then, does he?"

Liam snorts derisively. "Yeah, what with the babies dying and the planet on its knees, Dad's got all the time in the world to investigate why Ellis and her family decided to move away over the summer."

Lainey rolls her eyes and marches ahead, hoping to spot her friends, but Liam follows and grabs her arm.

"You don't have to listen, but please understand I'm only trying to warn you because I give a shit, Lainey. Remember that when you're there tomorrow. Okay?"

She hesitates, but people are watching, and it's easier to nod than argue in public. "I have to get to class."

"Me too." Inside the front gates he grabs her and hugs her, as though everything is fine, and when he steps back, he flashes her a smile. "I'll see you in art." Then his attention is diverted by the sight of two of his mates swaggering in through the gate, and he heads across to them, saying something out of earshot of Lainey, which makes them all smirk at her. Liam winks before they walk away, and Lainey feels herself bristle. Part of her wants to drag him back so they can continue arguing. It would take her mind off her bigger problems.

Making an effort to gather her wits, she joins the line for temperature checks and saliva tests. She pulls her phone from her pocket to see there's a polite message from her mum that nevertheless makes it clear she'd noticed Lainey's early morning disappearance. What the hell can she say to explain?

Nothing for now, she decides, switching off her phone to comply with school policy. She sees the increasing strain on her mother every time she comes home from the hospital. Last year, her mother had been slightly plump around the hips, but now she probably weighs less than Lainey. Emma rarely talks about the doll babies, but Lainey knows from the news reports that she'll be dealing with it almost daily. She's noticed Cathy's concerned eyes on Emma, when her mother isn't looking. And now, Lainey's going to add to all that stress, in the worst possible way.

8:50 a.m.

It takes Emma ten minutes to get through the security line inside the building. First, there's a pat down. Then a handheld infrared thermometer is pointed at her forehead to take her temperature, which is recorded again, the hospital not yet fully trusting the home-testing regime. The webbing between her fingers is swabbed. Her bags, jacket, watch, and phone trundle through the scanner, then are collected by another guard, labeled, and assigned a locker. As always, she is asked to witness them putting her belongings safely inside, then once the locker is secure, she is given a key on a small carabiner, which she attaches to the belt loop on her trousers. If she needs anything, she'll have to come down and repeat the whole procedure—only top management is exempt. This is one of the few places she's allowed to be without her watch.

When she's done all this it's only a few minutes until the morning briefing. The dozen or so seats are already taken by the time Emma arrives and she has to lean against the back wall. From the front row, Lynne gives Emma a sharp look, then turns away. Cara catches her eye and smiles. Emma can see Dorothy, Sylvia, and Isabelle in the second row, lined up attentively, chatting as they wait.

The room is calmer than it had been in the first few weeks of these briefings, when it had felt like they were all being battered by a great resurging wave. The shock has subsided, and now the atmosphere is more of a resigned, steely focus on the task ahead.

Angela from hospital management enters and heads straight for the front, a sheaf of papers in her hand. No eye contact or pleasantries. Her navy suit is teamed with a crisp white shirt, but the lapels are sticking up, as though she'd put on her jacket in a hurry.

"First up," Angela begins, her voice cutting across the chatter as she studies her notes, "the update from the National Birth Crisis Center. Latest science is considering looking at hormonal disruptors in both mother and child . . . and continues to rule out the baby's involuntary nervous system. Research is also focusing on the neurotransmitters of mother and child during birth. Unfortunately, as usual, the latest scientific findings are redacted to ensure the public doesn't panic. However, staff need to continue their extensive write-ups of both the live births and the still-births, as they are each of vital importance in these studies."

Emma doesn't so much hear the groan as feel the constriction of breath around her. The thirty-page reports have become a regular part of a midwife's day—documenting everything, from the temperature in the room to the emotional state and conversation of the mother. On top of this, all births must be recorded now. Unseen births are no longer toler-ated: each one has to be analyzed and dissected for any patterns that could solve the crisis. Emma grimaces as she thinks of those intrusive black cyclops eyes set up in prime positions, recording every detail of each labor and delivery with no regard for their subjects.

The presence of cameras has had a multitude of effects. Some mothers get lost in the moment and don't care who is there. Others have entirely different instincts, to slink like wary cats to a dark corner, where they can huddle protectively and turn inward. But after a couple of stalled labors and the resulting complications of forceps deliveries, hemorrhages, and emergency cesareans, Emma had resolved to do what is necessary. She's been reprimanded on a number of occasions for blocking the camera, knocking it over, or forgetting to check it is on.

"On to the media issues," Angela says. "Things have been a lot better since we officially banned all journalists from the hospital, but it's almost impossible to keep them completely at bay with the amount of staff and suppliers and visitors and patients we have coming and going. Management is working on new protocols for this, but in the meantime you need to be vigilant in your own areas. You must question people and ask to see their ID if you don't recognize them, and even if they have an ID, you must scan it *and* their watch to confirm their identity. We cannot afford any more mistakes. You must also ensure that birthing mothers are kept in their rooms at all times. We still have beefed-up security at the ambulance entrance, and that's the only way women in labor should be admitted. Directives are being distributed to all the families whose babies are due within the next three months, so fathers or partners, or whoever, know they can drive right up to the door. Other prenatal concerns continue to be rerouted to Heathfield Hospital wherever possible."

"Now," Angela says, looking around at all of them, as though trying to catch everyone's eye, "I know the reporting procedure is arduous, but I have to remind you to complete it to the best and fullest of your ability. Remember, you may be saving countless future lives. I understand your exhaustion and frustration, so take it steady. We do not want any more staff burning out. You are all needed. You are all *essential*. So prioritize self-care every moment you can."

Someone snorts in ironic laughter, but Angela is already halfway across the room, having learned she needs to make a speedy exit to avoid the clamor of questions and complaints. Emma would like to think that this final statement is born out of sympathy for the tremendous pressure the nurses are under, but lately she's grown more cynical. The hospital is struggling to cope. Half the staff have already resigned or are on sick leave with stress, and most of the current batch of midwives have been cobbled together from nurses across the hospital who are prepared to deal with the daily uncertainty of the situation. Some of the newcomers are great, matter-of-fact and kindly. A few are in it for the infamy of working in the maternity department, and others because their salaries have skyrocketed. Which often doesn't lead them to offer quality maternity care in anything like the form Emma had known in the past. She worries for the mothers who get caught in a shift of inexperienced nurses who haven't trained in midwifery. And there are many more cesareans nowadays, as staff tends to push the panic button faster. No one wants to make unnecessary mistakes, or begin a hospital-mismanagement disaster, resulting in harm to a mother or child who would ordinarily survive.

As Dorothy gets up, she catches Emma's eye, briefly flashing five fingers, a sign Emma knows well. She nods, and then finds Lynne is beside her.

"Just made it in time, then," Lynne says, smiling, but there is nothing convivial about her presence. Her eyes flash beneath knotted brows as she scrutinizes Emma. "You didn't complete the report for Jody McArthur yesterday. David wants it in his inbox by midday. You need to get on with it—we'll need all hands on deck, as there are seven on the ward already this morning."

A decade ago, Emma and Lynne had shared rides to work, swapping stories from the hospital, laughing at some of their more absurd experiences and supporting one another through the trauma of the pandemic. Then, five years ago, Lynne had been promoted, and slowly began to take her new role ever more seriously, until she had reported a nurse for a tryst in the store cupboard, after Emma had told her the story anecdotally, and the nurse had been fired. Emma had been furious, but Lynne was unrepentant, and things haven't been the same between them ever since. Nowadays, Emma knows from experience that if Lynne is in the mood to goad her, then it's best just to nod. She also knows that it infuriates Lynne if she copes too well with criticism, so she tries to act contrite. Behind Lynne, Cara makes a face and Emma bites her lip to stop the twitch of a smile.

But Lynne notices anyway and steps closer. "I saw your daughter on the way to work this morning," she says. "Hiding in a bush opposite your house . . ."

Emma's face falls into complete astonishment. *What the hell, Lainey . . . ?* She tries to picture this for herself and fails. Then she realizes Lynne is waiting for an explanation.

"Lainey's seventeen," she stutters. "I don't monitor her every movement."

"Well, perhaps you should," Lynne snaps. "I sure as hell wouldn't want Delilah trespassing in other people's gardens at dawn."

And she stalks away.

Automatically, Emma looks at her empty wrist before remembering her watch is confiscated downstairs. She sighs. As much as she hates to give Lynne points for anything, Emma's maternal radar is on full alert. She hurries back to the lockers to see if there's a message. She goes through the rigmarole of waiting in line to pass over the key so she can rummage in her bag, while security watches on.

No message on her phone or her watch. Irritation rises alongside her worry. *What are you playing at, Lainey?*

10:45 a.m.

Lainey can't take her eyes off the clock at the front of the classroom. Her eyes track the slender red needle that counts the seconds, sequestering the day.

Pregnant.

Below the clock are two daddy longlegs, gently swaying, spindle legs spread wide.

Pregnant.

At the front, Mr. Davenport is droning on about the First World War. She catches fragments of what he's saying. Gallipoli . . . Churchill . . . Lord Fisher.

Pregnant.

Time slips. Mr. Davenport has put a film on the smartboard. He's talking about Peter Jackson. *Lord of the Rings.* Lainey doesn't understand. On the film, dozens of men in uniform turn from black and white to color. The dead come to life. A smiling soldier pats a big black dog, and she thinks of Fergus.

I'm pregnant.

Surely, the day is a dream. There's another Lainey somewhere, with different choices. Because she's not an idiot. She's seen all the headlines.

BIRTH RATES PLUMMET.

A COUNTRY IN CRISIS.

ONE IN THREE BIRTHS END IN TRAGEDY.

She's heard her mother talking to Cathy: "No one with any sense would get pregnant now."

Pregnant.

The word had barely been on her radar until the past couple of months. Something for the future. Perhaps. Because none of Lainey's dreams right now include a kid.

And there's something else, too.

What if there's a doll baby inside me?

Some of her friends can't stop talking about them. Others, like Lainey, try to shut out the news. All lifelike dolls had been removed from shop shelves two months ago, condemned as too upsetting for the public until the crisis is deemed over. But a few school pranksters had found them at home and brought them in. Hapless victims would find a baby doll sitting on their seat in class or tucked into their bags. To receive a doll was to be given a curse. Most people had experienced it. Lainey had walked most of the way home before she realized there was a small plastic face poking out of the top of her bag.

In the beginning, it had just been a sick game. But things had gotten real for them all two weeks ago, when the PreacherGirl song had set the rumors about Ellis circulating, just before the start of term.

Lainey pictures Ellis at the desk beside her, one hand over her workbook to hide her scribbling. Most of her friends doodled simple shapes during boring lessons, but Ellis drew the outlines of women along a catwalk, modeling her very own signature styles.

Where is she?

The question comes, now, with an extra stab of fear, because Lainey isn't sure how long she can keep her own pregnancy a secret. If she doesn't want to disappear like her friend, she *has* to confide in someone. Her mum will want to help, and she's the one person who'll know all the options—but telling her will be the worst moment of Lainey's life. Still, perhaps they can talk about abortion. Even though it's illegal, maybe her mum can find someone who'll keep it confidential and get it done.

Could she go through with that?

She isn't sure.

"Lainey?"

Lainey jumps to find Mr. Davenport crouched down in front of her desk, staring intently at her. Around them, people are beginning to pack away their books.

She checks the clock to see time has jumped again and the spiders have gone. It jolts her. How long had she been lost in her thoughts?

"Are you okay, Lainey?"

She turns her attention back to the teacher. She doesn't know him well; it's only a few weeks into term and he'd come to replace Mr. Gowan, who'd finally agreed to retire after becoming legendary for falling asleep in class. Mr. Davenport's got a kind face: eyes that crinkle at the corners, a few weathered lines down his tanned cheeks that suggest he's spent more time outdoors than you'd imagine a history teacher would. He wears jeans and surf-brand sweatshirts to school, and hiking boots, and he's caused a few flutters amongst the older girls, even though he's obviously old enough to be their dad. Lainey hadn't got it until now, but with his face so close to hers, she's drawn to his reassuring smile. Or perhaps it's just the relief that he seems concerned rather than annoyed.

"I'm afraid I've bored you this morning," he says.

"It's not that . . . I . . . ."

She stops. He waits.

"I don't feel well today," she finishes.

He holds her gaze for a few moments. "You missed taking notes on the assignment. I want you to do some research on why the Allied invasion of Gallipoli ultimately failed, so we can discuss it next time. Okay?"

Lainey nods as she gets up and collects her books and pens, not bothering to put them in her bag, just wanting to be out of there. Mr. Davenport steps back, his eyes on her for another moment until Kamal begins talking to him about homework.

Sereena's waiting for her in the hallway. "Did you do it?" she hisses under her breath.

Lainey looks at her. Bites her lip. Nods.

"Oh, fuck," Sereena breathes, staring at her. Then her eyes divert over Lainey's shoulder, and Lainey turns to see Mr. Davenport behind them, locking the door.

"'Scuse my language, sir," Sereena says to him.

"Didn't hear a thing," Mr. Davenport says, smiling, but his expression grows concerned as it passes over Lainey. Before he can say anything more, Sereena grabs Lainey's arm and pulls her away.

They move outdoors to find a patch of grass far from everyone else. "Is your head all right now?" Lainey asks.

"It's a bit sore, but I'll be fine." Sereena can't stop staring at Lainey. "But this . . ." She glances at Lainey's midriff. "This is massive."

Lainey holds up a hand. "Don't say that—you're making it worse." She blinks away tears.

"Sorry, sorry, I know I am." Sereena motions to Lainey's watch, takes off her own, puts it on the ground and sits on it, then waits until Lainey's done the same. "So, what the fuck are you going to do now?" she whispers. "And why won't you talk about the dad? I know it isn't Liam. He's reporting back to Tom and Niall every day—they all think you're playing hard to get."

"No, it's not Liam. Thank God."

"Is it someone I know?"

"You know everyone I know, but I'm not ready to talk about it," Lainey mutters, picking at the grass. She wishes Sereena wouldn't push for details. It's strange keeping secrets from her closest friend, but every time she thinks about what happened she burns with embarrassment.

"My mind is literally exploding with this," Sereena says, searching in her bag and pulling out a lip salve. "I can't imagine what it's doing to you."

"It feels unreal—like I'm going to wake up any minute. Ow," she adds as Sereena pinches her.

"'Fraid not, sister, you're definitely awake." She lowers her voice again. "We need to make a plan, and luckily, you've got the best girl for the job. We'll figure it out, okay? If nothing else, I'll marry you and we'll raise it together—imagine what Liam will say when I tell him you're having my baby . . ."

Lainey lets out a brief snort of laughter.

"See," Sereena says, putting her arm around Lainey, "it isn't all bad. I can still make you laugh. But I need the deets, too, you sneaky little minx. Because I'm a good Indian girl, so at some stage I want a full description: length, girth, all that. Because whoever got you into this much trouble, I really hope he was worth it."

"I thought he might be," Lainey says. "But it turns out he's a dick."

"Are you going to tell him?"

"I don't know."

"Are you going to keep it?"

"Stop interrogating me. I don't know. What choice do I have, now that abortion's illegal. I need time to figure this out . . ." She hesitates. "And I can't stop thinking about Ellis . . ."

"I know." Sereena grows solemn and puts a hand on Lainey's knee. "Sorry. Try not to panic."

Despite her friend's words, another surge of fear runs through Lainey. "I'm trying, but shit . . . we screwed up this morning, didn't we . . . getting the test . . . I'm so sorry, I don't want to get you in trouble."

Sereena shrugs. "I wanted to help, and I'm more than capable of getting myself into a mess. Besides, perhaps we got away with it. They don't have our ID, and it's only one test. She might not even notice it's gone. I'm more worried about what you do next. They can't force you to have a baby."

"Can't they?"

Sereena hesitates. "Do you want me to talk to my mum about it?"

Lainey shakes her head as though to clear it. "Not just yet. I need time to think."

"Okay. Well, your mum will be cool, Lainey, I know she will. And she's the perfect person to help. She'll know what to do."

Lainey pictures her mother's pale face contorted with worry and worn out from work. Then she thinks of the babies again, and her insides clench.

"Can we just stop." Lainey jumps to her feet and grabs her watch as the bell rings. Sereena hasn't speculated on the chance of it being a doll baby yet, but if she keeps going, she just might. "I've barely had time to think about this. I need the weekend, at least."

"I know, I'm sorry, it's just . . . the world's upside down—all this crazy shit happening, I can't deal," Sereena says as they make their way back inside. "Thank God it's art next. I'm already regretting sociology. That last lesson was so frickin' dull. I might have to see if I can switch."

"To what?"

"I dunno. What's history like? Mr. Davenport's pretty easy on the eye, isn't he? Better than old-goat Gowan. Least if it's boring, I'll have something pretty to look at. Mind you, I think my mum's got her eye on him. They've got mutual friends—went out drinking together over the summer, you know."

"Really?" Lainey tries and fails to picture it.

"Yep. Hopefully, I won't wake up one morning and find him doing the walk of shame."

Lainey tries to smile, but they've reached their art class, and it's going to take all she's got to keep herself together. Behind them comes Liam, giving her an almighty smack on the bum as he goes past, turning to her with a smile that suggests he just gave her exactly what she wanted and can't wait to do it again. "Sit with me?" he says to Lainey, but Sereena clutches her friend's arm.

"I got her first, Leonardo."

"Lesbos," Liam calls out to them with a grin, before he shrugs and turns away. But as Lainey sits down next to Sereena, at a table in the middle of the room, she's aware of another person close by who hasn't said a word. Hasn't even looked at her since she'd walked in.

11:05 a.m.

Emma hurries to the second, unofficial briefing. A hasty affair with three of them crammed into the storeroom that served the staff as a makeshift meeting place, and sometimes a hiding place for a good cry, a five-minute stretch, or a snooze. Once upon a time, the boxes of surgical supplies had been neatly stacked along the rows of cold metallic gray shelves. Now the floor is crammed with items that haven't been properly stored, and there's barely space to stand up.

Emma is the last to arrive, and Cara is already talking in whispers with Dorothy. The central strip light illuminates them both like actors on a stage, surrounded by haphazard stacks of boxes that jut out of the shadows. They look like grandmother and granddaughter huddled together. A couple of Dorothy's springy gray curls have escaped from her hair clips, shivering as she speaks, her weathered hand resting lightly on Cara's arm. Cara stares at the floor and nods while she listens. Her long hair is coiled into a tight bun, not a strand out of place, but her plump face is pale and her shoulders slump.

"All okay?" Emma asks, squeezing in with them.

"Cara's still struggling to sleep. I'm saying she should try melatonin again, just for a bit."

"That's a good idea," Emma says. "Self-care first, remember, even Angela said so. You're no good to anyone if you're walking round like a zombie."

"I know," Cara whispers.

Dorothy catches Emma's eye. They've both had high hopes for Cara. She'd blown them away with her empathy and compassion for birthing mothers, despite her tender age. But those attributes are dangerous for the nurses now.

Cara offers them sherbet lemons, but Emma and Dorothy say no. They wait as she unwinds the plastic wrapping and slips a lolly into her mouth.

These hasty morning check-ins have become vital to Emma in the last few weeks. It's a way of orientating herself to the reality of the situation in the labor rooms, which can't be gleaned from the formal updates or the charts on the walls. But it's also a moment of connection between the nurses, who don't always agree with or follow the rules.

"Any young mums in today?" Emma asks. The recent lack of young mothers has added another level of mystery to the horror of the last few weeks, since the rumors online exploded after the PreacherGirl song.

Emma has been keeping a daily watch for teen mums on the wards, unnerved that she hasn't come across any.

"No. Youngest is twenty-four," Dorothy whispers. "Lady in Room Two's the main one to watch today. Name's Megan, and she's not coping well. Been here since the middle of the night. Not past three centimeters yet, but doesn't want to go home. She'll be a while, I think. Room Three has an active labor: the Swindells; nice, calm couple doing their breathing exercises together, and five centimeters on last check. A beautiful little girl arrived in the night, and a whopping great boy an hour ago. Both bawled their lungs out. Girl's in with her mother in Seven, already feeding. Boy's being checked over in the nursery while mum gets some sleep. It was a rough delivery, lots of stitches."

"It's been four days now," Cara says, before crunching her lolly loudly. "Perhaps . . ."

"Don't," Emma interrupts. She hates to deter Cara's obvious grasp for comfort, but she can't cope with unfounded hope. Better to be ready for the worst than to pretend it's over when the statistics suggest it's only just beginning.

They all handle the pressure in different ways. Dorothy prays a lot, while Cara's sweet tooth holds her hostage. She'll disappear from a labor room to surreptitiously pop another lolly into her mouth, but no one says anything, because she's young and they get it. And if she quits, there'll just be more strain on the rest of them.

"Anything else we should know?" Emma asks Dorothy.

"No, don't think so. A quiet night, all things considered. But Lynne is on your shift today."

Emma nods, and Dorothy holds out her hands to both of them. Emma takes one reluctantly, and watches Cara follow suit and close her eyes. Dorothy's voice is strong and steady.

"Lord, on this day, please grant us the serenity to accept all that we cannot change, the courage to change the things we need to, and your everlasting wisdom so that we may know the difference."

Emma feels Dorothy squeeze her hand and opens her eyes to find the older woman watching her. Assessing. Emma smiles back, although she senses there's no fooling Dorothy. She used to get comfort from Dorothy's words, but every day this feels like more of a charade. She seriously doubts there's a higher power listening to their pleas—and if there is, then all she has for this lackluster god is hot, venomous anger.

11:10 a.m.

Mr. Bailey, the art teacher, is ten minutes late. Lainey's eyes skim over the walls, usually peppered with pictures but currently cleared for the start of a new term. She won't turn around, won't give Dylan the satisfaction of looking. Of caring.

She leans over to get her pencils and sketchpad from her bag and can't help but take the briefest of glances toward him. She hasn't been this close to Dylan for months, but he seems exactly the same: slouching in his seat, wearing baggy dark jeans and a plain gray T-shirt under an open checked shirt. His floppy hair falls over his eyes as he doodles in his sketchbook.

There's no one close enough to talk to. Sereena is deep in conversation with Katie about tomorrow's protest, and Lainey's stomach begins to cramp as they wait. She wishes Mr. Bailey would hurry up. They all know what he's up to: he runs off for an illicit smoke on the breaks and has to move away from school grounds in order to avoid breaching policy.

Liam suddenly lobs a ball of scrunched-up paper at Sereena and Lainey, and Sereena picks it up. "Fetch, Fido," she says, throwing it back.

Lainey watches but doesn't smile. Sereena leans over. "You okay?"

"Uh-huh." Lainey pretends to rummage for something in her bag.

"Don't worry, we'll figure it out somehow."

"Figure what out?" Liam leans on the desk, having come to retrieve the pencil he'd just tossed at them.

"Mind your own," Sereena says, pulling out a lip gloss and smoothing it across her plump lips.

"If it's about the protest tomorrow, I'm telling you the same thing I told Lainey this morning. Don't go. You're going to get yourselves in a lot of trouble. Particularly if you start banging on about Ellis."

Lainey watches as Sereena's face falls. She leans across and says, "Sorry, Sez. Liam was annoying me earlier and I let it slip."

Sereena's face twitches and Lainey knows it's an inward groan.

"Of course we're worried about Ellis," she snaps at Liam. "Because she's our friend. And she's missing. But that's beside the point. Tomorrow is about the fact that women's rights are once again being eroded with no justification."

"Er, what's more important: your rights or finding out why the babies are dying?"

Sereena's eyes flash dangerously. "And what makes you think we have to sacrifice one to fix the other? I've got better things to do with my Saturdays, too, you know, in an ideal world. But some of us have to fight for our future."

"And how will you do that from inside a jail cell?" Liam says, arms folded, that irritating smug expression lighting up his face.

"The government won't allow free speech anymore, is that what you're saying?" Sereena raises her eyebrows. "Mary Walcott's a dictator now, is she, arresting everyone who dares to disagree with her?"

"But that's not why you're going," Liam says. "You've fallen for a conspiracy theory, and I thought better of you, Sereena. Like I was telling Lainey this morning, PreacherGirl's a con artist, and she's got you all sucked in and acting crazy. But you won't get anywhere: I've seen the tracking technology the government uses with the watches; Dad's showed me. They know where you are every second of the day."

Lainey feels her hackles rise along with her fear, but Sereena's calm exterior doesn't change. "It's okay for you, though, isn't it, Liam? What's changed for you, really? Will you be affected by having an illegal abortion, or suddenly disappear if the authorities think you're pregnant?"

"Seriously?" Liam laughs. "Don't you get it? Those laws are just temporary while they sort out the doll babies. And PreacherGirl has you all riled up and emotional because she knows how to press your buttons. There's always some uninformed twat ready to jump on the bandwagon and scare the shit out of everyone."

Sereena scrapes her chair around to face him. "Sometimes the government does bad things, Liam. Then the politicians pretend they're all innocent, so the people need to hold them to account. That's as old as time, too. Perhaps you should stop listening to Daddy and spend more time researching the facts. Go learn some history, Liam."

"You're so dramatic, Sereena," Liam says as he heads back to his seat. "Just don't say I didn't warn you. They won't let you off lightly because you're girls."

Sereena turns to Lainey. "We have to get that cretin to stop following you around," she mutters under her breath. "And I know you were stressed this morning, but I really hope you haven't fucked up the plan."

"I'll come tomorrow," says a gruff voice from behind them.

Lainey's stomach twists as they both look at Dylan.

"It affects all of us," he says. "And PreacherGirl made some good points. We should be protesting—women's rights are human rights." His face turns pink as he finishes speaking.

Sereena hesitates, and Lainey watches her thinking this through. Then she says, "Wow, thanks, Dylan," and glares triumphantly at Liam, who rolls his eyes. "I'd almost forgotten Dylan could talk," she whispers to Lainey, laughing.

Lainey leans close. "Should we put him off? We don't really want him with us tomorrow, do we?"

Sereena waves a hand as though to bat away Lainey's worries. "He probably won't show up. And even if he does, he can go and march with the main group if he doesn't want to stay with us."

Lainey opens her mouth to say more, then stops. This isn't the moment, but she can't cope with seeing Dylan tomorrow as well. Today is bad enough.

Until now, Dylan hasn't really been on Sereena's radar, and yet he's always been on Lainey's. They'd known each other in passing since primary school; however, in the last couple of years, as they'd both developed their passion for art, they'd found themselves working on more projects together, hanging out at the same events. Sereena was like most people who thought Dylan morose and strange, so Lainey hadn't told her that one weekend, a few months ago, they'd gone down to the old rail bridge together—climbing flimsy fencing and picking their way through long grass to paint a mural there. He wanted to try something different, he'd explained, as he used the twin arches of the bridge to form the under-curves of a pair of fiery orange wings, which spread out across the brickwork until it felt as if the bird was hovering above them, observing its own creation.

"Is this legal?" she'd asked on day one.

"Better to beg for forgiveness than permission," he'd murmured, focused intently on the orange outline he was daubing across the brickwork.

It had taken three days of painstaking close-up work, regularly standing back to check their progress. Lainey knew she was talented, but Dylan was something else. His vision was extraordinary. Slowly, the flaming phoenix had risen before them, captured midflight, eyes staring intently, wild and furious, like it wanted to swoop and pluck them from the ground. And she'd realized why he'd thought of it there—from a distance, the black boulders at the bridge's base were the perfect rubble of ashes.

On day three, as they'd finished, he'd said, "I brought something to celebrate," then he'd opened his backpack and pulled out a bottle of whiskey and two glasses. The sun had been setting behind the bridge. The fluorescent phoenix wings glowed in the twilight. They'd sat down and both knocked back two glasses, one after the other. There was an excited, nervous flutter in Lainey's chest. Dylan had picked at the grass, smiling as she told him about the tragicomic procession of the animals at the vet clinic, where she worked on weekends.

It was after the second glass of whiskey that he'd leaned in and kissed her.

Flushing with the memory, Lainey glances nervously across the art room, but Dylan is still doodling. He doesn't usually bother joining in the general conversation, and she wonders why he'd offered to go to the rally. Perhaps it was purely to antagonize Liam. Dylan has never had much time for Liam, and it appears to go both ways, yet somehow Dylan always avoids the sarcasm that Liam inflicts on other meek souls. Perhaps because he's the art teacher's son, but more likely because it feels like he can see right through you. His drawings are often of bilaterally dissected skulls with dark inner thoughts tumbling out of them like innards falling after a blade has struck. Dylan is moody and intense and definitely the most talented artist in the class, if not the school.

She really has to speak to him.

Everyone quiets down as Mr. Bailey finally enters. It's a hush born of respect rather than the grudging tolerance given to other teachers, because Mr. Bailey is almost one of them. His long, gray-flecked hair is in a ponytail, and he wears jeans and loose, unironed shirts. The only resemblance to Dylan is his deep-set brown eyes.

"Right, then," Mr. Bailey says, "we'll be doing a bit of art history this term, but first of all I have an exciting project for you guys. St. Stephen's Primary School has agreed to let us design an inspirational mural on the side wall of their new hall. The theme is 'regeneration'. It'll be a cooperative project with some of the kids there, and a mini-comp for us, because they'll get to pick the design winner. So, this is your homework for the next week; I'm going to get you working in pairs to come up with ideas."

As soon as he finishes, Sereena slides her chair closer to Lainey's and slips a possessive arm through hers. Mr. Bailey spots it straightaway and laughs. "Nice try, Miss Mandalia," he says. "We'll be deciding the teams without favoritism, and I've already prepared the draw." He pats a ceramic pot on the table. "All the boys' names are in here, and you lucky ladies get to come and pick a partner. Come on, then, Sereena, you can go first."

Sereena jumps up and heads for the desk, swirling her hand in the pot of names and pulling out a piece of paper. She opens it and groans. "Really?"

"Who'd you get?" Mr. Bailey asks.

"Liam," she says, shaking her head, as Liam lets out a loud whoop of sarcastic joy. She pulls an unimpressed face at him and returns to her desk.

Deon is paired with Brenda, Emily with Matt, Marina with Jeff. And then it's Lainey's turn.

She swirls her hand in the pot of half-a-dozen names, praying she won't pick Dylan. Then she opens the paper and sees five little letters. For the second time today, her prayers have not been answered.

"Dylan," she announces to the class, and dares to look at him. He barely responds, just raises his eyebrow as he taps his pencil on his paper. She wants to march over and slap him. Instead, she stalks back to her seat.

The next few names are pulled out, until everyone has a partner. "Great," Mr. Bailey says, putting the pot back on the shelf behind him. "Some interesting combinations there. Can't wait to see what you come up with. Get together with your partners now and start discussing your ideas."

Liam comes over to sit with Sereena, and Lainey joins Dylan at his table.

"Are you okay about this?" he whispers to Lainey, his eyes fixed on the sketchpad in front of them.

"Let's just get on with it," she snaps.

He glances up and catches her eye, stirring her memories. He looks as worried now as he had that night, when the air had finally rushed in between their lips.

"You know," he'd said all those months ago, with the dying sun behind him blazing in her eyes. "I've wanted to do that for ages . . . but . . ."

"But what?"

His face was so solemn. "I didn't think you liked me . . . like this."

She'd felt a shiver of nervous delight. "Really? Why?"

"I'm not like the others."

"And you think that's a bad thing?"

He'd looked surprised. Then he'd kissed her again. Harder. His body had pressed down on her, the grass tickling her ears. The ground was rough, and small stones dug into her skull. She'd ignored them, not wanting him to stop.

Her hands were inside his shirt, his breath hot in her ear.

"Do you want to?" she'd asked.

His reply had been breathless. Clipped. "I haven't . . . I haven't got anything . . . and I haven't . . . I haven't . . ."

"It's okay, just make sure you pull out before the end."

He'd stilled momentarily before he'd asked, "Really?"

She had felt she was losing him and sensed the moment might not happen again if she didn't take it.

"It'll be okay." She'd done sex ed. There was a window for fertility, and her period was due in a few days.

He'd hesitated as twilight crept over them. She could still make out the pure white skin of his chest and a smattering of jet-black hair running between his ribs, a dark circle of it around his belly button. He'd stared at the ample curves of her breasts. His face was red; his ragged breath an echo of hers.

"It's okay, you can touch me," she'd said.

His fingers had stroked her breasts, feather light at first, then firmer, circling her nipples. The ache between her legs had intensified, and she'd tugged at the zipper of his jeans.

He'd squirmed away. "Shit, Lainey, give me a minute, won't you." He'd sat back on his haunches, breathless, still staring at her, but then he'd laughed in a way she hadn't seen before. It was a deep, joyous laugh, like a part of him had suddenly slipped past the guardedness he wore as a shield.

After that, darkness had descended fast. Their jeans were down past their knees as he lowered himself onto her. She'd felt his penis probing, hot between her legs, as his long fringe tickled her eyelids.

"You're sure you want to?"

He wasn't like the others. She trusted him. "Yes."

When he'd pushed inside her, it had hurt more than she'd expected. She'd gasped, and they'd stopped kissing. Their eyes had locked for a moment, and he'd opened his mouth then closed it, and buried his face against her shoulder, thrusting and jerking for a few seconds, before he'd pulled away and his body had collapsed against hers.

He'd lain still and silent on top of her. She'd waited a moment then said, "Dylan, can you move? I can't breathe."

"Shit, sorry." He'd got up. Neither of them had spoken. The mood had changed, and she'd had no idea why, but they could barely see each other now, and it was dark and cold.

"We should go." He'd pulled up his jeans and hurriedly packed his bag, the cups clinking against the whiskey bottle. He wouldn't look at her. She'd fumbled with her clothes, aware of a cold stickiness between her legs, and before she was quite ready, he'd walked off, leaving her half running to catch up. He'd left her at the bus stop with barely a goodbye. After that, she'd hardly seen him over the last few weeks of term, and he hadn't spoken to her for the whole summer.

He's still staring at her now as she thinks of the secret in her belly. Half of her wants to hit him with it hard, right this second. The other half never wants to tell him.

Sereena leans back so her chair is balanced on two legs. She's watching them, curiously.

"We'll be meeting at midday tomorrow, Dylan," she calls across. "At the station."

Dylan takes a moment to answer, as though he's catching up with the words. "Right."

"Don't let us down. We need numbers to make an impact—the more of us, the better."

Dylan nods. "It's okay, Sereena, I get it."

"Don't waste your weekend, mate," Liam chips in.

"I won't. I'll be there," Dylan says with more surety.

"Great," Sereena replies as her gaze drifts between them.

Lainey can almost see the wheels turning in her friend's brain, cogs clinking together, ideas developing, swirling, strengthening. Suddenly, Sereena's eyes go wide. A question.

Lainey gives a small shake of the head. It's not *no*, it's *not now*. But Sereena can't resist mouthing one word at her. *Really?* Lainey gives her a desperate look. *Not. Now.*

Sereena's eyes are saucers. More silent words that Lainey can easily read. *What—the—fuck . . . ?*

Lainey turns away, back to Dylan, to find he's watching them both. She's not sure if he can read Sereena's lips from where he's sitting, but he's frowning in a way that makes her uncomfortable, and his cheeks are pink. What does he think? That she told her best friend about their awkward romp in the dark? That they're laughing about him? Perhaps she should've told Sereena, but she didn't want to laugh. It was so painful she only wanted to forget it.

Except we can't now, she thinks. A wave of nausea overtakes her, so that she suddenly jumps up and makes for the classroom door, not sure yet if she's heading for the bathroom or the exit, just anywhere but here.

11:55 a.m.

The administrative offices have always been colorless, soulless places for Emma. She stares at the computer, trying her hardest to compose her answers to the National Birth Crisis Center's post-birth questionnaire to the required standard. Once completed, it had to pass through a chain of obstetricians and management before reaching the NBCC. There's nothing worse than finishing one of these and being asked to do it again, with more detail.

She hates every moment of these write-ups. It feels like a betrayal of the mothers, recounting each woman's moods and words throughout labor and birth. Perhaps she's paranoid, but the questions seem to be worded to suggest some kind of maternal responsibility: as though the scientists might suddenly realize that if a mother swore or screamed from the pain more than a certain number of times, then that became the tipping point for a stillbirth. As though they didn't know that childbirth was as unique as the babies: that stoic mothers could end up rushed away for a cesarean, while anxious ones could suddenly settle into the rhythm of intense contractions and determinedly puff on gas and air. There were certain indications, of course, as to how births would go, but you never knew for sure.

Today's report subject, Jody McArthur, had been exceptionally polite during most of her labor, managing to thank the nurses even as she grunted and writhed in pain. Perhaps she'd decided that if she retained her manners, then the fates would look kindly on her, and if so, it had worked, because after ten hours of labor, Emma had passed a quivering, blood-smeared little boy over to his exhausted mother. Jody had taken him and stared at her child for a long moment, as if she couldn't quite believe he was there: breathing, squirming, *hers*. Her husband, Mac, had sobbed with joy and relief—and as she watched the couple's tears, Emma had felt her own little echoing rush of oxytocin.

Yes, she types, the child had latched well. *Yes*, the afterbirth had been delivered easily. *Yes*, she had given the baby an injection of vitamin K, and the mother a shot of syntocinon.

By the time the report is done it feels like she's been on shift for hours, but a check of the wall clock shows she's only an hour and a half in. She emails the documents to the attending obstetrician, copying in David Hargreaves, deputy CEO of the hospital, and Lynne, the head matron. Then she gets up and closes the laptop, bringing it with her to deposit it back at the nurse's station—ready for the next person who'll need it.

As soon as she pushes open the double doors to the ward, she knows what's happened. There's a certain kind of silence in the corridor, a gravitas to the way the nurses are moving, despite the cries of a laboring mother down in Room 2. Sorrow saturates the air.

Dorothy is at the nurse's station, checking the computer.

"Which one?" Emma asks.

"Room Three." Dorothy keeps typing, not meeting her eyes. "The Swindell couple."

Emma puts down the laptop and takes a few steps along the corridor. The door to Room 3 has been closed, and in the pocket on the wall, where paper-clipped notes are placed to wait for doctors, there's a laminated sign featuring three large black letters: IPX.

The nurses hate this symbol for the stillborn babies. They'd argued for something else—a pair of angel wings, perhaps—but the hospital ignored them, needing something stark and visual that warned people not to enter the area, which would now be going through the temporary quarantine procedure that happened with every one of these stillbirths: swabs and observations and temperature checks, and—somewhere in amongst it all—a mother and father allowed only a few minutes to grieve over their child. After, the body is taken to a special part of the hospital to await autopsy in the hope that this might be the newborn to give up its secrets and save the babies who are coming.

As Emma stares at the door, it opens and Cara comes out, weeping. She heads for Dorothy, who puts an arm around her and guides her away to somewhere more private. Emma watches them go, knowing that Cara doesn't have long left on the wards now. She's breaking a little more each time. They've seen it before, particularly in the younger nurses, because none of them had signed on for this. There are exceptions, but the older nurses tend to be more battle hardy, already experienced in the steady, numbing fatigue that comes from witnessing trauma and loss. And this place feels more like a war zone every day.

She hears a noise and sees Lynne exiting the delivery room, her mouth pinched in a tight line, a tightly wrapped bundle in her arms. Emma's eyes flicker away from the babe, because she knows what she'll see: a perfect little face that will never move, forever lost to the world at the moment he or she entered it. A tiny miracle, now the repository of a terrible secret that is slowly bringing them all to their knees.

Lynne pauses at the sight of Emma and frowns. Her eyes are tinged red, but hard and glassy.

"I'm sorry . . ." Emma begins.

"It's a Code Twelve, and I'm in the middle of protocols," Lynne snaps and pushes past her.

Emma steps back and watches her go. Lynne seems to take every one of these births personally, a slight on her midwifery skills, as though she alone might solve the country-wide crisis if she could just do better, work more expediently, get those damn babies out before they forgot how to bloody well breathe. Emma had been able to talk to her at first, but now there are no more discussions, barely any communication at all. Emma suspects the turmoil inside Lynne is greater even than Cara's, but to counter it Lynne has become a stickler for the rules, following each one ever more meticulously, admonishing anyone who dares to breach them. Her anger grows visibly with every deceased child, but she swallows it down, letting it blaze deep inside her. When Emma is around Lynne now, she senses danger. One more impending catastrophe that she doesn't know how to resolve.

3.

Lainey pushes open the heavy double doors of Whitehaven's veterinary practice, carrying the box of chicks and blinking the tiredness from her eyes. She'd been exhausted last night, mumbling one-word answers to her mother's stream of questions over dinner, until Emma gave up, hugged her, and went to have a shower and an early night. But despite Lainey's fatigue, she'd slept fitfully, waking from dreams where she was chased by unseen pursuers, always cornered just before she woke, until there was nowhere left to run.

Her Saturday job is usually the highlight of her week, but today it's the last place she wants to be. It could be the exhaustion that she now knows is the baby, draining her of nutrients and energy. Or it could be her reluctance to face the large bump protruding beneath Michelle's blue uniform.

A few months ago, Lainey had enjoyed Michelle's pregnancy updates, curious about the cravings, the strange pains, the nausea, the little kicks. Since then, Michelle has stopped mentioning the pregnancy, drilling Lainey for news from the hospital instead as her due date draws closer. It's been awkward so far. Today could prove unbearable.

"Morning, Lainey." Michelle greets her from behind the desk, pen poised in hand.

On the wall behind Michelle, a glossy poster shows a plump Labrador puppy and a sweet Ragdoll kitten gazing longingly at packets of Premier biscuits. In one corner, next to the padded sofas, a fish tank bubbles away, a few guppies cruising over a rainbow of colorful stones.

"Morning." Lainey places the box of birds on the countertop. "I've brought the chicks in for a checkup."

Michelle gently opens the lid, and Lainey holds her breath. The little creatures had been quiet on the journey, the box wobbling and rocking in the front basket of her bicycle. Now, as soon as the light reaches them, the three chicks burst into frantic chorus, mouths wide, demanding.

"Wow, still alive!" Michelle says, gently stroking their half-feathered heads. "I still can't believe we've got hatchlings this late in the year, but then the seasons are so out of whack nowadays. I'm surprised they've all made it this far. Great job, Lainey! You'd better give them something to eat."

Lainey nods and closes the box, although the birds keep on chirping. "And then what should I do?"

"You can start in the back room." The phone begins to ring and Michelle's hand hovers over it. "Just give it a once-over, sweep up, and do the restocks. It hasn't stopped this morning. I've got two emergencies coming in shortly, and Carol has just called to say she'll be late, so I might need you out here on reception."

"Okay." Lainey scurries off, grateful they'll be busy. At the moment, all she wants is to keep moving.

Her phone beeps in her pocket and she checks it. Sereena. Again.

> I know I'm fussing, but I still think you should stay home.

> I'm coming.

Lainey replies again.

> This matters to me more than ever now. See you at 12.

Then she switches off the phone so Sereena can't keep doing this to her all morning.

The large back room of the vet's office is a functional contrast of dull whites, grays, and chrome, and the only things tacked on the walls are sheets of protocols and information. The tang of disinfectant is overwhelming, and Lainey immediately wants to retch. She takes a few slow, steadying breaths and grabs an open tin from the fridge to feed the birds. Once they are full, she gets to work, cleaning out cages and restocking supplies.

Two sets of coal-black eyes watch her, noses pressed between the bars. The chart says they're miniature poodles, kept overnight after having their stomachs pumped for eating rat poison. "I hope you've learned your lessons," Lainey admonishes them gently, letting them sniff her hands. The only other occupied cage contains a sleepy cat. When Lainey squats down to peer closer, she sees three tiny lumps of black-and-white fur pressed against the animal's abdomen. "You had babies, did you?" Lainey whispers as the mother regards her with a baleful squint. "Well done, they're perfect."

Her voice cracks on the last word. The mother cat's eyes widen slightly.

"Lainey? You okay?"

She hadn't heard Michelle come in. "Yep, it's nothing," she says, getting to her feet. "I'm just really tired this morning. Sorry."

"No need to apologize." Michelle moves to the cupboard and begins to collect syringes. "Why so tired? Did you go out last night?"

"No, I was asleep by ten." Lainey grabs a cloth to wipe the stainless steel table in the center of the room, even though it's already glistening.

"I'm the same." Michelle peers into the cages as she talks. "I didn't know how exhausting pregnancy would be. I can hardly stay awake after dinner. It's better than it was, though—the first few months were terrible." Her voice drifts away as she rubs her tummy. Lainey waits, unsure what to say, watching the crease of Michelle's brow deepen.

"What's the latest from the hospital?" Michelle continues. "Has your mum said much lately?"

Lainey continues to wipe the table. "I've barely seen her. She's working long shifts."

"It's good she's still there. I've heard there're heaps of nurses on stress leave now. Does she see a counselor?"

"I don't think so. She doesn't talk about it much." Lainey wonders now if her mum talks about the babies at all. If she does confide in anyone, Lainey guesses it would be Cathy, not a counselor.

"She's got a brilliant reputation among the expectant mums, you know," Michelle says. "They all mention how good she is, how calming. Some of them have had her for previous births and they ask for her as soon as they get to the hospital."

"That doesn't surprise me," Lainey says. And it doesn't. Her mother is exactly the person for a crisis. Solid. Dependable. So, why have Michelle's words disturbed her? Why do they ignite a fresh blast of fear as Lainey thinks of Emma?

10:00 a.m.

Emma walks through town toward the river, past the newsagents with fluorescent yellow Closing Down Sale signs plastered all over its windows. Nearby, just beyond Marks & Spencer, there's another empty shell of a building, which had been a boutique gift shop the last time she came this way. Over a dozen high-street shops gone in less than a year. The town is slowly dying.

Or perhaps it's just changing. Nothing stays the same forever, after all.

She speeds up as she passes a group of teenage boys kicking cans off the bench in front of Aldi. They look so young, so unaware, and her thoughts turn to Lainey.

This morning, she'd lingered by her child's empty room. When Fergus had got up from his basket to stretch and trot across to greet her, Emma had bent down to ruffle his silky head. "What's going on with her, Fergie?" she'd asked, but the dog only regarded her stoically.

She realizes she's only a street or two from the vet's. She could pop in? No, that's a bad idea. Too unusual. Clingy. This irrational need to see her daughter, to hold her, has been increasing over the last few weeks, but it's not Lainey's problem. It's those little babies in the basement of the hospital, and the mothers four floors above, with their empty arms. They haunt her dreams, but they're not reasons to start fussing over her own girl, who's alive and almost grown, and doesn't need crowding. So she hurries on.

The Boathouse café is perched by the river's edge, with an idyllic view over the slow-moving, iron-gray water to the bluebell wood that Emma had loved as a child. She'd grown up in the care of her grandmother, who valued walks and wildflowers as staple weekend activities, and the bluebell wood was one of their favorite places. She'd taken Lainey there as a small child, too, but it's been years since she last visited, she thinks with a jolt. What had happened to her life that she couldn't find time for a walk in the woods?

The café is bustling. Customers line up to claim the few vacant tables, while waitresses weave between everyone, using their forearms to increase the number of plates they can carry at once.

Cathy is already at a table by the window, a mug of coffee in front of her. She gets up for a hug, then steps back to appraise Emma. "You doing okay?"

Emma shrugs. "Just about. It's getting harder, though."

"I'm not surprised." As they sit, Cathy puts the newspaper insert in front of Emma and taps on an article. "Seen this? You going to go?"

Emma grabs the paper and scans the text:

Local legend Geraldine Fox will appear at the Southbank Centre on September 13 as part of the London Literature Festival. A resident of Australia for the past twenty-five years, Geraldine will return to her roots to discuss her latest provocative book, *Last Woman Standing*. Known for three decades for her blistering feminist critiques of contemporary society, Geraldine's new work has been praised by the *New York Times* as "her best and fiercest book yet."

She passes it back to Cathy with her eyebrows raised. "Doubt I'll be buying a ticket. You know what I think of her."

Cathy smiles. "Yep, but right now I wouldn't mind hearing what she has to say. Perhaps she has a point. And I love the title."

"Sadly, I don't have the energy for anything except work at the moment."

"Speaking of which, I'm not sure what you'll make of my news." Cathy sets the paper aside.

"Oh?"

"Mary Walcott's paying us a visit. On Monday. Are you on shift?"

"Shit, really? Yes, I'm on day shift again from tomorrow. Why's she coming?"

"Well, I'd like to think it's because we're a shining example of hospital care, but I'm pretty sure Grant Whittaker set it up. He'll likely want the media attention, and he's buddies with a few of our board members. They're desperate for some positive publicity, to distract people from those embarrassing security leaks."

Emma sighs. "Even if the board is getting itchy because parents are choosing to go elsewhere, the reality is we're still short-staffed with the admissions we've got now. And with the new laws against giving birth outside a hospital, I can't see the maternity wards being empty anytime soon."

"I don't think Grant Whittaker or Mary Walcott give a toss about our admission figures," Cathy says. "They just want to put on a show to look like they're doing something, now that the stats are creeping closer to one in two babies affected. They must be panicking."

"Grant Whittaker doesn't panic about anything unless it involves his career. I still can't believe he's worked himself into such a prominent government position. I thought he was finished years ago when he had that affair with the nineteen-year-old, the one who wrote that slushy romance novel that everyone thought was about him."

"Ah, yes, *Slaves of Seduction*. That was a hell of a read." Cathy chuckles. "Must have been some interesting conversations in his house after that. I suppose you have to give some credit to the man for his sheer lack of shame and his efforts to claw back up the ranks."

Emma wishes she could see the funny side as easily as Cathy, but the man troubles her too much. "Well, he's made it almost to the top now, hasn't he? I'm surprised his kids still go to St. James's and he hasn't enrolled them in Eton or Harrow."

Cathy snorts. "He's a man of the people, Emma, surely you can see that. You can't have forgotten last year when he turned sports day into a campaign rally."

"Hmm . . . we should probably be grateful he's usually too busy to turn up at school events. I never see Lucinda anymore, either, now that the kids are old enough to get themselves to school."

"Well, you can be thankful for that, too. She's constantly trying to get me to her charity lunches at seven hundred dollars a pop. The whole family's insufferable. Beth pulls a face if Liam's name ever comes up. Apparently, he thinks he's king of the school."

Occasionally, when Cathy drops these things into conversation, Emma is reminded of how different their worlds are. They only live a few streets apart, but Emma's townhouse is a squat compared to Cathy's detached four-bedroom house with its double garage and large garden, thanks to her husband's success as a city broker. The only reason Emma has been able to keep Lainey at St. James's is thanks to her carefully eked-out inheritance and a number of sacrifices: no holidays, no car. Lucinda Whittaker has never invited Emma to a charity luncheon.

Cathy is still talking. "Anyway, let's get back to the prime minister's visit. This could all backfire, of course, but it's an opportunity for us to talk directly to power. And you know that comes around once in a blue moon. You can see she's under pressure at the moment, can't you? That speech the other day about all expectant mothers having a greater duty than themselves and their unborn child, that they also have to ensure the overall protection of human life. I mean, no pressure, ladies!"

Emma grimaces. "Yep, that was pretty awful. She has to be tough, though, doesn't she? She got so much crap for stumbling at the start and showing emotion. And with all the unrest now and the restrictions on travel and exports, you can just imagine all the ambitious bloodhounds circling if she doesn't draw a clear line in the sand."

"Well, when she comes to the hospital, you might get to meet her. She wants to talk to a few nurses and mums, apparently. Lynne has already put up her hand to show her around, of course."

Emma rolls her eyes. "No one else will get a look-in, then."

Cathy takes a sip of coffee before continuing. "Just remember, you have friends in high places, Em. If you want to show the PM around, I can make it happen."

Emma laughs. "No, no, that wasn't what I meant."

"Think about it." Cathy's face is solemn, her eyebrows raised. "It's saying here that the government's in turmoil and planning a range of new measures to try to safeguard future births. God knows what that means, but I don't think it'll be good for anyone actually having a baby. You might get a few points across that would really help the mums."

"Oh, I don't know." Even the thought of it makes Emma's shoulders tighten. "I'm not very eloquent. Perhaps you should ask Dorothy Suffolk, she's got a lovely way with words, and she's appalled by the lack of support on the wards."

Cathy's smiling as she shakes her head. "Only an eloquent person knows the word *eloquent*. You'll be great, but I'll keep Dorothy on standby, too."

Emma leans in. "Have you heard any more lately, officially or otherwise, about missing young mums? I hadn't even noticed until the online blowup, but now it's bothering me. I don't think we've had any teen mums on the wards since this started."

"We don't get too many young ones through, though, do we? Usually, less than a dozen a year are under eighteen, and that's a busy year. We can't go paying attention to wild conspiracies, we've enough on our plates."

Emma lets it drop, but she isn't sure Cathy's right. There's something disturbing about the stories, and she's struggling to let go of them. Perhaps it's because of the extra vulnerability she's seen in teen mums over the years. They tend to be more frightened and unsure. Easy to manipulate. And spread out across the country, their numbers were small enough that an unusual drop-off rate would take a while to be noticed.

Emma's misgivings have been exacerbated by the disappearance of Ellis's mum, Miriam, who'd cornered Emma in the school reception a week before the summer vacation and said she was planning to run for chairperson of the Parent-Teacher Association in September, and asked if she would have Emma's vote. Not the conversation she'd expect to have with a parent who knows they're moving away.

Her thoughts are interrupted by a waitress coming to bring them a bottle of water and take their orders. When she's gone, Emma leans forward again. "Maybe we should ask Mary directly what she thinks about the missing girls."

Cathy laughs. "Oh, dear, I hereby withdraw my offer," she says. "You're not allowed to spout conspiracy theories at the PM, okay? You can only rail about the situations we're experiencing directly! So, are you in?"

Emma holds up her hands in surrender. "Okay, I'll think about it."

Cathy nods. "Think fast, because plans are in motion."

"I will, but I'm trying to take a mental break from the hospital. Can we talk about something else for a bit? How're the kids?"

"Beth was out last night clubbing, and stayed God knows where. I keep telling her, whatever you get up to, just bloody well use protection. Obviously, she loves that. At least Archie is still young enough to like staying home with his VR headset." She pauses, her eyes never leaving Emma's face. "What's Lainey up to? Is she going to the march today? I'm nervous as hell about it, but Beth insists they'll be fine, and she's too old for me to ground her."

"You know what, I'm not sure," Emma admits, shamefaced. "She said she was planning to, but I haven't talked with her properly for a couple of days. Terrible, isn't it. I'll message her." She pulls out her phone and rattles off a message, then puts it away and rubs her eyes. "My shift pattern's been awkward, and I've struggled to have any decent conversations with her lately. I'm worried about her, to be honest. Her bedroom light has been on at all hours over the past few weeks, since she and her friends realized Ellis Scott might be one of the missing girls."

Cathy shudders. "Beth's struggling too. The whole situation is a nightmare." She stares at the view for a moment before her eyes move back to meet Emma's. "From what I hear, a lot of the girls are doing it though. As much as I want to lock Beth up and keep her safe, I think the protest march might be good for her if it means she feels a bit less helpless."

Emma shrugs. "Maybe you're right. I hope so." She tries to echo Cathy's optimism, but her smile falters.

Cathy leans across and pats her hand. "Lainey will be fine. Seriously, hon, she's always known what she's about: drawing her little heart out or rescuing sick animals. She's one of a kind."

Emma shrugs. "I know, and she handles herself well, but she can be pretty aloof. And it's hard to stop worrying."

"We're wired for worry, though, aren't we? No going back on that. It's biological."

Emma picks up the newspaper again and runs her eyes over the text. "Not for all mothers," she murmurs. "I hope the girls aren't putting themselves in harm's way for nothing today. These protests are pointless. Too many people agree with the government's position. Most of them don't even mind being surveilled anymore if they think it keeps them safe, and women's rights are always the first thing to go backward in a crisis."

"That doesn't sound like you," Cathy says, regarding Emma intently. "You're usually the first in line to challenge the powers that be."

Emma sighs. "I know. I'm just exhausted." As she speaks, her watch and phone buzz at the same time. She checks the message, hoping it's Lainey. Then grimaces.

"What is it?"

"They're short-staffed again. Lynne's asking if I can go in."

Cathy sighs. "It's your one day off. You don't have to, you know."

"I know. But I'm needed, aren't I?"

She doesn't add that she'd rather go in, because the alternative is an empty house, and pacing and fretting about her daughter. Cathy scrutinizes her for a moment but doesn't say anything more. They move on to other topics as the food arrives, although the hospital and the kids creep into the conversation. They're on their last few mouthfuls when Emma notices that Cathy is staring over her shoulder and turns around to look.

A heavily pregnant woman is standing by the counter, tears streaming down her face, while two women kneel in front of her, their hands on her belly, praying. A little girl of around two is clinging to her mother's skirt, eyes wide as she watches the women.

Emma pushes back her chair. "Em," Cathy warns. "Don't." But Emma is already on her feet.

Aware of the movement, the pregnant woman looks over.

You okay? Emma mouths from a few feet away. The woman gives a few small, hurried nods, and makes a discernible effort to stop crying, biting her lip and staring at the ceiling.

"Sit down, Em," Cathy hisses from behind her, pulling at her arm.

Reluctantly, Emma returns to her seat, keeping tabs on the women. When they stand up, the pregnant woman thanks them, and they smile kindly. One of them touches the woman's stomach gently before they move back to their table. The pregnant woman finishes paying, then scoops up her child as the little girl starts to cry. As they head for the exit, Emma leaps up and follows.

"Excuse me," she says, reaching them at the doorway, and the woman turns around. Her face is streaked with fresh tears. "Don't worry," Emma says, holding her hands up, "I'm not going to pray over you. I'm a midwife at the hospital, and . . . look . . . you deal with all this how you need to, okay? Don't let everyone else . . . I mean, it's okay to tell a pair of praying women to get lost—if you want to. And at the hospital, too, okay? You don't have to put up with all that."

The woman tries to smile. "Thank you. I don't mind, really. Their prayers can't do any harm, can they?"

Emma nods, chastened, unsure if she's getting her point across.

"But thank you for thinking of me," the woman adds. "What's your name?"

"Emma."

"I hope I see you at the hospital, Emma," she says, glancing at Cathy, who has come to join them, before she walks away.

Emma holds up her hand as Cathy opens her mouth. "Don't."

"You're a brilliant nurse, Ems," Cathy says anyway, "but you can't save them all."

11:55 a.m.

By the time Lainey reaches the train station, it's almost midday. Sereena is with Lexie at the entrance, and they're both focused on Katie, who is leaning on the wall, talking rapidly into her phone. Heart thudding, Lainey scans the area for Dylan and relaxes when she doesn't see him.

"Is Katie okay?" Lainey asks as she joins them.

"Her dad's threatening her with all sorts of consequences for this," Sereena replies with a shrug.

Lainey considers Katie, who's red-faced and animated, and wonders what that would be like. Neither she nor Sereena have had to deal with protective fathers. Sereena's dad died of a heart attack when she was small, and Lainey's father, Craig, had made himself scarce fifteen years ago and has a new family. Each Christmas he sends Lainey a card with a hundred dollars inside, and he pays the agreed amount of child support. Apart from that, they're strangers.

"You're gonna need one of these," Sereena says, producing a white T-shirt from her bag and handing it over. "But you need to go in the bathroom and put it on underneath your top until we get there."

Katie comes over, stuffing her phone back into her pocket.

"You good?" Sereena asks.

"For now," Katie replies, her jaw tight. "Dad's threatening to unleash hell. Don't know why, as he's always been pretty liberal. I think he's just scared, but he didn't like it when I said that."

"It's not just him," Lexie adds nervously. "I've seen the warnings online. The police are overstretched at the moment with having to guard all the hospitals. If they're not there, the march might not stay peaceful. The government's close to declaring a state of emergency because of what's happening with the babies . . . Are we sure about this?"

Sereena glowers. "I thought we were here for Ellis?"

Lainey goes to put a supportive hand on Sereena's shoulder but stops herself. She wants to be here for Ellis, too. But what she *really* wants is to go home and get back into bed. She stares at her feet, ashamed of siding with Lexie over her best friend and their missing friend. When had she become such a coward?

There's a beat when no one says anything, then Sereena throws her hands in the air. "Can't you see this is what they want? The government starts fearmongering, because they remember how powerful the climate marches were, so we'll get scared and stay home. Is that going to help any of us? Will it stop the erosion of our rights? Or find Ellis, or PreacherGirl, or the other missing girls?" She lowers her voice. "Next year, we'll be too busy doing shitty community service, and Ellis will still be missing if no one asks any questions. This is too important; we have to speak up now."

The group goes silent, heads bowed, contrite.

"The train leaves in ten," Sereena says. "If you're coming, let's go."

She strides away and Lainey hurries after her, linking her arm through her friend's. Sereena is trembling.

"Great speech," Lainey whispers.

"Are they coming?"

Lainey glances briefly behind them. "Yep."

A smile flickers across Sereena's face. "Good."

Lainey squeezes her arm.

"So," Sereena says, "Dylan didn't turn up, then . . ."

Lainey tenses, and Sereena seems to register it. "Sorry. We need privacy for that chat." She taps her watch. "But don't worry, he probably won't show. People are always saying they'll come and then finding something better to do. I knew you'd still be here," she says. "Although, I'm not sure it's such a good idea anymore."

Lainey stiffens. "Let's not . . . Don't start treating me differently, okay? I'm still exactly the same person."

"Okay, I promise." Sereena grins. "You can be on the loudspeaker, then."

Lainey stares at her and then her bag. "You haven't . . . Are you joking?"

"Only because I couldn't find one in time," Sereena teases. "Next time, eh. Come on, we still have to get through health and security, and we don't want to miss the train."

There's the sound of running footsteps behind them, and Lainey turns to find Dylan beside her, abruptly slowing his speed to a walk.

"Hey, sorry I'm late," he says, his face flushed, his words breathless. "I missed my bus. Had to run all the way here."

He stops speaking as they reach the line for the gate and he registers the police presence. Lainey catches Sereena's eye and raises her eyebrows.

They take it in turns to step through the security scanner into the health-check area, where a number of small mobile booths have been set up. In each is a robot, designed to appear human, with stationary legs but with disconcertingly realistic movement above the torso. Her mum and friends call them the Terminators, an apparent reference to an old movie Lainey hasn't seen. She can remember the first time she saw one of them, though, on a bus trip to London. They'd been introduced as a safety measure toward the end of the pandemic in places where there were crowds, but more and more had appeared across public services in the last few years, replacing the old-fashioned computer stations and health-scanning equipment. They were built with increasing realism. "One day soon," their science teacher had predicted a few years ago, "you won't even realize you're conversing with a robot because they'll seem so similar to us."

Today, the metal robots are scanning retinas for ID and taking temperatures, uploading and comparing each passenger's results to stored data on their watches, as half a dozen police officers observe from a distance.

"Hello, Lainey," the robot says in a soothing female voice as it scans her watch.

Lainey doesn't reply.

They get through without incident, and as they head to the platform, Dylan stays by Lainey's side. "I've had some ideas for the art project," he says.

"Oh. Right." Lainey had forgotten all about the mural.

"If you still want to work with me, we need to start sketching it. Maybe tomorrow?"

"Yeah, okay." She can't look at him, all too aware of his closeness as they wait together for the train. Yesterday, in school, seeing him had been horrible, but today is way more dangerous. Just a few words, and she'll change his life forever.

Should she?

No.

Yes.

When?

Once on the train, she goes into the tiny bathroom at the end of the carriage, taking out the T-shirt Sereena gave her. The black-and-white picture on the front is of Ellis, smiling happily at the camera, her long, straight, dark hair covering one eye. Lainey remembers the night it was taken: they'd been playing music in Sereena's room and laughing as they did each other's hair. It was only a few months back, but it feels like a million years ago.

The text beneath the photo reads, *Where Is Ellis Scott?*

She gulps as she turns it around and finds more words on the back.

Where Is PreacherGirl?

Lainey pulls it on and hurries out, the door behind her closing with a hiss as the automatic disinfectant sprays begin cleaning the cramped space. Back in the train car, she makes her way to her friends.

Katie and Lexie are deep in conversation. Lainey sits behind them, next to Sereena, who leans close, shouting in Lainey's ear to be heard over the noise of the train. "I'm just telling Dylan he might not want to hang out with us when we get there."

Dylan, who is on the other side of Sereena, also leans in. "And I'm saying I'm happy to be part of your plans. I liked Ellis a lot; we used to sing in the same choir at primary school."

Lainey smiles. "I can't imagine you singing in a choir."

"I got kicked out in the end," he says. "Couldn't concentrate or hold a tune. But Ellis always smiled at me, rather than rolling her eyes like the rest of them."

His breath is so close to her ear that Lainey's stomach does a weird little dance.

Which makes her think of the baby.

Which makes her pull away from him so quickly, he gives her a strange, slightly hurt look.

"Did you say you have a spare T-shirt?" he asks Sereena.

"Yeah, but it was for Sindi, and she's a beanpole."

"Well, give it here and I'll see if I can squeeze it over my six-pack," Dylan replies, grinning.

As he makes his way to the bathroom, Sereena turns to Lainey in surprise. "He really wants to join in?"

"It seems that way."

"Or is he just trying to impress you?"

"I really doubt it," Lainey says, but she can't hold Sereena's gaze.

"When did I miss all this?"

"A few months ago, when you went on your French exchange, I spent some time with him painting a mural. By the time you got back, it was all over."

"But I didn't even know you knew each other."

"We've been in a lot of the same classes and a few art events together. We hung out for a few days. And then we didn't."

"So, when are you going to . . . you know . . . tell him?"

Lainey's chest constricts. "I have no idea."

Sereena seems as though she's about to say more, then she stops and nods toward Dylan, who's making his way back to them. "One thing at a time, hey," she says quietly. Then, louder: "Did it fit?"

"It's pretty tight," he says, pulling a face. "But it's on."

It's another hour to central London, and the train slows regularly to pick up more passengers. Many are of a similar age to Lainey and her friends, some holding placards, and soon the cars are crammed to bursting. Sereena chatters away about a documentary she watched about the rapidly melting Arctic ice shelf, which is threatening to send a deluge of water toward Britain and Europe. Lainey tries to listen, but only hears snatches as her mind keeps drifting. At Liverpool Street station, everyone pours out of the carriage doors, watched by a long line of uniformed police, whose arms stay folded as they murmur observations to one another. Lainey marches with her peers along the platform toward the tube station. The atmosphere is excited, expectant, and tense.

The route to Westminster is awkward, with long walks down busy tube tunnels, and a line change at Bond Street. Half an hour later, they are at last above ground, breathing in the cold, clogged air of central London, and heading toward Parliament.

"You ready?" Sereena asks the group, and at their nod they all take off their jackets and tops to reveal their stark white T-shirts. Lainey ties her jumper around her waist. She's sweating despite the cold day.

"We need to reach the front before we get the banner out," Sereena says, and they follow her, weaving through the crowd, which is so densely packed they have to squeeze through in single file.

Lainey's heart is thumping by the time they get there, and her nausea is back.

"You okay?" Dylan asks, watching her with concern.

She pushes her hair away from her face. "Yes, fine."

It's beginning to drizzle. In the distance someone is speaking through a loudspeaker, but it's hard to make out the words. A chant of, *Walcott, stop the rot* gets louder and louder, followed by, *We'll always fight for women's rights*, and they join in, grinning at each other. Then it stops abruptly, drowned out by a buzzing so loud that Lainey covers her ears as she turns around to locate the source of the noise.

A convoy of thirty to forty drones are flying in low formation above them, four to a row, cruising across the crowd, staying just out of reach. Someone pokes an umbrella up at one of them and the machine neatly swings sideways to avoid it before righting its course. Lainey has never seen anything like this before, and it's silenced the crowd, whose eyes follow the drones as they line up in front of the Westminster barricades that separate protesters and police.

"What the hell?" Sereena calls to Lainey.

"They're creepy as fuck," Dylan says. "They're not going to open fire on us, are they?"

"We'd better get busy, or we'll miss our chance!" Sereena urges them, pulling the long white banner from her bag. It's made from old bedsheets, cut up and restitched. They're toward the front of the march now, and they unfold it and begin walking in a line, each holding a section at chest height.

Its words are a simple echo of their T-shirts: *Where Is Ellis Scott?*

And underneath, in smaller letters: *Where Is PreacherGirl?*

Lainey's legs are aching. The crowd presses around them. People catch sight of the banner, and their T-shirts, and the chant around them changes.

Where is Ellis Scott?

Where is PreacherGirl?

Where is Ellis Scott?

Where is PreacherGirl?

Sereena leans forward and catches Lainey's eye, obviously thrilled at the unexpected support.

They are nearing the Westminster barricade when, without warning, half-a-dozen of the drones let out a burst of white gas. It fills the air above the crowd, and people begin to scream, running haphazardly to get away. Lainey's eyes start to sting, and she drops the banner, staggering toward a low wall next to the footpath. By the time she reaches it, her eyes and throat are burning and her heart is pounding. She holds out her hands blindly as people bump and jostle her. A helicopter passes overhead, rotor blades thumping the air above them, as she leans against the wall, dizzy and nauseous. She listens to the shouts, her legs wobbly. People sound furious and fearful. Now and again there's a shriek, and time drifts. She's trapped.

"Lainey, are you all right?" As if from nowhere, Dylan is there, squatting next to her. She opens her eyes a fraction, finding them less painful, although they still stream with tears. Dylan's eyes are red and glassy, too, his face full of concern.

"My head is spinning," she says, straightening and swallowing her nausea. The air seems to be clearing, but the scene is confusing: some people have dropped to the ground, covering themselves with their coats. Others are running, or moving between those huddled on the floor, checking they're okay. She looks at Dylan, skinny-chested in his tight white T-shirt, and gets a crazy urge to laugh. He holds her wrist and pulls her out of the crowd, and they sit on the edge of the pavement. She waits for the world to stop swirling, aware of Dylan so close. Then it dawns on her that she can't see her friends anymore.

"Where are the others?"

Dylan follows her gaze. "I . . . I don't know." He stands up and tries to peer over the heads of the crowd.

A voice comes over a loudspeaker. *You are protesting illegally. Disperse now.*

It's monotone yet threatening. Lainey and Dylan stare at each other.

You are protesting illegally. Disperse now.

There are murmurs amongst those still on the road. The rows of police wait. The drones hover.

"I think we need to go," Dylan says, clearly beginning to panic.

As he speaks, there's a ripple through the crowd. Lainey notices two police officers in neon jackets standing a short distance away, conferring together, pointing at the T-shirts she and Dylan are wearing. One officer whispers something into his radio.

"Too late," Dylan mutters as the police approach.

"Could you two come with us, please?" the older officer says. His thick mustache trembles over his upper lip like a fat black caterpillar.

Neither Lainey nor Dylan moves. "Are you arresting us?" Dylan asks.

"If we need to, yes," the younger female officer says with some urgency, tugging at Lainey's arm so that she automatically stands up. "Let's go."

The two officers keep a firm grip on them both, pulling them behind police lines. As they retreat, the murmur of the crowd becomes a roar. Lainey sees the protesters pressing forward again, and the police surging in response. There's another spurt of white gas from the drones.

"Get in the van now!" the policewoman shouts, pushing Lainey so she stumbles on the vehicle's step. Dylan is close behind her, and as soon as he's in the van, before the doors are even closed, it begins to move.

Lainey grabs at the bench seat and pulls herself onto it, twisting around to find they're back with their friends. Katie looks shell-shocked, and Lexie is crying. Sereena leans across and touches Lainey's knee. "Thank God you're here, I was so worried about you."

Lainey opens her mouth to answer, then realizes they're not alone. Two policemen are sitting with them, openly watching as the van picks up speed. As they judder and swerve, Lainey desperately tries to hold on, taking deep breaths and closing her eyes. But she can't. Her stomach swells and surges, and she leans forward and throws up on the floor.

3:15 p.m.

When Emma walks into Room 13B, both mother and baby are crying. The TV fixed to the wall is on but muted, and Emma catches sight of a BBC news item showing an overhead view of the crowds around Westminster:

angry young faces, scores of placards, and drones belching clouds of gas. Her mouth goes dry. Surely Lainey and Sereena aren't caught up in that? She wants to fly across and turn up the sound, find out why that reporter is so damn serious. But she's learned not to panic, to wait for information, assess it, then act rather than react. Summoning her composure, she adjusts her expression and approaches the bed.

"Hey there," she says, picking up the chart and scanning it. Elise Cartwell, aged twenty-eight. Baby Maisie born early yesterday. Mum had some blood loss and ended up with a forceps delivery and lots of stitches. One of the tougher birth experiences.

"Hi," the woman says, sniffing and wiping her eyes.

"Looks like you've both had an eventful day. So, what's happening?" Emma comes closer, automatically tucking the bedcovers around Elise, who is topless, her chest flushed. Elise makes an obvious effort to gather herself, but Maisie continues to wail, her head between her mother's breasts, her tiny fists clenched tight.

"I just want to get out of here, but they won't let us go until she's feeding. They said if I can't get her sorted in the next twenty-four hours, they'll be using stored breast milk. I can't get her to latch on properly."

Emma hadn't needed to be told. Elise's nipples are red and blistered. Emma studies the woman's flushed face, noting the white fear in her tearful eyes.

"I understand, I really do," Emma says gently. "But don't panic yet, let's see what we can do."

"I'm just so frightened . . ." Elise strokes the baby's downy head as she talks. "What if there's something wrong with her?"

Emma's heart goes out to her. Lately, this has become a common refrain for new mothers. "I promise you that Maisie is fine. The problems—they always happen at birth, not afterward. She's made it already, okay?"

The woman nods, mutters, "Okay," and a fresh squall of tears escapes down her cheeks.

"May I?" Emma gestures toward the baby, and Elise nods. As soon as Emma takes the child, Elise's shoulders sag with relief.

"I could take her and give her a top-up bottle while you get some rest? We have special teats here, so they don't get used to guzzling milk from a bottle. It won't affect your chances of breastfeeding, and it might help her relax."

Elise's gaze flickers nervously toward the door. "They said I shouldn't."

Emma's jaw tightens. Of course they did. And Emma will be reprimanded if she pushes this too hard. Often it works out well, but occasionally an exhausted mother agrees to give a baby some milk, then complains to the hospital later, blaming the nurses' interventions when they can't keep the breastfeeding going.

"And I'd rather she wasn't out of my sight," Elise adds shyly.

"That's okay, it's your decision," Emma says, letting Maisie suck on her knuckle for a few seconds, feeling the little mouth working desperately, hard gums rooting for sustenance. When nothing happens, the child lets out another screech.

Elise bursts into tears. "Oh, shit, I don't know what to do . . ."

Emma puts the baby over her shoulder and rocks, going for the temporary fix. "What would you like to do, ideally? Ignoring everyone else for a minute."

"I'd like to feed her myself," Elise says, "but I didn't know it'd be this hard."

"Well, listen," Emma says, dancing from side to side as baby Maisie howls on her shoulder. "It's like this for many mothers, okay? You're not alone, and whatever happens, you haven't failed. I couldn't feed my daughter, so she had the bottle from a few days old, and she's always been healthy. She's nearly eighteen now."

At the mention of Lainey, fear surges through Emma. She glances at the TV again, but the news has moved on. As soon as she's finished here, she's going downstairs to grab her phone and find her child, because her instincts are screaming even louder than Maisie right now.

She brings the baby away from her body, cradling her in both hands. Maisie settles at the change of position, dark eyes squinting at Emma, as though trying to get the measure of her. Emma smiles at the scrunched-up little face. "Look, whatever you choose, this one will be just fine. Now, I'd like to try something with you. Lie flat on your back for me."

"They've shown me how to hold my boob and push my nipple into her mouth," Elise says as she moves a little farther down the bed, resting her head on the pillows and wincing in pain. "It works for a few seconds, but then she breaks off and bawls."

"It's not that." Emma pulls the sheets back a little farther, filled with compassion for Elise's vulnerability, her wounded body and her damaged areolae. "Here," she says, placing Maisie on the upper part of Elise's stomach so that the little girl's head is just underneath her mother's breasts. "Now, just breathe, try to relax and keep still."

Elise frowns at Emma for a moment, then peers down at her baby's head. Maisie has begun to strain her neck, her little head bobbing up and down like a chameleon with the effort of trying to control her neck muscles. Emma watches, and mentally crosses her fingers.

The head bob becomes an awkward little dance that gradually shifts the baby's body position, and slowly the little mouth edges toward Elise's left nipple. A few seconds later, and Maisie is locked on tight, suckling fiercely.

"How does that feel?" Emma asks.

"Sore," Elise says, smiling, her eyes shining through tears. They both watch the baby for a moment. "Wow, I had no idea she could do that."

"Do you want to try to sit up a little bit more?" Emma asks.

"Okay."

But their awkward attempts at shifting position break the seal of Maisie's mouth, and she bellows with rage. Emma scoops her up again and Elise lies back. They repeat the procedure. A minute later, the baby is sucking contentedly once more.

"This little girl," Emma says, stroking the downy hair on Maisie's neck, "knows just what she wants! She's a fighter, and that's good. We like hearing babies crying in this place; it's a sign that they're healthy and strong."

"Thank you," Elise says, tears spilling down her cheeks again. "The breastfeeding expert said either her mouth or my nipples probably weren't the right shape, so I'd almost given up. I've read all sorts of things online, but I haven't seen this before."

"It's called a breast crawl," Emma tells her. "It's not widely practiced, and it doesn't always work, but it's calming for both of you, and it shows you that she has good instincts." Emma perches on the bed. "Listen, who knows how she'll go long term—if she keeps coming off and yelling, then perhaps she's finding it too hard or frustrating. Babies have different shaped mouths, and she might have reflux or a sore tummy. But just remember this moment right now, and be kind to yourself. She's feeding; she's peaceful. You'll figure the rest out as you go. She was given to you. You're her mother. You'll work out what's best for her, no one else. Now, let me get you a bottle of water and . . ."

There's a cough behind them, and Emma turns to see Lynne standing there, hands on hips, watching. She moves to the bedside as though Emma is invisible. "That doesn't look like a very comfortable position for feeding," Lynne says, stroking the baby's head. "I don't know how you ended up there, but next time try sitting up, eh? You can't lie down like that every time she needs some milk."

"Can't she?" Emma retorts.

Lynne looks up. "Can I have a word please, Nurse Aitken?"

Lynne marches away and Emma follows, bracing herself. As soon as they're outside the room, Lynne turns around to face her, arms folded. "Stop talking to the mothers like that," she snaps. "You're giving them unrealistic expectations." Her eyes have a strange sheen to them. "For God's sake, motherhood isn't all flowers and cuddles, it's bloody hard work. And right now, they have to follow our procedures. I don't care if their nipples crack or they lose a bit of sleep, they need to prioritize their babies."

"That baby," Emma fires back, "is nursing properly for the first time in God knows how long, because I took the time to calm them both down. What good does it do to work everyone up by scaring them?"

"Oh, stop with the hippie bullshit, please. You know we can't afford any slip-ups," Lynne hisses. "Imagine if we lost a living child, alongside all the stillborns. There'd be uproar! This isn't a yoga retreat, it's a crisis zone. Anyway, that's not why I came to find you. Lainey's been arrested at the protest. I just took a call from the police station on Rowley Road. They're bringing her back to Whitehaven, and they want you to go and get her."

Emma is lost for words. Lainey's been *arrested?* She pictures her daughter in a cell, and her heart contracts.

"Go on, then, don't just stand there," Lynne snaps. "But, please, have a talk with her. We're so short-staffed, and she needs to understand how important your job is. Delilah told me about the march but thank God she wasn't silly enough to want to go."

Lynne strides away before Emma can point out that she shouldn't even be working. Today was her day off. One precious day, and she hadn't even tried to get Lainey to spend time with her.

She hurries down the corridor toward the lift. Perhaps Lynne's right. How can she help these women when she can't even take care of her own child?

5:20 p.m.

Lainey has been sitting in this small space for what feels like hours. It's more like a meeting room than a cell, but the door is locked from the outside by an electronic key card. The place is stuffy and airless and stinks of stale sweat. Her stomach is empty now, but she still dry-retches silently every few minutes, mouth hidden behind her hands.

They'd confiscated her cell phone and watch at the front desk, leaving her with nothing to do and no way of contacting anyone. They'd provided bottles of water, but Lainey drank hers quickly and now she wishes she'd eked it out. She picks at the hem of her jacket, studying the hangnails on her fingertips, wondering what's happened to her friends.

The police have been calling people out of the room, one by one, ever since she arrived. Sereena had been taken first, then Katie, then Dylan, and finally Lexie, who couldn't seem to stop crying. No one had talked much before that, since they were surrounded by strangers. Lainey is still mortified by the awful hour back to Whitehaven after she'd been sick, when the contents of her stomach had dribbled and dripped across the floor, and everyone had held their hands or clothing over their faces, trying not to breathe in the stench.

She's stuck between fear and exhaustion. She'd listened attentively to all the announcements at first, but her mind has wandered in the last hour or so. Therefore, it's a shock to hear her name being spoken by a stranger holding a clipboard, his shirtsleeves rolled up as he chews on gum.

She gets up and walks over to him. "Come with me," he says, and leads her out of that awful room. The cooler air is so welcome that she staggers slightly for a moment, giddy with relief. He leads her down a featureless corridor into a smaller area devoid of everything but one table and two chairs and shuts the door behind them.

It's horribly intimate, alone with him in here. She hovers by the table as he takes his seat and points to one of the chairs opposite his.

"Come on, sit down. This won't take long."

"Don't I need a lawyer or something?"

He raises his eyebrows. "You've watched too many movies. Nope, we're not charging you with anything. There are just a few formalities."

It's much colder in here. Lainey begins to shiver, tugging on her sleeves as she takes a seat. "My friends . . . are they okay?"

"Of course," he says, looking up from his paperwork. "Though some of their parents weren't too pleased when they collected them. We've been waiting for your mother; she'll be here in a second. Since you're a minor, we need to wait for her before I officially caution you."

Lainey's nerves are overtaken by a rush of righteous anger. "Caution me? What did I do wrong? We were at a peaceful march, that's all."

He leans forward. "You were lucky. After you were picked up it got nasty, and there are people in hospital tonight." He sits back, rubs his face, and sighs. "Listen, you might have been able to march like that a year ago, but it's not a good idea anymore. There are too many crises hitting us all at once. The government is determined to crack down on demonstrations. It's a different world now than it was five or ten years ago. So here's some free advice: if you want to stay safe, keep your head down and don't go hanging around large groups of angry people."

She doesn't say anything, but they both turn at the sound of the door opening.

A female officer in uniform turns to talk to someone, then steps back. And behind her is Lainey's mother.

Lainey gapes in shock. Emma's anguish and exhaustion are obvious.

She's so pale she appears ill, and so thin she's verging on frail. There are deep, dark shadows under her eyes.

"You okay, sweetheart?" Emma asks, hurrying forward, squeezing Lainey's hand as she sits down next to her.

The love and support in that brief touch almost breaks Lainey. "I'm fine," she says, blinking away sudden tears.

"Thanks for coming to collect your daughter," the policeman says. "I'm Inspector Taylor. Please sit down." As he says the words, Lainey sees the first signs of recognition in his eyes, before he does a double-take. "My God, Emma Aitken," he says. "I didn't realize. This is Craig's kid, then?"

Emma is frowning, her cheeks reddening, obviously struggling to place him. He laughs. "Bryan Taylor," he says. "I played football with Craig twenty years ago. Even came to your wedding reception. Sorry it didn't work out."

Emma relaxes and smiles. "Thanks. It was a long time ago now." Then she sobers. "Do you still keep in touch with him?"

"Craig? Nah—we weren't great friends, just teammates. I didn't always agree with what he did." The sergeant pauses, his gaze lingering on Emma, then he suddenly seems to remember where they are. "Okay, then, this won't take long." He peers at his folder. "We have all the details from your watch ID, Lainey. I just need to confirm them with you." He reads out her name, her address, and her date of birth, and Lainey nods. She'd quite like to ask more questions about her dad, but she can tell that the policeman's all business now.

"And you attend St. James's School, in Whitehaven?"

"Yes."

"Right, well, we'll be informing them of what's happened today, and they can decide on any repercussions on their end. We're not charging you with a crime, Lainey, but we're issuing you with a formal caution, which means you must stay away from the marches from now on. If you attend anything like this again, you'll be arrested and charged. Do you understand?"

"Yes," she whispers.

"Just hang on a minute," Emma says, leaning forward. Her tone is reasonably polite, but Lainey knows her far better than the policeman, so while he hesitates, Lainey cringes. "That's outrageous. If there's no charge here, then Lainey was just exercising her legal right as a citizen of our democratic country to peacefully march in protest. You're curtailing her freedom of speech. How do we object to this?"

The policeman puts down his papers and sits back, legs spread wide as he lounges in his chair and stares thoughtfully at Emma. "Well, I can put her in a holding cell again while we find a lawyer, but we're processing a lot of people today, so that may take some time. As I said to your daughter, Mrs. Aitken, we're living in a different world now, and a citizen's right to protest is not going to be a priority for much longer."

"It's okay, Mum," Lainey whispers, trying not to let the panic take hold of her at the thought of more hours in that airless room. "Let's just get it done and go home."

Emma turns and studies Lainey's face. "Are you sure? You know what he's saying is grossly unfair—and probably illegal."

"Let's ask Meena about it later. If anyone can sort it out, she can."

Emma nods. "Okay, but I don't like this at all." She hurriedly signs the form the policeman offers her.

Sergeant Taylor regards them both with what feels like paternal exasperation. "Mrs. Aitken—Emma—I'm sure you can appreciate that it's safer for Lainey to stay at home and focus on her studies and her social life than to put herself in the middle of potentially violent protests?" His eyebrows remain raised as he waits for her answer.

"It's *Ms.* Aitken," Emma says, leaning forward. "And I'm sorry to disappoint you, but I have no intention of encouraging my daughter to be compliant just to give the people in charge an easy ride."

Lainey braces herself, wondering if they'll both be back in the cells soon. But the policeman just tuts and shakes his head. "I'm trying to warn you," he says, his tone irritated as he gets up. "If you won't listen, then I'll probably be seeing you both again before long." He heads for the door, then pauses. "Now the country is in crisis, it's not about your human rights anymore. It's survival of the fittest, so for your own sake, be smart."

7:30 p.m.

Not for the first time, Emma wishes she hadn't sold her car. She'd given it up when gas prices skyrocketed, but it would have only taken minutes to get home under their own steam. As it is, they'll need to take two different buses, and the first one isn't due for another half an hour.

"Come on, let's get something to drink," Emma says, and they go to the nearest café, which has silver metal seats around silver metal tables.

"Tell me about the march," Emma says once they've ordered hot chocolates and found a place to sit.

Lainey stares into her cup. "It was much bigger than I expected. And Sereena had hatched this plan—to draw attention to Ellis. We had T-shirts and a banner, and the crowd liked it, but I don't think it made much difference, otherwise." She looks up. "What do you think, Mum? About Ellis and PreacherGirl? And all the other girls? Do you think they were taken?"

Emma hesitates. She can see the fear on Lainey's face, and her first instinct is to protect. But the second, more powerful urge, is to be honest.

"I don't know," she says. "But the system seems to be getting more draconian every day. I've wondered about it, too. Pregnant teenage girls are often vulnerable."

Lainey begins to fiddle with her watch. Emma senses she's closing down.

"You want to give Sereena a call, check she's okay?"

"I'll do it later . . . not here." Lainey indicates the busy café.

Emma frowns. Sereena and Lainey are never off the phone to each other. "You two haven't fallen out, have you?"

"What? No. We're fine." Lainey stares at Emma, then her gaze softens. "But what about you, Mum? I'm sorry you had to come all the way down here. You look exhausted."

Emma presses her fingers against her eyes for a moment. "I am," she agrees. "But not because of you. And I understand why you went to the march, but I'm worried. As much as I hate to admit it, that policeman's right: there's a different feeling about the protests this time. There's a different feeling about the whole world." She watches Lainey's face pale and wishes she could take back her words. "Oh, Lainey, ignore me, I don't want to frighten you. I'm just tired and I've definitely been working too hard lately."

Lainey shifts in her seat. "What's it like—at the hospital?" she asks tentatively.

"It's bad," Emma admits. "But I'm coping. And guess who's coming to visit on Monday?"

"Who?"

"Mary Walcott."

"Really? Will you meet her?"

"Maybe."

Emma watches Lainey taking sips of her hot chocolate and decides to wait for her to talk rather than fire more questions at her.

Lainey stirs her drink with her spoon, staring at the swirling liquid. "Do you think they'll ever find a cure for the babies?" she asks quietly.

"I don't know. I've read all the research I can get my hands on, but there's nothing conclusive. At the hospital we get daily briefings from the Birth Crisis Center, and thousands of scientists are trying to figure this out. We're told they're getting closer every day, but it doesn't help the babies born right now, or the women who're already pregnant. Although we're at the peak of that, I think. There won't be so many babies soon, until this is sorted. The prenatal clinics are already reporting a drop in new pregnancies. Most people are too scared to have a baby now."

Lainey nods, looking down at her lap.

"You want to tell me more about the march?" Emma tries, hoping to pull Lainey back out of her shell, dismayed she might have said too much and frightened her.

"Actually, I'm super tired." Lainey drains the remainder of her drink and stands up. "Shall we go?"

They collect their things, grab two bottles of water for the journey, and head to the bus stop. When they're standing on the bus, separated by a crush of bodies, Lainey puts her earbuds in and stares into space. Emma surreptitiously studies her daughter, amazed at the lithe young woman whose features still echo those of a little girl she once knew. She could reach out and stroke Lainey's hair, like she used to, but she doesn't. The space between them might be nothing, but the generation gap is unbridgeable.

There's no chance to talk again until they're walking toward the house.

Emma taps Lainey's arm, and Lainey turns off her phone and pulls out her earphones, winding the wires into a ball.

"What do you want for dinner?"

There's a pause. "Nothing. I'm really tired. I think I'll just go to bed."

Emma lets that stand while she unlocks the front door and takes off her coat, but her frustration is building. When Lainey starts up the stairs, she calls after her, "Lainey, stop. Can you come back and talk to me? I've barely seen you lately. I miss our chats. Tell me what's been happening with you."

Lainey trudges down the stairs wordlessly and collapses onto the chair in the lounge.

Emma sits next to her. "Right, then, talk to me."

Lainey picks at her fingernails. "I'm just sick of being treated like crap. The planet is struggling, and everything is frightening—what with the babies, the flood warnings, the iceberg. It's all horrible—and my generation is getting screwed with all these new laws . . . And now, on top of all that . . ."

Lainey stops and stares at her mother. The moment stretches.

Emma's stomach contracts as she studies Lainey's fearful face. "What is it, honey? You can tell me."

Lainey shakes her head. "No," she says with a sob. "I can't." And she bolts from the room and up the stairs, the thud of her feet matching the gallop of Emma's heart.

SUNDAY, 11:45 a.m.

When the doorbell rings, Lainey prays it's not for her. She's hardly slept after the frenetic text conversations last night as her friends shared their experiences at the police station, finding they were all cautioned by the police and banned from further marches. Their messages were clipped and concise. They stuck to the facts only, a tacit agreement in case of online eavesdroppers, but Lainey can still feel their shared fear and desperation. They're no closer to finding Ellis. *What now?*

There's a knock and her mother pokes her head around the bedroom door. "You're awake! There's a chap called Dylan downstairs. He wants to know if you have time to work on the mural today, says it's a class project you're doing together?"

Lainey pulls the pillow over her head. "Tell him I'm not here."

"Too late for that, I'm afraid."

Lainey sighs and flings back the covers. "Okay, I'll be down in five." She rushes into the bathroom to brush her teeth and get ready, then hurries down the stairs, trying to ignore her hammering heart.

"Hi, Lainey."

It's strange seeing Dylan standing in their lounge, his backpack over his shoulder. His stance is casual, but his hands are fidgeting in his pockets. Fergus appears at her heels.

"Hey, buddy." Dylan kneels to pat the dog.

She watches Fergus reveling in the attention. *Traitor.* "You're pretty keen to get this mural going, then?"

"Kind of." He stands up, his cheeks flushing pink. "I also wanted to check on you, after yesterday. You didn't seem well."

She bristles, aware of her mother somewhere upstairs. "I'm fine now. You want a drink?"

"Sure." He follows her through to the kitchen.

"We've only got Diet Coke or water." She holds up the options.

"I don't like bottled water. Coke, please."

She grabs two cans and passes one to him. "Come to my room, all my art stuff is there."

As they head up the stairs, her mother comes out onto the landing with her coat on. "I'm going for a walk. Won't be too long. Coming, Fergus?" When he sees the lead, the dog turns tail and bounds down the stairs after her.

As soon as Emma shuts the door, Lainey is very aware that she and Dylan are alone. It's weird and uncomfortable having him here in her personal space. Way too intimate. They haven't been alone since . . .

She really should tell him. And yet she falters, sitting heavily on the bed, sending a rush of air that causes the pillowcase over the bird box to flap up, setting them frantically chirping.

"What've you got there?" Dylan puts down his bag and sits beside her as she grabs the box and pulls off the cover. "Wow, Lainey, what are you doing with them?"

"Taking care of them. They're orphans," she says, grabbing the tin of food and scooping up some with the tweezers. "I'm taking care of them until they're big enough to fly."

"Whoa. What are their names?"

"Naming them only means you get more attached," she says, biting her lip. "Best not."

He watches her feed the first little starling. "Can I try?"

She hesitates, then says, "Sure," and passes him the tweezers. "Not so much," she adds as he picks up a large dollop of it. "Just a little at a time."

He laughs as he feeds the other two tiny birds. "That's brilliant."

She sees the shine in his eyes and feels a pull toward him, which makes everything hurt even more. She doesn't say anything as she puts the food away, replaces the pillowcase, and slides the birds back under the bed.

He must sense the change of mood because his cheeks go pink.

"Oh, crap, Lainey, I'm really sorry, you know." He gets up and goes over to the window as he talks, avoiding her gaze. "That day . . . I fucked up. I've wanted to apologize ever since." He turns around, and she can see his remorse: his brow heavy, his eyes downcast. "It's just . . . I really hoped it would be . . . different." He laughs bitterly. "I know I let you down." His expression grows desperate. "I felt like an absolute prick. I wanted it to be good. The whole thing. Because I don't know anyone else like you, and I wanted you to see me that way, because I think you're . . . you're amazing. But when it happened, I panicked and I didn't know . . ." His eyes drop to the floor and then he looks back at her, his cheeks mottled crimson now. "I didn't know how to make it right . . ." His voice deepens. "And the ground was freezing, and I thought I might be hurting you . . . And I should have stopped, but I . . . I didn't. I'm still embarrassed whenever I'm around you. I know I blew it. If it helps, I feel like a complete dick."

Lainey's thoughts swing wildly. They stare at each other before she says in a low voice, "You've said a lot about how you felt, but you didn't think to ask me how I felt, did you? I didn't feel used that night, because I wanted it to happen—I encouraged it. But I *did* feel like an idiot for the whole summer when you didn't call. *Then* I felt used. *Then* I felt embarrassed. *You* turned it into that, not me, because you couldn't talk to me, and acted like you didn't give a shit . . ."

Dylan returns to sit next to her on the bed. "I'm sorry, I know I'm crap at this, but I do care about you, Lainey, I promise. I wanted to talk to you, but then Mike told me he'd seen you with Liam-fucking-Whittaker, and I thought you'd moved on. And now, every time I turn around, you're together."

Lainey scoffs. "You think I'm with Liam?"

"Well, aren't you?"

"No! He's hanging around me like a foul smell, and I don't know how to get rid of him."

Dylan frowns. "How about telling him to fuck off?"

Lainey laughs despite herself. "You know it's not as simple as that. I don't want Grant Whittaker's son as an enemy, not when I have to come to school every day and take the same classes as him."

Dylan sighs. "Fair enough. I'm sorry, Lainey. I know I screwed up. But I . . . I like you a lot. Can we start over? I want to do this project with you. You're a brilliant artist, and I think we'll do an awesome job together. Please?"

Tell him.

She can't. Not when he's looking at her like this: so hopefully. So eager to fix things between them. And yet she doesn't want to make it easy for him, either.

"Okay," she says, "tell me about your ideas for the mural."

He seems surprised at the change of subject, but then smiles, obviously taking this as a good sign. "I've done a few different sketches, but the one I like most is the tree kids. Look." He pulls out a drawing of a row of smiling children, their hair morphing into trees and forests. "I reckon everyone will come up with some kind of nature sketch for *regeneration*, but I think we should have people in this—the kids themselves—so that every day when they see it, they're reminded that regeneration won't happen on its own. It's got to come through them and the work they put into it."

Lainey nods. "Yes, I like it, but I think maybe it would be more effective . . . hang on . . ." She grabs her pad and spends a few minutes sketching. "Like this."

Dylan stares at her drawing. It's a small girl with yellow ribbons in her curly hair, each tendril becoming a tangle of vines. Her hands are outstretched in offering and two small trees, visible from roots to leaf tips, are balanced in each of her palms.

"Yes!" He grabs the paper from her. "She's great. And maybe something like this, too . . ." He sketches a male child holding clouds with puddles of water at his feet. "And we need a rubbish bin to one side with whatever shit we can think of that's poisoning the planet. But you know what would be really great? Adding some holograms that you can see by using the watches. Get parts of it in 3D. Dad might think that's too complex, but I've tried it a few times. What d'you reckon?"

"Yeah, sounds good." She grabs her pad, and they begin to sketch their ideas, comparing notes, drawing kids that morph into flowers and plants and have roots for feet. Lainey is enjoying herself so much, she's forgotten her worries for a while, until Dylan says, "I reckon you guys are right about Ellis."

Lainey stiffens. "What do you mean?"

"I was thinking about it all last night. Not one of the policemen asked me about the T-shirt. About Ellis. And do you know, I researched PreacherGirl and the whole channel is gone now. Last time I saw it she had nearly two million followers. Why would she close that down without a word? There's no discussion about it on any other social media platform. Or perhaps there was, and it's been deleted."

Lainey stares at him, seeing the fervor in his eyes as he speaks; the belief he's onto a conspiracy. But it's still a distant concept for him, whereas she knows how caught up in it all they really are.

"That channel went down a few weeks ago."

"It did?" He looks astonished.

Hastily, she scribbles on the top of her sketchbook and shows him the note.

Remember our watches are probably recording conversations. Stop talking?

He stares at her, then picks up his sketchbook and writes again.

I think it's true: she was pregnant and disappeared. This is big. It's great we're all fighting for her.

Lainey's chest tightens as she reads,

But I don't think she's coming back.

PART II

transition

PREACHERGIRL LYRICS

So swiftly you've no chance to see it
So softly their strike can't be heard
They'll come at the darkest of hours
Swoop in like a carrion bird
Stick-bound and tarred with their feathers
You're away to a place no one knows
Left to rot down there forever
In a wasteland where nobody goes
While our leaders are lying
The babies are dying
And you just got caught in their game
So when this is done
Then the world will go on
And you'll be the one they will blame
But I'll still be calling your name.

4.

"**M**rs. Aitken, thank you for coming in this morning."

Emma nods warily as a tea tray is set down in front of her. She's the only one being presented with a drink, and she's not keen on being singled out for old-fashioned pleasantries. Lainey is next to her, and on the opposite side of the large polished mahogany boardroom table, there's a row of teachers: Mrs. Goodchild the headmistress, Mr. Bailey the art teacher, Miss Coats the biology teacher, and the new history teacher, too. He'd been introduced as soon as she entered the room, and his handshake was warm, his eyes dark and friendly, but Emma had been distracted by the worry of this sudden summons and now she's forgotten his name.

Her hand edges toward the china teacup with its foxgloves and peonies, just for something to do, but then she stops. She'd said yes to the drink without thinking, and it's making her feel traitorous, as though they've lulled her into complicity, so she can sip tea while they admonish her daughter. Beside her, Lainey is impassive, but Emma can see how hard her fists are clenched beneath the table.

Mrs. Goodchild turns her attention to Lainey. "I had a phone call from the police over the weekend, Lainey, and I understand that you and your friends were picked up by the police at a march in London and issued with a caution, is that right?"

Lainey nods without speaking. Emma watches. Her mouth is dry, but she'll be damned if she'll drink their bloody tea.

"It's our policy on these occasions, Lainey, to issue you with a formal warning. We cannot condone any form of illegal activity from our students. Do you understand?"

"Yes," Lainey says, as Emma's shoulders release their load. She closes her eyes, realizing she'd been terrified that Lainey was about to be expelled. Pure paranoia. Of course they wouldn't expel her for one march, what'd she been thinking?

"A formal warning is serious, Lainey," Mrs. Goodchild says. Her eyes drift to Emma as she talks. "We don't give them twice. The next time it's immediate expulsion, I'm afraid."

Emma bristles but doesn't have time to reply before Lainey pipes up. "What? So from now on, I can't exercise my democratic right to peacefully march in a protest, or you'll kick me out of school?"

Mrs. Goodchild's eyes flicker between mother and daughter. "Lainey, I'm trying to explain that our policy—"

"I'm sorry, Mrs. Goodchild," Lainey interrupts, "but your policy sucks balls." Lainey folds her arms and stares furiously at the headmistress.

Mrs. Goodchild glares at Lainey, her expression darkening, while Miss Coats looks astonished. Mr. Bailey is openly grinning, and the history teacher has put his hand up as though to rub his top lip, but Emma can see the upturn of his mouth and the amusement in his eyes.

"Lainey, I've never heard you speak with such insolence," Mrs. Goodchild says. She turns to Emma. "You might need to remind your daughter that we have a strict code of policy at school, and another serious offense is treating staff with such an open lack of respect."

Emma stiffens. "My daughter is sitting right next to me," she says. "Therefore, you've just reminded her yourself. May I remind *you* that the only reason I'm here is to support Lainey. And, quite frankly, I don't see why you're so offended. She didn't say *you* sucked balls, Mrs. Goodchild, she said the school policy did. And I have to say, I agree."

Mr. Bailey snorts with laughter, and the history teacher turns to the window. Miss Coats's mouth drops fully open, and her eyes take on a delighted gleam.

"Surely," Emma leans forward, "you're a little bit proud of the girls in this school for sticking up for themselves and their absent friends? Or do you happen to know where Ellis Scott is these days?"

Mrs. Goodchild stares furiously around the room at them all. "It appears this conversation is no longer constructive." She stands up and strides toward the door, then stops. "I've got a school to run, and other students to take care of, but I suggest you take this seriously, Lainey. Whether you agree with it or not, you now have a formal warning. Another one and you're out." She pulls open the door, marches through, and lets it slam behind her.

Miss Coats grabs her bag and hastens away, and the history teacher follows, casting a sympathetic smile toward both of them. Mr. Bailey comes around the table, still grinning, and pats Lainey's arm. "Don't worry, Dylan was read the riot act this morning, too. And the way the world's going, they'll soon have more to worry about than all this policy shite." His smile fades as he talks. "Thanks for making me chuckle today, ladies. See you in art, Lainey."

Once they're alone, Emma grabs her bag. "I really need to run—remember we have a special visitor at the hospital today?"

"Oh yeah," Lainey says. "Good luck with that. And thanks for backing me up."

"You know I always will."

As they hug, Emma feels Lainey tense. Surprised, she steps back and catches the momentary fear flitting across her daughter's face. "Sweetheart, are you okay?"

"Sure." Lainey smiles, and Emma tries to relax. She leans upward to kiss her child's cheek, which still seems strange, although Lainey's been slightly taller than Emma for some time now.

Lainey heads for the door. "See you later, Mum."

"Yeah, see you tonight," Emma says, watching her go before hurrying down the hallway to the school entrance, trying to shake off her nagging concerns. Perhaps it's just transference: the events she can't control at the hospital becoming anxieties about her own child. And yet, something is still off-kilter.

At the administration desk, the history teacher is chatting to one of his colleagues, but as soon as he sees her, he abruptly stops the conversation and holds out his hand. "It was good to meet you this morning, Mrs. Aitken."

"It's Ms. Aitken, actually," Emma says, shaking his hand. "And I prefer Emma."

"Well, Emma, Lainey is very lucky to have a mother who sticks up for her like you just did."

She's not sure whether it's the heat of his hand, the warmth of his words, or the kindness in his eyes as he smiles, but something—perhaps all three—suddenly makes her want to cry.

"Thank you," she says, trying to keep her voice steady. "I'm sorry, I've forgotten your name already."

"It's Nicholas Davenport. But I prefer Nick." He keeps hold of her hand for just a beat longer, then lets go.

"Nice to meet you, Nick." She smiles. "I've got to run, I'm late for work."

"Have a good day, Emma," he says. "Hopefully, I'll see you again sometime."

10:30 a.m.
Sereena doesn't wait long to gather them in. Lainey gets the text just before morning break.

> Meet in DC, 15M.

Lainey heads to the drama closet as soon as the bell rings and finds Katie and Lexie already there.

"You okay, Lainey?" Katie asks.

"Sure," Lainey replies with forced casualness, wishing everyone would stop asking her the same question.

Sereena bustles in and shows them a small black box sitting neatly on her palm, then she flicks a small switch on the side. "It's a jammer," she announces, laying it on the table. "Latest in anti-listening devices. Just in case. They block any sound being picked up by microphones within a ten-meter range, which means we can talk without worrying about these." She points at her watch. "I don't think just sitting on them is going to be enough anymore."

"Where did you get that?" Lexie asks, touching it tentatively. "Are you sure it works?"

"Mum gave it to me," Sereena replies with a grin. "Told me to guard it with my life as they're like gold dust and super expensive. Might soon be illegal, too. But she's sure it works. They use them at her office to ensure client confidentiality."

"Your mum is awesome, Sereena," Katie says with a sigh.

Lainey nods in agreement. As one of the country's top human rights lawyers, Meena Mandalia appears in the press regularly discussing high-profile cases, on TV shows from the *Morning Show* to *Question Time*. She'd come to prominence while working on the Windrush scandal, and had a landmark case representing a group of adolescent asylum seekers who'd found themselves stateless. While she'd fought and lost more than her fair share of battles against the rigid rule of government, she'd won some, too. At Sereena's house, there are often respectful discussions on everything from abortion to criminal justice to reality TV. And despite her vast experience, Meena always listens thoughtfully to the girls' opinions, pointing out flaws in their arguments and praising their insights.

"So," Sereena says, looking around at them. "Did you all get a formal warning this morning?"

Everyone nods.

"Okay, well, this school is driving me crazy. What the hell are they teaching us? Is it free thought in our lessons, then in real life just lie down and do whatever anyone says? Bullshit."

"Bullshit," Katie echoes. Lainey and Lexie say nothing.

"But we're gonna have to be careful," Sereena says. "The surveillance never stops, so we can't let our guard down if we're going to outsmart it.

Let's keep our ears to the ground. We might have to do things a bit less openly."

"You mean, like, undercover operations?" Katie asks, looking thrilled.

"Maybe." Sereena seems pensive. "We've still got to find Ellis somehow."

"Perhaps we should just lie low for a little bit," Lexie suggests, biting her lip. "For a few days at least. The police threatened us with jail, Sez, if we did anything else."

Lainey half expects Sereena to react badly to this, but instead Sereena puts her arm around Lexie. "They only said that'd happen if we protested in public, Lex. Nothing else. Remember, fear is their ultimate weapon, but it can't get you unless you let it. There are plenty of ways we can keep investigating things for ourselves. We just have to be clever about it."

"It's like the End of Days, isn't it?" Katie's eyes are gleaming. "But with babies instead of bombs. The babies don't want to come into the world, and who can blame them? Everywhere you turn, there's shit happening. The planet doesn't want us anymore, and the pandemic didn't work, so now it's giving the newborns a virus, and the human race will die out."

"Jeez, Katie, let's not start thinking like that," Sereena says, with a fleeting glance in Lainey's direction. "The world's always got problems. The government's just better at fearmongering now. Mum said last night that big marches won't be allowed or effective for much longer. The rebellion's going underground. She thinks we'll need new tactics in the Information Age, but we have to keep speaking truth to power. Especially when it affects our friends." Sereena briefly squeezes Lainey's hand.

"Does your mum say what it's like at the hospital?" Lexie asks, turning to Lainey. "Is it as bad as the media makes it out to be?"

Lainey hesitates, realizing she doesn't have the details they're hoping for. Emma never volunteers much information about work. She doesn't have to, because Lainey can see the strain written all over her: the dark smudges beneath her eyes, the fresh lines on her pale face, the slow way she moves around the house, as though she's made of glass. The last time she'd seen her like this had been back when Lainey was in primary school, during the long months of the pandemic.

"I don't know all the stats, but Mum's doing it tough and working all the hours she's got. She's always exhausted when she's home. I don't like to ask her for details or make her relive it."

"So, let's retrace Ellis's steps." Sereena stares at them all. "We know she was in the pharmacy on June twenty-fourth. She stopped all contact on the twenty-sixth. Let's go over those few days and see if anyone saw her. We should just focus on finding our friend without getting overwhelmed by the bigger picture."

"I can't believe they used tear gas at the weekend—on a peaceful march," Katie says.

"Me either," Sereena says, "and did you notice something? It's been taken off all the news sites. If you weren't there, it's like it never happened. And if you were there, sooner or later some part of you will start thinking you've made it up."

Lexie gulps. "I feel like that already. Like it didn't really happen."

"This is gaslighting, people," Sereena declares. "Keep on full alert. Report in regularly. Look after each other. Let all these lemmings fall off the cliff if they want to," she says, waving her hand dismissively beyond the door, "but we don't have to."

11:50 a.m.

"Sit still!"

"You know this isn't necessary—*and* it's against hospital policy," Emma says as Cathy dabs a thick makeup brush over her nose and cheeks. They're in Cathy's small office, surrounded by files piled high on both the desk and floor.

"Not today it's not. It's just a bit of color, I'm not doing your whole face. I just don't want you to look half dead."

"I feel half dead."

Cathy pauses and frowns at her. "That doesn't sound like you."

Emma sighs. "I know. It's just . . ."

"Lainey," Cathy finishes for her, continuing to dab her face with the brush.

"Lainey," Emma agrees. "Something's not right."

91

"Well, it must be frightening, getting cautioned by the police."

"It's not just that, though," Emma says, remembering Lainey's strange expression earlier. Then she flinches as Cathy flicks the brush and catches her eye with the bristles. "Ow."

"Oops, sorry. At least you stuck up for her this morning. She'll know you're on her side now."

"Yeah. I enjoyed watching her sock it to Goodchild. The woman might not suck balls, but she definitely sucks sour grapes. Some of the other teachers seemed to appreciate it, too. Bailey was chuckling. And have you seen the new history teacher—he's quite easy on the eye."

Cathy laughs. "That's more like it! I've heard Beth say something similar. And Paul Bailey is one of the nicest guys around. He and John go way back, you know, right to school days. They don't see much of each other, but John's really fond of him." Cathy sets down the brush and picks up a mascara wand. "Look up for me," she says, and then continues, "So, this history teacher sounds like a catch. Shame you don't do school pick-up anymore, or we could fix you up a bit so you could have a good flirt. It's just what you need, come to think of it."

"It's exactly what I *don't* need," Emma says, batting her away. "I have quite enough on my plate."

"You know what," Cathy says, stepping back. "You don't really have anything on *your* plate, Em, except other people's problems. Maybe it's time you got some stuff of your own going on."

Emma frowns, wanting to object but unable to find the words. She watches in dismay as Cathy picks up a bright-red lipstick, but is saved by the phone ringing. Cathy answers with a sharp, "Yes?" Then pauses, listening. "Uh-huh. Okay, we're coming." She puts the receiver back down. "Fifteen minutes till showtime. We need to go now. You ready?"

Despite the clamor of nerves, Emma nods.

"Right, then. She's coming in through the north trade entrance, basement level. Four of us heading there. You, me, Fred Allan and Phil Hammond from the board. She's got security staff and lackeys with her as well. God knows how many there are altogether."

Emma balks as she thinks of the chairman of the board and the CEO, neither of whom she's spoken to before. "I don't know if I should be part of this."

Cathy gives her a stern look. "Seriously? Neither Phil nor Fred have a clue. They get the reports, sure, but Phil plays golf three times a week, and when was the last time you found Fred down on the maternity wards? You're the one person who *should* be part of this. You and the other nurses."

"What about Lynne?"

"She's on Ward B. We said we needed her in charge there, in case of an emergency, but she's not happy about missing her moment of glory. She knows Fred, and he's promised to introduce her, so be ready for it."

"Right."

Cathy holds her by the shoulders. "Say and do what you need to, Em. This is your chance. Trust me. We'll deal with the flak later, okay?"

"Okay. Promise me I won't lose my job?"

Cathy gently turns her toward the door. "Not a chance while I'm here. And they can't sack me, I know too much. Come on, let's go."

12:00 p.m.

Lainey is getting her lunch from her locker, earbuds in, listening to an old Billie Eilish song, when she senses a subtle change in the atmosphere. She glances around to find two uniformed police officers a few feet away, pushing through the gaggle of kids. As the teenagers part to make way for them, Lainey sees they're with a woman she recognizes, and a small girl, still in St. Stephen's uniform, clutching a book to her chest. The woman is talking to one of the officers, her face flushed, gesturing dramatically with her hands. But the girl's eyes meet Lainey's.

They stare at each other, the little girl's gaze reeling her in. It's the child from the pharmacy, Lainey realizes, and it only takes a second before she understands that the girl is trying to tell her something.

As the group comes closer, Lainey instinctively turns away. Her blood pulses in her ears and her face burns as she waits for a tap on the shoulder.

It doesn't come. They go past, moving toward the main school hall.

Flustered, Lainey starts mechanically transferring books in and out of her locker, hardly aware of what she's doing.

"Lainey?"

The voice is close to her ear, and she flinches. When she turns, Liam is laughing.

"You're jumpier than my pet rabbit this morning."

"You have a rabbit?"

"As a kid. Little shit kept digging holes and then a fox got it. Anyway, why are you so stressed? Let me guess: you got in trouble for the protest. Next time you'll know who to listen to, eh?"

"Oh, fuck off, Liam." She zips up her bag, ready to go, even though she's not sure she's collected everything she needs. She doesn't even care anymore. She just wants him gone.

"Whoa there!" Liam laughs. "Hit a nerve, did I? Don't worry, we all make mistakes. You free for lunch?" he asks, leaning in, one hand on the lockers so that he can press himself toward her, suggestively. "We could go somewhere private, and I'll help take your mind off your problems." He leers at her breasts as he talks.

"I'm meeting Sereena." She turns around with her bag held in front of her, so he has to move back and give her space. She sets her jaw, determined to get rid of him. "Look, Liam, I'm not up for hanging out right now. I've not been feeling great lately, and I've got heaps of homework already. I'm struggling to keep up."

Liam doesn't seem offended or perturbed. "Really?" His eyes narrow. "I'm not struggling. Maybe I can help you catch up, and then you'll have more time for fun." He grins.

She stares at him, wondering how he can be so outrageously indifferent to taking the hint. Perhaps it comes from family connections and his certainty of his place in the world. He's probably never felt like an underdog. Inwardly, she despairs. Liam isn't a guy who deals in subtleties. She's going to have to spell this out for him.

She opens her mouth to try again, when an announcement comes over the school speaker system. "Could all the girls from years nine to twelve please report to the auditorium, straight away."

Liam steps back. "Sounds like you've got to go." He briefly strokes her cheek. "We'll continue this later, huh?"

He's standing between her and the double doors that lead outside. Lainey looks from him to the school hall to her left, then nods. Helplessly, she begins to walk down the long corridor, scanning all the faces she passes, desperately searching for Sereena. Where the hell is she? She checks her watch, but there's nothing, and she doesn't dare send a message right now.

All the girls are lining up to get into the hall, and Lainey hovers at the back of the line. Everyone is speculating, and a few people look worried. She can see Katie and Lexie not too far in front of her. They're holding hands, probably stressing this could be yet more repercussions from the protest.

But it isn't that. Lainey knows exactly what's happening. She's about to be taken away, in front of everyone. She'll be like Ellis Scott. Except it will be instant infamy, rather than quiet whispers. And what will come next? Where will they take her?

She touches her tummy briefly and thinks of her mum. There's just enough time to send her a message, but what can she say?

The line is shrinking as the girls file in. Her head pounds, and her cheeks burn. Soon she'll be inside, with no escape. She casts a desperate glance backward, toward the exit at the other end of the hallway. She could make a run for it, but it'll be so obvious.

Where the hell is Sereena?

A few feet ahead, Mr. Davenport comes out of his office, opposite the entrance to the hall, scanning the line of girls. Lainey's head swims and she staggers to one side, putting her hand on the wall to steady herself. The book under her arm drops to the floor, and the two girls in front of her turn around to stare.

She notices Mr. Davenport is watching her, too. As they make eye contact, he hurries over. "Lainey," he says quietly. "Can I have a word?"

His office is only a few steps away from the crowd. She nods and slips inside.

"You're very pale. Why don't you sit down," he says, closing the door. He studies her, then puts a finger to his lips, before moving to his desk and writing something on a piece of paper. He holds it up.

Are you in trouble?

He nods to the door and the hall beyond, then offers her the paper, placing a finger to his lips again.

She writes back.

Yes.

Do you want to go into the hall?

No.

He pauses, then scribbles.

Swap watches.

When she doesn't respond he nods at her wrist and makes an impatient gesture with his hands, conveying that she needs to hurry.

Confused and surprised, she unstraps her watch and trades it for his. He hurriedly fastens her own to his wrist and pulls his shirtsleeve over the top. She does the same. Then he scribbles more words on the paper and passes it to her.

Stay here, don't be seen.

Then he moves swiftly to the door and heads out, closing it behind him.

12:10 p.m.

By the time the prime minister's car pulls up, Emma's stomach is rumbling. It's lunchtime and she's not eaten anything yet. Hopefully, she won't embarrass herself by fainting at the prime minister's feet. She should have drunk that bloody cup of tea, after all.

Two buff security guys with sunglasses and earpieces emerge from the car first. One opens the door for Mary. Perhaps it's the contrast to their hulking size, but Emma is surprised to see the prime minister is so much smaller than she'd imagined. A bird of a woman really, slightly hunched, checking her handbag is closed and mentioning something to the security guards. From a second car, another man emerges: and Emma gulps when she sees it's Grant Whittaker. He fiddles with the buttons on his jacket cuffs and smooths down his white hair as he moves to Mary's side.

Finally, they turn and see the little party waiting for them. Both assume the same expression of enthusiastic greeting as they walk steadily forward.

"A pleasure to welcome you to the hospital, Prime Minister," says Fred Allan, stepping forward. She shakes his hand.

"Phil Hammond," says the CEO, blushing as he steps forward and enthusiastically shakes Mary Walcott's hand.

"This is Cathy Stubbs," says Fred. "She's managing the day-to-day aspects of this terrible crisis. And this is Emma Aitken, one of our most senior and respected midwives. She'll be accompanying you on the wards a little bit later."

"It's nice to meet you," Emma says formally.

"Likewise," Mary says as their eyes lock. "You're all doing a magnificent job under these terrible circumstances."

It's genuine enough, but Emma is flummoxed. She feels anything but magnificent. The prime minister regards her sympathetically, waiting for a response. Emma feels suddenly emotional, caught off guard.

Fred coughs.

"Thank you," Emma says, her heart sinking at all the formality. How can they hope for anything real to take place amid all this pomp and courtesy?

Grant Whittaker holds out his hand to Emma next, without saying a word. She takes it and almost lets go: his grip is clammy and cold. But his eyes are fixed intently on her as he squeezes her fingers hard while he shakes. His face is pinched and pale; the tendons in his neck clearly visible. She's stuck, her hand briefly held hostage in his grip, before he lets go and turns away to greet Phil and Fred.

"We'll take you up to the boardroom first," Fred says, "to meet the rest of the board and have morning tea. Then, as you requested, we have some time for you to visit the maternity wards."

The group sets off through the corridors, and Emma and Cathy take up the tail positions of the little train of people. There's not enough space for them all in the elevator, so the prime minister, Grant, and their entourage disappear with Fred and Phil up to the top floor of the building, and Cathy and Emma wait for the elevator to return.

"Looks like Grant's forgotten that he knows us, eh," Cathy says as they watch the floor numbers changing.

"Mmm." Emma's not sure what she'd expected, but it had been obvious that Grant recognized her, even if he'd tried to hide it. They'd both grown up in Whitehaven, after all, and while they hadn't gone to the same schools, they'd crossed paths a number of times as young adults at social events. Grant stood out, having always known how to hold court in a room. Emma avoided him as much as possible.

"I'd love to knock him off his high horse," Cathy says as they get into the elevator. "Maybe remind him his wife is not always discreet, and I know a few juicy things about the Whittakers that would probably make him cringe."

"He doesn't seem like a man who's easily shamed," Emma replies.

"True," Cathy says, as the doors close and the elevator begins to move.

When they get to the boardroom, Emma sees it's full of fresh flowers and sycophantic board members. On a nearby table sit at least a hundred bottles of sparkling and plain water and assorted healthy juices. Mary Walcott has already been given tea, and catering staff are offering her finger sandwiches and fine cakes, carried in on silver platters. Those lucky enough to be invited to the reception hover nearby, waiting for their chance to say hello.

Emma stands in the far corner, plate in hand, watching. She's lost her appetite, but Cathy brings little tidbits of food to her and insists she eats. She chews them like they're cardboard, as her mouth is so dry.

Close by, Fred is in animated conversation with Grant, his belly shaking with mirth as he regales some tale to the health secretary, who sips his tea, saying nothing, but somehow emanating disdain in the way he ignores Fred and studies the group of doctors closest to them. Farther along, people swirl around the prime minister in a deferential dance, blocking her from sight and occasionally parting to reveal her again. Each time she comes into view, she is listening intently to those around her.

"What d'you reckon she's thinking?" Emma asks Cathy.

"Probably wishing Phil would shut up and stop introducing her to all his cronies."

"How long is this bit meant to go on for?"

"Forty-five minutes."

"And how long do we have on the ward?"

Cathy keeps her eyes on the gathering. "Fifteen minutes."

Emma gives her a sharp look. "You're kidding."

Cathy sighs. "Fred told me the schedule this morning. You'll escort her into 14B, and we've prepared the mother there. She's the one whose little girl was stillborn on Friday. She's adjusting well in the circumstances, and said she wanted to thank the prime minister for all she's doing."

"But do we actually get time to talk to her? Is she going to leave here with any idea of what it's been like these last few months? Or is it just cake and condolences today?"

"I don't know."

Emma's chest tightens, and her blood begins to simmer. "So why drag me along? And why are you only telling me this now?"

Cathy turns to her. "Because I'm manipulating you," she says with the sweetest of smiles. "Because sometimes too much thinking time can be a bad thing. And I want to make sure you're as angry as I am by the time she finally heads our way."

12:30 p.m.

Mr. Davenport has been gone for twenty minutes.

Lainey waits, fiddling with the strange watch. It's big and awkward, and she's sure she must be breaking some law by wearing a teacher's watch, even though he'd told her to.

Suddenly, there's a loud wave of excited chatter surging along the corridor. Then the door opens and Mr. Davenport walks in. His worried eyes and drawn face convey only trouble. He puts a finger to his lips and goes back to scribbling on his pad, passing it over to her.

The police took Sereena.

The enormity hits her all at once, a punch to the gut. She gasps.

It's my fault, she thinks. *Sereena's been taken because she tried to help me.*

Suddenly, she can't breathe. Her lungs are pumping fast, but she's desperate for air.

Mr. Davenport hurries over to her. "Steady," he whispers, "you're okay, just take it easy."

She tries to get control of herself as he hovers close by. "Cup your hands over your mouth," he says, kneeling next to her to demonstrate. "And just breathe evenly. When you hyperventilate, your carbon dioxide levels drop too low, that's all. Your body will fix it when you let it."

She tries her best, and her breathing improves a little, but she can't stop trembling. "What happened?" she whispers, forgetting to write it down.

Davenport shakes his head and writes again.

There was a woman and a child . . . the students lined up and they walked along the lines. The woman picked out Sereena, and the police took her away.

Lainey goes cold.

Davenport writes again then holds up a question, his eyes on her.

Do you know why?

She nods.

More scribbling.

If you'd been there, would they have taken you, too?

She bites her lip and nods again.

Mr. Davenport writes and pushes the paper forward, looking intently at her.

You can trust me. If you're in trouble, I want to help.

She just stares at him. She's desperate for someone to confide in, but her problems are overwhelming. She's frozen in terror, still picturing Sereena being marched out of school. Where have they taken her? What are they planning to do to her?

Where will they take me?

Davenport is nodding at her wrist, indicating with gestures that they should swap back their watches. When he passes hers over, she sees a list of messages. Her phone is buzzing, but she doesn't dare take it out of her pocket.

Davenport watches her anxiously. "I have to get to class soon. Will you be okay?"

She lifts her chin defiantly, even though she can feel it wobbling. "I'll be fine. I don't feel too good right now, though. I think I need to go home."

"All right then." Mr. Davenport gets up and collects his bag. "Do you want me to call your mum?"

Yes, Lainey thinks. "No," she says. "I'll message her, but it might take her a while to get out of the hospital—they're not allowed phones on the wards. My house isn't far, I can walk."

She heads for the door, but Davenport calls, "Lainey!" There's a sharp edge to his voice that makes her pause and turn to him.

He grabs the paper from her and scribbles on it. She takes the proffered note with a shaky hand.

I promise that if you put your trust in me, I'll do everything I can to help.

She hesitates, but only for a second, then gives him a sad, apologetic smile and bolts out the door. And runs straight into Dylan, who looks terrified.

"Lainey? Are you okay?" he asks, his words interspersed with panicky breaths. "I've been calling you—did you know the police just took Sereena?"

Mr. Davenport appears behind them. "Do you have a class now, Dylan?"

"I do, but it's only art . . ."

There's a moment's pause. Lainey's sure Mr. Davenport is going to ask more questions, but he seems to be weighing some options.

"Could you walk Lainey home, if I clear it with your dad?"

Dylan's visibly relieved. "Yes, of course."

"Okay, then." Davenport turns to Lainey. "Remember what I said, won't you?"

He seems so genuinely concerned, and Lainey is so exhausted that she's tempted to blurt it out right then and there. But the fear on Dylan's face stops her. He's panicking already, and he doesn't even know the half of it.

Davenport senses her reluctance. "I'll see you both tomorrow, then," he says gently and walks away.

"Come on," Dylan urges. "Let's get out of here."

12:45 p.m.

Emma watches as a waitress collects Mary Walcott's teacup, and Grant Whittaker leans over to murmur in Mary's ear. The prime minister gives a tight nod but doesn't smile. They've been here for almost an hour now, waiting, and as far as Emma can see, no one has done anything more than make small talk.

"Nurse Aitken," Fred says, all smiles, "would you take us down to Maternity Ward B now, please?"

Emma nods and turns on her heel, leading them all to the lift. Phil keeps the conversation going as they travel through the corridors, talking the VIPs through all the enhanced security protocols at the hospital, sounding like a proud father boasting about his kid's school report.

Once on the third floor, as they come through the doors to Maternity Ward B, they find the nurses waiting in a line to greet the prime minister. Lynne is at the forefront and gives Emma a scorching glare before she turns to be introduced. The prime minister shakes hands with everyone and thanks Lynne for her good work with almost exactly the same phrase as she'd thanked Emma, and Lynne blushes as she steps back.

"How is everything today?" Phil asks Lynne loudly.

"Quiet," Lynne says. "Two women in the early stages of labor."

"Good, good." Phil sounds distracted. "And is Mrs. Swindell ready for us?"

"She is."

"This way, please," Phil says to the prime minister. Emma and Cathy exchange looks as they again follow at the rear of the little party.

Mrs. Swindell is lying on plumped-up pillows, her hair and makeup done, her fingers twitching nervously on the covers.

Mary Walcott goes straight to her. "Thank you for agreeing to see me—may I call you Gillian?"

"Of course," Gillian says, blushing. "It's an honor to meet you."

"And may I express my deepest condolences, Gillian, for your unbearable loss," Mary says, taking a seat by the bedside and reaching for Gillian's hand. "How are you doing?"

"It's been so hard," Gillian says, her eyes tearing up. "But everyone's been very kind."

Grant Whittaker stands nearby, his hands folded in front of him, his smile fixed, his eyes slightly glazed. His phone rings and he hurries from the room. One of Mary's assistants begins snapping pictures. It's subtle, but it makes Emma feel sick.

"I want to reassure you," the prime minister says to Gillian, "that we're doing everything we can to find out why we've been visited by this plague, and we'll keep you in touch every step of the way. I'm so sorry we couldn't save your daughter, but we'll save others in her name. We'll make sure we honor Abigail's memory."

"Thank you." Gillian bursts into tears, and Mary leans forward and gives her a gentle hug. "Thank you so much," Gillian sobs into her shoulder.

Three people are taking photos on their phones now.

"Ma'am," a security man says, stepping forward.

"It's time for us to go," Mary says gently. "Take care, Gillian, it was lovely to meet you."

"I'll never forget this," Gillian sobs. "I'm so grateful for your kindness."

Mary gives her another generous smile before they leave.

Lynne is hovering outside. "Mrs. Walcott," she says breathily, "thank you for visiting our hospital. I want to assure you that everyone here is very well taken care of. We're following your policies to the letter."

Emma doesn't know if she can bear this much longer. She coughs loudly, and Lynne glares at her.

"Let us show you the way to your vehicle," Fred says, and the whole party troops out of the ward and back toward the lift, where Grant Whittaker is still engrossed in his phone conversation. He sees them and ends the call, rejoining the group. Emma hasn't been asked any more questions or invited to talk. She's not sure why they even wanted her here.

Then she remembers. They didn't.

Cathy did.

As they wait for the lift, her fury reaches its zenith. When the double doors open, Mary steps inside with one of her security men, followed by Fred. Emma pushes past people to reach the front, with Cathy in hot pursuit. "May I ride down with you?" she asks the prime minister.

Mary looks surprised. "Of course."

Cathy quickly presses the button for the basement, leaving Grant Whittaker glaring and Phil Hammond gaping at them through the narrowing gap as the doors close. Before the lift even moves, Emma is gabbling. "Next time, Mrs. Walcott, you really should spend some time with the nurses who have PTSD. Or the less presentable mothers. Or even down in the morgue. I don't feel like the boardroom and one pre-prepared mother has shown you anything of the reality of the situation here. Which feels like living in a war zone, truth be told."

Mary's eyes widen, and Fred begins to bluster. "Well . . . I . . . I . . . I apologize for our nurse's rudeness. We fully appreciate that you can't possibly see everything, and we're grateful you've made time to visit us at all."

Mary holds up her hand. "This is obviously important to your nurse," she says. She eyes Emma intently. "What's your name again?"

"Emma . . . Emma Aitken."

The prime minister smiles politely. "I receive daily briefings, Nurse

Aitken. I'm sorry I didn't have the opportunity for a more in-depth visit, but the whole country is in crisis, and I have security meetings every few hours. Please be assured that we're fully aware of the deeper ramifications of what you're all going through."

"Then you'll know we need more support," Cathy interjects. "More funds for extra nurses. And counseling services for patients and staff that last more than a few days. More security so we don't have atrocious leaks like the video on YouTube. More of everything, Mrs. Walcott. Please."

Mary's smile falters, her expression becoming hard to read. Emma isn't sure if she's irritated or impressed, but they've definitely made an impact. "I'll see what I can do," Mary says, nodding, as the lift doors open.

"Ladies, we'll see the prime minister out from here," Fred says, glowering at them as Phil Hammond and Grant Whittaker emerge from the adjacent lift. Neither man looks happy. Grant Whittaker's mouth is a thin, disapproving line, his stare so contemptuous that Emma shudders as she watches the group disappear down the corridor. They listen to the dull clack of the prime minister's low-slung heels as Fred blusters more apologies.

"She listened, didn't she?" There's an excited tremor to Cathy's voice. "I think we got her to listen."

"We're going to get sacked," Emma says dully.

"Nope, we're not," Cathy replies with conviction. "We're going to get in deep shit for a bit, but they can't afford to lose any more staff and they know it. No one understands the ins and outs of this crisis like I do, because I'm working my arse off while they're taking tea with their benefactors upstairs."

The elevator doors close again, but they haven't pressed the button, so nothing moves.

"Thank you," Cathy says, flinging her arms around Emma. "I couldn't have done that without you."

1:00 p.m.

Lainey keeps her head down as she grabs books from her locker, while Dylan hovers beside her, shifting his weight from foot to foot. As soon as she's done, they hurry out of school and across the grounds. They're almost at the gates when Lainey hears her name.

She turns to see her friends rushing toward her. Lexie looks terrified, but Katie is eager to talk as she reaches them.

"As soon as Sereena saw them, she seemed to know what was coming," she says breathlessly. "She gave me this—and said to get it to you and tell you to make sure you use it."

The sight of the small black box is a stab in the guts. Even in her panic, Sereena had thought about Lainey and how to keep her safe. Meanwhile, Lainey had been hiding. She takes the box, scorched with the shame of it.

"Perhaps it doesn't work," Lexie says, nodding at the device. "Perhaps they heard everything this morning."

"If Sereena says it works, then it works," Lainey replies. "Thanks for getting it to me. I have to go home, but I'll message you both later, okay?" She strides away with Dylan at her heels, aware of both girls staring after her.

By the time they reach her street, Lainey and Dylan still haven't said a word to one another. The road is empty, save for a woman determinedly pushing a stroller on the opposite path. Lainey stares at the woman and tries to imagine herself in that life. She can't. It's too bizarre.

She sends her mum another message, asking her to come home, then straightens her back as she touches the jammer in her pocket, checking the switch is on. The moment of truth is here. After she's told Dylan and her mother what's happening, she'll go to the police station, tell them about the pregnancy, and face the consequences. Then at least they'll have to let Sereena go.

"Please, Lainey, tell me what's going on," Dylan says in an urgent whisper as she unlocks the front door and they head inside.

Lainey avoids his gaze. "Come upstairs—I need to check on the chicks."

In her room, the dozing birds are taken by surprise and stumble to their feet, falling over one another in an effort to get to the tweezers first.

Dylan smiles as he watches them. "They're so funny," he says. "It's like you're their mum."

She swallows hard and finishes the feed without answering him, then sets the jammer on the table and takes a deep, deep breath before she faces him.

"Dylan, at school today, the police took Sereena by mistake. They really wanted me."

Dylan frowns. She watches him trying and failing to make sense of it. "How do you know that?"

"Because . . . because I'm pregnant."

Silence. The words hang in the air, sucking all the oxygen from the room. Lainey desperately wants to snatch them back, because Dylan has gone very, very still.

"I didn't know for sure until a few days ago. There's been no one else but you. Dylan, it was us . . . that night . . ."

He takes a step away, his face aghast, his mouth slack.

Fergus trots in and puts his chin into Lainey's hand, staring up at her. Tears begin to roll down Lainey's cheeks. "Dylan?" she snaps, her voice cracking, desperate for something—anything.

"I . . . I need a minute," Dylan stammers and walks out. The bathroom door clicks shut, and she hears him retching.

She waits, listening, but it's gone quiet again. She lies on the bed, staring up at the ceiling, wondering if Dylan has managed to creep downstairs and let himself out without her hearing. But then the door creaks and he's back.

He sits down on her bed, and when she looks at him, he's almost a stranger. Older and haggard. As though they're trapped in a fairy tale and he's just aged ten years.

"I'm sorry . . . I just needed to . . ." He pauses, then takes a few shaky breaths. "You've done a test, then?"

"Yes. But I had to steal it, because you have to register to buy a pregnancy test now, and I didn't want to disappear, like Ellis. Sereena came with me. She's the only other person who knows. That's why they took her. The woman and her daughter who came in to school—it was the pharmacist and her kid. They were there to identify us. Now they'll be after me—there's no hiding anymore. I just want my mum to come home before they get here."

"Shit, shit, shit." Dylan's fists tighten. "And you're sure? You're . . . what, four months pregnant?"

"Yes."

He stares at her stomach. "And you can't get an abortion?"

"No. Not legally, anyway."

"So you—we—have to keep the baby?"

She shakes her head. "I don't know," she says, her voice rising. She makes an effort to control it. "I'm still in shock, too. I haven't made a plan."

They stare at each other.

"Can we just lie down for a bit?" Dylan asks eventually.

Lainey shuffles along to make room for him, pushing their art pads onto the floor, and they both lie with their heads on her pillow.

They don't speak for a while, then Dylan says, "Whatever you need, I'll help, okay?"

"Okay." She tries to let that sink in, but it's pointless. Too late.

"What can I do?"

"Probably not much. When Mum arrives, I'm going to explain and then ask her to go to the police with me. I'm not sure what'll happen after that, but presumably Sereena will be released. Will you wait here with me, until Mum gets home? I don't really want to be on my own if the police come."

"Sure. Yep. Do you want me to get you anything? A drink or something?"

"No, I'm fine." She feels terribly tired. "Let's just stay here while we can."

They lie side by side, bodies barely touching. Not talking, just staring at the ceiling together, as the afternoon ticks on.

5.

MONDAY, 2:30 p.m.

Emma has only been back on the ward for an hour when Cathy bustles up to the nurse's station, red-faced and flustered. "Okay, so Fred really isn't happy. Could you go home for the rest of the day while I try to calm him down?"

Emma sighs. "Really?"

"Yes, really?" a sharp voice says behind her. "I'm short-staffed as it is, and you've hardly been here today. What on earth did you do?" Lynne grabs two new patient charts and clipboards, then waits.

Cathy must sense how close Emma is to slapping the self-righteous expression off Lynne's face, because she steps forward and lightly touches Emma's arm. "We used the opportunity to tell the prime minister about some of the problems here and asked for more funding and support for the nurses and patients. Surely you agree with that?"

Lynne frowns. "So why is Fred unhappy?" Her eyes narrow. "Did you not consult him first?"

"Oh for God's sake," Emma bursts out, "we're not five years old! We had two minutes in a lift to tell the PM what it's really like here, and we did our best." Dizzy now, she puts her hand on the counter to steady herself.

109

"Right," Cathy says, watching her with obvious concern. "Emma, go home and get some sleep. Lynne, call someone else in if you need extra staff. I'll sign it off for you."

Lynne's jaw tightens. "Must be nice to have friends in high places," she says to Emma, before she stalks off down the corridor.

"You must need the patience of a saint to work with her every day," Cathy murmurs, watching Lynne go. "I've got to get back upstairs. Promise me you'll have a rest when you get home. And eat something."

"Only if you promise me I won't get sacked."

"I promise. This is just a temporary measure, so you don't get pulled into the fallout. The last thing you need today is another confrontation."

Cathy hurries off, and Emma finishes her notes on the mother and baby in Room 5A, then heads down the long corridor. Near the double doors, she hears a soft singing, and peeps into the room it's coming from. Lying on a bed, a new mother is cradling her swaddled baby in her arms, rocking the child and humming a familiar lullaby Emma had sung to Lainey, once upon a time. The woman's hair is unbrushed and she's pale, but she wears a look of wonder. Emma used to see this all the time on the wards, but now it's so rare.

The woman suddenly senses Emma watching, and stops. "I'm sorry," she says.

Emma smiles. "Don't be sorry, it's lovely."

"The last nurse told me to stop singing. Said I'll upset people, if they hear."

"Well, that nurse was just having a bad day. You carry on," Emma says, making sure she closes the door behind her.

But the mother has jogged her memories. To the first night of Lainey's life, when Emma had sung softly to that scrunched little face, who ended up swaddled with one fist poking out of the top of the blankets, pressed against her cheek. That night she'd stolen her newborn from the cot to sleep beside her, slipping down the bed so their faces were parallel, and she wouldn't accidentally roll on her, and she could breathe in those little milky breaths and study that tiny face lost in formless dreams. The wonder of this little being that was hers.

Then the years concertina in a heartbeat, and she's moving through security on autopilot, gathering her belongings and heading out to see the skies are a steely gray, and it's drizzling and cold. As she walks across no-man's-land toward security, she takes out her phone.

There are two messages there from Lainey. The first sent an hour ago.

> I love you, Mum. I'm sorry.

Her pace quickens as she reads the next one, sent a few minutes ago.

> As soon as you get this, please come home.

It's the moment she's been dreading.
She begins to run.

2:45 p.m.

It's impossible to rest with Dylan beside her. Lainey gets up and begins to sketch more designs for their mural, to keep herself busy. When he sees what she's doing, Dylan joins her, and they work in silence, the only sound their charcoal pencils scratching at the paper. Fergus lies on his side next to them, sighing regularly, lost in his dreams.

"I'm such an idiot," Dylan says. "And I'm sorry for talking about Ellis like I did the other day—before I knew. But perhaps we have it wrong. What's more likely? Pregnant girls going missing through some kind of organized kidnapping that the government won't acknowledge or care about, or us going nuts about a conspiracy theory online?"

Lainey grimaces as she weighs his words. "I know you're trying to make me feel better, but I don't want to talk about it."

"Okay, sorry."

They go back to drawing in silence. Lainey wants to tell him to leave, but she doesn't want to be alone with her thoughts. She prays her mum will be home soon and keeps her pencil moving across the page, resisting the urge to message Emma again.

"I like that," Dylan says after a while, pointing at her newest sketch of a little girl with clematis flowers that cascade from both her hands, looping through her curly hair and around her chubby legs, before trailing onto the ground. He puts down his pencil. "We've drawn so many kids now, we've probably got enough. We just need to choose which ones we like best."

She looks over and sees he's sketched a small boy in shorts and T-shirt, squatting down, hunched over, hands covering his face. The tears pour through his fingers like waterfalls, smashing into rocks at the bottom.

"That's different."

"Yeah. It's not for the mural."

Their eyes lock. She snatches his pad without asking and begins adding to the illustration. When she hands it back, he can see the silhouettes of half-a-dozen fish jumping through the spray, the hint of a rainbow behind them.

"I can't believe you drew on my picture," he says, feigning indignation. She smiles. "Yep."

He considers the changes. "It's . . . better. More layered, as my dad would say."

They both jump at the sound of the front door opening and Emma calling out Lainey's name, her voice stark with worry as she runs up the stairs.

In these few precious seconds, Lainey can feel part of herself breaking away, to stay behind, trapped in time. The girl she once was, before everything changed. She stands up and turns to Dylan. "You should probably go now."

Dylan hastily pushes his pencils and sketchbook into his bag. "Will you call me later?"

"If I can."

He pauses and his shoulders slump. "I can't believe this is happening, Lainey."

She shrugs. "Me either." But as she says it, she realizes she isn't as scared as she'd been this morning. Perhaps the loneliness of the secret will be even worse than the consequences had been.

The bedroom door opens. "There you are." Emma's face is red, her eyes fearful. "What's going on?"

She barely registers Dylan's presence as he says, "I'll let myself out." Once he's gone, she hurries across to Lainey.

"I got your messages, honey. What is it?"

"Oh, Mum, the police took Sereena from school today." And now it's back. The reality. The horror. She begins to sob. "And it's all my fault."

3:20 p.m.

"They *took* her?" Emma asks, trying to stay calm as she pulls Lainey close, feeling her trembling. "Why would they do that?"

"Mum," Lainey pulls away, her face blotchy, "I really don't want to upset you when you're working so hard and there's so much to deal with at the hospital."

"Lainey," Emma holds her gaze, "whatever it is, you can tell me, and I promise—I *promise*—I'll be on your side."

Lainey hesitates, and Emma sees her eyes flicker to a small black box on the table. "What is that?"

"It's a jammer—it interrupts microphones, in case the watches are recording us."

Emma's stomach flips unpleasantly. "And why do you need that?"

"Because I'm pregnant," Lainey whispers.

Emma stares at her daughter, fighting to breathe, understanding that every movement, word, and hesitation will be embedded in their relationship for all time. Her mind circles away to the hospital, the mothers, the morgue, Mary Walcott's smooth, prepared face, and Lynne's angry red one. So many people crowd into the room with them: her grandmother, Cathy, all the mums from school. But then she blinks and it's just the two of them, Emma and Lainey, in the chilly house she'd always promised herself they'd move away from, as soon as she could afford it, to a better garden, a bigger place, a calmer life. But this is it. Time went too fast, after all.

Lainey is waiting. And Emma knows what it takes to set aside her own emotions, to provide comfort to someone in greater need. She battles away all the judgments and despair and pulls her grown child into the moon-shaped crescent of her body. And holds her as tightly as she can and wishes she didn't ever need to let go.

3:30 p.m.

Eventually, the gap between their bodies widens a little, letting a

113

whisper of cold air slip through, and Emma asks, "How far along are you?"

"Four months . . ."

Emma pushes Lainey back to see her face, and Lainey's shaken again by the fear in her mother's eyes. "Four *months*? Oh, Lainey."

Fresh tears escape down Lainey's cheeks. "I had periods, Mum. Or I thought I did . . . I bled . . . so I didn't think . . ."

"How long have you known for sure?"

"Only a few days. Last Friday Sereena and I stole a pregnancy test, and I did it that morning."

"You *stole* a test?"

"I had to know for certain. But I was scared they might take me away, like Ellis."

Emma's mouth is a thin line. "And you're sure that's why they took Sereena today?"

"Yes. They brought the pharmacist in to school to identify us. They would have taken me, too, but Mr. Davenport hid me."

Emma shudders. "Oh, I wish you'd come to me, Lainey . . . I could have helped . . ."

Lainey can't bear the sadness in her mother's words. "You've had such a lot of stress lately. I thought . . . I hoped it would be negative, and you wouldn't even have to know. I didn't want to disappoint you like this, or make you risk your job."

"Oh, Laines." Her mother sweeps her fingers across Lainey's face, a gentle stroke that's one of her trademarks of affection. "I'm not disappointed in you. I'm just sorry this has happened, and that you've been dealing with it on your own. It would be scary enough under normal circumstances, but now . . ."

"You mean with the doll babies? Or the missing girls?"

Emma stiffens. "Let's not get too far ahead of ourselves. So, you did the test, and it was positive. Who else knows about it?"

"Only Sereena . . . and . . . and Dylan."

She sees the jolt of recognition in her mother's eyes. "Is Dylan the dad?"

Lainey grimaces. "Yes."

Emma falls silent.

"Mum, please say something."

Emma looks at Lainey and her eyes soften. "Sorry, I'm just trying to absorb it all and think about what to do next . . ."

"I already know what I'm going to do." Lainey takes her mother's hand. "It's only a matter of time before the police come here anyway, so I'm going there first. I'll tell them what happened and get Sereena back. Then I'll have to face the consequences."

Emma sighs. "Shit." She rubs her hand across her forehead. "Okay, I understand, but can we just talk it through? Have you tried messaging Sereena?"

"Yes, but she hasn't answered since lunchtime."

"All right, let me try to call Meena." Emma jumps up, but before she can go anywhere, there's a loud knocking on their front door.

They stare at one another, neither moving.

Lainey's heart pounds in her ears.

4:00 p.m.

Emma goes down the stairs slowly, unsure if she should answer or hide. When she can see through the frosted glass, she breathes a sigh of relief and opens the door. Meena is standing outside, dressed in a black trouser suit, arms wrapped around herself, staving off the bitter wind. Her face is pinched and frightened.

"Meena, come in," Emma says, as Lainey appears behind them on the stairway.

Meena steps inside and hugs them in turn, smelling of expensive perfume and coffee. Meena and Emma have always got on well, and their friendship has remained steadfast over the years, even though their shared circumstances as single working mothers had minimized their leisure time and often kept them apart.

"Have you heard anything about Sereena?" Emma asks. "Lainey just told me what happened."

Meena puts a finger to her lips, and points at her watch, but Lainey holds up the little black box. "Sereena got this to me before she was taken."

Meena nods and sets it on the table. "That's my girl," she says, her voice shaky. "The police called to let me know they'd detained her and said she'll be questioned and released within twenty-four hours." Meena wrings her hands as she talks. Emma can see she's close to tears. "I pointed out that she's a minor, and therefore I should be there, but they said she has a female officer with her at all times. I don't even know where she is, Emma. It's blatantly illegal."

Emma sits down hard on a chair, her legs weak. "Oh, Meena—they can't just take her like that, can they? I thought there were laws to prevent this kind of thing?"

"They said she's being held under national emergency provisions, but what the hell does that mean? I know she makes a lot of noise about the climate strikes and the iceberg watch, and PreacherGirl and all the other girls disappearing, but so do other people. My team is making calls, but I came here to ask Lainey some questions, if that's okay?"

Lainey steps closer. "Of course."

Meena takes a long, unsteady breath. "Forgive me my bluntness, Lainey, but I have to know. Is Sereena pregnant?"

Emma watches the color drain from her daughter's face, and then Lainey bursts into tears. Meena puts an arm around her. "No, sweetheart, don't cry. Sereena would want you to be strong right now. She needs your help, not your tears. Tell me everything."

"It's not Sereena," Lainey stammers. "It's me. She was trying to help me."

Meena's eyes meet Emma's over the top of Lainey's head. Their shared fear is palpable. "I'm so sorry, Meena," Emma says. "I'm still reeling. Lainey's only just told me all this."

"We stole a pregnancy test," Lainey continues. "We didn't want to break the law, but I was frightened because of what happened to Ellis." She explains about the police visiting her school with the pharmacist and the child.

"Okay, then," Meena says, nodding. "We have to hope that if they make Sereena do a test, once it's negative, they'll caution her and let her leave."

Lainey is still crying. "Thank you for not being angry with me."

"You're not the one I'm angry with," Meena says. "I'm sorry you're in trouble and I'm proud of Sereena for helping you. But, Lainey, you need a plan. As soon as they know you were together, they'll come here."

Emma senses more behind Meena's words. Her fear jumps up a notch. "What do you know?" she asks.

"I've been investigating the rumors about the missing girls for a while, with a few of my trusted colleagues," Meena says, her fingers fretting around a large ring on her right hand. "And look, we can't sugarcoat this. Twenty-four girls are unaccounted for. Of those twenty-four, fourteen of the parents are missing. The other parents will not talk, no matter how hard we try. The media is so ineffectual it's like it's been shut down. We need to take this very seriously."

"So, what do we do?" Lainey asks, her voice unsteady.

"Honestly?" Meena's gaze is pained but unflinching. "You need a plan, and fast. Can you go somewhere else for a while—or at least get Lainey away?"

Emma catches sight of Lainey's horrified face, and her thoughts whirl as she tries to find a way forward. An idea begins to form. "Maybe I can buy us some time. Just let me make a call," she says. She dials Cathy's number, praying she'll answer. When she hears her friend's voice, she doesn't waste a second.

"Cathy, I need your help. Are you still at the hospital?"

"Yes," Cathy sounds surprised, "but I'm leaving soon. What's wrong?"

"I can't say yet. I just need you to get me a small vial, the kind they use to take blood. The very smallest one. Can you do that?"

"Erm . . . I don't know. I'm not usually in the stockrooms or the treatment areas."

"Please, Cathy, I wouldn't ask if it wasn't really important. If you get it, can you text me and I'll meet you outside to grab it."

"Em, what's going on?"

"I'll explain, but not now. Please, Cathy."

"I'll see what I can do. Stay by your phone."

"Okay, thank you." As she hangs up, she turns to find Meena sitting with her arm around Lainey.

"I think I may have a plan," Emma says.

4:30 p.m.

Lainey hates her mother's plan, but it's the best idea they've got. The only one, in fact. So after Meena leaves, they get on the bus to the hospital. It seems safer to stick together.

It's growing dark by the time they reach the security checkpoint, and Lainey sees her mother wince as a tall blond man comes over, winding his scarf tightly around his neck and rubbing his pink hands together in the cold evening. "Hey, Emma, can't you stay away? Or is something going on in there?"

"Just waiting for a friend, Jase," she says. "And you know you can't ask me any more questions."

"Is this your daughter?" He holds out a hand. "Jason Langford with the *Online Times*."

Emma steps in front of Lainey before they have a chance to shake. "You can't ask her questions, either."

Jason takes a step back, holding up his hands. "Okay, Em, I'm just being friendly. Christ."

"After this is over," Emma says, "I'll buy you a drink, okay? But until then, do not talk to me, and do not get me sacked."

Jason grins. "All right, then, deal. You buy the drinks, and I'll get the dinner."

Once he's moved away, Lainey leans closer. "I think he's flirting with you, Mum."

"Christ, Lainey, not now," Emma says, hopping from foot to foot in the cold, her eyes lit up by the lights of the hospital as they wait. But Lainey sees the flicker of amusement even so, and it lifts her spirits. It's good to know she can still make her mother smile.

The wind is kicking up again, and leaves skitter over their shoes as they watch the dark figures hurrying across the empty parking lot. It's a while before they make out Cathy heading toward them.

"Come on, then," Cathy says as she reaches them. "I've had as much as I can stomach of this place for one day. Let's go get my car and I'll drive you home."

Emma leans close to Cathy. "Do you have it?"

Cathy simply nods as they walk.

"Did you get it . . . discreetly?"

"Of course! You know discreet is my middle name."

"Hmm," Emma replies, linking her arm through Cathy's as Lainey walks beside them. "I'm sorry to involve you, I just didn't know what else to do."

"Em, besides the fact that I'm your best friend, I think I owe you a good few favors after today. I'm the one who should be sorry that I got you in more trouble just when you don't need it." At this, she glances anxiously at Lainey.

"Have you told her?" Lainey asks Emma.

Cathy gives her a sympathetic smile. "I don't think she needs to, honey," she whispers.

As she says this, they reach the car. Once inside, Lainey holds up the black box. "It's a jammer. In case you're worried about our conversation being recorded."

Cathy raises her eyebrows and nods. "We really are the rebellion now, aren't we," she says to Emma. "All right, Beth called me and told me what happened with Sereena." She starts the engine as she talks. "She was pretty shaken up. Now there are rumors going around that Sereena is pregnant, and she's been taken like Ellis. So when you called, Em, I knew enough to start putting things together. I'm sorry, Lainey, and I'm here for you, okay? If you can't find your mum at any point, put me on speed dial, too." She turns back to Emma. "Mother's instincts, right?" she says, and they share a look.

They're all quiet on the short drive home. Lainey begins to drift a little, the weight of the day catching up with her, when Emma suddenly grabs Cathy's arm. "Keep going," she hisses. "Don't turn."

Lainey stares out the window and sees what her mother has already spotted. There's a police car outside their house.

"Shit," Cathy says, changing her course abruptly from the planned right turn. The car behind them gives a loud protest blast of the horn, and they all jump. "What now?"

"Can we come to your house? We'll only be five minutes."

"Sure, you can," Cathy says, "but everyone's there. What shall I say?"

"Tell them I'm borrowing more books."

Lainey listens to them, thinking of the police car. "Mum," she says nervously, "are you sure this will work?"

Emma leans around from the front seat. "Not a hundred percent, but it's a decent plan. We have to try."

They pull into Cathy's garage, and Cathy hustles them through the open-plan kitchen and living room before John or the kids can start talking to them. Upstairs, they head for the bathroom, and Cathy discreetly disappears.

Emma goes in first, while Lainey waits outside. When she comes out, she passes over the warm vial of urine.

"This is disgusting," Lainey says.

"I know. I'm sorry, love, but it might keep you safe. Try not to think about it. Just do it."

Lainey heads into the bathroom and scrunches up her nose before getting on with the repulsive task at hand: inserting the vial of her mother's urine inside her like a tampon, just as they'd discussed.

5:15 p.m.

Emma's dismayed at the sight of the busy police reception. Everyone seems stressed out, tired and hot, since the radiators are pumping heat and most are in thick jackets, rugged up from the biting cold outside.

Lainey hasn't spoken since she emerged from Cathy's bathroom, a look of deep distaste on her face, to find Beth on the landing, full of questions about Sereena and what had happened in the school hall. Cathy had hastily intervened and ushered them out of the house, dropping them here and promising to come back when they've finished. They hadn't dared bring the jammer with them in case the police discovered it, so it's safely stowed in the glove box of Cathy's car.

Emma squeezes Lainey's hand, and then they walk to the front desk together.

"We're here because there was an incident earlier today, at St. James's School, and my daughter was involved," Emma says, leaning on the desk.

As she talks, a middle-aged man in shirtsleeves and suit trousers comes out to the front desk with a couple of folders and stops when he sees them. Emma's heart sinks as she recognizes Sergeant Taylor from the weekend.

"Well, well," he says, "I thought I'd see you two again, but I didn't think it'd be quite so soon. What have you done this time?"

Neither of them smiles. Before Emma can speak, Lainey steps forward, her chin held high. "My friend was arrested at school today, and I think the police are searching for me, too. So I've come to explain, and then you can let her go."

The man leans on the counter, all business now, raising his eyebrows. "Is that right? Well, you'd better come with me, then."

"Sergeant Taylor, there's a witness waiting in room three for you. He's been there an hour," the female desk sergeant says with obvious exasperation.

"It's all right," he waves her concern away, "I won't be long."

They follow him back to the same interview room they'd been in two days earlier. He shuts the door and sits down opposite them. "Tell me," he says. "What's brought you here this evening?"

"Last week," Lainey says, "my friend and I stole a pregnancy test."

Taylor doesn't react, just waits for more.

"I recognize it was wrong," Lainey hurries on. "But I was scared, with all the babies dying. My friend Sereena helped me, and she was identified at school today by the police and the pharmacist, and they took her away."

Taylor doesn't say anything for a minute, then he leans forward and studies Lainey. "Yes, I know about this. Are you pregnant, Lainey?"

Emma holds her breath. *Please*, she thinks, entreating Dorothy's god in desperation. *Please make this work.*

"No," Lainey says. "It was negative."

Again, there's a protracted pause as Lainey and the sergeant stare at each other. "You'll take another test here to confirm that, will you?"

Lainey doesn't flinch. "Of course."

"Right." He gets up from the desk. "Stay here and I'll find a female officer to accompany you to the bathroom."

He leaves and they wait. Ten minutes. Twenty. Thirty. An hour. Emma is sweating in her coat but doesn't take it off. She needs to be ready to leave at the first opportunity.

They sit in silence, neither daring to talk. After an hour and forty-five minutes, a female officer appears and waves a pregnancy-test kit at them. "Come with me, then," she says to Lainey.

Lainey gets up and leaves with the woman without a backward glance. It was the right move; she's playing this to perfection. But Emma still wishes there'd been just one look between them; one more chance to channel all her love and strength to her daughter. Just in case this goes wrong.

7:10 p.m.

In the bathroom, the female officer opens the packet and hands Lainey the stick. "Go on, then." She gestures toward the stalls.

Lainey moves slowly, pushing the creaking cubicle door closed and locking it, half terrified that the officer will demand she keep the door open. But the woman doesn't seem that interested.

Once inside, she works fast. Sitting on the toilet, she removes the vial, thankful it comes out easily, pees into the toilet bowl, then opens the vial lid and pours her mother's urine over the stick. The glass is slippery, and she almost drops it, catching it with her free fingers. She balances the stick on her leg as she puts the lid on the vial and inserts it back inside her.

"You finished in there?" the policewoman asks.

"Almost," she says.

A blue latex-gloved hand comes under the door. "You can pass the test to me."

She gives it to the officer, fastens her clothes, and comes out of the cubicle to wash her hands.

"Right, we'll wait five minutes," the officer says, checking her watch.

Even though the plan has worked this far, it's the longest five minutes of Lainey's life. Five minutes to list all her worries. What if it doesn't work properly? What if they ask her to do another one? She should have only used half the urine. And what if they detain Sereena anyway? They'll both be in trouble for stealing, won't they? Something is bound to go wrong.

"Come on," the officer announces when the five minutes is up. "Let's tell everyone the good news."

Does that mean negative? Lainey daren't ask. She follows the woman back down the corridor to the interview room, her legs wobbly and her head spinning. Sergeant Taylor is back, chatting to her mother.

"It's negative," the officer says, holding out her blue-gloved hand so he can see the evidence for himself.

"What's that line for?" the policeman asks, pointing at the test.

"It's a control line. Shows she took the test properly, didn't just dip it in the toilet bowl."

"Okay," he says. "Bag that as evidence for now, don't throw it away."

The officer nods and leaves. Sergeant Taylor stares at Lainey.

"It's good news you're not pregnant," he says, "but what shall we do about you breaking the law?"

Lainey reddens.

"I've just checked, and Ms. Mandalia has been sent home, but she says she wasn't the one who took anything, she was the decoy, yes?"

"Yes," Lainey whispers.

"So, you were the instigator of this plan?"

"Yes."

"Well, I'll have to pass the report to our welfare team about the pregnancy test, and they might want to contact you to follow up. Now, what do we do about the theft?" Taylor taps his pen against his lips for a while, his eyes never leaving her, before he continues. "You know what, Lainey? It's busy out there. Everyone's manning the decks because we have so much going on. There are viruses, terrorism, climate change, and now we have babies dying every day." He sits forward. "I like you both, and I don't think you need more trouble right now, not with your mum having such an important job at the hospital. Maybe it's second-time lucky for you today, Lainey." He waves his pen at them. "Even though I should really be charging you for theft. But be very careful. Third strike, and you're out."

7:30 p.m.

Cathy collects them and drops them home with barely a word. It feels too dangerous to talk, so they make do with small gestures of comfort—a hand on an arm, a nod.

At home, Fergus is waiting by the door, having nosed his empty bowl into the hallway. Emma feeds him while Lainey goes upstairs to check on the chicks. When she comes back downstairs, Emma has poured herself a gin and tonic and is sitting in the semi-dark, still with her coat on.

"I've driven you to drink," Lainey says, flopping beside her.

"Nah," Emma says, putting her arm around Lainey, "but after the day I've had, I need this. Don't get me wrong—I'm so proud of the way you held yourself together tonight."

Lainey sits up again, rummaging in her bag before setting the jammer on the table. Then says, "But I'm still not safe, am I?"

Emma takes a long sip of her drink before answering. "I think we've bought ourselves some time." Her voice is low, too. "And at least we know Sereena's home safe. Meena just messaged me." She turns to Lainey. "Have you thought much about your options?"

"A bit." Lainey sits forward, rubbing her hands over her face. "I wonder if I could hide the pregnancy, and you can help me give birth."

"That would be really hard, Lainey, even if we could get away with it, which is unlikely. It'd be five months of torture. Plus, how would we explain the baby at the end of it? You might not be showing yet, but it won't be long."

"Maybe there wouldn't be a baby," Lainey whispers.

Emma shudders. "Don't say that."

"But it's true, isn't it? Although I know that plan sucks, and it puts pressure and stress on you as well. But what are my other choices? I could go away somewhere, but where would I go? I can't go to Dad—he's not interested. And there's no one else outside of Whitehaven."

Emma considers this for a while. "There's Aunty Bernie, but it's a long shot. I don't think I've even sent her a Christmas card for the last couple of years." She hesitates. "Honey, I just have to ask this. Have you thought of abortion? I know there're legalities to consider now, but if you could choose?"

Lainey hesitates. "Honestly? If I could have taken the morning-after pill or had an abortion early on, then maybe. But now it's gotten this far, I don't think I could. I know this sounds stupid, but I don't want an abortion or a baby. I just want the whole thing to go away."

"There's adoption?"

"Yes, maybe."

"You wouldn't be alone, if you kept it. I'd help you."

"Would you?"

"Of course I would."

"I don't think I want an abortion."

"Okay."

"But I don't want to disappear, either."

Emma's stomach drops. "No, but perhaps we're panicking unnecessarily. Cathy thinks that's all a hoax."

"Do you?"

Emma can't find the words.

"Because if it is, then where's Ellis, Mum?"

Emma puts her arm around Lainey and hugs her tightly. "I don't know."

"So, the best-case scenario is that I have the authorities watching my every move, but I get to stay here. And the worst is that I disappear—and perhaps you do too."

Emma gets up and pours herself another drink.

"I could do with one of those," Lainey says as she watches.

Emma shakes her head with a sad smile. "Under any other circumstances, I'd probably give you one."

"Are there no other options?" Lainey asks, moving down to the floor to cuddle Fergus, who has settled at their feet.

Emma's thoughts whir as she sips steadily at her gin and tonic. "Actually, perhaps there is someone else." She jumps up, takes out her phone, and begins tapping on it. Lainey waits, wondering what she's researching, until Emma shows her the screen. It's a ticketing website for Geraldine Fox's event in London.

Lainey stares at it, then at her mother.

Emma slugs back the rest of her drink then looks at Lainey, eyes blazing with determination. "I think it's time to go and see Grandma."

6.

MONDAY, 11:30 p.m.

Alone in her room, getting ready for bed, Lainey can't stop checking and rechecking her phone. She'd messaged Sereena hours ago.

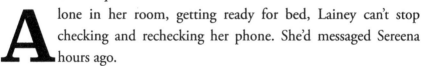

> I went to the police, and they said you were released and sent home. Are you okay?

There's been no reply.

Dylan, on the other hand, has checked in hourly. Each time his name pings up on screen, Lainey gets nervous, worried he'll forget there could be eavesdroppers. He must still be reeling, after all. But so far, thankfully, he's been discreet. He's asked to walk with her to school tomorrow, and she's said yes, of course, but she's dreading it. She wishes she hadn't told him. Too many people know her secret; she's losing her grip on it. It'll be out in the open soon, and then what?

She checks on the chicks, then wanders out onto the upstairs landing, the jammer clutched tightly in her hand, her fears swirling, needing to talk more. Disappointed that her mum's room is already dark, she's tiptoeing backward when Emma's voice calls out, "Lainey? You can come in, I'm not asleep."

Lainey climbs into the empty spot beside her mother, who turns and props herself up on her elbows. She peers at the screen Emma is holding and sees an image of Geraldine Fox sitting amongst a panel that includes an old man in a gray suit, a middle-aged woman in a navy suit, and a young guy in jeans and T-shirt. Geraldine wears a large black beret, bright-pink glasses, and a low-cut black T-shirt with the slogan *Nothing to see here* printed across her ample bosom. "What are you watching?"

"She was on *Question Time* recently." Emma tries to put the device aside, but Lainey takes it.

"Can I see?"

"I'm not sure it's . . ."

Before she can finish, Lainey presses play.

An audience member stands in front of a microphone, an older man in a suit and tie with neatly combed white hair. "Geraldine," he says. "We've watched the government clamp down on reproductive rights over the last few months, but Mary Walcott has made it clear that this is necessary to protect the population. Do you agree?"

Geraldine lets out a puff of sarcastic laughter. "Look, quite frankly, this is a terrifying moment for women." Her voice is striking: low and gravelly. "Was there any consultation with women's groups before this law was passed? Have there been any discussions of alternative ways forward that don't include a clampdown on women's rights? Of course not, because a patriarchal system will never pursue collaboration as a method of progress or restitution." She waves a pen in the air like a tiny jousting stick as she speaks. "The system, and those behind it, only want one thing, and that's control."

Beside her, the host leans into his microphone, smiling broadly as he asks, "So, do moments like this prove that feminism is doomed to fail, if we can so easily go backward in regards to women's rights?"

Geraldine sighs. "The Intrapartum X babies are a unique humanitarian crisis, and we shouldn't conflate them with an ideological stance. I think we should be suspicious of anyone, man or woman, who sees humanity as a pyramid with one group seated at the top and claiming eternal dominion while deciding how everyone else should live. It's very likely these people are brainwashed or have something to gain by keeping the system in place, while the rest of us have much, much more to lose." As she finishes, Geraldine sits back with a gleam of triumph in her eye, as though daring anyone to rebut her arguments.

"She doesn't hold back, does she," Lainey says.

"Nope—and she talks like a textbook. She'll probably eat us for breakfast."

"You think so?"

"Who knows, but she's our only hope right now. You okay?"

"Mmm. Kind of." Lainey snuggles into the covers and lets her eyes close. "I'm just wishing I hadn't told Sereena and Dylan."

"Well, you needed support, and what's done is done." Emma lies down beside her. "Besides, if we can get you away from here, it won't matter anyway."

"Are you sure you want to bring Grandma into it? I thought you didn't want to talk to her?"

Emma's voice is firm in the semi-dark. "Well, I've changed my mind." There's a rustle of covers as she turns over. "I know we haven't seen her for years, but she once offered help if I ever needed it, and I haven't asked her for anything before. Not even money when I thought we were going to lose this house and she was doing regular stints on TV. She might just help us . . . and we have to get you away until the dust settles."

"But leaving the country . . . isn't that breaking the law, too? And I haven't got a good track record of late." She thinks of Sergeant Taylor's warning: *Three strikes and you're out.* She realizes she's clenching her teeth and tries to relax, wiggling her jaw and massaging her temples.

"You're no threat to the nation, Lainey," Emma says firmly in the darkness, with such surety that her words reach right into Lainey, seeding hope amongst her fears. "This isn't a virus, or the problem would have spread very differently by now. However," she hesitates, "this country may pose a threat to you."

Lainey swallows hard. "And you're sure that's our best option? You want me to go to Australia, with a stranger?"

"She's your grandma! You've met her before."

"When I was eight! She's a stranger, Mum."

There's a long pause before Emma says, "And if your pregnancy is discovered and you're taken away somewhere, do you think you'll be with friends then?"

Lainey doesn't reply. She lightly touches her tummy and imagines the tiny being inside her, curled up like a peanut, doing nothing wrong. Just like the chicks, who would have died without her intervention. A wave of protectiveness rushes over her. Their helplessness is horrible. As is her power over them.

She shivers, and her mother must feel it. "Oh, I'm sorry, Lainey, I don't mean to scare you. We're both exhausted. Let's sleep, then we can consider all this with fresh heads tomorrow. I know it's easier said than done, but we should try."

Lainey hesitates. "Do you mind if I stay here?"

"Of course not," Emma says. "I'd like that."

Lainey stares into the darkness for a while, her head replaying the horrors of the day. "Thanks for everything you did today, Mum. I probably should've told you sooner."

"You told me when you were ready. That's okay, Lainey. It's your life, your decisions. I just want to support you." There's a pause. Then Emma adds softly, "I've missed you lately."

"I've missed you, too."

Emma snuggles closer and begins to stroke her daughter's cheek, but it still takes Lainey a long time to settle. When she finally begins to drift, her mother's fingers still sweep gently across her skin, in a simple language without words.

I'm here.

TUESDAY, 7:00 a.m.

Emma jumps up at the first wail of the alarm, grabbing her dressing gown to stave off the cold. It had been a fitful night of sleep, with terrible images rolling across her mind like stricken ships tumbling in ferocious waves. At one point, she'd woken up groping blindly in the dark, hands outstretched, before realizing there was nothing to hold on to.

Thankfully, Lainey still looks to be fast asleep. Emma unplugs her phone from the wall socket as she checks it, and sees that Cathy left a message fifteen minutes ago, asking her to call. Not wanting to wake Lainey, she hurries for the stairs, nearly tripping over Fergus, who has taken up a sleeping sentry post outside the bedroom door.

Once in the kitchen, she returns the call. "Cath?" she says when her friend picks up. "What is it?"

"Are you guys okay?"

"Yes, for now."

"Okay. Well, you need to take today off work."

"Why? Is Fred still on the warpath?"

"Kind of." Cathy hesitates. "I'm sorry, honey, but yesterday evening, Lynne made a formal complaint about you. She says you're putting mothers and babies at risk by not following hospital protocol."

"What?!"

"Something to do with a breastfeeding mum."

"Seriously . . . ? As far as I'm aware, Elise Cartwell is still breastfeeding thanks to me."

"Well, you'll be told about it as soon as you come in, and I'd just rather you two didn't cross paths today. She's making a big fuss, saying you're dangerous to have around, and that you're not focused because your daughter and her friends have been in trouble at school."

"How dare she!" Emma splutters, beginning to pace up and down on the cold kitchen tiles.

"You do know it's not really about any of that, don't you? It's about Lynne's bruised ego after Mary Walcott's visit, and her need for control."

"I know, I know," Emma says, "but she doesn't get to take me down so she can feel better."

"Exactly, and I'll sort it out. It's just that Fred is still mad with both of us because of yesterday, so he's jumped on it a little too eagerly. I'm sorry, Ems, you were having a hard enough time as it is and now I've made it worse."

"Just tell me it'll be okay."

"Absolutely. I'll get it sorted ASAP. It's my only priority today, I promise. Hang tight and try to make the most of your day off."

"I'll try." Emma grimaces. "Though I'd rather spend my time without worrying I'll be sacked."

"I promise you, nothing will come of this." Cathy sounds exasperated. "They know how much they need you. This is just a power play, trying to make sure they keep you in line. Now go back to bed and take it easy."

"I bloody well hope you're right," Emma replies, a little more snappishly than she means to. Then, "Sorry, Cath, I know you're doing your best." She pauses, wondering whether she should say more, then decides it's time. "She's not coping, you know. Lynne, I mean. She's so tightly wound up that everyone is tiptoeing around her terrified they'll be the one to push her over the edge. And she's close to losing it, Cathy, I can feel it. She's taking every Intrapartum X birth as a personal failure. This isn't anything to do with the troubles between us, I swear. I've watched it getting worse for a while, I just haven't known what to do about it."

"I'll bear that in mind, Em," Cathy says, her tone grim. "But Fred's in her pocket—he's big buddies with her father. I'm pretty sure it'll be impossible to do anything to help her unless she requests it. But keep telling me your worries anyway, won't you? We might just have to be prepared, so we can catch her if she falls."

It's a magnanimous statement from Cathy, always so caring yet practical. And it's more generous than Emma's felt of late, because Lynne has become so unbearable. Emma's grown less concerned about what will finally make the woman crack, and more worried about whom she'll take down with her when she does.

8:00 a.m.

"If you're staying home, maybe I should too," Lainey says, already dressed in her uniform and brushing her hair.

"No, it's better that you carry on as normal." Emma hands her a plate of toast and a glass of apple juice. "Besides, catching up with Sereena will make you feel better, I'm sure."

"She hasn't texted me yet." Lainey automatically checks her phone again. "I'm worried she's mad at me." She turns away, not wanting her mum to see how upset she is. She's called five times so far with no answer. Each time she'd followed up with messages and watched the little circles next to them change to blue ticks, then to Sereena's profile image. Each time she'd known Sereena had seen them and waited for a reply. It happened instantly most mornings. But not today.

"Sereena wouldn't hold a grudge like that with you," Emma reassures her. "Besides, it was her choice, Lainey, you didn't force her."

"No, and I didn't come to her defense, either. I hid."

"Well, you're not going to feel any better staying here to brood. Go, and if there's music to be faced, then get it done. I can chat to Meena, too, and help smooth things over if need be."

"All right." Feeling brighter, Lainey takes her toast upstairs to gather her things. She's just pulling on her jumper when there's a persistent rapping at the door. She stops in her tracks, knowing exactly who knocks like that.

She'd completely forgotten about Liam.

Downstairs, her mum is already opening the door.

"Oh hi, Mrs. Aitken," she hears Liam say in surprise. "Is Lainey here? We usually walk to school together."

"Er . . . I don't think she's quite ready," Emma replies as Lainey grabs her bag and hurries down the stairs to stop their conversation before it starts.

"Hey, Lainey," Liam says, grinning as soon as he sees her. Emma catches her eye, raising her eyebrows before she disappears.

Lainey hesitates, a band of nerves tightening around her belly. "Sorry, Liam. I promised I'd walk with Dylan today."

Liam frowns. "Seriously? You'd rather hang out with that loser? Come on, I want you to fill me in on yesterday—I can't believe Sereena got escorted out of school." His eyes are alight with intrigue. "So, is she pregnant?"

Lainey bristles, her face burning. "For God's sake, Liam, don't believe everything you hear. Of course she isn't."

"It's not just me, the whole school's talking about it! Well, I guess we can ask her ourselves—if she ever comes back. Perhaps she'll be whisked away and become part of one of those conspiracy theories she loves so much."

Lainey stares at him. "You're an arsehole," she says, as he beams back at her. But inside she's mortified. *Just how much trouble have I caused my friend?*

Before they can say more, Dylan comes up the path, bent over from the weight of the huge black backpack on his back. Despite the glower on his face as he spots Liam, Lainey's heart lifts to see him.

"You cutting my grass now, Bailey?" Liam calls as he nears.

"Don't be a dickhead," Dylan replies with a sigh. "We're doing the art project together, and it's got to be in on Thursday."

"Yeah, I know, I've just been asking Lainey if my partner is going to show up or if she's got herself up the duff and gone missing."

"Well, if you get to school, maybe you'll find out," Dylan snaps. "So jog on."

With a snide smile, Liam turns to leave, moving left to bump against Dylan, who stumbles off the path into the flowerbed.

"Laters, Lainey," Liam says at the gate as he blows her a kiss.

Dylan shakes his head as they watch him disappear along the road to school. "You really can't get rid of him, then?"

She sighs, flushed and flustered. "He just keeps turning up, even though I'm always telling him to get lost. But you helped this morning, so thanks. Are you dreading this day as much as I am?"

"Yep."

"You know, if Sereena doesn't come to school, then everyone's going to ask me if she's pregnant."

"Just give them all the same answer: *I don't know, so piss off.*"

Lainey smiles. "That might do it. Not sure I'll have many friends left by the end, but okay, then, let's go." She calls out, "I'm leaving now, Mum."

"Okay." Emma comes to the front door. "Was that Liam Whittaker?"

"Yeah." Lainey's surprised to see her mother's face is flushed with irritation. "He's been coming around a lot. I can't shake him off."

Emma grimaces, then spots Dylan and makes a visible effort to relax. "Oh, hi, Dylan."

He can't quite meet Emma's eye as he mumbles, "Hi."

"Don't worry, we can talk later," Emma says to both of them, pointing to her watch. "For today, take care of yourselves and each other. Call me when school finishes, Lainey, and let me know how you're doing and if you see Sereena."

Lainey collects her bag and follows Dylan down the path. "Your mum seems pretty cool, considering," he says once they're on the road. "Sounds like she's not a Liam fan."

Lainey doesn't reply, focusing on the walk and watching out for people they know. She takes long, deep breaths to try to steady herself, since she's light-headed this morning, as well as fighting the vague nausea that's plagued her lately.

"Do you want to talk about stuff?" Dylan asks eventually.

"Okay. Can we sit down for a minute?" She gestures toward a low redbrick wall in front of a nearby gas station, where the trash bins are overflowing, and half the pumps seem to be out of service. Dylan follows her, putting his bag by his feet.

She grabs her art pad and writes fast, passing the message across.

We went to the police station last night, and Mum helped me with the test, so it came up negative.

He reads it and looks up at her. A question.
She shakes her head.

No. I'm still . . . It was just to protect me. For now.

His face falls. He nods.

So what next?

Mum has some ideas, to get me somewhere safe.

Away from here?

Yes.

Do you want to go?

Might not have a choice.

I'm sorry.

They stop writing and sit on the grimy wall, staring into space and breathing in faint petrol fumes as cars speed by. Dylan's fingers touch Lainey's for a few seconds, and she jumps up. "We should go, or we'll be late."

Dylan heaves his bag onto his back. "Wonder if we'll get time to work on the mural today. I think we're almost ready anyway. We have all the sketches, we just need to compile them for the presentation."

"You're really into this challenge, aren't you?"

"You know I love painting walls." He grins. Then he remembers, reddens, and turns away.

Minutes later, they're within sight of the school gates, walking with a few other stragglers, all quickening their pace to beat the first bell. Inside the school grounds, Lainey braces herself, expecting the questions to begin as soon as she's noticed. But it's quieter than usual here, with only a few students sitting on the grass, staring intently at devices. Dylan raises his eyebrows at Lainey as they head toward the main entrance, waylaid by the health-check station, as robotic arms take their temps and dip their saliva swabs into test tubes for analysis.

Once cleared, they head inside to find the corridor is packed. People huddle in groups, all staring at their phones. Some chatter excitedly, while others look scared.

Lainey exchanges a confused glance with Dylan as they head to their own lockers. Then she spots Lexie and Katie nearby.

"Hey," Lainey says nervously. "What's going on?"

"Oh, hi." Lexie is clearly shocked.

Katie holds out her phone. "You haven't seen this, then?"

Lainey takes the phone and sees an article on a news website with the headline, PREACHERGIRL'S IDENTITY REVEALED, next to a photo of a girl their age with a short black bob and piercing brown eyes. Lainey scans the text, a nerve in her neck beginning to throb.

Alyssa Roberts, a seventeen-year-old singer whose potential was once showcased on *Britain's Got Talent*, hasn't been seen for a fortnight, after she and her parents went missing sometime on or around August 25. Police were unaware of Alyssa's possible alter ego until yesterday, when friends of hers came forward to share their concerns after recognizing her voice. Voice analysis experts now believe it likely that Alyssa is at least partially responsible for the online viral video hit by an anonymous artist known as PreacherGirl, which claimed that young girls across the country have been disappearing, and caused a reaction nationwide, as concerned teenagers put forward more names of missing friends. Police and journalists have stalled in their efforts to track those mentioned, due to the limited information provided—only names and places, often in cities with hundreds of thousands of people.

Alyssa is the second missing teen from Chelmsford, after Jessica Abbott—a friend of Alyssa's, whose name was listed on the PreacherGirl music video—was reported missing at the beginning of August. Concerns are also held for Alyssa's mother, Janet, a policewoman, and her father, Richard, a lawyer, who have not been at home or work for the past fourteen days.

Lainey shudders. "Jeez, this is scary. And Chelmsford is only, like, half an hour away."

"Aren't Meena's offices in Chelmsford?" Katie asks Lainey. "Do you think they know this girl somehow? D'you reckon that's why they marched Sereena out of here yesterday?"

Lainey looks helplessly at Dylan. "Hard to know," he says solemnly, returning the phone. "Probably best not to speculate. When she comes back, she can tell us herself."

"*If* she comes back," Lexie says dramatically, her eyes wide as they stare at each other. Lainey sags against the lockers as Lexie continues, "If she's pregnant, she might not come back at all."

11:00 a.m.

After a failed attempt at sleep and a strong cup of coffee, Emma reluctantly returns to the ticketing website she'd found last night. The Geraldine plan irks her, but it's the only thing she can think of, and a sense of urgency she doesn't altogether understand is screaming at her to take action and not wait passively for the worst.

She hasn't seen Geraldine for nine years. At Nell's funeral, when Geraldine had asked Emma if they could keep in touch, Emma had shied away, feeling it would be disloyal to the woman who'd raised her. Nell had never gotten over Geraldine abandoning them and wouldn't hear her daughter's name spoken in the house. Emma had known she was loved, but it hadn't been an easy childhood. Her grandfather had died before she was born, and while Nell made sure Emma had everything she needed materially, she was a reserved woman who loved needlework, gardening, and church, and always praised Emma for her attentiveness and caring. When, as often happened, Nell got a bad bout of arthritis and took to her bed for a few days, Emma had learned how to handle the cooking and housework. Only much later, when she began nursing, had it hit her that it probably wasn't arthritis at all, but rather depression.

As a teenager, Emma had eagerly sought out information about Geraldine, shocked by the nude photos published in the press and Geraldine's plain talking about subjects such as rape and abortion. Unsure how to handle her mother's eccentricities, she'd decided her grandmother was right: they'd both been abandoned by someone who preferred the adulation of strangers to real relationships. The hurt had been compounded when Geraldine had talked publicly about her inability to mother and the child she'd left behind, with no shame at all, only a conviction that she'd done the right thing.

In her early twenties, Emma had been plagued by a year of constant fatigue, and a therapist suggested that her body couldn't cope with the continual tide of anger that Geraldine invoked in her. Since then, she'd avoided her mother's news as much as possible, and things had been a lot better. For a few years, there hadn't been much about Geraldine online. She'd suddenly seemed to shun the limelight she'd once loved, but then came the new book in April, and with all the surrounding publicity, she's been hard to miss. What's more, she continues to talk publicly about Nell as the mother who disowned her, and Emma as the baby she didn't want, couldn't cope with, and left behind.

Stifling her anger, Emma holds her breath and presses purchase on two tickets for Geraldine Fox's London event tonight, which are ridiculously expensive because all the cheap seats have sold out. The extra cost means they'll also get copies of Geraldine's book and can attend the VIP signing line to meet her personally.

Perfect, Emma thinks. Time to give Geraldine the shock of her life and see what she's really made of.

1:30 p.m.

Lainey has never been so grateful for lessons. In classes she can't be quizzed by her classmates, although she can still hear continual whispers of Sereena's name. She manages to hide in the bathroom for most of the morning break, thankful she has a double period of history to get her through to lunch.

Mr. Davenport is acting like nothing happened yesterday. If anything, he is avoiding eye contact as he explains next week's field trip to Coventry Cathedral as part of their project on how artists commemorate and reexamine war. Lainey should be thrilled at a day out, with two of her favorite subjects colliding. But while the rest of the class chatters excitedly, she's trapped in a bubble of fear. She doubts she'll be here by next Friday.

Where will I be?

Where is Sereena?

It's unbearable. Toward lunchtime, she plots her escape. She hides her phone under the table to send Dylan a message.

> Cover for me in art? I'm going to find S.

He replies in seconds.

> Okay, can do.

"Miss Aitken?"

Of course, *now* Mr. Davenport is looking at her.

"Can that wait?" he says mildly.

Her face reddens as she puts the phone back in her bag.

She hurries out of class when the bell rings, before Mr. Davenport can ask her to stay behind for a chat. Head down, she's out of the school and through the gates in less than a minute. On the way she sends a message to her mum.

> Can't take school anymore. No word from S. On my way there now.

The reply is almost instant.

> I'm coming. I'll meet you there.

The relief is immense. She's dreading what they might find, but at least she won't be facing it alone.

2:00 p.m.

The day is gray, and a light drizzle is just starting. Emma wishes she'd worn her thicker coat as she watches Lainey hurrying up the wide street of large, semidetached houses, her shoulders slumped.

"How was school this morning?" she asks, giving her a brief hug as they meet.

"Awful."

Without another word, Lainey marches up to Sereena's front door and knocks. Emma follows and they wait, both jiggling with cold and nerves.

There are footsteps, a hesitation behind the frosted glass, then the door swings open.

Meena stands there, tired and somber. "Is Sereena okay?" Lainey bursts out before Meena can say anything.

Meena doesn't answer, but her troubled eyes meet Emma's as a small, tired voice behind her says, "It's okay, Mum, you can let them in."

Meena steps back, and there's Sereena, in her pajamas, her hair unbrushed, dark circles under her eyes.

Emma keeps her dismay hidden, but Lainey flings herself at her friend. "Oh, Sereena, I'm so sorry, this is all my fault. I've been mad with worry. Why didn't you answer my texts?"

"Come in here," Sereena says, grabbing Lainey's hand and pulling her into the lounge.

"What's happened?" Emma asks Meena as they follow the girls. "Is it safe to talk?"

"Yes," Meena assures her, "although, I'm so angry right now I'm not sure I can speak."

Sereena and Lainey sit together on the cushioned window seat in the large bay window. Emma has always been envious of Meena's spacious home, the large fireplace, built-in bookcases, and colorful throws and wall hangings. Despite her busy career, Meena has still managed to make this place feel much more inviting and homely than the worn furnishings in Emma's cramped front room.

"Are you okay?" Lainey asks, holding Sereena's hands. "I've been so worried about you. I'm so sorry I wasn't in the hall—I should have thought—but it all happened so fast."

"It's okay," Sereena says, smiling. "You can cool the vibes, I promise I'm not cross. I'm just glad they didn't get you as well."

Emma glances from Sereena to Meena. "So, what happened—can you tell us?"

Meena doesn't reply but raises her eyebrows at Sereena. A question.

"It's okay, Mum, we can tell them." Sereena turns to Lainey and takes a big breath. "They didn't take me to the local police station, it was another one. I'm not even sure where. I was in the back of the police van and the windows were blacked out. They put me in a cell, made me pee on a stick, took my blood . . . and then they just left me there for hours." Sereena shudders. "With no food or water. No explanation. I was terrified."

"That's surely illegal, isn't it?" Emma splutters in outrage, watching all the color leeching from Lainey's face.

"Absolutely." Emma can see the suppressed fury in Meena's stance and hear it in her voice. "She's a bloody minor, Emma."

Sereena pauses while they speak, then continues. "Finally, another policewoman came in and listened and seemed to recognize Mum's name. After that, I was literally out of there in fifteen minutes, although they said I'm not allowed to go anywhere until they call us. That's what you missed, Lainey, and I'm so glad you did. Imagine if they'd done that to you."

Lainey is stunned. "But they can't . . . they can't do tests and stuff without consent, can they?"

Sereena shrugs. "They did. The scariest thing is that I'm sure it was only Mum's name that got me out in the end. Without that, who knows what would have happened."

"I'm so sorry," Lainey says, hugging her friend tightly, her tearful, terrified eyes meeting Emma's over Sereena's shoulder. Watching them, Emma is overwhelmed by the same dual agony of anger and distress that she can sense coursing through Meena.

Lainey sits back to look at Sereena again. "As soon as I told Mum, we went to the police station. But I only did the basics, peeing on a stick, nothing like what you went through."

"What?" Sereena is horrified. "You had to do a test? Then how are you here?"

"Oh, God." Lainey covers her face with her hands, and Sereena stares at Emma as Lainey explains what they'd done. As Lainey reddens, Sereena grins. "Seriously," she says to both of them. "That is badass! You guys are badasses!"

"Yeah, but probably not for long," Lainey says. "After what you went through, I don't understand why they didn't do more to me."

"Maybe you just caught them off guard, turning up like that."

"Maybe."

Emma remembers the intrigue on Sergeant Taylor's face. On both occasions, she'd felt he was condescending, but perhaps he'd been warning them, too. He'd let them off lightly twice, after all.

"So, what can you do now?" she asks Meena. "Can you file a complaint?"

"A year ago, yes, there would have been uproar. But now? No one cares, Emma. Honestly, I don't know where to begin. Sereena heard them mention the NBCC a few times. If this scenario was created by the government, where do we turn for protection?"

Everyone is silent. Then Sereena asks Lainey, "What are you going to do?"

"We're going to my grandma's event tonight. Mum wants to ask her for help."

"Hang on." Sereena's eyes widen. "You're going to see Geraldine Fox?"

"Yep."

"You're so lucky! I love that woman. Still can't believe you've got her genes. You should really be more experimental, clothes-wise, you know."

Emma pastes on a smile at Sereena's enthusiasm. Why can't she admire her mother in the same way everyone else seems to? It's so hard to negotiate the mismatch between Geraldine, the truculent absent mother, and Geraldine Fox, the charismatic public figure. The thought of turning up at her event tonight and having to beg for a favor is especially upsetting. But she'll do it for Lainey.

Meena is watching her, nodding in approval. "You're doing the right thing. There are too many stories of pregnant girls disappearing, and now, after what happened to Sereena, I think it might be more than that. I hate to say it, but I think the government may be involved." She focuses intently on Lainey in a way that makes Emma's knees weaken, as Sereena's arms go around her friend. "If your grandma will take you with her, Lainey, you should go."

6:00 p.m.

The lights dim, and a woman in a smart black trouser suit walks out onto the stage. "Ladies and gentlemen, I'm Claudia O'Grady, and it's a pleasure to welcome you here tonight. But I know you're not here to see me, so without further ado, please welcome the one and only Geraldine Fox."

Geraldine emerges from the wings with a smile, both hands aloft as she waves to the audience. She has bright-pink hair, purple glasses, and wears a long, flowing patchwork dress paired with Doc Martens. Lainey studies her curiously, thinking that Grandma doesn't look much like their savior. Grandma looks more like a crazy eccentric, even if she does pull off the outfit better than anyone else could.

Lainey and Emma had been among the last into the auditorium, caught in the London rush hour as they struggled to get across town. They'd hardly spoken since leaving Meena's. It's all happening so fast and Lainey feels breathless and afraid.

"All right, all right, thank you," Geraldine says as she sits down, waving her arms to stop the applause. "Maybe you should wait and see if I've got anything interesting to say first before you clap too hard."

Everyone laughs except Emma; her mouth is a fixed flat line.

"So, Geraldine, it's been a while," Caroline begins, "but we're very pleased you're back to talk about your latest terrific book, *Last Woman Standing*. I love your insistence that we've lost sight of the knotty complexity of the big issues of the day, and your dissection of the 'greatest battle our species has ever faced,' as you call it: to separate and regain truth from perception and belief, which has been going on for over a decade now. My first question is, would you have said the same thing back when you published your seminal work, *The Femme Fatale*, or was the truth a more straightforward concept then?"

Geraldine thinks for a moment. "There are two answers to that," she says. "Let's start with the personal one. When I wrote my first books, I was burning with anger and injustice, and so I came from a very strong, focused position on the enslavement of women, and I don't regret that. I think it was incredibly important to write from the standpoint of my convictions, which remain my convictions, by the way. At that point in my life, I wanted to change the world."

Geraldine pauses, thinking, and Lainey waits, fascinated.

"Now, it's more like I want the world to change. I feel sadness and frustration rather than fiery outrage when I consider what's happening, watching humanity repeating the same flawed patterns over and over, and everyone falling for those well-worn, shonky spin-doctor tricks."

"Well, you still seem pretty outraged in your latest book."

"No. I remain passionate about my arguments, but I'm world-weary, too. Besides, fiery outrage hasn't been good for my nervous system, and I can't bear another mental breakdown, so I've learned to channel my anger differently nowadays."

She's had mental breakdowns? Lainey looks sharply at her mother. Was that why Geraldine had left Emma behind?

"But the second answer," Geraldine is saying, "is that when I first began writing, I felt that academic work was generally respected in society. If you have a PhD in something, even the man in the pub knew that meant you'd worked hard and studied and perhaps knew a little more about what you were discussing than the average Joe. But now, Joe will spend all night arguing the point with you and presume you're on an equal footing. In the information age, because we all have access to information, everyone considers themselves an expert. It's a horrible twist to something that's essentially so wonderful and should have finally allowed for classless access to education."

Lainey is mesmerized. She's watched Geraldine online before, but it's so much more powerful hearing her in person. *Sereena would love this*, she thinks. She tries to stay tuned in, but the conversation that follows about the paradox of belief goes over her head. However, her mind snaps to attention as Claudia says, "Let me ask you this: you've become an outspoken critic of Mary Walcott, but you two were close at one time, weren't you? You went to Oxford together?"

Lainey leans forward. This is news to her.

"Yes, but I don't know her well anymore. We're just two old spinsters with some mutual friends. I haven't seen her for a number of years, but I have to say I'm very disappointed in Mary." Geraldine takes a long sip of water before continuing. "I don't know what it is about power—I've never been in a government myself—but it corrupts people so often, and Mary's proved to be no different. Why on earth she's let Grant Whittaker play such a major role in this new crisis is beyond me. They've always been rivals, and for a while Mary managed to stop him and the other party extremists from using politics to line their pockets, but perhaps not anymore. As a former lawyer, she's well aware of the complex issues we're discussing, but these new laws she's introducing, they're insane."

"You don't think her hand's been forced with the number of stillbirths increasing?"

Geraldine leans forward. "I want to say as forcefully and as *vehemently* as I can: surveilling women is NOT the same as supporting them."

The audience bursts into the biggest spontaneous round of applause of the night. Lainey claps too. So does Emma.

"Did you see that the prime minister visited your hometown of White-haven the other day, to meet mothers who've lost their babies?"

"Who cares! The truth lies in the policies," Geraldine insists, "not the media show and tell. It's the oldest trick in the political playbook to garner sympathy with a photo op. Why are we still falling for that?"

"What do you think Mary Walcott should be doing?"

"Showing some proper bloody compassion *in* the policies. The women—the mothers—are the *victims* here, not the perpetrators. At the moment, all expectant mothers are being treated as potential criminals, even though no one seems to have the first clue why this is happening. And what about these missing teens, and all the PreacherGirl rumors. Who's searching for these girls? The government's barely said a word about it."

"You think the government is getting it wrong?"

"Not just wrong," Geraldine insists. "*Horrifically* wrong. In fact, I'd say the government is using the situation to instill panic and excuse the draconian level of surveillance, which flies in the face of any human rights. And people are so apathetic, they're not even bothered that they spend half the time writing notes to each other because they're not sure if they can speak without being recorded." Geraldine turns to the audience. "If you want to stand up and be counted, the time is now. Don't wait any longer, because we're heading back to the Dark Ages. This may be my last chance to speak to you all in person, because next year I won't be allowed into the country, I'm convinced of it. I realize the stillbirths are making the headlines every single day, and I understand that each one is a personal tragedy of mammoth proportions, but as a society, it's blinding us. Your heads are being turned toward the daily horror, but look beyond it, please, if only for a moment, and try to see what's happening to the freedoms you take for granted. Too many of you and your fellow citizens are falling for the party line, believing that the government will keep you safe, and that's allowing this terrifying New Conservative ethos to infiltrate all corners of life and every corridor of power. Consider this an urgent public announcement: it's time to wake up."

The applause is rapturous. Amidst the clamor, Emma leans over to Lainey and says, "What do you think of her now?"

"Honestly?" Lainey replies. "She's pretty amazing."

"Yep." Emma examines the book she's holding, turning it over in her hands. "She's always been amazing. Except when it comes to us."

7:20 p.m.

Emma wants to be angry and righteous, but she's nervous and uncomfortable as they wait in the book-signing line. She's been letting people go in front of them, and Geraldine's publicist is now eyeing them warily as she moves along the line, taking people's names and putting them on sticky notes to make it faster for Geraldine to sign.

"You don't have to keep letting others in front of you," she says sweetly when she reaches them. "I'm afraid Geraldine won't have time to chat."

"Oh, I think she'll want to chat to me," Emma demures.

The woman gives her a strange look and backs away, but returns when Emma lets a few more into the line.

"May I ask why you keep letting people in?"

"I think Geraldine will want to see me at the end."

"Could you explain that assumption, please? She won't have much time to talk."

Emma leans toward her. "I'm the daughter she never wanted," she whispers.

A defiant part of her enjoys the utter shock on the woman's face as she backs away again.

"Mum!" Lainey says, sounding half surprised, half amused.

They watch as the publicist goes to whisper in Geraldine's ear, gesturing toward them. When Geraldine sees them, her face opens briefly in astonishment, before she shakes her head fervently and looks down at the book she's signing.

Emma's heart sinks. Will Geraldine not even speak to them? She's expecting the publicist to approach them again and ask them to leave and is wondering how much of a scene to cause, when she notices the woman isn't moving. She's still at Geraldine's side, gesturing for the next people to come forward.

As the line edges closer, Emma tries to rehearse what she'll say, but her thoughts are too blurry, and she can't seem to pin the words down. Lainey squeezes her hand just before they are beckoned forward by the publicist, as Geraldine stares at them.

"Well, I never thought I'd see you two at one of these events," she says.

"I need to talk to you," Emma replies.

Geraldine slowly gets up from her chair and collects her bag. "All right, then, I think we might go somewhere a little more private to talk, if you don't mind."

They follow her down a long corridor into a room that has a desk and mirror lit by a row of lightbulbs, and a large black leather sofa pushed against a wall. "So," Geraldine says, closing the door and gesturing to the sofa, "what brings you here tonight?"

Emma seems to have lost the ability to speak.

"It was a great talk," Lainey pipes up beside her.

"I'm glad you enjoyed it, Lainey," Geraldine says. "And look at you—a girl the last time I saw you, but a woman now. Are you both well?"

Silence.

As Geraldine waits for an answer, Emma suddenly realizes how crazy this is. Her mother is a stranger—Lainey's right. They've come to see someone they hardly know and ask her for an enormous favor, after ignoring each other for years. Where should she begin?

"Emma," Geraldine says, "are you in trouble?" She seems neither compassionate nor judgmental, and her tone is matter-of-fact.

"Yes," Emma replies, finally finding her voice, sitting stiff and upright on the edge of the sofa. "I know we're springing this on you out of nowhere, but we're in a lot of trouble, and after listening to you tonight I'm hoping you can help."

Geraldine shifts forward. "All right, tell me."

Emma nods at Lainey, who returns the gesture and puts the audio jammer on the seat between them, checking it's switched on. Emma takes hold of Lainey's hand. "Lainey's pregnant."

There's a long silence while Geraldine sits there, not moving, perhaps absorbing all the ramifications of this news. Then she says, "And you want Lainey to come with me?"

Lainey's hand squeezes Emma's.

"Yes," Emma says. "I think we need to get her out of the country, fast."

"I'm sure you're right. But, Emma, my plane leaves in four hours. I haven't got time to organize it. Perhaps . . . perhaps she could follow me later." The furrow in Geraldine's brow deepens.

"No," Emma insists, hearing the desperate note in her voice, "it's not safe on her own. And I want her to go soon. Please. I've never asked you for anything before now. But you have to help us."

"Mum," Lainey says softly, "it's okay if—"

"No." Emma jumps up in agitation, one hand massaging the nape of her neck, where a migraine seems to be starting. "You heard what Meena said. Geraldine, I don't want you to make me beg, but please."

"Emma, it's not that I don't want to help." Geraldine stands up too, her arms spread in appeasement. "But I can't miss my plane. Do you know how difficult it is to get flights at the moment? But I understand how serious this is, and I'll do everything I can to help when I'm home."

"Okay," Emma snaps, "well, that's it, then."

She doesn't dare catch Lainey's eye. She's so close to breaking, and she won't let Geraldine see her cry. She turns and storms away, horribly aware she's acting like a petulant teenager but unable to stop herself. She's out of ideas and terrified.

She can hear Lainey apologizing and hurrying after her. "Mum, wait. It's okay."

"No," Emma says, leaning against the wall, trying to steady herself, "it's really not. Come on, let's go."

They head outside, amongst the crowd on the South Bank. "I should complain about the show and at least get a bloody refund," Emma says, stuffing Geraldine's book into the nearest bin.

"Mum, stop!" Lainey pauses to pull the book out again. "We sprang it on her. She didn't know, and her flight is tonight—it's not her fault."

"Not this time anyway," Emma mutters, and then catches sight of Lainey's stricken face. "Oh, Lainey, I'm sorry, I know I'm behaving like a child. I've tried so hard not to be resentful, but she just walked away and never came back, not even when her own mother was dying. Then she had the gall to turn up to the funeral and say she wants to know me. She told me she'd always be there if I needed her, and it's taken me nine years, but this is the first thing I ask her to do, and of course she can't help."

"Mum, this wasn't a little favor, it was huge. And she *did* say she wanted to help. She just can't take me straightaway, but perhaps she'll think of something."

"Maybe." Emma shrugs, turning on her phone. "But for now, our first job is to get ourselves home."

As soon as the phone lights up, she sees a message from Cathy.

> Have you seen Mary Walcott's due to make an announcement tonight?

Emma clicks on the link. There's a countdown timer in the corner of the screen and an empty lectern with microphones surrounding it. The press conference is only a few minutes away. She spots a nearby bench. "Can we just stop and watch this?" she asks Lainey.

They both take a seat, peering at the screen as they wait. Emma is trying to figure out where the footage is coming from. It isn't Downing Street. The double doors behind the lectern look more like a hospital. Then she sees the letters in the corner. NBCC, the National Birth Control Center. Her heart lifts. If the prime minister's been with the scientists, this could be something promising.

Right at 8:00 p.m., the doors open and Mary Walcott emerges, wearing a cream-colored trouser suit, with a sheaf of papers in her hand. A few others troop out after her: three men in suits, and a man and woman in lab coats.

The prime minister heads for the lectern as the others form a semicircle a short distance behind her. She puts on her glasses, giving the people in front of her a large smile.

"Thank you for coming out at this late hour," she begins. "I know this is an unusual time for a press conference." She takes a deep breath, appearing a little nervous. "I'm here at the National Birth Control Center, where scientists have been working hard, and there's been a significant—"

There's a sudden noise, like the crack of a whip, and the prime minister clutches her chest. Her face slackens with shock and her jaw drops in surprise. Emma's eyes are drawn to Mary's left hand, held at her heart, where crimson blood is beginning to pour through her fingers.

Lainey screams, an echo of other screams around them, and Emma jumps up, still watching as Mary Walcott's shoulders slump, and her whole body pitches forward heavily past the lectern, beyond the camera's small, square eye, and drops out of sight.

PART III

second stage

@BarberJohn: Jesus Christ WTF just happened? #Walcott

@LucifersChild: Was that a bad joke? Please tell me that was a f-ing bad joke? #Walcott

@CatDogLover51: I live 5 mins from NBCC. Sirens everywhere right now. It's real. #Walcott

@WhitehavenTimes: Sources saying Mary Walcott shot and killed by sniper while speaking live on TV. Awaiting official confirmation. #Walcott

@ChelmsfordPolice: Emergency announcement for suburb of Hasledon. Gunman in the area. Armed and dangerous. Please lock all doors, stay inside, keep all lights on, and move away from windows. #Walcott

@DopeDude: I think I musta smoked somethin bad. #Walcott #RIP

@JennySims79: My mum works @NBCC. Not answering her phone. Can someone please confirm all the workers are safe? #Walcott

@NBCC: Building evacuated due to gunfire. One known casualty. Updates as we get them. #Walcott

@SandyShawBBC: Journalists saying Mary Walcott died in front of them. Raw footage appears to confirm. Tragic news for our country tonight. #Walcott

@DowningStOfficial: Please stand by for an official announcement #Walcott #MaryWalcott

7.

"**W**e need to move."

Emma's voice is low, determined, and hard around the edges. Fear pulses through Lainey as they rush along the pedestrianized walkways of the Southbank Center, past tableaux of shock and confusion. People sit on the curbs, hugging, crying, and staring at their phones. The pubs are still packed but strangely quiet. Occasionally, a group that hasn't yet heard the news comes by, laughing and chatting, beginning to look around them, their liveliness fading to concern. Lainey watches two men in their twenties approach a crying woman to check if she's okay. She says a few words to them, and they stare at each other in horror.

Emma has hold of Lainey's arm so tightly it throbs in protest. "Mum, slow down, you're hurting me."

Emma loosens her grip slightly but doesn't let go. "Come on, the country just got plunged into chaos. We'll be much safer at home."

They hurry across the Jubilee Bridge with a growing swarm of people, some with them, others against the flow, all movement rapid and anxious. As they come down the steps toward Embankment, it's clear that everyone has the same idea. Crowds are pouring in the direction of the station, jostling to get inside. The space around them shrinks and constricts, as they're bumped and pushed by those moving faster.

Emma is knocked to the side, and for a moment Lainey is alone in the surging throng, but then Emma is there again, grabbing her arm to pluck her out of the confusion, guiding her away from the station entrance to huddle against the opposite wall.

"Perhaps not," Emma says, as people continue to rush past.

"They all look so frightened," Lainey murmurs.

"This is uncharted territory. Everyone wants to get home."

"Are you . . . are you sure she's dead?"

Emma turns to Lainey. "Yes. You don't bleed from the chest like that and survive."

Orange-jacketed security guards are forming a line across the station entrance, calling out for order, warning people it's too crowded inside and they'll need to wait.

"Come on," Emma says as they near the Strand. She sets off at a jog, and Lainey follows.

Close to Charing Cross, a procession of black cabs are pulling up and moving off again in seconds as the line for them quickly builds. Emma ignores the line and marches to the nearest taxi, yanking open one of the doors. "Get inside," she says urgently to Lainey.

"Hey, no, you can't do that," the driver objects in heavily accented English. "There's a line over there." As he speaks, others notice and begin to shout. A group runs toward them, and Lainey slams the door closed as the driver roars away. "What the hell are you playing at?" he shouts. "You're gonna get us all beaten up."

Emma leans forward, talking through the speaker set into the security glass. "We need to get to Whitehaven, and you'll earn a chunk of my week's wages if you'll take us there."

"Okay, okay," he says. "Just everyone calm down now, yeah?" He switches off the Brahms symphony that's been playing in the background. "And while we drive, you can tell me what the hell is going on."

10:15 p.m.

It normally takes two hours to get to Whitehaven on a clear run, but they seem to hit traffic at every turn. Emma watches the taxi meter on the central console screen with growing dismay. She hardly dares think about how much this will end up costing.

On her phone, a live stream shows a journalist providing updates outside the NBCC. Behind the journalist, a huge screen has been erected, shielding the podium and emergency services from view. Nevertheless, ghostly blue and sickly white emergency lights strobe across her face as she talks. In the front of the taxi, the driver is listening to the news, exclaiming loudly at every update. "Oh, my Lord. Oh, Lord help us." At one point he rings his wife, who's convinced Arabs will be blamed, and insists he come home. Their discussion digresses into a language Emma doesn't understand, except for the tone: shock, alarm, and foreboding.

A dry, stifling heat blasts into the back of the car from two air vents that seem to be broken. As Emma fiddles with them, trying to turn them down, her watch pings at the same time as Lainey's, and she checks the screen to see a short message:

> Please return to your homes. Stand by for further announcements.

The scrolling text is accompanied by a miniature coat of arms.

It has always been a specific function of the watches: to provide real-time information, instructions, and updates in states of emergency, but this is the first time she's seen it happen like this. The coat of arms adds a solemn officiousness, even though the instruction is unsigned.

"What does that mean?" Lainey asks, eyes wide.

"I don't know." Emma squeezes Lainey's hand, just as Lainey's phone chimes.

Lainey reads the message and starts typing a reply.

"Who is it?"

"Sereena."

"What's she saying?"

"She's freaking out. Says there're rumors online that we're at war."

"At war with who?"

Lainey shrugs, typing furiously.

Emma can't bring herself to check her own phone. She leans her head against the cool glass of the window, watching the blur of the dark night streak by. She's so tired, but when she closes her eyes, all she can see is the shock on Mary Walcott's face as she'd instinctively put her hand to her heart, the way her mouth fell open in horror as her blood poured through her fingers.

If only everything would stop, just for a day. Emma needs the world to pause while she plans her next move, but instead it's speeding up, trauma upon trauma, fear upon fear. She knows exactly why everyone had run for the trains and buses home. If this was a terror attack, then history shows they often come in clusters. Could this really be the first shot of a war?

After the last few months of distraught mothers and their lifeless babies, Emma had thought nothing could truly shock her again. All those never-to-be lives cradled in her hands, their infinite possibilities dispersing into the ether. But Lainey's secret and now this horror tonight have reawakened every numb part of her. She'd forgotten how much there is still left to lose.

When Lainey nudges her, she opens her eyes and sees familiar empty streets. A tortoiseshell cat pads along the pavement, slinking underneath a gate as their cab passes. The squat lines of townhouses have never looked so comforting, with their soft, steady lights seeping through rows of closed curtains. They're almost home.

She relaxes a little, until Lainey says, "Mum?"

Lainey's tone is uncertain, and Emma's instantly back on high alert. She peers through Lainey's window. Outside their house is an unfamiliar black sedan, parked and waiting.

"Pull up here, please," she says hastily.

"All right, Miss." The driver swings the car to the curb and stops.

"Who is that?" Lainey asks.

Emma doesn't answer. Her arm shakes as the driver scans her watch. She briefly notes the three-figure sum in dismay, before she climbs out of the taxi and hurries to Lainey. "Let me go first," she says, wishing they weren't so conspicuous. But surely this isn't to do with Lainey? Not tonight, with everyone still reeling.

Warily, they approach the car. The windows are blacked out and there's no sign of movement. They walk around it, toward their front gate, casting uncertain glances at one another.

They're almost past when there's a whirring sound and the back passenger-seat window slides down, revealing a familiar face.

"Looks like I've missed my flight," Geraldine says wryly. "May I come in?"

10:50 p.m.

Lainey sits on the sofa in the lounge, hands resting on the cool leather, while Emma and Geraldine stand on opposite sides of the low-ceilinged room, eyeing each other warily. Geraldine is wearing a multicolored knitted patchwork shawl that appears warm, cozy, and ridiculously unfashionable. Emma still has her coat on and is massaging a point on the nape of her neck.

"We have a lot to sort out tonight," Emma snaps. "Just tell us, have you come to help or not?"

"Mum!"

Geraldine just glares at her daughter before she turns to Lainey. "So," she says, "you want to come to Australia with me?"

"Actually," Lainey replies, "that's what Mum wants." She pats the audio jammer in her pocket, then turns to Emma. "Can't we think of another option? I don't want to leave you or my friends. And doesn't tonight change things?"

"Maybe," Emma says. "It was one idea, but perhaps it's not the right time." She shoots a stern glance at Geraldine. "We've managed so far without help, I'm sure we can figure something out."

Geraldine purses her lips and sighs. "I'm afraid things may be about to get worse."

At this, Emma's attention jerks from Lainey to Geraldine. "Do you know something?"

Geraldine grimaces. "I don't *know* anything, but I can't say I'm entirely surprised about tonight's events."

"You thought Mary Walcott would be *murdered?*"

"No, no, not murdered. But have you watched her speeches these past few months? She was always touching her neck, like she could feel an invisible rope slowly tightening."

Lainey shudders.

"And why do you think that was?" Emma asks. "The babies?"

"Could be the babies. Or the flooding. New diseases. Or the iceberg. Who knows? Things are changing fast now—there's a new crisis every month. But some of her recent announcements haven't been anywhere close to Mary's original manifesto. She was always too conservative for my liking, but at least she was a moderate until the babies began dying. Lately, she's looked—well, the term I'd use is *haunted*. I wonder if she's known a lot more than she's been able or willing to say."

"I met her yesterday," Emma murmurs, "when she came to the hospital."

"Really?" Geraldine's eyebrows shoot up. "What did you think of her?"

"I liked her more than I thought I would." Emma sinks into an armchair. "She listened to us—even when we'd essentially cornered her in an elevator without permission to ask her for more help. She seemed tired, but she was still composed. Although, perhaps she did seem a bit haunted on TV. We probably all do when we're talking about the babies. I know you said on stage that you're disappointed in her, but maybe she was doing the best she could."

Geraldine sits easily on the sofa next to Lainey. "Perhaps she was," she murmurs, but with just the right amount of sarcasm to make it clear she doesn't agree.

Lainey is trying to think of something she can say to appease them both, when her phone chimes at the same time as Emma's. She rummages in her bag and pulls it out. "There's an emergency school assembly in the morning?"

"They'll want to reassure everyone," Emma says as she flips open her phone case to check. "I've already had a similar message from the hospital."

Geraldine's ample frame tilts toward Lainey on the soft-cushioned sofa. "Shall we get back to the problem at hand? How long have you known you're pregnant, Lainey?"

Lainey outlines the whole story, from the stolen test to her mother's help at the police station, grimacing as she details what they've had to do. By the end, Geraldine is grinning at both of them. "Quite the mutiny. Bravo!" Geraldine pulls her shawl tighter around her shoulders, sitting forward, and Lainey notices for the first time her sparkly velvet leggings and the little bows on her sateen shoes. "However, these small victories are one thing, but every time you challenge the status quo, you put your head above the parapet, and that only increases the danger to both of you. Look," she says, "I want to help. If I can find a way for us to get out of the country, will you come with me, Lainey?"

Lainey glances from Emma to Geraldine. Her mother is astonished; whereas Geraldine seems calm and collected. "Yes, okay, but Mum needs to come too," she says. She turns to Emma. "I won't go without you. I'm not leaving you here alone."

Geraldine holds up a hand. "I get where you're coming from, Lainey, but let me explain why it's not such a great idea. First, it's going to be much harder to get three seats on a flight right now. It'll be the devil's job to get two, I should imagine. And second: you'll be missed sooner if Emma comes. Third, a bigger group naturally draws more attention to itself, and—"

"Whatever. I don't care about any of that," Lainey interrupts. "The fact remains, I'm not going otherwise."

"But she's right." Emma comes to sit on the arm of the chair next to Lainey, stroking her back. "Aside from those problems, it would be tricky just to abandon my job or this house, however much I'd like to. And what about Fergus?" She gestures toward the sleeping spaniel, whose ear twitches at the sound of his name. "Give me more time, and I can come later. But *you* need to go now."

The words are small, sharp stones that chip at Lainey's heart, leaving a trail of spreading cracks as her choices narrow. She thinks of all the people she'll have to leave behind: her mum, Sereena, Dylan, even

Fergus. Michelle will struggle on the weekends without her help at the busy surgery. And what about school?

She's vaguely aware of Emma and Geraldine making plans over her head and tries to refocus. "How are you going to get tickets?" Emma is asking.

"Well, I travel a lot." Geraldine stifles a yawn as she talks. "And there's no law against leaving the country yet—although I'm sure they're working on it. I've heard some parts of the world are reluctant to accept UK citizens, but Australia won't be keen to slow the record numbers of tourists—it's gone bonkers since things opened up again. So, I hope I can find someone to help us. At least tell me you have a passport, Lainey?"

"Yes."

"Thank Christ, that's one hurdle we don't need to worry about. Okay, you need to get it for me . . ." She stands up as if about to leave.

"Where are you staying tonight?" Lainey asks.

Geraldine shrugs. "I'm not sure yet. Hopefully, the hotel still has a room for me."

Lainey looks at Emma, who says nothing. "You could stay with us?" she offers.

There's a hint of amusement in Geraldine's eyes. "Thank you, Lainey, that's a lovely offer. It's late, isn't it? So I might just do that. I'll go tell the driver to come back in the morning, and I'll get my bags."

Once she's gone, Emma rolls her eyes at Lainey. "Seriously? I hope you're giving up your bed for her and not expecting me to sleep on the sofa?"

"Yeah, she can have mine, and I'll come and listen to you snore," Lainey jokes, trying to lighten the mood. Then she turns away, before her smile fades.

WEDNESDAY, 6:30 a.m.

The faintest smudge of dawn pushes through the curtains as Emma huddles on the armchair nearest the television, a blanket over her legs. Unable to sleep, she'd gotten up just past two, turning the sound down low so she wouldn't wake the others.

Breakfast news is filling in time with a historical commentator, wild-eyed at his moment in the spotlight as he regales the story of Spencer Perceval, the last prime minister to be assassinated, over two hundred years ago. The hosts nod politely, letting him ramble until their demeanor suddenly shifts and they straighten, shuffling their notes. They swiftly wind up the segment, then the camera zooms in close on news anchor Sara South's solemn, tanned face.

"There's been an official announcement from Ten Downing Street," she says, her expression carefully neutral. "I'll read it verbatim."

As she takes a breath, Emma leans in.

"It is with great sadness that we confirm the death of Prime Minister Mary Walcott, who was killed on the steps of the National Birth Crisis Center in Chelmsford, at 8:03 p.m. yesterday evening. The perpetrator has not been apprehended, and anyone with information should dial emergency.

"The remaining members of the Security Council and the COBRA emergency committee met overnight and will be working rapidly to restore national security over the coming hours, days, and weeks. There is no need to panic. You may see more army and police on the streets for a short time to ensure your safety. Please go about your business as normal.

"In light of recent events, Health Secretary and Deputy Prime Minister Grant Whittaker will not automatically become prime minister until we fully assess the threat to our government, our democracy, and our country. Instead, the remaining cabinet and committee members will unite as one voice, to restore the well-being, fortunes, and foundation of our great nation. Therefore, each announcement will be signed as this one is: *from your government.*"

"Now that's just weird," says a raspy voice close to Emma.

Emma jumps, turning to watch as Geraldine sits down. She's still wearing her clothes from the night before, and her uncombed pink hair sticks out in tufts.

"What are they playing at?" Geraldine nods at the television, her eyes puffy. "How can they refuse to appoint a leader?"

"You don't think it makes sense?" Emma asks as doubt swirls in the pit of her stomach.

"Well, of course they were clever enough to present it as logical, but I don't like it." Geraldine's eyes meet Emma's. "In fact, as I listened to that, I distinctly felt a shiver down my spine."

They sit in silence for a while, before Geraldine speaks again. "Look, Emma, can we try to clear the air a little?"

Emma stills, waiting.

"I realize we're not going to fix things overnight, but you think I abandoned you, and that's not quite right. I just knew I wouldn't be a good mother, so I left you with your grandmother, who could nurture you in all the ways you needed."

Emma's pulse begins to race. "You didn't think it might put a strain on her, caring for a young child in her sixties?"

Geraldine sighs. "She insisted on it. She persuaded me that your life would be so much better with her, and I have to say that even though we disagreed on a lot, I think she was right. I did what I could. I sent a lot of money over the years."

Emma snaps to attention. "You sent money?"

"She never told you, did she?" Geraldine tuts. "I hope you can hear this, but I think my mother didn't mind the rift between us. She wanted you all to herself. I tried to visit, but she said it would be confusing. Instead, I paid off the house and took care of her debts, which meant she didn't have to work. I became the provider."

Emma glances back to the television, unsure how to respond. Her thoughts are spinning.

"I won't say any more," Geraldine adds. "I'm not trying to twist things. Mum gave you everything she could, and I'm grateful. But I'd like you to see me as a person now, not as Geraldine Fox the feminist, or the mother who abandoned you. Just another complicated human being, doing her best."

Emma can't stop Geraldine's words from permeating the protective shell she's always constructed when she's around her mother. "Okay," she says softly. "I'll give you a chance."

Geraldine lets out a long sigh of relief. "Thank you. Now, is there any good liquor in this house? I haven't slept a wink from thinking about all

166

this. And besides, your dog kept coming in, and those funny little birds in the box were rustling about. What's going on there?"

"Lainey's nursing them back to health. She's always loved animals. We've had all sorts—she even tried to keep ants once; she collected thousands before they all escaped. We were infested for months."

"Sounds delightful. Another nurse in the house, then. So what about this tipple?"

Emma has never connected Lainey's care for animals with her own nursing skills, and she smiles at the thought. "You really want alcohol at six in the morning?"

"There's no bad time for a good drink, particularly on such a portentous occasion. We should toast the future, now we've cleared the air, and try to put a bit of a spark in the day."

"You sound like an alcoholic. Which makes me very nervous about my daughter going away with you."

"Oh for Christ's sake, I'll just make a cup of tea, then, if you'll point me to the kettle."

"No, I'll get you a drink," Emma says, getting up and heading to the kitchen.

When she returns minutes later with two tumblers of whisky and ice, Geraldine is standing by the mantelpiece, holding something in her hand. As Emma gets closer, she sees it's the Russian dolls that once belonged to her grandmother.

"Matryoshka dolls—I remember these," Geraldine says with a wistful smile, shaking the wooden doll gently so they can hear the other smaller dolls rattling inside. "I used to play with them when I was little. Even gave them all names."

"I loved them, too! So did Lainey. Don't remember naming them, though. Lainey used to like putting the tiny one in her mouth when she was a toddler, which was terrifying. I had to hide them for a couple of years."

"It would have been an original way to go. Choking by nesting doll."

"Ha ha."

"Are they all still inside?"

"I think so—take a look."

Geraldine sits down and tips them onto her lap. From the single doll, four others emerge, the last less than an inch tall. "You should take care of these," she says as she restacks them, hiding them away one inside another. "They're pretty old and obviously well painted. They're probably worth something as a complete set."

"Maybe," Emma says, placing the dolls back on the mantel and handing Geraldine her glass of whisky. "Or maybe I should keep them for Lainey's daughter." She says it without thinking of Lainey's situation, but then casts a nervous glance at the jammer, still lying on the table. Anxious knots tighten inside her. Geraldine follows her gaze, then indicates Emma's watch.

"It must be awful," she says sympathetically, "being branded with this thing."

Emma stares at the innocuous little device. "You know what," she answers, "the worst thing is, it's not as awful as it should be. The surveillance crept up on us. Everyone got so used to it that there's hardly been an outcry about keeping them on overnight, or not using cash anymore. It's like nobody cares."

"That's terrifying," Geraldine says with a shudder. "I suppose now that they're beginning to chuck out all the foreigners, I'm one of the few people in the country without a tracker. Perhaps they'll hunt me down and strap a temporary device on me at some point."

"Probably," Emma says bitterly. She holds her glass high. "Cheers. To the future and our freedom," she says, feeling momentarily like an eighteenth-century French revolutionary, clinking her cup against Geraldine's and slugging it back. She enjoys the burn as it rolls down her throat, the small rebellion of drinking before the day starts.

"Bottoms up," Geraldine says, echoing the action and setting the empty glass on the coffee table. "Now, let's talk about Lainey."

Emma flops heavily onto her chair, wondering if the drink was just a ruse, as Geraldine continues, "I've managed to book two tickets on a flight at seven thirty tonight."

Emma sits up, the pleasant burn turning to acid in her throat.

"What? I thought we'd discuss it first. I'll need to sort out the money somehow."

"Don't worry about the money," Geraldine says firmly.

Emma opens her mouth to argue but can't summon the energy. She sinks back on the chair again. "It's just so . . . fast."

"I think it needs to be. Don't you?" Geraldine gestures toward the television. "The country just watched the prime minister die. Whatever this new government says, we're all primed now, waiting for the next bombshell. It's going to be fraught in the coming days and weeks. And all those young girls are still missing." She grimaces. "I've been going over it all night. Don't you think it's curious that Mary was at the NBCC, about to make a speech? There was chatter online about a possible breakthrough with the babies. I was watching a replay in the car: when Mary came down those steps, she seemed hopeful. Like she was about to tell us something important. Moments later, she's dead."

Emma's chest tightens. "You really think there's a conspiracy?"

Geraldine nods. "Yes. And it could be big. The question is: what was she about to say, and who doesn't want us to know?"

8:45 a.m.

There's a lot Lainey wants to tell Emma as they walk to school together for the assembly, but it's a jumble of thoughts and emotions that she can't organize into sentences, so the journey ends up a quiet one.

The morning so far has been surreal. She'd woken to find the circumstances of the prime minister's death being analyzed on TV, and Geraldine Fox sitting in her kitchen telling her about plane tickets and travel arrangements while her mother watched on in silence. If all went to plan, she'd be leaving home after lunch, and be in another country by the end of the day.

Emma had been keen for Lainey to come straight home with her after the assembly, but Geraldine had said they should feign normality for as long as possible. Lainey had agreed, although her reasons are more about seeing Sereena and pretending this isn't happening.

Here and now, everything seems so ordinary. There are cars and buses and cyclists on the roads. Mums in yoga pants push strollers and power walk past ambling retirees who stop to chat or let their dogs sniff at flowers. It's only as she passes close to people that Lainey notices the same thing is happening over and over: a momentary eye contact full of wariness and confusion. A shared question with no answer.

What happens now?

At school, the line for health checks is almost out the gate, and inside the main hall is more crowded than Lainey has ever seen it. There are hundreds of chairs set out, and all are taken, leaving latecomers to lean against walls or sit on the floor. There's a distinctive, brooding atmosphere, and everyone looks drawn and anxious. Parents have their arms around teenage children, who normally wouldn't be caught dead being hugged. Teachers are positioned like sentries, spaced out around the hall.

Lainey and Emma find a spot under a portrait of a headmaster from the 1960s in mortarboard and gown, who stares stoically into the distance. Katie is up ahead, flanked by her parents, while Lexie hovers to one side with her dad and younger sister. Dylan is sitting near the front, and Mr. Bailey leans against a wall close to his son, hands in his jeans pockets, watching the room.

Sereena rushes over to give Lainey a hug, with Meena close behind. "What happened last night?" Sereena asks as they embrace. "Is there a plan?"

Lainey nods, and sees Meena and Emma exchange glances.

"Good," Sereena says, squeezing Lainey's hand.

Before they can talk further, Mrs. Goodchild takes to the dais, wearing a black dress offset with a string of white pearls. "Thank you all for coming," she says to them, her voice tremulous. "I know we're all in terrible shock after the tragic events of last night, and so I feel it's important to assure you that while the country navigates these uncharted waters, your children are safe here.

"We also have some new emergency measures during this period of transition. For the time being, all students are to sign in by scanning their watch at reception and must then stay on the premises until the last bell, unless they are signed out by a parent. This includes seniors."

"What the actual fuck?" Sereena murmurs, but Lainey is distracted by a prickle on the side of her neck, the sensation of someone watching her, and turns to look. Liam is standing a few feet away. When she catches his eye, he raises an eyebrow, without smiling. Uneasy, she turns her attention back to Mrs. Goodchild, who is telling everyone that counselors are available for anyone traumatized by video footage.

"The police have also informed me," Mrs. Goodchild continues, "that it's become fashionable for teenagers to put watches on animals in order to be able to disappear for a while. They asked me to let you know that the watches monitor your pulse, and that cat and dog heartbeats are easily discernible from those of humans. They can also tell if people are wearing multiple devices. Therefore, may I remind you," she says, peering at them over the top of her glasses, "that the watches are there to keep us all safe, and are not to be removed at any time." She glares at them for a long moment. "That's all for now," she finishes, "but I'll keep you informed of any changes. Now, I just need the following students and their parents to stay behind." She recites a list of names, and before long Lainey hears her own, and those of her friends and Cathy's daughter, as well as others she doesn't know. There are about thirty names in all, and as the room clears, she can see pockets of people who remain sitting, all fidgeting nervously.

"Please make your way to the front," Mrs. Goodchild says brusquely, waving them forward. Once everyone has retaken seats, she continues, "I received a phone call from the police this morning, asking me to talk to you all specifically." She hesitates, assessing them. "Because each student present has attended a protest march recently, you will now be subject to a strict evening curfew of eight o'clock. Every night your locations will be checked via your watches to verify you're at home. And of course, you must also tag yourselves in and out of school at reception, along with everyone else."

Meena already has a hand raised. Mrs. Goodchild spots it and looks irritated. "Yes?"

"How long will this go on for?"

"I have no idea."

"So, these kids are stuck at home every evening, indefinitely. That's ridiculous."

"Mrs. Mandalia, these are unusual times. I'm sure these restrictions will be relaxed once the government has confidence that order is restored. And circumstances like these are at least a chance for the students to focus on their studies," she says with an encouraging smile.

Next to Lainey, Sereena pretends to retch.

Lainey leans closer to Emma. "What about our plan?"

"We'll figure it out," Emma whispers back. "Don't worry, you'll be gone by eight."

Lainey feels sick.

There's a babble of rising voices shooting questions at the headmistress now, but she holds up her hands to stop them. "Please remember, I'm just the messenger. I've told you everything I know. Now, I have a lot to do today, so if you'll excuse me." And she practically runs from the hall, accompanied by two secretaries, who simultaneously gabble at her.

"How pathetic," Sereena hisses to Lainey as they watch her leave. "But you know what? I think we're stuck with it for now. If you'd asked me a week ago, I would have gone out at eight tonight just to piss them off and see what happened. But shit just got real, and I don't fancy another visit to the police station for a while." She grimaces at Lainey. "We're not giving up, though," she adds, nudging her. "It's just time for a tactical rethink. I've got to find Katie before sociology, but I'll catch up with you at break, yeah?" She squeezes Lainey's hand again, and Lainey nods, absorbing the touch of her friend.

"Sereena," Meena says, "I need to go. I'll see you tonight, and don't worry. It's a big overreaction at the moment, we'll sort it all out." She smiles at Lainey, but there's concern in her eyes. "Take care, Lainey, won't you?"

"I will," Lainey says uncomfortably. Their sympathy isn't making her feel any easier about the day ahead.

Emma is already by the door, talking to Cathy. Lainey grabs her bag and trudges toward them.

". . . you have no idea what she was about to say?" Emma is asking.

"No, there're all sorts of rumors at the hospital, but we haven't heard anything official from the NBCC."

Mr. Davenport pauses on his way out the door and turns back to join their discussion. He's unshaven and looks short on sleep. "Did you just say the NBCC?"

"Yes." Cathy frowns at him. "Do you know something?"

"No, not really. My sister Rachel works there—she was with Walcott yesterday. I've been trying to get in touch with her since last night, but so far, no luck. The family's panicking a bit this morning . . . we just want to know she's safe."

"We only get official briefings through the hospital," Cathy says. "Same ones that are sent across the entire country. Other than that, we're told nothing, and questions certainly aren't encouraged. I'm sorry—I wish I could be more helpful."

Mr. Davenport nods, then notices Lainey listening and adjusts his posture. "You ready for our lesson this morning, Lainey?"

"I guess." Lainey smiles, trying to conjure the mask of normality she'll need to get through the day.

"Right, I'd better go and get ready then. Thanks anyway," he says to Cathy, then adds, "Nice to see you again, Emma."

Emma?

They watch him go before Lainey turns to her mum. "You're on first-name basis now, are you?"

"I guess we are," Emma replies with a small smile.

"You know all the girls in school have a crush on him?"

"You're not the only ones," Cathy adds with a laugh, just as Beth joins them. "I should think he's featured in more than one school mum's night-time fantasies."

"That is revolting," Beth says, pulling a mock-horrified face at Lainey. Cathy winks at Emma and bursts out laughing. Beth and Lainey follow suit, and Lainey's aware they're drawing attention to themselves, people obviously wondering what they could possibly find funny on a day like this. She wants to hug Cathy and her mother for somehow finding a way to make things feel brighter and more normal, even if only for a few seconds.

"Just remember," Cathy says to Lainey, leaning close, "I love your mum like a sister. You know what I'm saying? She's always got me, so you don't have to worry about her."

Lainey bites her lip as tears prickle. "Thank you," she says, just as someone knocks into her and she stumbles forward, caught by Emma and set back on her feet again.

"Sorry," says a sarcastic, not-at-all-sorry voice behind them. She catches a brief glimpse of Liam's contemptuous smile before he walks away.

"Prick," Beth mutters.

But it's more than that. Lainey swallows hard. Liam is deeply unhappy about something, and he's making sure Lainey knows it.

9:30 a.m.

Parents congregate outside the school in groups, holding animated conversations. Emma spots Meena chatting to a group of mothers and hangs back, waiting. As soon as Meena sees her, she hurries over.

"Have you heard anything?" Emma whispers.

"Yes," Meena replies. "Let's not talk here—I can come over later."

"Okay. You still think we're doing the right thing?"

"Absolutely. Now more than ever."

The compassion in Meena's eyes threatens to pull Emma apart. She searches for a change of subject. "How's Sereena?"

"Recovering well," Meena says with a smile. "There's too much fight in her to stay down for long, but they frightened her for sure. I just want her to keep her head down at school. Goodchild seems a bit of a government clone, don't you think?"

"It seems that way." Emma steps closer. "There are so many of them nowadays. And what do you think of the government announcement this morning?"

"Honestly?" Meena drops her voice even lower. "I'm wary. No, correct that: I'm terrified. It's not normal, is it? They'll say it's to protect society and the system while there's a killer at large, but the UK now functions under rules made by an unknown, perhaps unelected group who appear to have the full consent of Parliament. I mean, where's the opposition? It's already being condemned overseas as authoritarian, and quite possibly the inception of a dictatorship. And all we've got in response is resounding silence. What's happened to all the dissenters? And how will we fight against anything if we don't know who's in charge?" She looks around at the milling, chattering adults. "People may not realize it yet, but this has been building for a while. Whatever is going on at the top, I fear it's just taken a drastic turn for the worse."

11:15 a.m.

Lainey is heading to history class when someone grabs her arm, fingers pinching hard.

"Hey," she protests, turning to see it's Liam, who gives her another oblique smile.

"Come with me to the tech shed for a minute, I need a word with you." He lets go and strides away without waiting for a response.

Lainey's fury rises. She's had enough of his bullshit and begins to walk the other way, but he circles back. "You either come with me, or we can have our little chat in front of everyone."

Her heart skitters. Whatever he has to say, she'd rather not have an audience. Reluctantly, she follows.

There's a patch of grass next to the tech shed, some distance away from the main school buildings. It's an unofficial no-man's-land, too conspicuous for any contraband activity, but not on the way to anywhere, either. Somewhere to go for a private spot to chat or study. Today, it's empty.

Ahead, Liam turns and waits for her on the grass bank, leaning on the shed wall. As Lainey gets closer, she can see the scowl on his face, and her nerves nudge up a notch.

"So," Liam says as she nears, "Sereena got arrested."

"Isn't that old news after last night?" Lainey stops, keeping her distance from him. "Besides, she was back this morning, didn't you see her?"

"Yeah, I saw her. But I'm more interested in what my dad said when we spoke about it. Apparently, a couple of girls stole a pregnancy test, and she was identified as one of them. Now, they just need to find the other thief."

The words turn Lainey's stomach. "How did he know that?"

Liam laughs scornfully. "He's a government minister. He knows everything."

"But . . . but Sereena isn't pregnant," is all she can think to say.

"No." He glares at her.

"That's all sorted, then . . ." She turns to walk away and sees Sereena coming across the field toward them.

"Maybe her friend is, though," Liam says, stepping closer, his voice next to her ear.

She stares at him, her face burning, unable to speak.

He grabs her arm. "You thought you were pregnant." He leers as he looks her up and down. "You even went to the station last night and took a test. You've been giving it out somewhere, and yet you've been stringing me along for weeks. That's not nice, Lainey. I don't like that at all."

"Hey," Sereena calls, closing in fast now, "get off her, you fuckhead."

Liam drops Lainey's arm but doesn't take his eyes off her. "I'm just asking Lainey about her baby daddy."

Lainey watches Sereena's mouth drop open. Her face forms the question: *You told him?*

Lainey shakes her head, a small, swift gesture. *Please don't say anything.*

Liam looks intently at them, and Lainey prays he can't see the truth. They're all frozen for a moment, before Sereena says, "Time to go?" and links arms with Lainey and pulls her away.

Liam remains smirking, arms folded, as they hurry across the field back to school.

"He's creeping me out," Lainey says when they're at a safe distance. "He knows I went to the police station. What if he still suspects something?"

"Unlikely. Even if he does, he's got no proof."

As they reach the school, Lainey's legs are leaden, and she sinks down against a wall in a corner out of sight. "How did it get like this? We're carrying jammers around just so we can have a conversation, and it turns out that Liam can find out all the intimate details of our lives anyway."

Sereena sits down next to her and sighs theatrically. "We're just gonna have to talk in code, I reckon. Like those weird dot-dash pigpen-code grids we messed around with in primary school."

Lainey laughs despite herself. "It's gonna take us a long time to have a conversation using those!"

"Probably." Sereena pauses. "How many classes have you got left now?"

"Just history."

Sereena puts an arm around her. They don't say anything for a while, then Sereena rummages in her bag, finds a pad, and starts to draw.

"You know how much I love you, don't you," Lainey says.

"Of course I fucking do." Sereena doesn't take her eyes off the paper, concentrating for a few more seconds, before she pushes it into Lainey's hand as the bell rings. "Read this when I'm gone."

They stand up and share a quick, tight hug that makes Lainey's eyes water, then head into school. Liam jogs up behind them, hissing, "Sluts" under his breath as he passes.

They look at one another, astonished, before Sereena smiles sympathetically as they part for different classes. "Thank God you won't have to worry about him soon."

Nevertheless, Lainey is shaken by his open animosity. It's clear she has an enemy now.

Only once she's in history class does she examine the slip of paper Sereena had given her. It's a grid code. While Mr. Davenport is distracted setting up the whiteboard, she takes out a pen and works out the letters.

FUCK LIAM.

STAY SAFE.

LOVE YOU.

KICK ARSE.

2:15 p.m.

As she walks into the lounge, Emma's stomach drops at the sight of her daughter's packed bag and backpack. Lainey is waiting, fresh-faced and frowning. She's wearing jeans and a sweatshirt with her hair in two braids, and she looks so young. "The car's almost here," she tells Emma. "I've left the jammer for you." She indicates the little box on the table.

"You should take it," Emma replies.

"Geraldine says we won't need it, and we can't take it through airport security."

Emma is aware of Geraldine watching them but refuses to meet her gaze. Outside, a car gives two short beeps.

Lainey gets to her feet, her eyes moist. "I've left the chicks on the bed upstairs. Can you give them to Dylan and ask him to talk to Michelle? I think he'll like taking care of them."

"Okay," Emma says, watching as her girl, her beautiful girl, pulls her backpack onto her back.

"Have you got your passport?" she checks, unexpectedly grateful for their dismal week in Mallorca a few years ago, an attempt to get a last-minute break, where they'd both caught a stomach flu on the plane over and spent all but two days in their room. It was the only reason they'd needed passports in the last ten years.

"Yes."

"And the credit card I gave you?"

"Yes. I have everything, Mum, I've checked twice."

"I know, it's just . . ." Emma's voice cracks.

"Come on, then, let's not make this harder than it needs to be," Geraldine says from the doorway.

Emma wants to punch her, but it's also a good thing she's here as it's stopping Emma from completely falling apart. She pulls Lainey into a tight hug, kissing the wetness of her cheek, where Lainey's tears run freely. "Go and have fun with your crazy grandma," she whispers.

"I heard that."

Lainey laughs through her tears. "Love you so much, Mum."

"Love you more. Don't message me before you go, just in case, but let me know as soon as you're safe."

"I will." Lainey picks up her bag, squeezes Emma's hand, then heads down the path.

Emma watches her go, drinking in the sight of her.

"Okay, then," Geraldine says awkwardly, patting Emma's arm on the way past. "I'll get in touch as soon as I can."

"Hold on a second," Emma says in a rush as Geraldine reaches the door. She walks closer. "You're taking my daughter." Her voice sounds strange and threatening to her own ears, blighted with emotion. "There's nothing more important to me, Geraldine. Protect her. Don't leave her alone anywhere. Promise me?"

Geraldine's expression becomes a mixture of sadness and irritation. "Of course I promise. I don't just abandon people, Emma. I think through all my decisions carefully, and this one's no exception."

"I'm sorry," Emma says. Her emotions are getting the better of her, and she doesn't want Geraldine to leave feeling angry.

Geraldine's lingering look is intense and assessing. "Just so you know, I'm not doing this because I think I owe you. I'm doing it because I want to. We all have to make difficult choices to protect those we love." She pauses, her gaze lingering on Emma, then her voice softens. "I promise I'll take care of her. Call a friend, won't you, after we've gone."

She puts a hand on Emma's arm and lets it stay there for a moment before she hurries down the path and climbs in next to Lainey.

As the car pulls away, Emma remains frozen by the front door, breathing heavily, until the loss breaks over her in a crushing wave of grief, sending her charging outside to scan the empty street, willing them back to her.

But they're gone. She runs into the house, slams the door closed, and slides down the wall, sobbing.

Eventually, when she stops, she becomes aware of a small scratching noise. She gets up and walks to the kitchen door. As soon as she opens it, Fergus bounds in, heading to the front, as though aware he might be late for something.

"I think she locked you out, buddy, so she didn't have to say goodbye," Emma calls after him.

Usually, he'd go straight upstairs to curl up in Lainey's room, but this time he sits down in the kitchen, watching her, head cocked to one side.

Emma laughs through her tears. "Told you to look after me, did she?"

His tail wags in reply.

She makes a cup of tea and takes it into the lounge, switching on the TV, thinking she might never turn it off if it helps her avoid the confronting silence of the house. Fergus curls up beside her on the sofa, and she leans her head back and closes her eyes.

When she opens them again, the phone is ringing. She grabs it, on alert for Lainey, but the screen shows Dorothy's name instead.

"I couldn't see you on shift today." Dorothy sounds frazzled. "There's a woman here in distress, and she's asking for you. Can you come in?"

3:00 p.m.
"You're doing the right thing, you know."

Lainey tenses but doesn't reply, unsure if it's safe to talk in the car. She puts a hand over her watch and Geraldine notices the movement.

"We're okay. This is an elite chauffeur service for VIPs. The cars come with built-in signal jammers—not just for the private conversations, but also because they don't want their drivers killing the wealthy customers by checking their mobiles at the wrong time. It's a key part of their marketing material." She smiles. "So let me repeat, you're doing the right thing. Over the years, I've studied government responses to women in times of change and crisis, and I haven't seen anything like the last year—not even in the seventies. Which is ironic, because back then I was bonding with Mary Walcott over our love of Betty Friedan and Gloria Steinem, and look at the way things turned out. I'm glad I can help you, but first we're going to have to separate—at the airport."

A knot of fear tightens inside Lainey. "Really? Why?"

"Well, we need to keep as inconspicuous as we can—and I am not very inconspicuous, I'm afraid. That's why it's good we also have separate seats on the plane."

"Oh. Okay. You're not disowning me, are you?"

Geraldine shakes her head, smiling. "You're as suspicious as your mother. No, I promise. The driver will drop you first, then drive a little farther and let me out. We'll keep an eye out for each other in the airport, but don't acknowledge me when you see me. I'll be behind you in the security line, and then, once we're through all that, I'll see you on the plane."

The thought of being on her own is daunting, but neither does she want the extra attention. "What do people do when they come up to you?"

"Depends. Sometimes they want me to sign something, and sometimes they want to yell at me, but the worst ones are the huggers." She shudders. "No, they're the second worst, actually. The worst are the ones who want to debate the entire concept of feminism with me, while we wait in line for the toilet or the grocery checkout. Sometimes I end up telling them I don't give a shit about feminism at that moment, I just need to pee, or buy food, or whatever. Anything that gets them off my back."

Lainey laughs.

"I loved hearing about your escapades lately," Geraldine continues. "I greatly admire your mother, you know. She has qualities I just don't possess. All the prerequisites of nursing—the nurturing, the patience, and kindness—she gets most of that from my mother. I could never do it. But I know enough to see that she's a rebel, too. And that fire inside her, that sense of injustice and determination . . . now that," she says, waggling a finger at Lainey with a smile, "I'll take a little bit of credit for. And I can already tell you have it, too. I think we'll have fun together, Lainey. I'm a terrible cook, and housework isn't my thing, either, but I know how to have a good time. Let's get through this next bit, and then we can really enjoy getting to know each other."

Lainey leans back in her seat, thinking, *Perhaps this isn't going to be so bad, after all.* Then she turns to the window, sees a sign for London and the M25, and the nerves flood back in. They can't afford to relax. Not yet.

3:30 p.m.

Emma keeps her head down as she goes through security, health screening, and up to the ward. Her jeans, boots, beanie, and padded jacket feel like a disguise. Nurses who would normally greet her walk straight past, leaving Emma with an unbidden impression of the hospital through the patients' eyes: surrounded by strangers, the outer layers of life stripped away at the door, all vulnerability exposed.

On Maternity Ward B, Dorothy is at the nurse's station, typing away at a computer. Two empty rows of chairs for visitors line the space in front of the main desk, but no one else is around. The only background noise is the hum of overhead striplights and the clank and whir of hospital paraphernalia.

When she sees Emma, Dorothy does a double-take.

"Emma! You're as white as a sheet. Are you all right?"

"I'm fine," Emma replies, knowing her smile is wholly unconvincing.

"I shouldn't have called. I didn't know you weren't well."

"Really, I'm okay. But I'm unofficially suspended, so I'm here as a private doula."

"What do you mean suspended?" Dorothy sounds horrified. "We need you. We can't lose you, too."

Emma grimaces as she sanitizes her hands. "Hopefully it won't be for long, but Lynne might not be very happy to see me today. Where is she?"

"She's in with your friend in Room Three." Dorothy's expression darkens. "Please don't tell me she got you into trouble."

"Everyone's under pressure." Emma shrugs, bracing herself for Lynne's officiousness.

"Is this a good friend of yours?" Dorothy asks.

"It's Lainey's boss at the vet's—Michelle. Do you happen to know who her doctor is?"

"Brandow. We've paged her, but she's been held up."

In part, this is good news. Sharon Brandow is firm but respectful, and not overly interventionist, unlike some of the other obstetricians, who act like gods of the maternity wards, and whom the midwives regularly second-guess to stop panicking mothers from sliding down the whole cascade of intervention: where a cervical check leads to an induction, then to a botched, uneven labor, resulting in an exhausted mother taking a hasty trip to the operating theater.

Emma thanks Dorothy and heads to Room 3, taking a deep breath before pushing open the door. Inside, Michelle paces, one hand pressed against her back, as though to counterbalance the mountain of her belly. Her husband, Jack, hovers, while Lynne stands to the side, arms folded, watching.

"Oh, thank God," Michelle says, straightening a little as she sees Emma, her face scrunched with discomfort. "Everyone's freaking me out. Dr. Brandow is at a birth in bloody St. Thomas's, so we don't even know if she'll make it—and that nurse over there isn't doing anything."

"That's because you don't need anything at the moment," Lynne counters primly, before glaring at Emma. "And what are you doing here? I thought you were on leave?"

"I'm here as a friend today," Emma says, smiling at Michelle and Jack.

"Can I have a word?" Lynne glowers. She gestures toward the door.

Michelle suddenly groans, and Jack goes to her. Reluctantly, Emma follows Lynne outside.

In the hallway, Lynne turns on her. "This is my patient, and you're not supposed to be here," she hisses. "I can handle it—she's not even three centimeters yet."

Emma's grateful for the hushed hallways, although she can see Dorothy peeping around from the nurse's station. "And I told *you*," Emma snaps back, "I'm supporting her as a friend. You know how quickly things can change. You don't have to stay. I can call you when she gets close to delivery."

Lynne growls with frustration and stomps away. Emma watches her go, half frustrated, half relieved. Dorothy, she sees, has wisely disappeared.

She returns to the labor room and hurries over to Michelle, who's decided to get onto the bed. Once she's propped up with pillows, Emma grips Michelle's hand and gets close to her ear. "I'm here, Michelle— you've got this. Now, try to slow down your breathing. Focus and count, like they showed you in the classes. It will help."

Michelle's eyes widen as she inhales, then she pushes the air out in a long, shuddering breath.

"That's the way," Emma encourages, stroking her arm. "Another big breath in, that's right. You can control this, Michelle, just focus. Your baby isn't far away, so *breathe*." Jack casts a nervous glance at Emma, and she nods to reassure him all is well. "There you go," she tells Michelle as the contraction subsides. "Now rest. Just rest. Your body knows what it's doing. Don't be frightened. You can do this."

Emma is a master of hiding her own anxieties. Over the years, she's grown better at concealing even the smallest tell, whether movement or sigh. Nevertheless, her heart is pounding. The statistics are severe, and if this baby doesn't breathe, it will be only the second time she's known the parents personally. The other couple, Jim and Martha Rhodes, were a family from St. James's. They'd had a late-in-life, unexpected pregnancy, and it had been Emma's worst experience to date. Martha still runs the other way when she sees Emma, riven by grief.

Focus on Michelle, she tells herself. *One step at a time. Don't think ahead. Don't catastrophize. Soothe. Encourage. And stay alert.*

Within an hour, the contractions have become a barrage of relentless surges. Michelle no longer talks between each one, and Emma helps her sip water and rubs her back, while Jack soothes her and holds her hand. This, Emma knows beyond doubt, is her gift. She can teach mothers to ride each wave of pain, particularly when it begins to push away all reason, and fear takes over. It doesn't always go smoothly—there are plenty of complications to impede labor—but it always helps. She knows how to comfort, encourage, to make her voice heard over the panic. Most of all, she knows that these women will never forget how they are treated in the most vulnerable moments of their lives.

But today her heart is broken. In just a few months, it will be Lainey's turn to do this. How many babies will be born sleeping by then? How can Lainey possibly be ready for this? She's just a child, and Emma has let her leave, to face it alone. *This is wrong*, she thinks, with a desperation that floors her. She needs her daughter back so she can care for her and *be there* when this wretched thing happens to her. Because what has all her work and experience been for, these past fourteen years, if she can't be there when Lainey does this?

"I can't do it anymore," Michelle wails suddenly, crying snotty tears onto Jack's shoulder. "It's going to be dead, isn't it? Happens to almost one in two they're saying now. Please, I can't bear it."

Emma's eyes are moist as she nods, understanding, but she won't let Michelle go down that path. "There's an excellent chance this baby will be healthy," she says as she presses a buzzer to call for support. "Don't fret now. You're doing great. Try to rest for a minute. I think you're in transition."

They've reached the short pause in labor when Michelle's body will shift focus from dilation to expulsion. Emma has watched countless mothers float here for a few giddy minutes in the eye of the storm, sometimes weeping, sometimes laughing, as they surrender to the inevitable. It's at this point Emma can almost see a ghost girl rising from the exhausted mother-to-be and silently taking her leave. No woman goes through birth, whatever the method or outcome, without leaving something of herself behind.

In another ten minutes, the room is an efficient workplace, with Michelle at the center, steadily laboring her baby into the world. Each time Michelle pushes, Emma remains outwardly calm, but there's a fire building in her chest. No one has come since she called for help fifteen minutes ago. There's been no on-duty nurse with her since Lynne stormed off, and they'll soon discover if this child will breathe. She can't leave Michelle now, but if there's a problem, she will need help resuscitating the baby. Is Lynne doing this deliberately? Is she really that malicious?

It's irrelevant, because the baby is already crowning, its face blue and scrunched up tight, eyes closed to the world. Michelle's grunts and Jack's frantic encouragement both fade behind the pounding in Emma's ears. *Please be okay.*

As Michelle rears up for another push, Emma sees a thick loop of umbilical cord wrapped around the baby's neck. "DO NOT PUSH YET, MICHELLE," she shouts, hitting the emergency button.

Lynne runs in, followed by Dorothy and Cara, and together they flip Michelle onto her back, while Emma makes a space between the cord and the child's neck.

"Cut it now," Lynne urges, and Emma deftly slices through the cord. Blood flows from the severed ends, while the midwives urge Michelle to push. She puts everything into it, roaring as she bears down, and the baby finally slips free.

Lynne rushes the infant to the resuscitation table as Michelle and Jack watch on, distraught. "No, no, no," Michelle cries in a long wail of anguish.

"She had the cord around her neck. We just need to check her airways," Emma calls to them as she runs to the table, letting Dorothy and Cara take over with Michelle. "Where the hell's Brandow, or one of the other doctors?" she hisses at Lynne.

"It's only Philips on duty, and he's doing an emergency cesarean."

The baby is still floppy and blue. While Lynne massages the heart, Emma works the bag-valve mask to manually ventilate the child. Dorothy has pulled the curtain around the bed and is trying to comfort Michelle and Jack. "Hold steady," Emma hears her tell them in that beautiful, calm voice. "Let them work now. Just hold on tight."

They have been working on the baby for nearly ten minutes when Doctor Brandow rushes in. "I've broken every speed limit to get here. What's happening?" she asks, beginning her own checks on the infant.

"It's a Code Twelve." Lynne stops and steps back. "There's no heartbeat."

"No," Emma barks, continuing heart massage. "It's not."

"Nurse Aitken, you're not officially on duty," Lynne snaps. "She's here as their friend," she confides to the obstetrician. "She's emotionally involved. It's been ten minutes now."

"We need to try," Emma insists, sweat gathering on her forehead and dripping onto the baby's towel. "The cord was around the neck," she implores Dr. Brandow. "It's not a straightforward Code Twelve."

Brandow nods. "Okay, ten minutes more," she says to Emma, and they settle into the resuscitation rhythm together.

Lynne tuts beside them. "You're torturing those parents now," she hisses in a low voice.

"Matron," Dr. Brandow says sharply, "stop talking and watch the time for us."

All Emma's hope and energy soak into the disappearing minutes as they work desperately on the baby. There's no change. She tries to ignore the sobs from behind them, but her heart is aching for Michelle.

"Fifteen minutes," Lynne announces.

"Come on," Emma whispers to the baby. "I know you're not a Code Twelve. It was the cord. Come on."

"Wait," Dr. Brandow says, holding up her hand while she puts the stethoscope on the baby's chest. Emma stops. "There's a slow heartbeat. Keep going."

They go back to work with renewed fervor, and thirty seconds later the heartbeat is established. A minute after that, the baby is breathing, and Lynne and Dr. Brandow are hastily wheeling her away.

Emma rushes over to Michelle and Jack. "She's alive," she says, wrapping them both in a hug.

Michelle sobs inside Emma's embrace. "It's a girl?"

"Yes," Emma says joyfully, "and after we get you cleaned up, they'll take you to her if she can't come to you." She turns to Jack. "You can follow her if you want."

At one nod from Michelle, Jack rushes from the room.

Dorothy and Cara continue tending to Michelle, helping her with the afterbirth, but Emma's head is buzzing with adrenaline. She has to move, and goes out to the nurse's station, surprised to find Lynne sitting on a swivel chair, hunched over.

"Lynne?"

When Lynne turns her eyes are red, but Emma can't feel anything other than fury.

"What the hell were you thinking?" Emma's voice is louder and harsher than she intends, but the rage comes from nowhere and explodes before she can stop it. "That baby could be in the morgue right now."

"I thought you'd be along to rub it in," Lynne sniffs. "Brandow asked me to wait here. You've no doubt got me in a heap of trouble—you must be delighted."

"How dare you!" Emma shouts. "You've been a danger to these mothers for months. You're a disaster waiting to happen, and today it almost did. And do you know what, I sympathized with you! I did, even when you were trying to make my life a misery. I know what it's like to be tired and burnt out and stressed as hell, even if I don't agree with the way you handle it. But you're petty and vindictive, too, Lynne. You wanted me to go home today. Imagine . . . just imagine if I had . . ."

Lynne dissolves into sobs and Emma sees Dorothy running toward them. A few people have come out of rooms to stare. Only in the ensuing silence does Emma realize how loudly she's been shouting.

"Enough now, Emma," Dorothy says, her face sympathetic, but her tone brooking no argument. "Time to come away."

5:45 p.m.

As the line at airport departures edges closer to the scanning machines, Lainey's whole body is trembling. She tries to hide it with continual movement, checking her bag is zipped up, flicking through her passport, but even so she feels horribly conspicuous.

The uniformed guard dishing out trays is solemn and efficient, as are those stationed at intervals behind the conveyor belt. People make their way steadily forward as bags and trays are swallowed into the X-ray machine one by one.

There are health-check stations to go through, then two X-ray scanners ahead, and Geraldine had flagged the larger full-body scanner in the car, as they'd talked through this part of the journey. "I've checked, and it can't see inside your body. Nor will it harm the baby." But Lainey doesn't like the look of it.

As she moves past the health checks and nears the front of the line, the security officer notices her, and he beckons her toward the smaller scanner. She walks through and there's a beeping noise. Her heart thunders in her chest.

They move her to one side, inspecting her, trying to figure out where the noise came from. A female officer points at her jumper. "Lift that up."

Reluctantly, Lainey slowly pulls up her jumper. Surely, they don't suspect and want to see her stomach? But the woman taps on her belt. "Take that off and go through again."

Lainey's hands are sweating as she slides the belt from her jeans. It's collected and placed in a separate tray, then handed down the line to be scanned, before they ask her to go through the scanner again.

This time there's no beep. The officers' attention moves straight past her to the next traveler, no longer interested.

Lainey tries to relax as she collects her belt and searches around for her bag. Geraldine hovers a few feet ahead of her, fussing over repacking her belongings.

"Is this yours, Miss?" another officer says, both hands on her bag.

Her heart quickens again. "Yes."

"May I take a look inside?"

"Sure."

He opens it, rifling through. On Geraldine's advice, Lainey had deliberately brought a small backpack to keep cabin luggage to a minimum. He pulls out her headphones, and a little bag of her favorite jelly sweets that Lainey hadn't known was there. With a pang, she realizes her mother must have slipped them in. Next, he takes out her cosmetics bag and unzips it, then holds up a pair of nail scissors with blunt tips. "You can't take these."

"Oh, sorry."

He tosses them into a bin behind him and repacks her bag for her. She hovers, moving her weight from foot to foot to ease the tension. He hands the bag back to her, and she smiles, but he just turns away.

She joins the line for passport control, aware of Geraldine taking up a spot a few places behind her. She wants to share the relief, but doesn't dare even catch her eye. Besides, they're not done yet.

The line progresses slowly until it's Lainey's turn at the counter, in front of a female officer with short, gray hair and gold-rimmed glasses.

The woman takes her passport wordlessly and flips it open, flicking a glance in Lainey's direction. "And where are you traveling today?"

"Australia."

"Long way to travel on your own?"

"I'm going to see my grandmother."

The woman nods as she types into the computer. "How long for?"

"A month," Lainey answers, thinking fast.

"Are you still in school?"

"Yes."

"But they're happy for you to go?"

"Yes," Lainey says, stopping her urge to explain, thankful Geraldine had had the foresight to warn her about questions. "Don't give them anything more than they ask for," she'd said. "First rule of resisting interrogation," she'd added with a wink. Geraldine seemed to be enjoying this a little too much at times.

"And you're in your final year?"

"Yes."

"Odd time to choose to visit a relative."

"She's . . . not well. I might not get the chance for much longer."

"I see. Do you have a return ticket?"

"Not yet. It's been hard enough to get this flight, and I don't know how long I'll be needed."

The woman's gaze flickers toward her again, for another long, assessing stare.

"It's all happened so suddenly," Lainey blurts, then holds her breath.

The woman turns to her computer and taps a few more times. "Well," she says, handing back her passport. "Good luck, then, Lainey."

Is Lainey overreading it, or is there some knowledge in the woman's eyes? Some sympathy? Why the luck?

She grabs the passport and hurries through the exit doors, into the transit lounge. Once there, she squeezes her hands into tight fists to release the tension, and in a small celebration.

A glance behind her shows Geraldine coming through the double doors. Geraldine gives her a brief, subtle nod. They did it.

Lainey gazes back at the long glass window, at the rows of planes on the other side. She's really leaving.

She rushes to the bathroom, locks herself in a stall, and takes a few minutes to feel the weight of what's happening. She retches into her hands . . . quietly, of course, so she doesn't attract attention.

5:45 p.m.

Emma is tucked away in Cathy's office, a hot mug of tea beside her. Cathy had brought her up here and made her a drink in silence. Emma waits, trying to predict if Cathy will be annoyed or sympathetic. Coursing through her is the same thought, over and over: *What if I've done the wrong thing? I shouldn't have let her go.*

"So, why are you even here?" Cathy begins, then holds up a finger, grabs a piece of paper, and writes a note.

Has Lainey gone?

Yes, at lunchtime.

Emma writes back, eyes glistening despite herself.

"Christ, Emma," Cathy's tone is thick with exasperation, "I can't imagine how you're feeling right now, but you're not fit for work. You know if anything had happened to that baby, you'd have faced the wrath of the whole bloody hospital. The lines are blurred when you're not on duty. I might not have been able to help you."

Emma rubs her forehead. "It was my decision, and you don't always have to protect me. Michelle asked for me, and I wanted to be there for her."

Cathy nods. "Well, thank God you were," she says. "Dorothy filled me in. She said that Lynne put off coming to help you until the last minute, that she ignored your call in transition, and that she seemed to want you to get into trouble. Thank God you turned the tables on her. You've averted a disaster, and there will be consequences, I can assure you. Brandow is furious, too." She sighs. "And at last we have some evidence that Lynne is falling apart."

"You know I've been worried for a while that she might put someone in danger."

"I know, and I hate the fact that we have to wait until these incidents happen before we can take action. This bloody retrospective style of management gives me the shits. However, you can leave me to deal with all this now. I promise you she'll be taking an extended break, so hopefully it's at least one thing off your mind. However," she says, leaning in, "you're no use to anyone either if you keel over."

"I know, you're right, and I'm exhausted. Perhaps you can call a muscly security guard to carry me out. You might even pretend he's escorting me from the building. Lynne and her cronies would enjoy that."

Cathy snorts. "You're a hard woman to look after, Emma."

"I know." Emma grabs her bag.

"Promise me you'll head home now and rest?"

"I promise."

She leaves Cathy's office fully intending to keep her pledge. But there's a side trip she wants to make first.

Downstairs, in the special-care nursery, she peers through the plastic top of the crib, watching Michelle and Jack's squirming, pink-cheeked newborn. One tiny hand has escaped her swaddle. The baby's gaze is intent but unfocused as her gums root against her fist.

"So, what will you do with your life?" Emma asks her. *"Will you be a doctor? A dancer? A dreamer? What gifts do you bring? What did we so nearly lose out on?"*

"Emma?"

Lost in thought, she hadn't noticed Jack enter the room, pushing Michelle ahead of him in a wheelchair.

"You've got a beautiful baby girl here," Emma says to them, beaming.

"We'll never be able to thank you enough," Jack murmurs, shaking her hand.

Michelle touches the crib, her face radiant with joy. "I can't wait to tell Lainey this little one's finally here. She's been listening to me drone on about pregnancy and babies for months."

The words cleave Emma in two, and it's the hardest job in the world to smile back and say, "Yes, she'll be thrilled." But Emma manages it, then collects her bag. "I'll leave you all to enjoy getting to know each other." She gives them both a hug and hurries from the room. The tears won't hold for much longer. She needs to go home.

7:10 p.m.

Waiting to board, Lainey can't settle to anything. Most people around her appear switched off from their surroundings, some sleeping, others wearing headphones as they check phones and devices. In contrast, she feels horribly conspicuous, and can't stop watching the clock. Now that they've come this far, she just wants to get on the plane.

For a while, she'd thought Geraldine's assessment of her own fame might be overkill. But Geraldine, sitting a few rows away, has been approached numerous times over the past hour for brief discussions, mostly with older women, who are obviously delighted to have spotted her. Lainey can't see Geraldine's face to know how she's handling it, but no conversation lasts more than a few minutes.

"Ladies and gentlemen, boarding for flight EK one zero five is now open."

Lainey grabs her bag and moves to join the line, noticing Geraldine is reading a magazine. Then she's through the final boarding-pass check and walks purposefully down the long ramp to the plane. She's one of the first on, taking her window seat in row twenty, pushing her bag under the seat in front of her.

She watches the passengers making their way on board as the plane fills up. The more they squeeze in around her, the more claustrophobic and desperate she feels. There's no sign of Geraldine as an older couple sits next to her, the woman smiling briefly at Lainey and the man in the aisle seat ignoring her. She tries not to fidget, staring as people continue to edge their way down the narrow aisles. There aren't many vacant seats left now.

Perhaps Geraldine has managed to get an upgrade. She'd moaned numerous times about traveling in economy, but she'd also said theirs were the only two seats she could get. But what if she isn't coming? What if, for some reason, she's helped Lainey this far and now she's leaving her on her own? Or what if something's happened to her?

Lainey's heart hammers in her ears as her panic grows. There are no more people coming in and the aisles are clear. Should she get up, or stay on the plane?

She checks her watch. It's after seven thirty now.

But then Geraldine comes down the aisle, obviously irritated as she scans the rows for Lainey. There's murmuring around them. "Is that Geraldine Fox?" the woman next to Lainey says sotto voce to her husband.

"I bloody well hope not," he replies gruffly, staring at Geraldine.

Geraldine is too far away to hear, but her face relaxes when she sees Lainey. As she comes past, she rolls her eyes, saying, "They wanted a photo with the crew. Wouldn't take no for an answer."

She stops a few rows down from Lainey. People have to get up so Geraldine can sit down in one of the center aisle seats. Lainey turns back around, trying to relax. Now they just have to get moving.

She pulls out her phone and plugs in her earbuds, listening to music and closing her eyes. She's vaguely aware that they haven't moved yet, but only returns to her surroundings when someone taps her on the shoulder.

She opens her eyes.

And her whole body goes cold.

Two middle-aged police officers, a man and woman, are standing in the aisle, watching her. The woman is short with sun-damaged skin, her uniform straining at the seams around her ample figure, and her dark hair pulled back into a lank ponytail. The man is thin and sour-faced and appears to be bald beneath his cap.

The couple next to Lainey are staring, their expressions wary, as though she might attack them at any moment.

She whips out her earbuds, her face burning. There's suddenly no air in the cabin; she can't catch her breath.

"Lainey Aitken?" the woman asks, sounding tired and vaguely bored.

"Yes."

"You need to come with us."

"Why?" she asks hesitantly, not moving while she weighs up her options.

"We can discuss that once you're off the plane," the policeman says sternly. "Let's not hold these people up any longer."

Lainey can't see a way out of this particular situation. The couple next to her get up so she can squeeze into the aisle. She's shaking as she collects her bag and begins to move. The whole planeload of passengers is turned in her direction, staring. Perhaps she's drifting off to sleep and the plane is moving, and this is just a projection of her very worst fears. But if so, she doesn't know how to wake up.

"Excuse me," comes a strident voice from behind them. Geraldine is on her feet. "Where are you taking that girl?"

"Ma'am, sit down," the policeman says, gesturing with his hands that she should do as he asks.

"Not until you tell me why you're taking that girl."

The policeman walks farther down the aisle. "Ma'am, if you don't want to get yourself arrested, please sit down."

"Go on, Geraldine," someone in another aisle shouts. "Give 'em hell."

"Come on," the policewoman instructs Lainey. "Let's go."

She's sandwiched between the two officers as they head down the aisle, their bulky presence meaning she can't turn around to see Geraldine, but she can still hear her calling, "Hold on a second there. Stop! Stop!"

Other people are chiming in now, annoyed, telling Geraldine to sit down.

But then her voice comes again, doubly strident yet with a note of despair. "Get off me, you arsehole. That's my granddaughter they're arresting! Now let me off this *fucking* plane!"

8.

THURSDAY, 9:05 a.m.

Fergus is barking. Emma comes to on the sofa, fully clothed and fuzzy-headed. Her eyes are sticky, her mouth dry. The light of the morning is relentlessly gray.

She checks her watch, startled to find it's past nine. She hadn't slept until the early hours, tracking the flight from London to Dubai, the dragging ache in her heart deepening as the little white line of progress lengthened and arced across Europe.

Fergus is still barking, and now she hears knocking. She hauls herself up, nudging back the curtains to see a gray BMW parked outside. She groans, sick of unmarked cars and unwelcome surprises, but before she can decide whether to answer the door, Sergeant Taylor steps into view, backing away from the front step and squinting up at the house.

He spots her watching, waves, then points at the front door. *Damn.* Sparks of alarm shoot through her as she combs her hair with her fingertips, hurrying to greet him. She fumbles with the lock, finally opening it with a feeble attempt at a smile.

Sergeant Taylor's expression remains somber. "May I come in?"

It's strange seeing him away from the station. In the natural light, his curly, dark hair is peppered with more gray than she'd noticed before, and his eyes have a sorrowful slope to them. His smile is kind, though, but she hesitates, not keen on letting him inside. "Isn't it pretty early for a house call? Why are you here?"

"I think you know. But I'd rather talk about it inside."

Emma relents and leads him through to the kitchen, trying to focus, to gather her wits. *Does he know about Lainey? What does it matter, if she's gone?*

"Would you like a cup of tea?" she asks, expecting him to say no.

"I'd love a coffee, if that's possible."

His tall, broad presence fills the small space, adding to her growing unease. She pulls a jar of coffee from the cupboard and turns on the kettle. He sits at the kitchen table without waiting for an invitation, watching as she makes the drinks. He replies to her queries about milk and sugar but doesn't offer another word until she puts the coffee in front of him and sits down. Then he asks, casually, "Is Lainey here?"

It's a huge effort to keep her movements slow and steady. His eyes don't leave hers, and she holds his gaze.

"Not right now," she replies, taking a sip of tea.

He leans his elbows on the table, fingers interlinked in a pose of prayer, his mouth hidden behind them as he ponders her answer. "Okay, then. Only, there was a report on my desk this morning, asking me to send an officer here to talk to you. When I saw it, I decided to come myself to check you're okay, since I've seen you and Lainey a couple of times recently." His eyes bore into hers, searching. "According to that document, Lainey attempted to board a flight last night."

Emma stiffens. She's suddenly cold and shivery. Her hands stay clasped tight around the hot mug, as though if she moves, everything will shatter.

"*Attempted?*"

Knowledge floods across Taylor's face.

She doesn't know what she expects—judgment, probably, or another lecture?—but it isn't the intense sympathy that's plainly evident.

"She didn't get on the plane?" Emma can't help but ask, hoping he can't detect the pleading undertone to her words.

"She got on the plane, but her name was flagged in the system shortly before takeoff, so police boarded and arrested her."

"She was flagged? Do you know why?"

Taylor grimaces. "I'd assumed it was the curfew, but when I read the file, it said that one of her classmates made a report about her suspicious behavior. So her watch was tracked, and they saw her at the airport."

The news is a ten-ton boulder dropped from the sky, smashing all hope and crushing the air from her lungs.

"Emma?" His voice is distant. Worried. "Are you okay?"

"Was . . . was anyone with her?" Emma stammers, desperately trying to steady herself. She has to stay strong, for Lainey, but she's cursing Geraldine for rushing her into this. Why had she gone along with it? Why hadn't they made a contingency plan?

Taylor frowns. "Not that I'm aware of. Was she traveling with someone?"

"Her grandmother."

"I see."

"Where's Lainey now?" Emma can't hide the desperation anymore. "Is she okay?"

Taylor takes a gulp of his coffee before answering. "Apparently, she fainted twice while the police were talking to her, so they decided to transport her to the local hospital, just to be on the safe side. While she was there, the staff discovered she was pregnant. She's currently detained under provision five of the Act for the Protection of Human Life, which asserts that every pregnant woman must cooperate fully with medical guidelines and protections to ensure the health of their child."

Emma closes her eyes, wishing she could unwind the last twenty-four hours. All their efforts had been for nothing. And yet, from the sounds of it, they'd come so close to getting Lainey away: she'd been sitting on the bloody plane. Her head swims at the thought of how frightened Lainey must have been.

"I don't know how you pulled off that charade at the station the other day," Taylor continues, and she opens her eyes, back to reality. His tone betrays a certain respect as he leans forward. "I did try to warn you, Emma."

"What else could I have done?" Emma snaps. "She was already

pregnant. There was no way of keeping our heads down and staying out of trouble. This was her only option."

He looks affronted. "I'm not the enemy. If you'd told me the truth, I would have tried to help."

His tone riles her. "Pregnant girls have been going missing for a while now. I'm sorry, but I haven't been in a very trusting mood lately. Please, just tell me where she is."

Now he has the decency to seem embarrassed. "I'm afraid that's classified."

Emma stands up in a rush. "Seriously? After what you just said? How dare you! She's my daughter. I have a right to know where she is."

"You don't understand." He holds his hands aloft to appease her. "When I say it's classified information, I mean I'm not even privy to it. The police have a dedicated team for underage pregnant girls now, and they report directly to the government outside the usual chain of command. I know that Lainey was in the hospital in Hillingdon but left around midnight. The notes stopped there. I'm sorry, Emma, but I don't know where she's gone."

Emma jolts at his words. "You have no idea at all?"

Taylor gets up, the chair scraping roughly on the tiles. "Don't panic, I'll see what I can find out at the station. I'm not here officially, but when I saw your name, I thought I'd come and . . ." He trails off at the expression on her face, as though sensing the molten rage that bubbles beneath her stillness. "I'll be in touch as soon as I hear anything."

He waits, but she doesn't move.

"I'll let myself out."

She barely registers him leaving until the sound of the door slamming closed makes her jump, and she rushes to the living-room window to watch his car drive away. She circles the house, pacing up and down the stairs with a confused dog at her heels, wishing she'd thought of more to ask him, trying to work out what to do next. Despite Taylor's promises, she's not confident he'll be able to help. She tries Geraldine's mobile, but it's switched off. *Damn you, Geraldine. Where the hell are you?*

She runs through the options of who else to call. The list is so short it's terrifying. She tries Cathy but gets her voicemail. Next is Meena.

"Have you left for work?" she asks when Meena picks up. "I need to talk to you, urgently."

"I'm driving there now, but I can come back. Is it Lainey?"

"Yes."

"Are you at home?"

"Yes."

"I'll be there in ten."

When Meena arrives, in her tailored dark suit, Emma almost collapses on her in gratitude.

Meena hugs her hard, then steps back, taking in Emma's disheveled, distraught appearance. "What's happened?"

As she tells Meena, Emma's remaining composure crumples, her voice cracking on each word.

Meena puts a finger to her lips, her intent gaze a question. She gestures toward the lounge and follows Emma inside.

"Lainey left me this." Emma's fingers fret across the jammer as she briefly holds it up, swaying as she talks. "They were so close to getting away, Meena. Now I don't know where she is, and I haven't heard from Geraldine. What if Lainey's been taken, like all the other girls? Please, I need you to tell me everything you know."

Meena lets out a long breath, but before she can speak, Emma's phone begins to ring. Emma snatches it up, praying it's news, but it's only Cathy.

"I can't talk right now," Emma tells her, hurriedly.

"Wait a sec, I'll be quick. Lynne's been signed off sick and we're super short-staffed. I've just had it out with Fred. Do you want to start back today?"

"No, no, I can't. Lainey didn't make it onto the flight. She was arrested, and now I don't know where she is."

"Oh, *Christ.*" There's a protracted silence. "Ems, I'm so sorry. What happened?"

"I'm trying to find out. But there's no way I can work."

"Of course. I'll sort it out somehow. Oh, Ems."

Cathy's sympathy is close to tipping her over the edge. "I need to go."

"Okay, call me later. I can come over straight after work," Cathy says, before Emma hangs up.

"Was that Cathy?" Meena asks.

"Yes. My hospital suspension is over, and I can resume my duties." Emma snorts bitterly. "Only right now, I couldn't care less if they sack me. Tell me about the girls, please."

Meena takes her time to reply, appearing to measure her words. "I think it might be better if we go to my office. I'm not sure it's wise for you to be here alone."

"Shouldn't I stay here in case Lainey turns up, or there's news?"

"Emma, listen to me," Meena's tone is a gentle rebuke, her brow deeply furrowed. "I told you before that some of the missing girls' parents have gone too, and the others are obviously keeping silent for a reason. If something happens to you, how will you help Lainey then?"

Emma frowns.

"Let's get to the office." Meena points to the jammer. "Make sure you bring that, and don't let it out of your grasp."

Once in the car, they don't talk much on the journey to Chelmsford. Emma keeps her eyes closed, warding off a migraine, until the car slows. Meena reverses into a space in a parking lot next to a squat three-story building, stops the engine, but makes no move to get out.

"Meena, are you okay?"

Meena's expression is a mixture of apprehension and concern. "I've been debating whether to tell you something," she says. "But I think it's important."

Another squall of fear hits Emma in the guts. "Go on."

"I presume you don't know that, as of last week, all pregnant girls who are under eighteen automatically become wards of the state, thanks to those sneaky laws in that horrible act that supposedly protects life."

Emma's pulse skips into a patchy staccato rhythm. "No, I didn't know that."

"Neither did I." Meena sighs. "It wasn't flagged in any legal or general news, which is outrageous and terrifying, quite frankly. I only found out after Sereena was arrested. It's hidden away in some pretty oblique language in a subsection of a subsection—difficult to spot. I'm sorry I didn't tell you—I weighed it up, but your plan was in motion and I thought it would only frighten you. But now, if the government has Lainey . . ."

". . . it's going to be very difficult to get her back," Emma finishes. The news scorches through the complexity of her emotions, until all that remains at the center of her is a white-hot crucible of rage. *We are good people*, she thinks. *I've devoted my life to caring for others. I don't deserve this, and Lainey certainly doesn't.*

She hadn't even realized she'd spoken aloud until Meena answers her.

"It's not about what you deserve," she says with compassion. "It's never about what you deserve. So many people have come to my office feeling like you. It's my job to show them that power doesn't work like that. The powerful don't seek to reward. They seek to control."

"Please," Emma says desperately, "just tell me you know how to get her back."

"Come up to the office first," Meena says, opening the car door. "Then we'll talk."

10:00 a.m.

The first thing Lainey sees is a chandelier, its myriad crystals shimmering and winking in the soft light. She stares at it in confusion, pulling herself up onto her elbows and looking around.

She's lying underneath soft white linen on a comfortable four-poster bed in an intricately decorated room. The walls are papered with elaborate patterns of flowers and buds in shades of brown and pink. There's a polished sideboard next to the bed, underneath an ornate gilt mirror, with a platter of fresh fruit on it: bananas, pears, oranges, and bright-red apples. At the end of the bed is a deep-blue velvet sofa, next to that a long table with a vase of roses at its center. The large windows are hidden by heavy wooden shutters.

Her mind works fast, trying to piece together what's happened. She remembers the policewoman holding her up when her legs had buckled as she'd walked off the plane. There'd been a few awful hours in a bare room at the airport, with officials barking questions at her, while she'd grown woozy and light-headed from fear and lack of food. Then a hasty journey to a hospital, where she'd lain on a gurney in a cubicle delineated by a thin blue curtain and listened to hurried footsteps, heated discussions, and the clatter of equipment, all the while assailed by an unrelenting stench of vomit and disinfectant. A nurse had come in when she couldn't get up without feeling faint and helped her to provide a urine sample in a cup. Soon after, a question had been whispered in her ear.

"Do you know you're pregnant, Lainey?"

And, in the small hours, fatigued and alone, she'd whispered back to the kind voice, "Yes."

She sits bolt upright. What happened after that? Why can't she remember?

As she surveys the lavish room, she realizes she's not alone. A young woman sits in an old-fashioned, high-backed armchair, a magazine on her lap. As Lainey moves, the woman looks up and smiles. Her eyes are air-hostess bright, just like the women who'd welcomed her onto the plane but who'd avoided her gaze when she'd been taken away again. Her lips are plump and pink, and her teeth gleam.

"Where am I?" Lainey asks, heart hammering, becoming aware of the soft pink chenille pajamas she's wearing, which don't belong to her. Her right hand goes to her bare left wrist, clasping at the clammy skin. Her watch is gone.

The woman hurries across to the bed, holding out her hands in reassurance. She's about Lainey's height and dressed all in black, her tunic top similar to the shape of her mother's nursing uniform, but with no logo or features on it to give Lainey a clue as to where she might be. Just two deep pockets at her hips and long, slim-fitting trousers beneath.

"It's okay, Lainey. You're safe. You've had a nice, long sleep, which is perfect. You were exhausted when you got here."

Lainey shrinks away. "I don't remember getting here. Where am I?"

"This is Horcombe House." The woman beams. "Welcome! It was once a hotel, but it's been repurposed for the time being to help girls like you."

"Girls like me?"

"Pregnant girls," the woman says with a breezy smile. "I'm Jenny. I'm here to help you settle in."

"I was on a plane . . . with my grandma. Do you know where she is?"

"I'm sorry, I wasn't told anything about your grandmother."

Lainey flings back the covers. "Please, I need to go home now."

Jenny lays a firm but gentle hand on Lainey's shoulder. "Really, it's okay, Lainey, try to relax. I'll check on your grandmother, but I'm sure she's fine. After the hospital staff discovered you were pregnant, you were taken to a local police station, where everything was explained to you. Since pregnant girls under the age of eighteen are especially vulnerable to the trauma surrounding the Intrapartum X births, it's been decided that the government will take temporary responsibility for your welfare until the baby is born. You agreed to come here for the duration of your pregnancy. When you arrived late last night, you were so overstimulated you couldn't sleep, so you were given a sedative to help you rest—for your own good as well as the baby's. I understand this may have caused some temporary memory loss and confusion, so let's get you up to see the doctor." She bustles across, putting her arm around Lainey's shoulders and encouraging her to sit up. "Can you stand?"

Lainey gets slowly to her feet, her body swaying for a moment.

"Oh, well done. All right, then, follow me."

A strip of soft blue carpet cushions Lainey's bare feet as she trails Jenny down a long, wood-paneled corridor. To her right are a series of windows that overlook a grassy bank, which gradually rises and gives way to a thicket of trees in the distance. On her left are intermittent varnished wooden doors with gold-plated numbers on them: 213, 211, 209. The corridor is deserted, their breaths and footsteps the only sounds.

"In we go," Jenny trills as they reach an elevator, the doors already standing open. Lainey follows. Every step feels like a mistake, but her brain is sludgy, and she doesn't know what else to do.

Jenny scans her watch against a dark electronic pad, presses number 4, then her eyes stay fixed on the floor numbers for the short ride up. Lainey's fingers encircle her bare wrist. Where has her watch gone?

When the door opens with a ping, Lainey falters. She'd been expecting another corridor, but instead, they step into a large room with an assortment of hospital equipment lining the walls. In the center is what looks like a dentist's chair, with flimsy paper covering it.

Jenny gestures to the chair. "Hop up there and the doctor will be with you in just a minute."

After Jenny disappears through a side door, Lainey scans the space. The floors are polished wood, the curtains a heavy burgundy velvet, and the walls papered in a similar way to the room she'd woken up in. This place definitely wasn't designed for medical purposes.

There's rustling from beyond the doorway, then footsteps, and a small, slim woman appears. She's wearing gold-framed glasses and a white doctor's coat with a smart gray suit beneath it. Her face is narrow, her chin an angular V, while her lips are a deep, unnatural red. Her gaze is not hostile, nor especially kind. Her natural attractiveness is marred by the pockets of bruised flesh under her eyes.

"Lainey," she says, her tone nasal and clipped. "I'm Dr. Kennedy. It's good to meet you. Please," she pats the chair and waits.

Lainey walks slowly across and sits down. When she's swung her legs onto the long, cushioned seat, the doctor covers them with a blanket.

"We estimate you're about seventeen weeks pregnant, would you agree?"

"Yes," Lainey says shyly.

"Hmm," Doctor Kennedy says, "it's not ideal. We like these procedures to begin as early as possible, preferably around twelve weeks, but once we've caught up, then I'm sure it'll all be fine."

"Procedures?" Lainey pushes her fingernails into the padded arms of the chair.

The woman glances up sharply. "I'm sorry, that was an unfortunate choice of words," she says, her smile tight. She moves closer to the bed, her eyes intent on Lainey's. "You're in the best place possible here, Lainey. We get updates directly from the NBCC and can implement their findings straightaway. Our job is to protect you and your baby, to give you the best possible medical care and attention so that this child doesn't suffer the fate of those poor babies in the hospitals. Your mother is a nurse, yes? So I'm sure you know more about it than most."

The mention of her mother is jarring. Lainey bites her lip to stem the sudden rush of emotion. *How do they know about my mum?*

"We'll begin by conducting blood tests and sonograms over the next few days to get up to speed," Dr. Kennedy says as she gathers equipment, "and from then on, we'll do this once a week, along with a few other checks when needed. Every day we'll do some basic health checks on you and your baby, and keep detailed records of the results." The doctor frowns as she attaches a blood-pressure cuff to Lainey's arm.

"It's so quiet," Lainey ventures. "Are there others here, too?"

"Of course," the doctor says. "Mornings are about rest, exercise, and health checks. There's a schedule here, and we all stick to it. When you've had a chance to settle in, I'm sure you'll meet everyone. Now," she starts to puff up the cuff, and the padding tightens around Lainey's arm until it's almost unbearable, "let's see. One twenty over eighty-five, can't ask for better than that, Lainey. Good job."

"Thanks," Lainey says, uncertain she merits the praise. She waits for the release of pressure, but instead, there's a sharp sting in the fold of her arm.

"Okay, then," the doctor says, "that was easy while that vein is nice and visible. Just something to help you relax, and next we'll take some blood."

More needles are produced, and Lainey closes her eyes, trying to ignore the series of stings, one after another.

"Well done, Lainey." When she opens her eyes again, the doctor appears pleased. "You did great. It won't be like that every time, don't worry. We just need some results for our baseline. And now . . ." she says, wheeling across a table with a TV monitor perched atop it, "let's see your baby, shall we?"

She doesn't wait for Lainey's answer, but pushes the pajama top up a little, exposing Lainey's stomach and squeezing cold gel onto her skin. Then she holds the scanning device firmly against Lainey's tummy, and they both stare at the screen.

"And there we are," Doctor Kennedy says as the black-and-white outline of the baby's head and body come into view, one tiny arm outstretched as though poised to catch something that's just out of sight. "There's your baby."

Lainey watches the little being on the screen shift and wriggle. She can make out arms and legs, even toes. Every single bit of this is real, she realizes, with a flash of despair. She's trapped in this strange, unknown place, with a tiny being growing inside her, and she has no choice about any of it.

"Looks like you're having a healthy girl," the doctor announces, collecting a piece of paper emerging from the base of the screen and passing it across. "Congratulations, Lainey, I'll see you tomorrow."

As she leaves the room, Lainey stares at the picture in her hands. A girl? The baby is frozen in the same posture she'd seen on the screen. The shape is so clear: she can see the bump of its nose, the long spinal cord. She'd thought it would be a blob. She hadn't ever thought about how quickly a baby became a baby.

A little girl. She holds the shiny picture right at its edge, her thumb and finger in a pincer grip so as not to mark the image. The paper is as flimsy as a feather; it could so easily fly away.

When Jenny comes to lead her back to her room, Lainey tries to remember the details of the short journey, but her head is foggy and her skin clammy. At her door, she hesitates.

"Come on, Lainey," Jenny says, her voice soothing and gentle. "You must be tired again now. Come and rest."

She follows, even though she doesn't want to go back into that airless room. And yet, when she sees the inviting bed waiting for her with its soft, plush covers, she falls onto it, gratefully. What happens next doesn't feel like sleeping so much as passing out.

11:00 a.m.

Meena's offices are huge, light, modern, and open plan, with matching beech furniture, enormous computer screens, and ergonomically designed chairs. Emma can't imagine what it would be like to work somewhere so calm and orderly every day.

"Emma, this is my colleague, Kelli Frame."

Kelli is young, short, and stocky with close-cropped red hair, a pale face and thick, red-rimmed glasses. She politely shakes Emma's hand.

"Can you join us, Kel?" Meena asks.

"Sure."

"Then let's talk." Meena leads them into a glass-partitioned room on one side of the large, open-plan floor, then closes the door behind them.

Emma catches Meena's eye and taps her watch—a question.

"It's safe to talk in here," Meena assures them, and they all take seats at a boardroom table. She glances at Emma as though checking it's okay to begin, and Emma nods.

Once Meena has finished outlining Lainey's situation, Kelli watches them curiously. When Meena finishes, Kelli exhales loudly. "Jeez, I'm so sorry."

"Thank you," Emma says, grateful for her compassion.

"Emma works at Whitehaven Hospital as a midwife," Meena continues, "so she's had lots of experiences of the Intrapartum X babies there. Lainey and Sereena are close friends. You might have heard Sereena talk about her?"

"Not the artist? The one with the birds under her bed?"

"That's the one."

It makes Emma want to weep, hearing them describe Lainey like this, as her dynamic, unique girl, rather than the pregnant statistic who's been abducted.

Meena turns to Emma. "Kelli has been helping to investigate the missing girls and she knew the Abbott family. They've all disappeared—the parents and the pregnant daughter, Jessica, who was friends with PreacherGirl. So far, we think that the girls have either been taken against their will, or they're being paid by a private partner of the NBCC so their pregnancies can be more extensively tracked and possibly manipulated. If money is changing hands, that would explain some of the stonewalling we've encountered from the families we've been able to locate."

"How many families have you found?"

Meena holds her gaze. "Nine out of the twenty-four whose daughters are still listed as missing."

"And the others?"

"Seem to have packed up in a hurry."

She pauses, and Emma thinks that both women seem nervous. "You said you're investigating?" Emma asks. "But why? On whose behalf?"

Kelli and Meena exchange worried glances, then Meena turns back to Emma. "You must keep this between us," she says.

"I will."

"The government asked us to investigate."

Emma stares at them both in confusion. "I don't understand. Do you mean the government doesn't know where the girls are? But the whole ward-of-the-state thing comes from them!"

"We were employed by Mary Walcott's government," Meena elaborates. "But when she was killed, we requested further instructions from the new government. Yesterday, they came and took our files and wiped our computers. We've heard nothing else from them since, so we're not officially investigating anymore."

"But you are still . . . *unofficially* investigating?" Emma asks cautiously.

Meena lays both hands on the table and interlinks her fingers. "Emma, I need to make sure you understand the gravitas of what we're discussing. Breaking client privilege is one thing, but leaking classified government information is another. We could all go to prison."

"But you'll help me, right?" Emma asks desperately. "You'll help me find Lainey? Why the hell was Walcott's government investigating if they'd made laws to allow girls to be taken?"

Meena glances at Kelli, who nods. "Mary was persuaded to put the item about wards of the state in the new laws, but she received assurances that it wouldn't be acted upon unless there were no other alternatives. She wasn't aware of the girls disappearing until PreacherGirl brought them to national attention. She'd had intelligence briefings that people in government were using the legislation to round up a cohort of young pregnant girls for medical trials—it was known as Project 9—but she wasn't able to find proof of how close to the top this went. And technically, because it's in the new act that her government had agreed to, the legal issues were going to prove incredibly tricky. So, her people began liaising with us."

"And now we've become amateur sleuths," Kelli explains, her expression grim. "Every time we've tried to talk to someone in police or government over the past two days, we've been shut down."

"But if the government won't cooperate anymore, why are you still pursuing it?" Emma asks.

Kelli raises her eyebrows. "Aside from the infringement of basic human rights? A few things. I studied forced disappearances as a specialty at university, particularly those in Argentina and Sri Lanka. When Preacher-Girl's video exposed all the missing girls, it struck some uncomfortable chords with me. The suddenness of it. The way her website was so swiftly shut down. And now with Walcott gone, the new 'government'," Kelli says, making quote marks in the air with her fingers, "seems extremely authoritarian in tone, don't you think? We're concerned that there's a bigger endgame in play."

Emma goes cold. "What kind of endgame?"

Meena takes over. "As far as we know, no one has figured out the cause of the stillbirths," she says. "So the first to do so will have incredible power. They can sell it to the highest bidder. Or they can decide how to distribute the cure—or whether to withhold it. But in order to solve the situation, you need test subjects—and who's likely to agree to that? So what do they do?"

"They exploit the vulnerable," Emma cuts in.

"Yes," Meena answers, eyes fixed on Emma, her expression a mix of compassion and concern. "And these missing girls certainly belong in that category. There's plenty of evidence showing that the girls on Preacher-Girl's list were pregnant. And there are definitely rumors about private companies collecting information from the NBCC. This number of girls is significant but not extensive—which makes sense if someone is running covert clinical trials. I would love to know what Mary Walcott was about to tell us. The press are obsessed with who killed her and whether it was a terrorist attack, but there's almost nothing about what she might have been about to say."

"And what about the girls' whereabouts?" Emma asks. "What do you know about that?"

"I wish I had better news," Kelli says. "But we've been looking into this for months now, and there's hardly anything to go on. I'm sorry, but we don't know where they've gone."

1:30 p.m.

Lainey is disorientated again after her nap, and this time, compounding her confusion, there's a series of round Band-Aids on her arms and a picture of a baby—*her baby*—on the bedside table.

Her head is fuzzy, trying to drag her back toward sleep again, but she resists, getting up and padding slowly around the room, aware she'd had company the last time she woke. But this time she's alone.

She goes to the window to pull back the shutters and let the light in, but they seem to be locked somehow. Next, she tries the door that leads to the hall—it's locked too. She leans against it, listening, the silence suffocating.

She steps away from the door in a hurry as she hears it click. Jenny enters, beaming as though she's never been so happy to see anyone. "Well, hello, Sleeping Beauty! My goodness, I thought you'd be out for the count for a while yet—"

"I need to talk to my mum now," Lainey interrupts. "She'll be wondering where I am."

"Of course." Jenny nods. "We don't have outside phone lines in rooms, as we have to be careful with security. We need to keep all stress to a minimum and make sure we're looking after you properly. I know it's a lot to take in, but the director will talk you through it tonight; he's really keen to meet you. So hop back into bed, now, won't you."

Not knowing what else to do, Lainey climbs between the plush sheets.

"Excellent, you're doing great. I think you're going to love it here, Lainey. Now, I'll leave this with you," Jenny says chirpily, handing over the remote. "Enjoy your relaxation time, and I'll be back later."

Within moments, the door closes with a small click. Lainey doesn't move for a few minutes, hoping Jenny will have gone far enough away, and then tiptoes to the door again. She turns the handle as slowly as she can, trying not to make a noise, then gives it a push.

It doesn't budge.

She stumbles back to the bed, looking around, convinced there are cameras in the room, trying to figure out where they are. How can she search for them without any spies noticing?

She idly flicks through the channels, settling on an old film called *Ever After*. She stares at the screen so that to anyone observing she'll appear absorbed in the story, but her brain is sprinting through the last twenty-four hours, remembering Geraldine's words in the car.

"You'll need a Plan B," she'd said.

Lainey had been horrified at first, as Geraldine matter-of-factly outlined all the ways their plan at the airport might fail.

"If this happens," Geraldine had said, "you'll be alone. You'll probably be frightened, too. Who wouldn't be! Just make sure your fear doesn't dull your senses, because you'll need all your wits about you. You should be gathering information everywhere you go, observing and recording all you can." Geraldine had tapped her finger against her temple and grinned conspiratorially. "For bargaining power, for escape routes, whatever you might need."

It had all sounded so dramatic and outlandish at the time, but now that Lainey's locked in this strange, imposing room with none of her belongings, she realizes her grandmother was preparing her, giving her strength for precisely this moment.

She considers the long corridor and all those closed doors. The gardens and the strange medical room on the top floor. Everything here is so visible, there are few places to hide. It's very likely there are cameras all over the place, too, and she's being given God knows what in terms of drugs—she's still sluggish from whatever they'd injected her with this morning.

"You can do this," Geraldine had said to Lainey in the car, a mischievous smile on her face but fire in her eyes. "You have plenty of rebellious blood inside you, Lainey. You can lie your way through passport control. You can refuse to talk to the police. Trust your instincts and don't give up, whatever happens."

She tries to recite her grandmother's words, to keep them close for courage. But this place has obviously been designed to keep her in, and she has no idea how she'll ever escape.

1:45 p.m.

Back at the house, Fergus is in a huff and has dragged his bowl into the hall to make the cause of his displeasure clear. Emma feeds him, exhaustion kicking in as the adrenaline of the morning subsides. She's been researching online, and now her mind flips between all the faces of the missing girls, each of them overlaid with Lainey's. She can't stop thinking about all she's learned.

"Get some rest. Don't answer the door unless you have to," Meena had said as she left. "I'll come over this evening and we can keep talking."

She heads upstairs for a shower, glancing at Lainey's bedroom with a pang, as though this could all be a mistake and she'll find Lainey lounging on her bed, sketching with her headphones on, Fergus curled up beside her.

Instead, she spots a box sitting on the empty covers.

"Oh, no, no," she cries, rushing over to it and opening the lid. Two chicks squint warily back at her and begin to squawk. But the third is keeled over, eyes closed.

She hasn't fed them since Lainey left. Michelle's labor and the events of the morning had completely wiped them from her mind. She pulls out the little body, hoping she might massage it back to life, but it's already floppy and cold. "Oh, my poor darlings," she says, putting the lifeless chick on the bed and grabbing the tub of food to feed the other two. "I'm so, so sorry."

The remaining chicks attack the food greedily, snuggling into each other once they're done. Emma closes the lid and takes the tiny corpse outside to bury it in the back garden. She lays it next to her on the grass, and Fergus sniffs solemnly at it while she digs.

She places it in the hole she's made in the soil, covers it over, then bends double, keening for the loss, dismayed that she'd overlooked this important thing she was supposed to do, when Lainey had dedicated herself to keeping them alive for the past fortnight. One slip-up, one morning of forgetfulness, and all Lainey's hard work is undone.

She's overcome with despair, unable to move, until Fergus pushes his furry face onto her lap and peers up at her with his big brown eyes, whimpering gently.

"All right," she says as she forces herself gingerly to a stand and checks her watch. "Shall we go for a walk? We might make the end of school."

She hurries upstairs and grabs the box of birds. Fergus bounds about her feet when he sees his lead. Once outside, Emma stares at the road, not wanting to run into anyone she knows today. She's not up for small talk. Nevertheless, she feels conspicuous. There's a recurring prickle between her shoulder blades that makes her swing around occasionally to check if someone is behind her. There never is, and she's annoyed with herself. The last thing she needs is to give in to paranoia.

At school, she rushes into the administration building. "I need to speak to Dylan Bailey," she says, nodding at the box. "I have something for him."

"I think Paul just went into the staffroom," the receptionist replies, getting up, her eyes shifting from Emma's unkempt appearance to the cardboard box. "Let me go and check."

Emma hovers by the desk, waiting, her gaze falling on the rows of pictures of school sports teams that line the walls. Lainey will be there somewhere in the hockey team, but she can't bear to search for her face today. Despite this school being a daily part of their lives since Lainey was eleven years old, today it feels like another world. One they don't belong to anymore.

"Mrs. Aitken?"

Heart sinking, she turns and gives the headmistress a wan smile as Mrs. Goodchild comes hurrying toward her. "Where's Lainey? She's not signing in and out properly. I've been trying to call you. Has she been in school?"

Emma braces herself. This conversation was going to happen sometime; it might as well be now. "Could we go to your office for a moment?"

Mrs. Goodchild warily eyes Fergus. "I don't usually allow dogs in the school, you know."

"He's well trained."

Mrs. Goodchild sighs. "All right, this way."

The headmistress's office is a dark, gloomy place, lined with bookshelves crammed with thick books that have faded jackets and cracked spines. All the technology—phones, computer, chargers—are huddled on a small desk that's been squeezed into the available space, leaving an imposing chestnut-colored desk completely bare in the center of the room. Perhaps she'd designed it this way to make it easier to glare at students and parents without obstruction.

Emma gets straight to the point without taking a seat. "Lainey won't be coming in for a while. She's gone overseas with her grandmother. We thought it best at the moment, since my work at the hospital with the newborns and the mothers has proved arduous over the last few months, and I haven't been able to give Lainey the time she needs."

This, she thinks sadly, is not much of a lie.

"Oh?" Mrs. Goodchild sounds shocked. "How long is she likely to be away? Her final year is very important, you know. She does history and art, yes? And what else?"

"Biology."

"Well, they all have coursework as a component of her final grade. She'll miss vital work while she's gone."

"I'm aware of that. She may have to finish her studies in Australia."

"Australia! Mrs. Aitken, this is all very sudden."

Emma bristles. "It's *Ms.* Aitken. My mother was leaving last night, so it wasn't a decision that could wait. It happened in a rush for us, too, and I'm not sure of the length of the visit. I'd rather not withdraw her yet. I'm just letting you know that our circumstances are difficult."

"Well, then," Mrs. Goodchild nods, flustered, "we also have procedures here, you know. We can't hold her place indefinitely. Please keep me informed over the next week or two, and then we'll have another discussion. If you do want her to stay with the school, she'll need to continue working while overseas. But I hope you understand that it may not be easy to coordinate. Our teachers are overworked as it is."

"I'll keep you informed. Thank you," Emma says, eager to leave, pulling at Fergus, who's settled down as though intending to snooze.

She steps out of the office to find both Paul Bailey and Dylan waiting for her. Dylan is flushed, while his father's flipping a cigarette packet open and closed, releasing the mixed scent of fresh tobacco and stale smoke.

"You were looking for Dylan?" he asks.

Dylan's face turns a darker shade of red, and Emma realizes he's uneasy about the potential topic of conversation. She has a momentary flash of irritation. *You caused this.* She tries to rein in her anger. It's not going to help Lainey if she makes a scene, and she can tell her daughter is fond of this strange, pale-faced boy.

"Yes," she says hurriedly. "Lainey's had to go away for a while. She wanted to give you these—can you take care of them for her?" She holds the box out to him. "I'd take them to the vet, but Michelle's just had a baby, and Lainey thought you'd like to look after them."

Dylan opens the box and frowns. "Weren't there three birds?"

Her jaw clenches. "There were."

His color deepens. "Sure, no problem. How often do I feed them?"

"Every few hours. And you'll need this, too." She passes him the tweezers and the half-full tub of food, which she'd covered with cling film and popped in a clear plastic bag. "Thanks for helping out. My shifts make it difficult for me to take good care of them. If you get stuck or run out of food, call the vet clinic."

"All right." Dylan nods, then kneels to pat Fergus, who nuzzles him then tugs at his lead. Emma lets the dog pull her away, calling goodbye, glad the errand is done.

She's almost at the school gates when she hears her name being called. "Hey, Mrs. Aitken."

She can't place the boy's face at first, then remembers. He was at her house two days ago. Her heart jolts. It's Grant Whittaker's son.

"How's Lainey?" he asks, stopping beside her, eyes bright, face flushed.

He knows, she realizes. *He did this, and now he's playing with me.*

Emma steps closer. "You have a nerve," she hisses.

He pushes his tongue against the inside of his cheek, and Emma's left in no doubt. *He's enjoying this. He's just like his dad.* She can't decide whether to walk away or slap him, when another voice says, "Liam, soccer practice started a few minutes ago."

Nick Davenport is jogging toward them, and Liam turns to go—but not before one last smirk at Emma.

Nick waits beside Emma until Liam's out of earshot. "Was he bothering you?"

"It's okay." Emma shrugs, working hard to hold back a rush of emotion.

"Well, he bothers a lot of people, so I hope he didn't speak out of turn." He pauses. "Where's Lainey? She wasn't in class today."

Emma stifles a sob and makes a decision. "Lainey's in trouble."

Nick's posture stiffens and he steps closer. "What kind of trouble?"

She hesitates. "You said you couldn't contact your sister at the NBCC —have you heard from her yet?"

He frowns, and she can see his thoughts turning over, reaching conclusions, his eyes questioning her, filling with compassion. "No, not yet."

Emma thinks fast. "Could we meet somewhere later, away from school? I'd love to chat more, but," she says, indicating the milling students and teachers, "not here."

"All right." She's grateful he doesn't press her for details. "How about the Rose and Crown at five-thirty? Would that work?"

"Yes, I'll see you there."

She walks away, acutely aware that he's watching her. It's a leap of faith to trust him when she doesn't know him well, but he's helped Lainey before. And if she wants to find her daughter, she needs to start taking some risks.

4:50 p.m.

"Lainey!" Jenny says breezily as she enters the room. "I bet you're hungry? Are you ready to get dressed and go and meet the other girls?"

"Okay." Lainey is curious despite herself. She'd laid waste to most of the fruit platter hours ago, and her stomach is rumbling.

"It looks like you don't have much to wear," Jenny pulls open Lainey's wardrobe. "There are some clothes in here. I'll leave you to change and come back in ten minutes."

"Jenny?" Lainey asks before she leaves. "Where are my bags?"

Jenny shrugs sympathetically. "I'm not sure. You didn't have any bags with you when you arrived."

"Please, could you ask someone?" Lainey persists, wondering if her backpack had traveled to Australia without her. But she's certain her hand luggage had been with her up until the hospital.

"Okay. Now get dressed or you'll miss the food."

When Jenny has gone, Lainey stares at the clothes. There's nothing in here that she'd normally wear. The bright flower patterns on the dresses, blouses, and long skirts are for someone more girly.

Whose clothes are these?

She doesn't dwell on that, choosing a dark-green slip dress with a subtler purple-and-blue floral motif. She uses the plastic hairbrush and disposable toothbrush, briefly catching sight of her sallow face in the gilt mirror. She can't find any shoes, and the white toweling slippers seem silly, so she goes barefoot instead.

By the time she's ready, her hunger pangs have morphed into nausea and dizziness. As she emerges from her room, Jenny claps in delight. "Oh, you look lovely, Lainey."

Jenny is really starting to get on her nerves. The best she can manage is a lukewarm smile.

What's this woman on? You look like shit. It's Sereena's voice in her head, and her smile becomes momentarily genuine.

Jenny appears pleased by her reaction. "Just one thing before we go down," she adds, lowering her voice. "We need you to keep a little secret for us. We haven't told the girls that Mary Walcott died so tragically." Jenny's eyes widen as she emphasizes the last word. "We thought it might upset them too much, and we need to protect their emotional state. I realize it might be hard not to mention it when it's so recent, but you're welcome to discuss your feelings with me or the doctor. Just not the girls, okay?"

Lainey shrugs. "Okay."

At the elevator, Jenny scans her watch, and they head down. Lainey braces herself as the doors open into a silent lobby. There's a long reception desk, but no one's around. Old-fashioned sets of keys hang redundant on the wall, alongside empty pigeonholes.

"There are some fantastic facilities on this floor," Jenny trills as they walk down another soft-carpeted corridor. "There's the library"—she points to a closed door—"you'll see that after dinner. And there's the breakfast area," Jenny says, and Lainey peers in to see it: it's spacious with lots of small tables already set up for service, "and at weekends we have a select buffet, but during the week, breakfast is taken in your room. And here we are. This is a bit fancier and more fun."

They've arrived at a long dining hall with a tall fireplace at the far end, and a well-established fire burning in the grate. The center-piece is the longest table Lainey has ever seen, with rows of studded deep-green leather chairs down either side, but Lainey's eyes are drawn high, to the four stag heads mounted, two on each side of the room, grotesque half-bodied sentries with coal-black eyes that stare absently at nothing. Light sconces on either side of them underscore their chins and cast their antlers in shadow, leaving dim outlines of thorns on the walls.

Five women wearing black tunics are seated in the chairs close by, while at the other end of the table, sitting nearest the warmth of the fire, are about a dozen girls. Some wear dresses or leggings and T-shirts. A couple are in their pajamas. They are talking quietly, but fall silent as Lainey and Jenny come closer.

"Everyone, this is Lainey," Jenny beams. "She'll be joining us from now on."

No one speaks. The girl closest to Lainey gently pats the seat next to her, moving the chair back so Lainey can sit down.

"I'll be right over there if you need me," Jenny says, gesturing to the group of women in black and heading across to take a seat.

"Hi," Lainey says to the girls, sitting down as they all stare. In the silence she's crippled with shyness, wondering how she can break the ice, when there's a voice from the far end of the table. A girl with long, dark hair is leaning forward, her thin face flushed and her eyes squinting as though she's having to work hard to see clearly. There's an expression of utter amazement on her face.

"Oh my God," she says slowly, staring around at her companions before refocusing on Lainey. "Lainey Aitken, is that really you?"

5:40 p.m.

Emma arrives at the Rose & Crown ten minutes late. The Tudor-fronted pub, with its sweet little window boxes bursting with color, is halfway between Lainey's school and their home, and a known haunt for St. James's teachers. In hindsight, it isn't the greatest choice for a private chat. If it's full of people they know, they might have to take a walk.

A blast of warm air hits her as she opens the door. Nick Davenport is already waiting at a corner table, close to the fire.

"Thanks for meeting me," she says, shrugging off her coat as she sits down. That's when she notices again how strained he looks. "Any word from Rachel?"

"No, not yet." He rubs his face tiredly and nods toward the bar. "Can I get you a drink?"

She almost says no, but changes her mind when she sees how empty the place is. "A gin and tonic would be good."

She watches him walk to the bar, her nervousness intensifying because of the conversation they're about to have, and her awareness of how much she's drawn to him. He's broad-shouldered and obviously fit, judging by the way his blazer and jeans cling to him. While she's studying him, he turns around with the drinks in his hand and she swiftly focuses on the row of wineglasses hanging above the counter.

Back at the table, he slides her gin and tonic across and takes a sip of his pint before setting it down.

"As I said earlier, Lainey's in trouble," Emma says.

He holds up a hand to stop her and leans closer. "Hang on." He taps his watch. "These things have ears."

She nods. "I know. That's why I'm carrying this thing around." She briefly shows him the jammer in her coat pocket as she flicks it on. "It disrupts the microphones."

"Wow," he says, sitting back a little, eyebrows raised, the ghost of a smile on his weary face. "I'm impressed. Although I should have known, since you're a friend of Meena's." Then he appears to register what she just said about Lainey, and his smile fades to apprehension. "I'm really sorry about Lainey. Is she . . . is she . . . ?"

"Yes, please don't say it out loud. And it's worse, because now she's missing, too."

"Oh, shit." He leans forward, his tone a mixture of shock and concern. His fingers brush her hand in sympathy. "What happened?"

"My . . . her grandmother tried to get her out of the country last night, on a flight to Australia. It didn't work—or so I presume, since my mother has gone abruptly silent." Her shoulders tighten at the mere mention of Geraldine. "Unfortunately, she has a nasty habit of disappearing when she's needed. However, I know Lainey was arrested and taken off the plane, but no one will tell me where she is." Emma runs her finger along the rim of her glass. "Meena has a theory about the PreacherGirl conspiracy and the missing girls: that if they're pregnant, they're being bribed or coerced to take part in private testing, via the NBCC. So, I wondered if your sister might have said anything to you about that? I'm sorry to ask at such a bad time when you're so worried yourself, and I know I'm clutching at straws."

To her surprise, Nick shakes his head. "No, I don't think you are," he says in a whisper.

"Really?" His intensity flips her stomach. "What can you tell me?"

He holds her gaze. "My sister's a star in medical-research circles—she's spent ten years examining rare diseases caused by damaged DNA. She wasn't happy about the circumstances of this job, obviously, but she really hoped she'd be able to help get a breakthrough." He glances around for eavesdroppers, then leans back in. "She was telling the family about it to begin with—they'd found some evidence of a faulty gene sequence in the Intrapartum X babies. It had proved difficult to identify, but they were getting closer to confirming it. But a short while before the PreacherGirl thing blew up, she stopped talking. Her husband told us she'd even been sleeping at the center, and when I tried to talk to her about the Preacher-Girl rumors, she was angry. Said she'd been told to sign new confidentiality agreements and could get in serious trouble. They'd had death threats at the center even before Walcott died, and we haven't been able to contact her at all for the past couple of days. My parents are frantic with worry—and so's her husband." He pauses, pulls his phone from his pocket, presses a few buttons, and holds up the screen so Emma can see. "This is the last time we saw Rachel," he says, pointing to a slim woman with wavy, dark hair standing a little distance behind Mary Walcott as she took to the podium in the seconds before she was killed.

Emma takes the device from him and studies the photo. "You haven't heard anything from her since this?" She can't help but notice the sheen of excitement—or is it nervousness?—on the prime minister's face. How terrible it is to rewind time like this and return to the past with full awareness of her fate.

She hands the phone back. "Are any other scientists missing?"

Nick shrugs. "I don't know. Not that I'm aware of, but I suppose there could be."

"And she said nothing else about what they were doing?"

He stares at her and she can see him weighing up how much more to say. "Once," he says, "early on, she said that the DNA damage made her think of the Thalidomide babies. That she was convinced there was a man-made cause behind it. She's been expecting something like this for a while; she's always nagging us about checking the chemicals and hormones in food. She thought there'd either been a huge cover-up or some kind of covert terrorist act."

Emma gulps. "You mean this was deliberate? That babies are dying, and the people who know why won't talk?" Her head swims with scenes from the hospital. To think that anyone would deliberately cause such devastation makes her heart falter into heavy, broken beats.

Nick frowns. "I'm sorry, Emma. It's understandable that they have to be careful with announcements about breakthroughs. But now, with Walcott dead and so many girls missing, things appear much more sinister."

"Meena found something else. She told me they don't need anyone's permission to test the girls anymore. The new laws say that all pregnant girls under eighteen are wards of the state. Lainey belongs to the government, and there's nothing I can do about it."

"What?" he splutters midsip, and has to wipe beer from his chin before continuing. "Which law is that?"

"It's tucked away in the Act for the Protection of Human Life, but there seems to have been a media blackout on it."

"You've got to be kidding." He looks at her, aghast. "That's ... horrific."

They fall silent. Emma can't bear to imagine what this might mean for Lainey. The sense of danger around her is growing by the second. The walls are closing in.

5:45 p.m.

There's a short commotion while Ellis swaps places so she can move next to Lainey. As Ellis sits down, Lainey stares at the neat bump protruding beneath Ellis's T-shirt, before she presses her hand automatically to her own stomach, which is still only slightly rounded. Then Ellis wraps her in a hug that makes her eyes sting with tears.

"I can't believe you're here," Ellis says. As they study each other, Lainey sees not just her friend's eager smile, but also the tired hollows beneath her eyes. There's a gray tint to her skin and a dull sheen to her dark hair, which hangs loose around her shoulders, so different from the usual high ponytail Ellis had always preferred. There's so much Lainey wants to ask her friend, but she's suddenly aware of all the girls watching them. She opens her mouth, but Ellis gives a small shake of the head, her eyes taking in the group of black-clad women who shoot regular glances at them in between their own conversations. Then Ellis turns to the girls. "Everyone, this is Lainey."

The girls offer an array of greetings, then take a while going around the table introducing themselves. There are thirteen of them altogether: Bianca, Christine, Britta, Farida, and Kirsten sit opposite, while alongside Ellis and Lainey are Drew, Celia, Jessica, Sandra, Hannah, and Judith. Lainey tries to remember the details of where they're from and how many weeks pregnant they are, but there are too many of them and it's hard to keep track. She stares hard at Jessica. She can't remember the pictures in the media very clearly, but the name is surely not a coincidence. Is this the Jessica that PreacherGirl had spoken of? She longs to ask her, if they get the chance to talk privately.

They're interrupted by two stout, middle-aged women wearing full-length navy aprons who bring in platters of food and place them in the center of the table, avoiding eye contact. Soon, there are at least a dozen different dishes: an aromatic chicken curry, a rich, creamy lasagna, a plate of spicy chicken wings, and a number of salads and sides. The black-clad women at the other end of the table appear to have a similar-sized spread and are collecting their food and chatting among themselves. They all look so similar in their black uniforms, with tied-back hair and glossy lips. Lainey can sense them watching, on alert.

"Who are they?" she whispers to Ellis, nodding at "the Jennies," as she's beginning to think of them.

"They take care of us," Ellis says. "You did well getting Jenny. She's nicer than some of the others."

Lainey tries not to stare at Ellis, whose cheeks are still pink and whose movements are slow and deliberate. As the girls set about piling their plates high, Lainey follows suit, observing them all while they eat, gleaning everything she can. She's constantly aware of the revolting stag heads and tries to avoid staring at them so she isn't put off her food.

As they eat and talk, the differences between the girls begin to show. Sandra and Kirsten seem exhausted, and while they fill their plates, they leave a lot of their food untouched. Both are dressed in pajamas like Lainey's, and have the largest pregnancy bumps. It makes Lainey queasy imagining her own stomach distended like theirs in just a few months. Judith and Drew pick at their food and don't say much, but Christine and Britta chat about the TV programs they'd watched that afternoon, while the others chuckle sporadically or occasionally contribute to the debate in between mouthfuls.

Lainey tries to relax. They're all being nice, and they don't seem scared or worried. And yet there's something a little off about most of them: they speak slowly, and they seem to drift in and out of each conversation. She watches a few of them staring into the distance, their eyes glazed.

"What's been happening in the outside world over the last few months?" Britta asks Lainey. "We don't see any news."

Lainey stalls for time. "Nothing much," she answers, remembering Jenny's warning and wondering how good the girls are at detecting a lie.

All their attention is on her again, and it's uncomfortably warm so close to the fire. Her forehead prickles with sweat.

"Is everyone still listening to the Rebels and freaking out about community service?" Christine adds.

"Pretty much." Lainey tries to laugh, but even here, surrounded by girls in the same predicament as her, she feels disconnected and adrift. Her old life already feels like a distant dream.

The dinner plates are collected by the same two women, still acting as though the girls are invisible.

"Are you sure you're okay?" Lainey asks Ellis, while the others are distracted watching the dessert platters being brought in. "We've all been really worried about you."

"Yeah," Ellis says, spooning fruit salad into her bowl and avoiding Lainey's eyes. "I mean, check out this food. They look after you really well."

Lainey hesitates, unsure what to ask next. Despite Ellis's obvious delight at their reunion, something has changed. The old Ellis was spontaneous and full of fun. The new Ellis is guarded; her movements careful. Each sentence seems not quite her own, as though she's choosing her words to shut down any chance of discussion.

"And have you seen your family?" Lainey asks eventually.

Ellis's eyelids droop a little. "Not lately. I miss them, but it's for the best."

"Really?"

Ellis seems surprised. "We have to take care of the babies, Lainey. If this treatment works and these babies all survive, then we could help save so many lives."

"And the only way to do that is to lock us up here and not let us see anyone we love?"

Ellis's hand pauses a moment on the way to reaching for a chocolate eclair. A couple of girls nearby have fallen silent. "Stop, Lainey," she says. "It's not a good idea to talk like that."

Lainey's face is scorching from her proximity to the fire. She gulps water and pours herself more, and tries another tack. "Do you remember signing any kind of agreement?"

Ellis bites into a piece of eclair, the cream squirting down her chin before she scoops it away with her finger. "No, I don't think so, but there're benefits to being here. The director says after this baby is born, I'll get a lump sum to help me with my studies, and whatever happens I'll be exempt from community service—even if . . . you know." She gulps. "The exemption is a bloody relief, to be honest. It sounds awful."

"And you haven't spoken to your mum and dad at all?"

"No—they told us it would be too distressing to speak directly. I had a message from them, though, saying they love me and understand why I have to be here."

Lainey tries and fails to imagine her own mother agreeing so readily to this arrangement. "So they . . . they treat you well here?"

"Of course," Ellis says, with only a slight hesitation. "They're really good at making sure we all stay healthy. Don't worry, it's a pretty cool place to live for a while. There's a gym, and a swimming pool with a spa. There's even a games room. It's like being on holiday. The days can get a bit samey, with all the health checks and the mandatory rest times, but at least I'm not getting crushed with homework at St. James's," she finishes with a weak laugh.

The dessert trays are nearly empty by the time Jenny comes in with a tray bearing mugs of hot chocolate and begins handing them out.

"You need to eat, Lainey," Ellis says, pointing to the trays as she hastily munches on a mini chocolate muffin. "We're on a timetable here; the food gets taken away after an hour."

"What happens after dinner?" Lainey asks Ellis, helping herself to a cinnamon doughnut.

"The director usually comes in to say hello, and then we can go to the library for a little while to read or play games," Ellis says. "Or back to our rooms if we're tired, but we're not meant to watch TV in the evening. It does something to our brain waves, apparently, and overstimulates us." She shrugs.

Suddenly, Lainey is desperate to pry apart Ellis's contentment. "Ellis, Sereena's spent weeks searching for you. We all have. We've been really worried about you."

Ellis's face drops. "That sucks," she says with a frown. "You know I would have contacted you if I could, right?"

"You're really okay with being here?"

Ellis shrugs, avoiding her eyes. "It's not forever, is it?"

Lainey wants to ask more. She wonders how much she dare say, but Jenny had only told her not to mention Mary Walcott.

"People outside think you've all just disappeared," she says, nodding at the others, too. "Like, been kidnapped or something. There's been a big fuss about it."

Silence falls across the table. Ellis frowns at Lainey, whose thoughts begin to swim. The stag heads seem to tremble behind the rising heat from the fire.

"All right, then," a booming voice says from the doorway, making Lainey jump, the girls all turning as one toward the sound. "Where's Lainey Aitken?"

6:15 p.m.

Walking home in the dark, Emma feels giddy from all the noise and commotion and that vague sensation of being watched: the fast-moving traffic, the bikes that swerve around her, the people coming toward her on the pavement and veering away at the last minute, tutting at her for not making way. She longs to be home but dreads it, too, since every inch of the space will remind her that Lainey isn't there. She thinks of her talk with Meena and Kelli this morning. Afterward, she'd searched online for Argentina's *Niños Desaparecidos*. The sons and daughters who had disappeared. She'd seen the mothers of the Plaza de Mayo, who had refused to stop searching or go quiet: their haunted, grief-stricken, angry faces. The black-and-white photography had switched to color as the mothers aged, and their protests continued. Some of those mothers had disappeared too, but one thing never changed: the endless rows of photos of the lost ones.

She turns onto her street with weary resignation: so tired, but with little hope of sleep. Her mind begins replaying her conversation with Nick, and every time she ends up with more questions and more worries.

As she heads up her garden path, she startles. There's a figure sitting on her doorstep in the shadows, bags piled next to her, and Emma reels as she realizes who it is. Before she can react, Geraldine hears her coming, jumps up, and rushes over.

"Please tell me she's here?" she asks desperately, looking scared and gaunt and very old.

Emma had imagined all the things she might do the next time she saw Geraldine. Shout in her face. Slap her. But it melts away when she sees how worried Geraldine is.

"You'd better come in," Emma says, hurrying up to the door and turning the key in the lock. Only once they're inside with the door closed does she answer. "No. She didn't come back." She tells her about the detective this morning and what he'd said. "I've spent all day trying to find out where she is."

"Did you just say 'a ward of the state'?"

"Yes," Emma says tightly.

"For Christ's sake, what century are we living in?" Geraldine sinks onto the sofa, her hands over her face. Emma waits. When Geraldine looks up, she is obviously stricken. "I'm so sorry, Emma. I thought we were going to make it. We got so damn close."

Emma sits down beside her, placing the jammer box between them. "Tell me everything."

Geraldine stares into the distance as she talks. "She was incredibly brave. She must have been so frightened going through all those checkpoints, but she held her head up and kept going. I floated around, keeping my distance so that I could watch her without people noticing we were together. She got on the plane first, and I waited and was last on, just to make sure all was well. I was bloody hallelujahing as the stewardesses began shutting the doors behind us. But something happened. We sat on the tarmac for a while, then the police came in and took her. I don't understand what went wrong."

"A schoolkid with a grudge tipped off the police," Emma explains grimly. "A police sergeant told me this morning. They tracked her location because of it, thanks to the watches. So, how come you're here? How did you get off the plane?"

"I made such a fuss about her arrest that I was taken off, too, but they wouldn't let me see her. They arrested me and took me to another station overnight. I've been there all day, hanging around, answering their ridiculous questions and asking for Lainey. They released me a couple of hours ago, and I came straight here, but they took my phone and returned it with a flat battery so I couldn't call."

"We knew it was risky," Emma concedes. "You did your best. Now I just have to focus on finding her."

"Yes, and I want to help," Geraldine says fervently.

"I thought you needed to get home?"

"I do. I really do. But not till I know Lainey's safe."

Emma regards her mother curiously. "Really?"

Geraldine's jaw tightens. "Of course. I didn't get involved just to turn my back on you now."

She says it lightly enough, but Emma still feels the rebuke. "Okay, I'm sorry. Well, thank you. Can we walk while we talk? I need to take Fergus out before my friend Meena comes over. She's been helping me today, and I'm lucky to have her on my side." She explains about Meena's involvement with Mary Walcott.

"Really? Mary was looking for the girls? Well, the plot thickens." Geraldine indicates her bags. "Do you want me to stay here tonight, or shall I find a hotel?"

Emma is close to dissolving. "Can you stay here? To be honest, I've been dreading being in the house alone."

"Oh, Emma."

Emma allows herself to be pulled into Geraldine's ample frame for a hug. She fights the ever-present urge to push away, letting Geraldine hold her for a few seconds, and even though it's strange, it's comforting.

"Right, let's get something straight," Geraldine says as she steps back.
"What?"

"Can you stop the nonsense of blaming yourself. Because if there's one thing I'm sick of, it's hearing women torture themselves for believing they created problems that were forced on them. You didn't ask for this situation. You have no choice but to react to it. You can be mad as hell, but no guilt, okay?"

Emma purses her lips. "You're right. Deal."

They gather their coats, Fergus dancing at their heels when he realizes what's happening. They set off into the darkness of the evening, neither talking for a while. Then Geraldine says, "The system that supports you can also be used to control you, Emma. Don't ever forget that, will you."

Under the dim light of the street lamps, in the drizzle of the chilly September evening, their eyes lock. Emma doesn't need to reply.

6:30 p.m.

The director leads Lainey into a compact room farther down from the dining hall, which is a cross between an office and a store cupboard. The shelves on the walls are filled with an assortment of paraphernalia: everything from brass candlesticks and stacked serving trays to overflowing boxes of pens and paper.

He sits behind a redwood desk and taps a few keys on his laptop, peering at it over his wire-framed glasses. As she waits, Lainey's gaze is drawn behind him to a tall glass cabinet, where two stuffed birds are positioned with wires: one diving in flight, its wings spread wide; the other waiting on a narrow branch. The seated bird's feathers are dry and drooping, its beak strangely off to one side.

"All right, then, Lainey," the director says, his smile exposing his long, slightly yellow teeth. "I like to say a personal hello to all new arrivals, so take a seat and let's get to know each other." He sits back, heavy-set and round-faced with short, gray whiskers that stray across his cheeks and the wide double chin of a toad. His hair is thinning badly on top, revealing a smooth pink crescent of skull. He's wearing dark suit trousers and an orange shirt, the buttons straining around his middle when he leans forward, occasionally exposing pockets of white flab.

"I'm Doctor Hallston, but you can call me Darius. No doubt you'll be feeling a bit discombobulated at the moment, but I'm happy to answer any questions you have, so don't hold back."

"Okay, what does discombobulated mean?"

He roars with laughter. "Great first question. I like you, Lainey. It means confused and unsure."

She sits without a word as he reads his computer screen. "It says here that they did thorough blood work and scans on you today and everything looked really good." He leans back with a satisfied smile, his legs spread wide as he swivels toward her. She resists the urge to scoot her own chair backward. "That's great news, Lainey. Now you're here, I hope we can help you to stay healthy and happy for the duration of your pregnancy."

She really hopes he isn't about to start asking her intimate questions about her body. "Do I have to stay here?" she blurts, her attention flickering between him and the macabre display of dead birds. "Or am I free to leave if I choose?"

The director's smile fades. "No, you're not free to leave, Lainey. According to the law, you are now a ward of the state, which means the government needs someone to care for you while you are vulnerable. And we've been assigned that job, and I can assure you we will take excellent care of you."

Ward of the state? The phrase is surely an anachronism, something Mr. Davenport would teach them about in school, but she doesn't know enough about the law to challenge it. Instead, she asks, "And who are you?" while maintaining eye contact, seeing his eyes flare in response.

"We're a company called Ambrose Medical. We've been contracted to help the government investigate the cause of the Intrapartum X babies. Our job is to take the groundbreaking work done by the NBCC and make sure you girls are the first to receive the benefits. We work with cutting-edge technology and we're in the business of saving lives. I can tell you, Lainey, you're very lucky to be here."

"So everyone keeps saying."

He regards her as though she's a particularly disappointing student. "All pregnant mothers would love to be here, if they knew about it. But this place is top secret because we can't take them all, only a chosen few." He leans forward. "We want to prevent you from having an Intrapartum X baby, Lainey. We're so close to unlocking this puzzle, even finding a cure, but we need to monitor you all for the remainder of your pregnancy. Your cooperation is greatly appreciated, and you'll be well compensated overall, I promise you that."

"Why us? Why a load of schoolgirls?"

His smile hardens. "Your youth makes you great candidates for this. There are far fewer health issues and complications to contend with. We can't offer our services to mothers with other children, or with underlying health conditions. There'd be work implications, too—it would be far more disruptive for an older cohort. This is just like a top-class boarding school for you, without all the homework." He chuckles. "Although, did the girls tell you we can help you with your studies if you want to pursue them? We have a gym, a pool and a huge library next door, but it's entirely up to you whether you want to study or swim." He flashes his long teeth again.

Lainey keeps her expression neutral. "Have you told my mother where I am?"

"Not in person, but she'll be kept well informed. We'll be following up on that, shortly." He taps his teeth with his pen. "A few parents choose to come and live close by, for the duration. Perhaps your mother would be interested?"

The suggestion hovers between them—a dangerous jewel of temptation—waiting for her to snatch at it. "I . . . I don't know about that. She works at the hospital, helping the mothers there. She's a midwife."

"Yes, I read that in your file," the director says. "Well, I wonder, considering our line of work, we might be able to gainfully employ her here. Just think: she could live close by and help out with you and the other girls as your pregnancies progress. Would she like that?"

Lainey has a flash of longing for her mother to be here, but the notion also seems absurd, that they could both be content while locked away for months. "I don't know, but right now she'll want to know I'm safe. Please, can you make sure she gets that message? Lots of people think the girls staying here have just disappeared."

"Yes," he says, and pulls a pained face. "PreacherGirl was . . . unfortunate. We were trying to keep this facility confidential, and she rather blew it up. But the next of kin have always known where their daughters are. To explain it to the general public would complicate our vital work here and cause a debate we just don't have time for. So, we've allowed the conspiracy theories to run their course."

He waits, as though expecting her to respond.

"I think I'll feel better once I've seen or spoken to my mum."

"Of course. I'll investigate that possibility for you, and we can talk about it again tomorrow evening." He pauses, then gestures to the cabinet behind him. "You seem intrigued by the birds."

"They're swallows."

"Really?" He looks impressed. "How do you know that?"

"The shape of their tails. The size. The color."

"Would you like me to have them brought up to your room?"

"No," she says. "Thank you."

He seems disappointed, sighs and wipes his palms on his thighs. She sees that the back of his hands are covered in thick, dark hair. "Well, if that's all for tonight, you can head into the library. Second door on your right." He checks his watch. "I think the girls have about half an hour left."

She gets up slowly. Warily. He's still seated behind the desk, so she isn't sure why it feels like he might suddenly pounce. Perhaps it's the way he watches her, like he's assessing her every move.

Outside the office, she's thankful to be away from him, and hurries toward the welcoming yellow light of the library, thinking over his words. This place is unnerving, but not entirely unpleasant. The premise is all about staying well and healthy, to give the babies the best chance of survival, and the other girls seem content to go along with it. The food is amazing; the surroundings are luxurious. It's not like they're treated badly. When the director had explained the reasoning behind the secrecy, it kind of made sense.

So why is she so nervous? Is she just too paranoid?

The doubt lasts only seconds: long enough to recall the stings of needles in her arms, delivered without permission. The locked doors. The closed shutters. The weird, forced gaiety of everyone here.

Don't get lulled into complacency. It's Geraldine's voice in her head. *Observe. Make a plan. Make multiple plans. Stay on your toes.*

The girls greet her as she enters the library. There are only five of them now, sitting on cushions on the floor, playing a game of Spot It. Ellis is there, with Jessica, Britta, and Christine. Lainey can't recall the name of the final girl.

"Where are the others?" she asks.

"They've already gone to bed," Ellis explains.

"What about our minders?"

The girls cast nervous glances at one another, some smiling, others not. "They're just helping the others. They'll be back shortly. Come, you want to play?"

"It's okay, I'll watch." She takes a cushion and joins the group, staring curiously at Britta, who has an obvious baby bump and is stroking it so absent-mindedly that Lainey wonders if she realizes she's doing it.

"How was your chat with the director?" Jessica asks.

"Fine. He told me a bit more about this place and tried to reassure me."

Jessica looks up from the game, curious. "Reassure you?"

"I wasn't given a choice about coming here." Lainey pauses, but then, emboldened by the fact they appear to be alone, and the lack of watches, adds, "Were you?"

An undercurrent of alarm ricochets around the group, visible only via fleeting eye contact and the stiffening of postures. Everyone huddles in closer.

"It was a good opportunity," Britta replies carefully, looking at the other girls for backup. "In the circumstances."

"You don't mind being locked in your room for half the day?"

There's silence for a moment, then Jessica says in a small voice, "That part's not great."

"What are they doing to you all?"

"It's just medical procedures—mostly blood tests and ultrasounds. There's one that's a bit scary with a really long needle they put straight into your tummy, but not all of us have had it."

Lainey frowns. "Sounds like an amniocentesis. I can't remember what it's for exactly, but they only do that on older mums."

Britta laughs. "Are you a nurse?"

"No, but my mum is a midwife. A friend of hers had to have it. I remember her being really scared about the needle and asking my mum about it."

"I've had it," Ellis says. "It doesn't hurt—it just feels like someone pushing hard on your tummy."

"You'll have it, too," Britta tells Lainey. "You have it if you come here when you're over twelve weeks pregnant."

Lainey feels her chest tighten at the idea of it. "And what else?"

Jessica shrugs. "Nothing much. We only stay here till we're thirty-two weeks pregnant. Then we get moved to a birthing center. Quite a few girls have gone already."

Lainey frowns. "Sounds a bit weird to send us to a birthing center that early—when there're still eight weeks to go."

The other girls stare at her, and she can see their alarm. They agree, she realizes, but no one dares say.

She can hear voices coming toward the room and begins to panic, desperate to find out as much as possible. "Do you have a friend called Alyssa Roberts?" she asks Jessica, keeping an eye on the open library door.

Jessica seems astonished. "Yes."

"She was searching for you. Making a fuss. It didn't go down well with the authorities."

Jessica's eyes widen. "Really? What happened?"

"They shut down all her accounts." Lainey suddenly remembers Jessica's parents are missing too, and is wondering how to ask about them without scaring her, when one of the black-clad Jennies suddenly puts her head around the door. The girls spring apart, their spell broken by her voice. "Fifteen minutes, girls," she announces.

It disrupts their willingness to talk openly, and Britta deals more cards. They play in silence, Lainey's words sitting between them all like unexploded grenades. She's not sure what she's done; whether they're happy enough here, or if they're grateful for her questions.

She shuffles closer to Ellis. "Are there more girls somewhere, apart from those who were at dinner?"

"No." Ellis's brow furrows. "Why do you ask that?"

"I only counted thirteen. I thought there'd be more. There's a list of names online, and I'm sure it was longer than thirteen."

Ellis thinks for a moment. "Sandra and Celia are from the Midlands— they said they were in another place, with other girls, before this one."

"Really?" Lainey shudders at the thought of more houses like

Horcombe. She thinks for a moment, trying and failing to figure out what this all means, then notices Ellis rubbing her belly. "How far along are you now?"

"Twenty-two weeks. And you?"

"Seventeen."

"This stage isn't too bad," Ellis says. "I'm not sick now, or so tired. And a few weeks ago, I could even feel it kicking." She turns to Lainey, and for a moment it's a different Ellis, her face shadowed and scared. "But that doesn't happen so much anymore," she adds, and holds Lainey's gaze for a long moment, before she looks away.

7:15 p.m.

Meena arrives ten minutes before Cathy, who is bearing takeaway. Emma introduces them to Geraldine, who greets them like old friends. They sit around the dining table, the jammer as a centerpiece beside the pizza boxes. The others help themselves, but Emma isn't hungry.

"Did you see the government announcement today?" Cathy says. "Pregnancy tests all around! At fourteen! It's like something out of the Dark Ages."

"What?" Emma asks, stunned. "I haven't heard about this."

"You'll have an email," Meena says grimly, pulling out her phone. "Mine came through half an hour ago. Listen to this." Her voice deepens to gruff mockery as she begins to read. "Twenty percent of women will not realize they are pregnant until the eighth week of their pregnancy, well after the fetal heartbeat is first detectable. That's why we're introducing compulsory pregnancy tests for all females over fourteen years old, with immediate effect. If you are a woman of childbearing age, you can visit your doctor for this easy test, which you'll need to take every three months from now on. Reminders will be sent via the government smartwatch app, which is a compulsory download, and preinstalled on most watches. This practical measure will allow us to monitor developing fetuses from the earliest stages and help us to intervene with Intrapartum X complications at the earliest opportunity. By protecting each one of us, we can protect us all. Thank you for your cooperation. Signed, your government."

"Our government," Emma scoffs. "Do they really think we're buying that?"

"It's a bloody patriarchal coup, that's what it is," Cathy splutters. "And do you know what they were talking about at the hospital?" she continues, wine sloshing around in her glass as she waves her arms animatedly. "Whether to put women to sleep to give birth, so they don't have to go through the horror of finding out if their baby is an Intrapartum X. I kindly suggested that might be a question for the mothers themselves, not hospital management, and said I'd bet a year's salary that ninety-nine percent of women will choose not to be gassed like they were a century ago."

"I fear we're only going to hear more of these preposterous suggestions," Geraldine murmurs.

"It's all horrific," Emma agrees, "but can we make finding Lainey our only focus this evening. When I have my daughter back, I'll fight like hell about everything else, but I only have one priority right now."

"Absolutely," Meena agrees. "So, the question is, where to begin? A while ago, Kelli sourced a map of the NBCC building, and we don't think there's space or facilities to accommodate that many girls on site. Plus, it would be difficult getting them in and out, and taking care of them without people noticing. We're convinced there'd also be more rumors. While none of the scientists are likely to talk, there are plenty of support workers—cleaners, catering staff, et cetera—who are happy to discuss what they see. And what they see are scientists working long hours in labs and having meetings. There are a few small lounges where scientists can sleep if it gets too late to go home, but no evidence of anyone other than staff using them. Any additional postmortems of the babies are conducted in the basement, but the only restricted areas are the morgue and the autopsy rooms, four in total, which obviously wouldn't be suitable for hiding these girls.

"Therefore," she continues, "our first supposition is that even if the disappearances are connected to the NBCC, the girls are being held in an external location. And our next is that the location might not be too far away from the NBCC, since there may well be key workers traveling between the two. I'm aware this involves a horrible amount of conjecture, but if we draw a twenty-mile radius around the NBCC building in Chelmsford, then a lot of the larger towns such as Colchester, Bury, and Luton are excluded. In fact, when we saw how much countryside there is in this projection, we began to think it would make sense to keep the girls out of the way somewhere. If we take out villages, which tend to breed gossip and whose inhabitants would definitely notice this number of girls, we're left with business parks, halls, country hotels, farms, and other ambiguous buildings. Of course, it could also be the case that the girls are on a secure hospital floor somewhere, but Kelli has been researching this for a while and come up with nothing so far." She takes a sip of water. "My best suggestion for tonight is that we divvy up the map and make a list of possible locations. It might be clutching at straws, but at least it's something to do."

Emma sighs. "It's worse than a needle in a haystack."

Meena offers her a concerned smile. "Yes, it is, but it's worth a try. And Kelli is retracing all the parents we've attempted to talk to, so tomorrow we can start appealing to them."

"We'll find her," Cathy adds, squeezing Emma's hand, "because we won't stop searching until we do."

They wait anxiously for Emma to give the signal to begin. "Thank you," she says, "all of you, for caring about us and sticking your necks out to help us. I'm grateful you're here."

Meena raises her glass to Emma. "Lainey might be the one in trouble," she replies, "but this affects us all. We can't stand by and watch girls disappear, then line up for our pregnancy tests without question. If we act like that's acceptable, what the hell happens next?"

The conversation fades as they begin to pore over maps of the areas nearest to Chelmsford, using Google Earth and Street View to focus on places of interest. Occasionally, Emma is grateful for their intense concentration but wonders if they find it all as ridiculous as she does. The chances of finding Lainey like this are minuscule. Perhaps they are humoring Emma, just keeping her busy so she doesn't have so much time to fret. She can sense Geraldine's apprehension, too, and is half irritated and half appreciative of her sympathetic glances.

As the clock nears nine, Cathy gets up apologetically, saying she needs to get home to check on the kids. "But call me if you need me," she says, grabbing Emma's arm. "I can be back in a jiffy."

Emma puts all her pointless notes into a pile, not knowing how she'd ever prioritize which buildings to search first. "I'm not sure this is going to work," she says, hugging Cathy, "but thanks for trying."

Once Cathy's gone, she turns to Meena. "Do you need to get home to Sereena?"

Meena checks her watch, then nods. "Kelli is with her, but I shouldn't be too much longer."

Geraldine clears her throat. "Before you go, I think we have a mutual acquaintance: do you know Marian Suffolk?"

"I should have known," Meena says, smiling. "You're RGN, aren't you?"

Geraldine beams. "I'm RGN."

"Can someone please explain what the hell you're both talking about?" Emma cuts in.

"You know you've completely broken protocol," Meena says to Geraldine.

"I don't give a stuff about protocol," Geraldine replies. She turns to Emma. "This might take a while. Perhaps you should sit down."

THURSDAY, 9:10 p.m.

By the time Jenny ushers Lainey to her room, she's floating. The sensation had begun in the library, just a whisper of it at first, but now she feels worse than the time she and Sereena had shared a bottle of Meena's red wine. Once Jenny has said goodnight, Lainey teeters over to the bed, clutching the wooden struts like they're ballast, before collapsing onto the mattress, not even bothering to undress. Before she passes out, she has one last thought:

I've been drugged.

THURSDAY, 9:15 p.m.

"Let me start at the beginning," Geraldine says, once Emma has taken a seat. "As you know, a decade ago the world was heading toward catastrophe, with authoritarian agendas everywhere, climate change playing havoc, fracking poisoning the water supply, and the virus upending millions of lives. The world seemed pretty troubled in the years that followed—oscillating between hope and despair—desperate for recovery but mourning all we'd lost. And then there was the great worldwide effort to pull together on climate change—instigated, of course, by the people, not the leaders, as it usually is. Well, at that point, a few thinkers began having a conversation about what might happen next. They were people who were aware that history works in cycles and progress toward true democracy would still be heavily impeded by capitalism, extreme religious groups, misinformation, et cetera, et cetera. We were all aware that the world couldn't afford to lose a few more years if there was another uprising, and that keeping this new balance would be critical if we were to stand any chance of rescuing ourselves as a species, not to mention saving the planet."

"I'm not sure my goals were quite as lofty and overarching," Meena interjects. "I was just fed up with the corruption and injustice."

Geraldine shrugs. "We all have our reasons, and we're a diverse group. RGN stands for Recovery Groups Network—although, personally, I prefer Rebel Groups Network." She winks at Emma. "We're basically an alliance of spies, informants, and do-gooders, watching out for trouble, trying to preempt problems before they happen, rather than sit back and watch. To participate, you must agree to a number of simple principles. There are no official gatherings, no paperwork, nothing traceable, and we don't meet anyone beyond our closest circle unless there's a reason. We just pass information along the line until it reaches the right people."

"And we were doing quite well until the babies began dying," Meena says. "But we've never faced such a test before."

"In the last few months, the group has seemed quite ineffectual," Geraldine agrees. "Of course, we couldn't predict the situation with the babies, but it's been clear for a while that the government would like to have more control over the rate of reproduction—and that's not just here, it's happening the world over, now there's so much more stress on supplies and resources, and the planet is in such a precarious and unpredictable state. But with this particular crisis, we've been on the back foot from the beginning—with no real notion of what's happening to the babies or the missing girls—although there's been plenty of speculation, of course. And we couldn't prevent what happened to Mary," she says sadly.

"So am I part of this, now I know about it?" Emma asks.

"It doesn't quite work like that," Meena says. "There's meant to be agreement between at least three in the Network *before* we ask someone to join us," she adds, looking pointedly at Geraldine.

"Oh, we haven't got time for that," Geraldine says. "Besides, none of my contacts know Emma, so how would we manage it? I just took a punt on you being involved, once Emma told me that Mary had asked you to investigate the missing girls."

"Was Mary part of RGN?" Emma asks, amazed.

"Not officially." Geraldine smiles. "Politicians aren't allowed. But I gather she knew about it and she left it alone, so I think she appreciated the ethos."

Meena suddenly sits forward. "Now Emma knows, it might be easier to get her to one of our safe houses."

"Hang on a second," Emma says. "Why do I need a safe house?"

"It's just a matter of time before something happens," Meena says gently. "You're too vulnerable here. In fact," she says to Geraldine, "I think someone should stay with Emma at all times until we can get her away, so there's no chance of a quick snatch."

Geraldine nods, and Emma stares at them, aghast.

"You haven't noticed anyone following you today, have you?" Meena adds.

"I . . . I'm not sure. I felt watched, but I'd decided I was just being paranoid. Right now, I feel like I'm in a dream. Please tell me you're having me on, and this isn't my life."

"I'm sorry," Meena says sadly. "Chances are you're already under surveillance because of Lainey. We should get you away as soon as possible."

Emma sits back and tries to let all this sink in. Her brain throbs from the turbulence of her thoughts, and she still doesn't know the answer to the only question that matters:

Where is she?

Her eyes fill with tears. "I know you mean well with the safe house, but how can I go and leave this place behind? What about Lainey? What if she comes home and I'm not here?"

Meena leans forward and puts a hand on her knee. "What if she comes and you've been taken by the government? Then she won't be able to find you at all."

Emma sits up again, grappling with a weird combination of panic and exhaustion. "Okay, I think I need to get some rest first. I'm sorry, I know you're both looking out for me, but can I at least sleep on this?"

"Of course." Meena stands up. "We can't do much more tonight. But you need to think fast, Emma. The other side won't wait for long. We have to make our move as soon as we can."

"I understand," Emma says, "and I appreciate everything you're doing. Just let me have a few hours' rest and we can talk some more."

"And I'll be here," Geraldine reassures them both. "Playing body-guard." She raises her eyebrows, indicating her bemusement at the role.

When Meena has gone, Emma lets Fergus out the back door and stands in the cool night, watching him sniff the weeds that have sprung up between cracks in the paving. *This place is so neglected,* she thinks. *But it's mine. It's home. Can I really leave? And how will Lainey find me if I do?*

Geraldine comes to stand beside her. "I'm sorry it's all so hard, Emma."

Emma doesn't respond.

"I saw something special tonight, though," Geraldine adds. "A real kinship of women, and wow, it's powerful. Your friends are completely invested in finding Lainey, and you're fortunate to have that in your lives. So often, women are set apart by the system, taught to compare and compete before they can even figure out who they are, and some of them end up spending their whole lives climbing over one another to rise to the top of female righteousness."

Instantly, Emma thinks of Lynne, who is so officious, such a stickler for the rules, whereas Emma has never been able to let laws and regulations override her instincts. She's not sure if that's a good thing or not, but after tonight it's obvious she'll have trouble with the painstakingly methodical approach. What she really wants is to light fuses and blow things up until she finds her daughter.

It's a clear night, just a scrap of moon poised in a fetal curl. *Where is she?* Emma asks the heavens, imploring some omniscient being to help them.

"When I was with Lainey," Geraldine continues, "I told her I could see the rebel in her, and I tried to prepare her, in case things didn't go to plan. I see the same spark in you, too, Emma. You're not content just to follow the rules. You'll do what you believe is right, and you won't stop until you get Lainey back. When they see you won't give up, hopefully they'll decide she's not worth the trouble."

"You make us sound so similar," Emma murmurs. "Whereas I've felt disconnected from Lainey for quite a while. She looks at me like I'm such a . . . a disappointment."

"I know that feeling," Geraldine laughs.

Emma shakes her head with a small smile, registering her faux pas, but Geraldine doesn't seem to mind. "For all you know, Lainey thinks she's a disappointment to you! But it's not your fault—or hers—or mine. Have you ever considered what society does to a mother and daughter—the demands we're taught to make of each another? The impossible, exacting standards we're expected to meet? These are man-made, not innate. You didn't feel that way in the beginning and nor did she, but life wears you down. You don't even notice how tightly you're wrapped in all of society's norms and expectations—and if you don't keep fighting them off, then you'll be slowly smothered by them. It's *Sophie's Choice*."

Emma knows the words are meant to galvanize her, but she's so close to breaking that she sways on her feet, unable to reply. "I'll fight for her forever," she says, almost choking on the words, "but if the government is behind this, how will we ever win? This is far bigger than any of us: they have so many resources and so much power at their disposal. What do we have against that? Most of the country agrees with the new policies. They think we're safer if we abide by the rules."

"Yes, the government enjoys keeping its citizens meek and frightened," Geraldine says, her expression grim. "But, eventually, enough people will see the truth. Even when people wake up, these things take time, because all battles for change are exhausting. Often it looks like nothing is working, and just as we're all about to give up and embrace the gin bottle, suddenly, there's a tipping point. When it comes, it's fast, and you can't miss it."

"So how do we make that happen? What's our advantage?"

"Well, we have truth on our side, and infinite passion for what we're fighting for," Geraldine replies. "Plus, we know what's at stake. We might not be able to outrun the mighty and the powerful, but we can still outsmart them. Don't count us out yet."

9.

"**M**orning, Lainey, breakfast time!"

Lainey reluctantly opens her eyes to the sound of a woman's tinkling voice. It takes her a few seconds to place it, and then she remembers.

Jenny.

The woman looms into view above her, smiling broadly. Her manicured hands, bright-red talons on each finger, grip the handles of a large tray table, poised to set it down.

Lainey forces herself awake and struggles to sit up. She's assailed by a variety of smells; some making her mouth water, others turning her stomach. There's orange juice, pancakes, a fruit platter, and a full English breakfast. She spots the bacon and sausages on a side plate. "I'm a vegetarian."

"We wondered if you might be," Jenny answers, her smile unwavering, so it looks like she's talking through gritted teeth. Her face is heavily made up and her hair pulled back in a tight bun. Beside her, Lainey feels unkempt and unwashed. "That's why it's on the side. I'll leave you to it—just set the tray by the door when you're done, and I'll pick it up later. If you can get yourself ready for your health check at nine thirty, you'll

245

get that out of the way and then you can spend some more time with the girls." Jenny picks up the remote from the bedside table. "Don't forget there's plenty to distract yourself with on here, too," she says, clicking on the TV to a rerun of *Alexa & Katie*.

Jenny vanishes, and Lainey is left staring at the cooling food and listening to canned laughter.

Everything's a little more familiar today, which isn't good at all. She has no intention of getting comfortable. She picks up a pancake and bites into it—it's soft and sweet, but her mouth is so dry that it's an effort to chew. She stares at the rest of the food as she mechanically moves her jaw, unable to remember the last time she'd had breakfast in bed like this. She usually makes a hasty morning toast with jam before school, often after her mother has left, but sometimes, when Emma isn't working, she comes downstairs to find it already waiting for her. Emma knows to make the toast so it's not too hard or soft, and exactly how much butter Lainey likes, with just a thin smear of jam.

Her eyes prickle. She just wants toast with jam.

She sets the tray aside and switches off the TV, plunging the room into silence. She listens a moment for the other girls but hears nothing. Her mind chews over the numerous undercurrents she'd felt at dinner, and the girls who'd seemed too tired to even say a word. The way the others chattered happily about nothing but paused to listen when they thought Lainey and Ellis might be discussing something important. The close circle of their heads in the library in the few moments they'd had to talk unobserved. The director's smile stretching and contracting as he worked on convincing Lainey everything was as it should be, frustrated when she wouldn't play along. The areas that were obviously designed for other purposes: empty receptions, long tables, and heavy curtains. The luxury of this place, but the weariness, too. It's like a storybook home, hidden in the forest, where the occupants appear welcoming at first, but transform into ghouls and demons overnight.

She shudders. Why is she torturing herself?

Her head is heavy. The pancake is a ball of paste in her mouth that she still can't swallow. Beside her, the orange juice glistens. She reaches for it, then stops and thinks of the warm drinks last night. Despite napping a lot yesterday, she'd somehow still managed a whole night of deep, dreamless sleep.

She gets up, collects the juice, and puts the glass to her mouth, pretending to drink it while she walks, hoping any cameras are fooled by her performance. In the bathroom, she looks around, trying to figure out if she's being watched in here, too, hoping it's harder to hide something between the tiles. She spits the food into the toilet and pours the juice in before she flushes, washes her hands, holds her hair back, and gulps water from the tap.

9:30 a.m.

Emma recognizes the police officers at the cordon this morning and they smile and greet her by name. She does her best to act casual as she walks past them, hurrying across to the press tent, instead. For once, she's grateful that they've closed the roads around the hospital; it makes it easier to spot anyone following her if they're on foot. But it's quiet, and there's no one loitering suspiciously. She'd left home while Geraldine was still asleep, aware of her probable disapproval, but unwilling to stay and negotiate. She wants answers right now. She wants her daughter back today.

There's not much to the press tent, just a gazebo set up against the parking lot wall, and a small camp table with mugs on it. Three people sit under the shelter: Jason Langford is sandwiched between an older man with a ruddy face who wears a bright-orange fleece that strains over his ample belly, and a younger woman in a smart black suit and heels who cowers into her chair as though she's chilled to the bone. Jason is rocking back on his seat, the collar of his navy sports jacket turned up around his neck, talking to the others, eyes down as he scrolls on his phone.

The woman notices Emma's approach first and says something to the men. Jason looks up, his eyes widening in surprise as he sees Emma coming straight toward them.

"Got time for a chat?" she asks, trying to sound nonchalant in front of the others, keeping her cold, trembling hands pushed deep into her pockets.

He jumps up. "Sure."

"I'll buy you a coffee." She points to a little deli in the distance, which sells takeaway sandwiches and salad packs to the hospital trade, and has optimistically set up a few tables and chairs outside, despite the persistent cold wind. No one else is there. She's as confident as she can be that they're not being watched.

"What's changed?" he asks as they walk toward the café together. "You've been scurrying past me for months."

"I'm sorry, it's not personal, it's hospital policy. You know we can't talk to the press. But I'm not on duty today and I need your help."

She adds nothing more until they've gotten to the deli and ordered drinks. Once they're sitting, she rummages in her bag, finding only a pen. "Can I borrow your notebook?" She doesn't want to show him the audio jammer, fearing he might be too curious about how she came by it. She can't get Meena into trouble.

"Notebook?" He laughs. "It's the digital age, Em. I take notes on my phone."

She grabs a napkin from the cutlery tray instead, and writes on it.

Exclusive for you. My daughter, Lainey, is missing, seventeen weeks pregnant. Taken by police yesterday. I don't know where she is. I think it might be connected to the PreacherGirl rumors. What do you know about missing girls?

Jason stops smiling, stares at her, then at her written words, as though he needs to be sure he read it right the first time. He blows out a long breath and grabs the pen.

Nothing concrete. Only rumors. I'm sorry, Emma.

She nods curtly, not wanting to waste time on sympathy.

Tell me about rumors.

He hesitates, then writes.

Pregnant girls being used in private medical trials—someone outside NBCC trying to fix babies fast.

Anyone know where?

she scribbles.
He shakes his head. "I don't know. Sorry," he says aloud.
She nods furiously at the paper, and tries again.

Where did you hear this?

A few places. Lots of chatter after PreacherGirl, and again after Walcott's death.

Why is no one investigating?

Jason sips his drink, seeming to weigh up his response. He pulls another napkin across and spends a while on his reply before he hands it over.

I've tried. So have others. Editors won't publish. Owner wanted me fired if I didn't stop writing about "government conspiracy theories." That's why I'm here, sitting outside the hospital. If Duncan (editor) doesn't have a job for me covering sports or charity balls or lottery winners, he keeps me tied up here so I can't follow other leads. And he edits my copy if he doesn't like what I write.

She reads it twice, trying to think through the implications. Every time she speaks to someone new—Geraldine, Meena, Nick, and now Jason—the conspiracy plot gets bigger and bigger. And Lainey is ensnared somewhere in this vast web of deceit.
She tries another tack.

Do you know what MW was going to say?

He pauses after he reads her question, stares hard at her as though trying to figure something out. She entreats him with her eyes, holding his gaze until he leans over to write again. When he's finished he pushes the napkin across.

Don't connect this to me, okay. Contacts at NBCC say the government knows a lot more than they've announced.

Emma's breath stalls. She points to the word *knows*. A question.

There'll be an increasing number of deaths without intervention, he writes. *But they're working on a cure and making progress. Government was waiting until they had something positive to announce, to give people hope at same time as bad news. To avoid panic/despair.*

Emma tries to think this through but can't make sense of it in relation to Mary Walcott's death.

So, if she was about to announce something, why would someone kill her?

Jason shrugs.

Chatter says it's a power grab, while most distracted by babies. Keep hearing Whittaker is in charge, backed by frightening number of New Conservatives. Collusion goes across party lines. People disappearing/ resigning if they don't support. His hand pauses for a moment, before he adds, *Could be a war we don't know we're fighting.*

Emma snatches up the napkins and pushes them into her bag as the waitress comes to take their empty mugs. She catches sight of the hulking gray slab of the hospital and thinks of everyone she knows inside. The mothers whose babies are kept below ground, their tiny bodies lined up in a row of metal lockers. Babies that would have gone home with their families a year ago. How many more will join them before they can stop this new plague? Before this waking nightmare ends?

Once the waitress has gone, Emma grabs a new napkin.

Is there anything else that might help me find Lainey? I'll give you any info I can if you'll help me.

Jason studies her intently for a while, then seems to come to a decision. He scribbles again as she waits.

Don't worry, I have a few eyes and ears in the hospital. But I found an old name connected to Whittaker: Darius Hallston. I haven't reported it yet—I'm working up the courage after what happened to Walcott.

He hesitates, then adds,

Don't look him up—too dangerous. Give me until 1.00 pm. Go to 33 Cranbrook Road. Postbox behind the white pillar. I'll gather what I know and leave it for you. Please be careful. If you're caught with this there'll be repercussions for both of us.

A middle-aged man with dark hair and a navy blazer is walking toward them. Emma tenses, feeling Jason doing the same, and she pulls the napkins out of sight.

"You still running?" she asks Jason abruptly as the man passes close by them, heading into the café.

"No. Didn't go for much longer after you left. Work took over and I got lazy. You?"

"No. It feels like an eternity ago. When life was . . ." She struggles to find the right word, appalled at how exhausted she's become; so unfit; her tired body all bent out of shape.

"Normal?" he suggests with a sympathetic smile.

She's searching for a response when the man emerges from the shop carrying a small paper bag and walks away.

She smiles at Jason, but there's no getting away from this new overwhelming world of paranoia and mistrust. She wants to leave now, to be alone, to think about what he's said. She stands up. "Thanks for the chat. I'd better go."

He nods, then holds up a hand to indicate Emma should wait. Taking another piece of flimsy tissue paper, he writes intently, his expression grim as he hands the napkin to her.

I spoke to Ellis Scott's parents twice before they disappeared. First time they were worried about her, couldn't talk enough. Second time, someone had put the fear of God into them. They were so frightened they wouldn't talk to me at all. Be very careful, Emma. Whoever's in charge, these people aren't messing around.

10:30 a.m.

Same gown.

Same room.

Same doctor.

Lainey's mood, however, is different. She's groggy and irritable; her skin pimpled with goosebumps. She doesn't want anyone's hands on her today.

"How are you feeling this morning, Lainey?" Doctor Kennedy asks as Jenny disappears into the side room.

"Fine," she says as the doctor feels her belly, listening to her baby's heartbeat with a doppler.

"Tired?"

"Not really—I must have slept for eleven hours, so deeply I didn't even dream. I hardly ever sleep like that." She risks a glance at the doctor just as Kennedy's eyes flicker up to meet her own.

Yes, she thinks, hoping the woman perceives the weight of her stare. *I know you're drugging us. I am not compliant.*

"Well," Dr. Kennedy says, moving away to peel off her gloves and sanitize her hands, speaking to Lainey with her back still turned, "your baby's fine, and your pulse is steady. You seem very calm this morning, which is great. The best way to keep you both healthy is to stay rested. We did all the blood tests yesterday, so we don't need to do anything more today, but please let me or Jenny know if you have any concerns. Your iron is low, so we'll keep an eye on that and get you some supplements, but otherwise everything's looking really good."

"When will you do the amniocentesis?"

"You seem to know a lot about what we're planning?" Dr. Kennedy sounds bemused.

"The girls mentioned it."

"Okay. Well, I hope they also told you it is painless. I'm not sure when we'll do yours. Not yet!" She laughs as though the discussion is a silly one.

Lainey ignores her. "Is the baby okay?" she asks. And can't help adding, "Do you know if it's . . . normal?"

Kennedy's thin-lipped smile resurfaces. "The baby's fine at the moment. Some tests take longer than others, but all indications are good. Just relax, Lainey."

Just relax? Screw you.

Lainey smiles sweetly in reply, adding in a low voice, "Does it bother you, Doctor, that I want to go home? That I'm here against my will?"

Dr. Kennedy's smile tightens, and she offers her hand to help Lainey sit up. Lainey finds herself pulled upright with surprising strength, the doctor's mouth close to her ear for just a second. The whisper is barely discernible. "You assume it's different for me."

A moment later, the doctor steps back and drops Lainey's hands. "Oh, I don't think that's right, Lainey." She laughs. "You must realize this is the safest place for you, but it's completely normal to feel homesick in the first few days. Let me know if you still feel like that tomorrow. You might need a short course of Valium to help you settle."

As Jenny bustles back in, the doctor turns away.

11:00 a.m.

> Where are you? There are two people waiting for you at home. They say they're case workers for Lainey.

Geraldine's text message has Emma running for the bus, spending the journey home in a panic, her mind giddy with all they might have to say. Once home, she bursts into the house to find her mother waiting in the lounge with a man and a woman. Geraldine raises a sardonic eyebrow at her and makes no move to introduce them, but the woman jumps up and holds out a hand as Emma approaches. She wears a dark-purple tailored coat and patent black shoes with stout heels, a dress code that reminds Emma of royalty. Despite the friendly smile, there's an air of imperiousness about her.

"Nice to meet you, Emma. I'm Philippa Regan, and this is Edwin Decroix. We work as a liaisons between the NBCC, the home office, and the private medical facilities employed by them."

Edwin offers his hand, too. "Nice to meet you, Emma."

Emma's hand disappears inside his warm grip. Edwin's a snappy dresser: his tailored suit looks pricey. He's bald with dark skin, designer glasses, and a graying beard.

Emma perches on the armchair next to Geraldine, and the other two sink back into the sagging sofa.

"Where's Lainey?" Emma asks immediately.

Philippa lets out a brief, infuriating chuckle. "Emma, please, let me explain who we are first and why we're here." She turns to Edwin, and Emma catches a small raise of eyebrows passing between them. "Could we talk alone?"

Geraldine starts to object, but Emma puts a hand on her arm. She stares at Philippa. "This is my mother. Lainey's grandmother. She'll want to hear what you have to say."

Philippa holds up her palms as though placating them. "Okay, then. First of all, please calm down, both of you." She titters, which might be due to nerves, but it still makes Emma want to lunge at her. "Lainey is safe, I can assure you. I'm her caseworker and your point of liaison: I work for all the girls taken into temporary care under the new provisions of the Act for the Protection of Human Life. I'm here to explain the situation to you and to let you know your rights and responsibilities during this time."

"Okay," Emma says, "tell me what rights I have?" She keeps her hand lightly on Geraldine's arm, reminding her to let Emma take charge.

Philippa blinks a few times as they stare at one another. "To begin with, you have the right to ask after Lainey's welfare on a weekly basis and be kept informed in general terms."

"Can I see her—or talk to her?"

"No, not until after she has the baby."

Emma freezes, and Geraldine seizes the opportunity. "That's five months away—you really want us to spend the next five months without having any contact with her at the most vulnerable time of her life?"

Philippa sighs as though she's an exasperated teacher dealing with unruly children. "I'm sorry, let me try to help you understand. These girls are extremely vulnerable. In this cohort, over fifty percent of them would have chosen abortion under normal circumstances. Now, this is something we cannot permit until we know exactly why so many babies are dying and we have a cure. So, we have to protect them. I promise you, Lainey is not alone, she's with a group of her peers, and is under the best medical care the country has to offer. We know from experience that family contact and interference is *distressing* for these girls. It makes them yearn for home, rather than focus on how to get the best out of their situation. However, on this note you'll be pleased to know we do allow one initial piece of contact, which is partly why we're here." She waves her phone at Emma. "You have the opportunity to make a short video that we can show to Lainey, to reassure her that she's safe and you're still supporting her from afar. We find this to be incredibly comforting for all the girls."

Emma stares at the phone. "Is that all you're here for?" she asks steadily. "To get me to make a video?"

They both nod and smile. "And to reassure you of Lainey's welfare," Edwin adds.

"But I'm not reassured. I don't know where she is. I can't see her. I only have your word, and I've never met you before. You haven't even shown me any credentials."

Philippa's expression changes to disappointment, and her tone becomes coddling. "Emma, I know this is hard, but just consider it from our perspective. We need to keep these girls safe. Parents can get desperate to see their children and vice versa. If we were to tell you where Lainey is, could you

255

really stay away? You might promise us now, but what about in a month or so, in a moment when you're really missing her? Parental instinct is understandably powerful, but in this case, it doesn't work in the child's best interest. And there's the media to think about: as usual, some sections of the press are being incredibly combative, wanting to sensationalize everything rather than support the government's urgent work to help stop this daily tragedy. It's a real fight keeping the lies out of the news. I know you work on the labor wards, Emma. I know you've seen this for yourself. Don't you want it to stop? Don't you want to give your child—your grandchild," she adds, looking from Emma to Geraldine, "the best possible outcome here?"

Her argument is persuasive, sending traumatic images of the hospital swirling through Emma's mind.

"This is ridiculous," Geraldine huffs as she gets up, going to lean against the door as though blocking it. Emma catches her eye, and they hold one another's gaze for a moment, trying to read the other's thoughts.

Philippa smiles tightly. "Come on, Emma. This is your chance to reassure Lainey that she will be safe and well cared for. Tell her you love her and that you'll see her soon. It will only take a moment."

Uncertain, Emma sinks into the armchair. Philippa takes this as assent, holding up the phone. "Just tell me when you're ready."

Don't.

The voice in her head is sudden but crystal clear. She hesitates. Opens her mouth.

Don't. They're making you complicit.

Emma has always trusted this inner voice, even when it leads her toward turmoil. And yet, its the hardest thing to shake her head and say, "I can't. I'm sorry. This will only upset Lainey. She knows I love her. She doesn't need this."

Philippa sighs and puts the phone away. Edwin comes to kneel in front of Emma. "Can you really not think of your daughter?" he asks gently, a scolding edge to his tone. "Can you not do this one thing for her?"

"Oh, for God's sake," Geraldine mutters.

Emma shuffles backward a little. "The thing is, I think—I *know*—she'll cope better without this."

Edwin purses his lips. "I'm just not sure you understand. We need your cooperation, Emma, just as we need Lainey's. You saw what happened to Mary Walcott. There are dark forces all too ready to use this situation for their own ends."

Emma gapes at him. Was that a threat? A warning? His expression is closed and impassive. It's impossible to tell. She jumps out of the chair, goes to stand next to Geraldine, and opens the door. "I am cooperating. I'm telling you, she won't want to see me on video. Please, could you leave now."

"I think she's made her decision," Geraldine adds.

Edwin gets slowly to his feet. "All right, then. We'll get back in touch later when you've had time to think about it. But remember, if Lainey does show signs of instability, she may need to be sedated until the baby can be removed from her care. For both their safety."

And they troop out as Emma reels in horror, imagining Lainey strapped onto a bed in a room, day after day, not knowing who or where she is, her baby being taken away while she's drugged. She stares blindly after them as they leave, and Geraldine closes the front door.

"Nice little threat at the end," Geraldine murmurs once they're alone. "Still, well done. Round one to you."

"Are you sure about that?" Emma replies unsteadily, closing her eyes as she collapses back onto the cushioned chair.

Geraldine nods. "It's a wise move. If Lainey sees you encouraging her to stay, she'll lose the will to fight. And if you tell her everything's going to be all right, she'll know you're a liar. You can't possibly say what you want to—well, you can, but I doubt they'll show it to her."

Emma's eyes tingle. "But I'm so frightened for her, I can hardly breathe," she says, unable to rid herself of the terrifying images. What's more, she's beginning to understand why Ellis's parents didn't want to talk to Jason. If this is only the beginning, she dreads to think what might come next.

11:40 a.m.

"You'll love the pool house," Jenny exclaims, leading Lainey toward an external door.

Lainey tries to focus on Jenny's singsong words and her flashing white teeth, but the few whispered words of the doctor still ring in her ears.

You assume it's different for me.

Had she really meant that she's a hostage here, taking blood samples and running medical tests against her will? Or had she just been messing with Lainey's head?

She wants to ask Jenny the same question. And yet, she knows she won't. Jenny is definitely not on her side.

She follows the woman out of the main house and across the grounds to a large stone outbuilding with narrow church-style windows set high in the walls. It's a sunny day, but there's no real warmth in the air. "This is such an amazing building," Jenny gushes. "It's completely repurposed from the old barn. At this time of day, we encourage some form of exercise, even if it's just a walk in the fresh air. We try to open the pool house for you girls at least twice a week."

She pauses as Lainey hurries to keep up and tries to appear interested. A flash of irritation passes across Jenny's face. Perhaps she'd been expecting a thank-you.

"That's great . . ." Lainey mumbles, although the last thing she wants to do is swim. Her skin feels sore and sensitive, and a dull ache has settled into the base of her skull.

She looks back at the house, longing for the solitude of her room. Tangled ivy spreads over the gray stone walls like a network of veins, and rosebushes surround the four-story building. A circular gravel driveway rings the entirety of it, like a dry moat. She turns and shivers as she stares at the repurposed barn. They're nearly at the large double doors, which are framed by trellises covered in more ivy. To their right, a steep grassy bank leads toward a thicket of trees.

"Can we go walking there?" Lainey asks.

Jenny pulls a face. "I'm not sure—no one else has asked. There's nothing up there but trees."

Lainey stares at the small patch of woodland, thinking of the last tree she'd climbed to rescue the starling chicks, scooping them out of a hollow in a sturdy sycamore. She has a pang of longing, hoping they're doing okay without her.

Jenny is holding open the door. As Lainey enters, she almost gasps at the sumptuous, sparkling blue pool running the entire length of the interior. Above it are three huge old-fashioned chandeliers, each of their brass rings a coronet of electric candles. The place is well lit thanks to them and the large arched windows.

Half-a-dozen loungers are scattered on the light-gray tiles. Most are empty; only two girls have chosen not to swim. Those in the water gently float or stand idly, chatting in groups. Three of the girls are swimming lengths.

"Lainey!" Ellis breaks off her conversation to wave as she treads water. "Are you coming in? It's lovely and warm."

"There are plenty of bikinis you can borrow." Jenny gestures to a basket of garments on a nearby bench, beside a pile of fluffy white towels. "Swimming is excellent for pregnancy. The water will relax you, and as you get bigger, it'll take the weight off your joints."

Lainey notices that a few of the Jennies are spaced at regular intervals down each side of the pool, inappropriately dressed lifeguards in their smart black trouser suits. A couple of girls sit on loungers set back from the pool area. Lainey tries to recall their names. Bianca, she thinks, is the one with a short strawberry-blond bob and pale freckled skin, who had seemed friendly yet shy at dinner, but hadn't been in the library. She's stroking her large belly, staring absently at it, lost in her own world. Drew, who has wavy blond hair and apple cheeks, had picked at her food last night, saying little. Lainey watches her studying the girls in the pool, while they ignore her. As Lainey peers closer, she sees the bandages on each of Drew's wrists. Her heart skips.

"You want to go in?" Jenny cuts across Lainey's thoughts.

Lainey bends down and tests the water with her fingertips. It's bath-warm. Part of her really wants to show compliance. To be like the others. But then she thinks of the cameras she suspects are hidden in her room and wonders where they are in here. She imagines the director watching them with his wolfish grin.

"I don't feel like it today. I'll just sit on a lounger." She gestures to the seat near Bianca and moves toward it.

"You've got just under an hour," Jenny calls after her, before turning away to talk to one of her doppelgangers.

"Hi," Lainey says as she reaches Bianca.

Bianca barely looks up from stroking her bump. "Hi."

"You don't want to swim?"

"I have problems with my ears."

"Oh." Lainey searches for something they can talk about. "Is Drew okay?" she whispers.

Bianca frowns at Lainey, then stares across at Drew. "I don't know. The bandages appeared two days ago. She won't talk to anyone."

"Oh."

Bianca says nothing more. It's hard work to talk, so Lainey lies back instead, watching the girls in the water. Ellis catches her eye, waves, but carries on swimming. Lainey still can't believe how disinterested she seems in life back home. *It's not the same Ellis*, she thinks, with another little spark of fear. Being here has changed her. Or they've done something to her.

Maybe both.

"Do you know if you're having a boy or a girl?" Bianca suddenly asks.

"Girl. You?"

"Girl too. When are you due?"

"Another four and a half months. And you?"

"Nine weeks to go." Bianca strokes the bump again. "I'd be counting it down, but I'm scared for her." She pats her stomach. "I'm worried about going to the birthing center—they're taking me next week. I wish there was a cure."

"Me too," Lainey says, staring at the small mound of her own stomach. "But I don't trust this new government one little bit."

As soon as she's said it, she freezes. The hairs on the back of her neck prickle.

"*New* government?" Bianca asks, confused. "What do you mean?"

In the few seconds before she replies, a series of images flash through Lainey's mind. Mary Walcott's chest bursting open with blood. Her mother's frightened face during the taxi ride home. The way families had leaned against each another haphazardly at the emergency assembly, like the remnants of a demolished house of cards.

Jenny asking her to lie, with that horrible fake smile plastered onto her face.

"Mary Walcott is dead," Lainey whispers to Bianca. "She was shot and killed on live TV a few days ago. No one knows who's in charge anymore."

Bianca's mouth drops open for a few seconds. She stares and stares, while Lainey holds her gaze, trying to convey the truth of her words. But then Bianca's face twists into outrage. "You're a liar," she shrieks as Lainey recoils. "Liar!" she screams as tears stream down her face and the Jennies all rush toward them. "*Liar! Liar! Liar!*"

1:00 p.m.

"Are you sure we can trust your journalist? They're not always known for their ethics," Geraldine says as Emma attaches Fergus's lead to his collar, and the dog fusses at their feet. Emma has spent the last hour explaining where she'd been this morning, since Geraldine hadn't been impressed to wake up and find her gone.

"Yes, I've known him for a long time. Besides, I approached him, didn't I? He wouldn't have had a chance to plan anything."

"Trust nobody, Emma," Geraldine says blithely. "People regularly surprise us—and usually not in a good way."

"I have to follow this up—it could be important," Emma insists.

"All right, all right, well at least we can stick together this time." Geraldine grabs her coat. "Don't go giving me the slip again, will you? You're making me look bad at this minder malarkey."

They hurry along the terraced street, Fergus trotting at their heels. Emma is thankful for the dog, since he makes the purpose of their outing less suspicious.

"I think we've got company," Geraldine murmurs when they're a few streets away from home. "There's a white car behind us."

Emma doesn't want to turn around. "Are you sure? Perhaps we're just paranoid."

Geraldine doesn't falter. "I'm sure."

Emma stiffens. "Okay, so how will we do this?"

"Ordinarily I'd say let's split, but that might suit their purposes. Let's get to Cranbrook Street and suss it out."

"Okay," Emma says, a flurry of nerves spinning in her stomach. "The address isn't far ahead. Two streets on the right."

Soon they're walking up Cranbrook Street, past number 33, and Emma can see the white pillar and letterbox. They don't stop, turning up the next side street, slowing down so Fergus can sniff at some rosebushes. A white hatchback drives past them and pulls in about fifty feet ahead.

"Not very subtle, are they?" Emma grumbles.

"I don't think they intend to be. They'd rather keep you on your toes. But they've done us a favor. Now, let's pretend we've dropped something. You search here and I'll go back down Cranbrook Street. Hopefully they won't know what to do, but since they can't see me from where they're parked, I'll grab the package and be as fast as I can. Just don't go getting kidnapped, will you."

"Why do you have to talk about everything as though it's amusing?" Emma says, half irritated but also trying to stifle a smile.

"Gallows humor, dear. One of life's essentials," Geraldine answers wryly.

Emma bends over Fergus like she's checking his collar, while Fergus waits patiently, panting.

"Right, I'm off," Geraldine says, retracing their steps at a hasty trot.

As soon as she's gone, Emma becomes very aware of the car parked up ahead. "You're not very scary, Ferg," she says, wishing she could turn him briefly into an Alsatian, something a little less approachable than a sweet-faced spaniel. There's no movement from the car, however. They seem content to watch as she pretends to search the area around them while muttering, "Come on, Geraldine," under her breath. Fergus makes her smile by putting his nose to the ground like he's joining in the charade.

It's a relief when Geraldine rounds the corner again, her hands in her pockets. "Let's go," she says, shrugging as if whatever they've lost couldn't be found.

"Right," Emma says. "Success?"

"Oh, yes. Let's just say my bra is currently holding more than two double Es," she answers. "Praise be for big boobs."

They walk steadily back home, the car trailing them from a discreet distance. As they go inside, it pulls up a little farther down the road on the opposite side, with a clear view of the front of the house. Once Emma has shut the door, Geraldine pulls an envelope from beneath her blouse and hands it over.

Emma slides out the contents, about a dozen folded sheets of paper, and takes them through to the kitchen table. They sit in silence for a long time, reading and absorbing Jason's research, occasionally exchanging glances as they pass the papers between them.

Eventually, Geraldine puts everything down and sits back and says, "Fuck."

Emma scans the last few paragraphs of the final article and meets her mother's eyes. There's no merriment in Geraldine's expression anymore, only fear and foreboding.

5:30 p.m.

"Do you see what damage you can do if you don't listen to our instructions?"

The mask has slipped now, Lainey thinks as Jenny berates her. The veneered smile has cracked. She's been waiting for this ever since Bianca was helped from the pool house, wailing, while the other girls stared in frozen horror.

Lainey has been locked in her room for five hours. No lunch. No fruit. She'd been frogmarched out straight after Bianca by a sullen Jenny, those red talons locked around her arm.

While held prisoner, she'd alternated between trying to rest and pacing the plush carpet, growing faint and claustrophobic as the hours passed. She'd wanted to keep her anger burning, sure it would serve her better than the terror underneath, but the hours had slowly tamped it down, and she's fighting tears as she answers Jenny now.

"Yes, I'm sorry. Is Bianca okay?"

"No," Jenny snaps. "She's not okay. She's distressed, Lainey, thanks to you. We've spent all afternoon calming her down. Why would you do such a thing when we asked you not to? The girls are so vulnerable—pregnancy is a frightening time, as you must know yourself—why would you want to add to that?"

"I didn't . . . I just . . . I told the truth." Lainey bites her lip, suspecting this isn't what Jenny wants to hear.

"And what use is the truth if it's terrifying?" Jenny hisses fiercely. "What use is the truth if it leads to absolute hysterics? We don't need the truth here, Lainey, we need calm, peaceful mothers-to-be so that we end up with calm, peaceful babies. You're so damn lucky, Lainey. You should try having a baby out there." She points to some unknown point beyond the house, her breaths heaving from the anger of her words. Then she moves closer to Lainey. "Thankfully, only Bianca heard you, but I need your assurance that you won't have any more slips of the tongue around the other girls."

"I won't," Lainey says keenly, hoping that's the end of it.

"Good," Jenny replies. "However, I don't quite trust you yet. Therefore, you will be chaperoned to dinner, and you will not be allowed into the library tonight."

"Okay," Lainey agrees. She doesn't want to talk to anyone anyway. Food is all she can think of.

Jenny checks her watch. "Come on, then, dinner's already starting." She eyes Lainey's chenille pajamas. "You can come like that."

Lainey wonders if this is supposed to be some kind of punishment; if it is, she couldn't care less. She hurries after Jenny down the corridor. They don't say anything more to one another in the elevator, and the hall is empty. As they pass the director's office, it's so dark that Lainey assumes he isn't in there. But he's working by lamplight, staring at a screen. His head snaps up when Lainey passes, and he glares at her coldly and calls her name.

Reluctantly, Lainey changes direction, stumbling on the carpet. As soon as she enters his office, he jumps out of his chair and closes the door.

"I heard about what happened today." All pretense of niceties is gone as he growls at her, staying way too close for comfort. "Let me just state

264

plainly that it must never happen again. While you are our guest, we will treat you kindly for as long as you abide by our rules. But if you seek to disrupt this house, frighten the other girls, put them and their babies at risk, I will personally make sure that you end up somewhere more befitting a troublemaker. A place without any of the protections for you and your child that you're currently enjoying. Do I make myself clear?"

She tries not to flinch at his warm breath close to her ear. "Absolutely."

He steps back slightly, his eyes gleaming in the low light, his lips wet. He suddenly smiles, and she jolts at the change in him.

"We'll put this one down to a rookie mistake, then," he says affably. "I hope you and your baby enjoy your evening, Lainey."

He returns to his desk, and Lainey gathers she's dismissed. Her hand gropes for the door handle, and she exits to find Jenny waiting for her. As their eyes meet, she sees the glint of satisfaction in Jenny's stare.

Most of the girls are already in the dining room, and Lainey's heart skips as she sees Bianca closest to the fire, another Jenny sitting beside her. There are spare seats opposite her, and Lainey heads for them, ignoring the questioning glances of the other girls.

As soon as she's seated, she says, "I'm so sorry I upset you, Bianca."

Bianca has her head down, slurping soup, but looks up when she hears her name, and it's all Lainey can do not to leap out of her chair. Bianca's eyes are red and glassy, a sign of her prolonged crying, but there's something else wrong with them. She stares vaguely, as though she can't quite see Lainey clearly. Then she smiles. "Don't worry," she says, the words slurry and spoken like a sigh, before she turns back to her food.

What have they done to her?

Lainey casts around anxiously for support, but the girls are trying to focus on their meals, sensing the atmosphere; no talking tonight. When she briefly catches Ellis's eye, Lainey smiles, and although Ellis returns it, her expression is wary. The others keep their heads down.

Are they all scared of me now? Lainey wonders with growing despondency. *They think I caused Bianca's meltdown. Are they frightened of what I might do to them?*

She'd thought there would be nothing worse than being in here, but now she realizes there's always another level of dread. The notion of having no one to talk to—to trust—is unbearable.

Courage and despair duel deep inside her, and she can't tell which will win. She stares at the food, desperately hungry but certain she'll retch at the first mouthful.

She has to get out of here. She groans, bending double.

"Lainey?" Jenny is instantly close by. "Are you okay?"

"I feel like I'm going to throw up," she says breathlessly. "Please, I need to go back to my room." She covers her mouth for effect, and Jenny seems irritated.

"You should try to eat—for the baby."

Lainey heaves into her hand, and Jenny tuts. "Come on, then. I'll have to bring you something later."

Lainey keeps her eyes averted as Jenny helps her away. The girls don't make a sound.

7:30 p.m.

"I'm still not sure we should share this," Emma says as she and Geraldine walk to Meena's. They'd spent the last few hours debating what to do with the information Jason had provided, and every idea had felt fraught with danger. Then Meena had called, and they'd agreed to walk over.

"Meena's already put herself out on a limb. She'll want to know," Geraldine replies with remarkable assurance considering she's only known Meena for a day. And yet Emma suspects she's right.

"If the government is doing what it looks like it's doing, anyone who gets a whiff of it is probably going to get killed."

"I know." Geraldine stares at the road ahead. "But try to act normal. I can't see the car at the moment, but it doesn't mean they're not watching."

Emma's phone buzzes as she walks, and she pulls it from her pocket. It's Cathy.

> Want me to come over and keep you company?

Emma feels a surge of protectiveness toward her friend.

> Geraldine is with me. Stay with the kids and have the night off from worrying about me

> Okay, I'll call you tomorrow. Love you xx

> Love you too,

Emma types, and then adds,

> Bye.

It feels horribly final. There is no coming back from this. No more snatched lunches and long brunches with her best friend. The only thing she can do now is keep her distance so that Cathy, at least, might avoid the fallout.

When they arrive at Meena's, Sereena opens the door to them, smiling but obviously tired. Meena appears behind her. "Sereena hasn't felt so well today," she says. "Go on up to your bed, honey. I'll bring you some food, shortly."

Emma watches them with a mix of envy and longing before the women troop through to the lounge. "She's feeling Lainey's absence today, I think," Meena says.

"She's not the only one," Emma replies.

Meena reaches out and gives her arm a squeeze. "So, what's been happening? Kelli kept studying the maps and making calls all day, and she's narrowed down some possible places to investigate. There's an abandoned farmhouse and an industrial site—a few grand houses around there as well. We could start scouting them out tomorrow."

"That's good," Emma says, "but we have some things to tell you first."

Meena's expression darkens. "Sounds ominous."

"Is it safe to talk here?"

"Yes, it's fine. Come into the lounge."

They follow her through, and as soon as Meena has closed the door, Emma outlines the caseworker visit, and her refusal to do the video.

"Brave move," Meena says.

"I just hope it was the right call."

"For you and Lainey? Of course. But when you're clearly not going to cooperate, I don't know what they'll do next."

"And it gets worse," Emma says. "We were given some papers today showing evidence of a relationship between Grant Whittaker and a man called Darius Hallston."

Meena's eyes widen. "Really? I know that name—tell me more."

Geraldine retrieves the envelope from under her shirt. "It looks like thirteen years ago, Whittaker was caught up in a scandal involving a medical-research company called Protec, because he had heavily invested in Hallston's research. Emma's friend gave us a whole catalogue of information: names, timelines, and some frankly terrifying theories. You'll need to sit down for this."

They move to the lounge chairs, before Geraldine continues. "It seems Hallston and Whittaker have known each other since university days—there're pictures of them together campaigning for the local Tory party—but it went a lot further than that. Both before and after they graduated, while it was de rigueur to aspire to a dictatorship, Hallston and Whittaker shared a number of platforms at ultra-conservative events, talking about the inevitability of eugenics thanks to medical research that was becoming increasingly successful at manipulating the human genome. Whittaker said, and I quote," she pauses briefly to riffle through the papers,

"'A weakened world cannot sustain a weakened populace, and it will take all our strength to defeat the scourges of plagues and overpopulation. Medical advances have moved us away from the natural order of things: the survival of the fittest. Now, the precarious state of our planet compels us to use our scientific prowess to eradicate weakness and disease, to ensure mankind's survival.'"

Geraldine waits for a moment, allowing the words to sink in.

Emma takes over. "However, while Whittaker built his political career and gradually toned down his lofty speeches, Hallston gained his doctorate and turned his attention to medical research on the human genome. He was probably beginning to put their ideas into practice, but he went too far: illegally manipulating the DNA of IVF fetuses whose parents had a family history of known genetic diseases, while promising them miracles. It was a botched project without proper trials that resulted in a number of babies dying and he served a paltry four years in prison for it. Meanwhile, Whittaker claimed he hadn't known the extent of Hallston's work, and this has never been disproved. Nevertheless, Hallston's company, Protec, went under, and the entire board, including Whittaker, faced wide condemnation for turning a blind eye to Hallston's actions."

"Oh my God, I remember that case." Meena's eyes go wide. "And so how does this connect to the babies now?"

"Well, here the plot thickens," Geraldine says. "Whittaker did his time in political purgatory, and was beginning to be allowed back into the fold just as Hallston was released. Hallston seems to have laid low for a year or two, but then he moved to a small town called Briarstone. Does that ring any bells?"

Meena frowns at them. "Should it? Oh, hang on—wasn't that the illegal fracking site that caused all those problems for the Tory Government?"

"Yep. The water was heavily contaminated as a result, and in the aftermath the town had a marked increase in unexplained stillbirths. Hallston is on record as attending a number of the autopsies, and some scientists that worked alongside him in Briarstone authored at least three peer-reviewed articles highlighting the dangers that this kind of incident posed to the general population, should it reoccur. Infertility, birth defects, and stillbirths are all listed."

Meena doesn't speak for a moment, her face slack with shock. Then she says carefully, "You're saying you have direct links between two proponents of eugenics, one of whom is quite possibly now the unelected leader of the country? And that you can connect them to a previous stillbirth crisis, albeit on a much smaller scale, which was caused by contaminated water?"

"Yep, that's exactly what we're saying," Geraldine replies. "Plus, Hallston has been spotted twice at the NBCC in recent months. For years this man has presented himself as a researcher trying to find a fix, but he's not actually helped anyone. He only causes death—or arrives in its aftermath." She waves the papers at them. "He's just been using them all, researching, learning everything he can about genetics and how to manipulate the human body right up to this moment. And now he's hanging around behind the scenes again. From reading all this, it seems far more likely that Hallston and his friend Whittaker don't want to solve the baby crisis, they just want to control it for their own ends. The journalist told Emma about rumors inside the NBCC: that the numbers of Intrapartum X babies will keep increasing. If you control the cure, then you get to stamp your mark on the entire population for the rest of time. You get a say in every single life. No more weak children or adults with health problems taking up time and resources. No more families with a dozen kids on welfare. And no more rebellion, because unless people want their family line to die out, they have to dance to the government's tune. It'll be a country of puppets."

Meena glances at Emma. "We'd come up with some similar theories, even without all this evidence," she adds. "And you said there was a long list of names attached to this?"

"Yes. And job titles. Plenty of people in high places are suspected to be colluding with this shady new government. Take a look for yourself." Geraldine hands over the papers.

Meena glances through them, and they wait in silence until she speaks again. "So, not only do we have a plausible link between Hallston, Whittaker, and the current crisis, we've also got a murdered prime minister who was trying to uncover a possible conspiracy around the missing girls. And there are shuttered circles of knowledge throughout the government, the police, and the judiciary. Well, this explains why it's so hard to ask questions through any official channels now."

"It's all so revolting," Emma splutters. "It contravenes every human right you can think of."

"Yes," Geraldine says, "but the corrupt never see people's rights, do they? They just see pawns in their game. You know what they're doing, don't you? Looking at the world, the floods, the food shortages, and the population problems, well aware that it doesn't stack up for much longer. This way they can take full charge of all births with minimum unrest. Some people might even be grateful if they play it right, and persuade them that they're safer this way. Particularly if they've spent most of the year scared out of their minds, with the endless news cycle force-feeding them the daily horrors of it. For all we know, this was a setup from the start."

There's a sharp silence. Then Meena blows out a long breath. "You do know what we're saying," she says. "Because if this wasn't an accident, then every one of the stillbirths is murder. That's over twenty thousand . . ."

"Stop!" Emma says desperately. "Don't. My daughter is part of their grand experiment, and right now they could be testing her and the baby, seeing if it's an Intrapartum X, and running trials. I have to find her." She tries to catch her breath, to stay calm, even though her skin is tingling as if insects are crawling all over her.

"I think the Network is our best shot at disseminating this information," Meena tells them. "As far as the authorities go, we just don't know who we can trust. I've seen a few people trying to speak out, but they're not getting much airtime. I don't think we can rely on mainstream media either, and much of the opposition appears to have been silenced. We have to get you to a safe house as soon as possible, Emma, and then we'll work out how to find Lainey and Ellis and the other girls."

Emma thinks fast. "We need to let Jason know too, before we share it much further. He's been trying to get this information out, but he might be in danger if we release it and they can trace the source. Can someone from RGN get to him?"

"Yes, I'll look into that—"

She's interrupted by a few loud knocks coming from the back of the house. Everyone jumps, then Meena puts her finger to her lips. "Let me see who that is."

They hear Meena whispering in the corridor, then the door opens and Meena returns, followed by Nick Davenport.

"This is Geraldine, Emma's mother," Meena says. "And you know Emma."

Nick nods. "Meena's been filling me in. Sorry if I worried you—there's a car outside, watching the house, so I had to come round the back way." He sits on the sofa next to Meena.

"Nick's going to help get you out, Emma," Meena tells her. "He's RGN, too."

There's a beat of stunned silence. Emma's mouth falls open. "You are?"

"Yes." Nick nods. "And while I do enjoy teaching history, I don't think my cover will hold for much longer. I've been working at the school to keep an eye on the Whittakers, but my background is military."

"And what about your sister?" Geraldine asks.

"Rachel's still missing." He pulls an old-fashioned flash drive from his pocket and holds it up. "Remember these things? She got this to me before Walcott was shot. It's a copy of all her research. Not the only copy now—there are a few more hidden until I know she's safe."

"Nick came over to tell me they've just pulled a body out of the Blackwell River," Meena adds.

"I tried to get down there," Nick says, "but they won't let anyone close. I'm praying it's not her." He rubs furiously at his chest as though trying to scrub away a pain.

No one speaks for a moment, then Geraldine says, "Can I ask exactly what's on there?" She nods at the USB.

"Proof Rachel can fix the babies," Nick says. "And proof there are people who don't want her to."

8:30 p.m.

In bed, Lainey stares at the blank television screen. Now she's alone, her stomach is growling again. The evening has stirred up her adrenaline, and sleep feels a long way off.

The lack of view and outside access is adding to her claustrophobia. She's desperate for some gulps of chilly fresh air and wishes she could open the shutters so she could at least see the night sky. It would calm her to feel connected to the wider world, even if it's only staring at an empty landscape and stars light-years away.

As she considers the sprawling mattress, she thinks of home, and

Fergus, who always takes her presence on the bed as a sign to jump up and join her for a nap. She fights the tears that threaten, teeth clamping down hard on dry lips, the dull pain distracting from the deeper one. She makes a vow to herself: she will not cry in this place. She's certain there are cameras watching, and she will not let them see her break down, however much she wants to.

She goes to turn on the TV again but can't access the channels. There must be a curfew, and she'd been so keen to talk to the girls in the library last night that she'd forgotten to grab any books before they were ushered out. With no distractions, there's nothing to do except think. If only she could draw to relax, but they haven't even left paper or pens around. Frustrated, she gets down from the bed and paces the room, checking it in detail, hoping anyone watching thinks she's interested in exploring rather than searching for an escape route. She notices other things she hadn't before: chipped paint on the radiators; the way the wallpaper peels off at the corners. The black scuffs on the skirting board and the scratches on the wardrobe. The ostentatiousness of the place hides a lot of the wear and tear, but she sees it now that she's looking.

How on earth would she break out of here? The Jennies are watching the cameras, and there are probably security guards outside somewhere. The main doors and elevators are electronically coded. And now that Lainey's caused obvious disquiet among the girls, she's not convinced they'll help her fight back. Any anger they have is trapped beneath their fears, and there's a lot to be frightened about.

She climbs back into bed and grabs the sonogram picture. Pressing her hand onto her stomach, she tries to comprehend that this little person is inside her. It's surreal. She'd watched it wiggle on the screen, and yet she can't detect anything moving now. She lies as still as she can and tries to concentrate, but there's nothing. Strangely disappointed, she sets the picture down.

She switches off the lamp and attempts sleep, but although her thoughts begin to float, her body keeps urging her back to consciousness. She sits up with a rush, breathless, and switches the light on again. Getting out of bed, she splashes water on her face, inhales, and exhales in a steady rhythm, channeling her school yoga classes. But her body doesn't want to relax. The more she tries, the more she feels edgy and light-headed. Fidgety.

Trapped.

8:35 p.m.

"Tell us more about this proof," Geraldine says to Nick.

He nods. "In all the babies Rachel has analyzed, there's hard-to-spot catastrophic damage to a tiny part of the DNA sequence. It's so specific that the first genome-sequencing processes couldn't find it, but Rachel saw there was an error and kept searching. And now she's close to establishing its mutagenic pathway."

"What's a mutagenic pathway?" asks Emma.

"In simple terms, it means that there's a chemical coming from an external source causing a change in the DNA of cells. The body's cells are replicating all the time, and this chemical, whatever it is, is mutating those cells as they change. That part works in the same way as radiation causing cancer, but in this case she's discovered that it's disrupting something in sperm, and therefore damaging any embryos created by that sperm. She said it's in many of the recent samples they've analyzed."

Geraldine lets out a sudden breath. "The problem's in sperm, you say? My, my, no wonder there are covert operations going on."

"So, Jason's right," Emma says. "It will affect more of the population before long."

"Who's Jason?" Nick asks. He listens, obviously shocked as they explain what they've uncovered. "Okay," he says, "this makes terrible sense. But I don't get how it can be in the water supply. This is happening right across the country. There are numerous different water authorities. Whether it's malicious or accidental, it's unlikely they would all have been infiltrated."

"I've been thinking about that, too," Emma jumps in, one hand running nervously through her hair. "What if it's bottled water?"

The others stare at her. She can almost see their thoughts whirring.

"So many people are drinking it now, ever since the illegal fracking caused all those problems and the floods contaminated the water supplies up north. Remember the pictures of rotting animals in the reservoirs? And shares in H2OBlue skyrocketing when they began using that new biodegradable packaging? We've even got H2OBlue dispensers all around the hospitals."

No one speaks for a moment, then Geraldine shrugs. "Pure hypothesis until we can test it, but it's a decent theory."

Emma's whole body is trembling. "If something like H2OBlue were contaminated, it would be a nightmare—exactly like the one we're having." She turns to Nick. "Do you really think your sister can fix it?"

"Absolutely," he says fervently. "Rachel's a whiz at this. Her work is cutting edge—her mentors won the Nobel Prize for their research into gene editing, and they use this technique known as 'genetic scissors.' To begin with, Rachel had been collaborating on this with Walcott and her team, and making good progress . . ." He hesitates. "All the Intrapartum X babies go to the NBCC, and they've done lots of autopsies . . . but then Rachel began to notice some anomalies. She was asked to look at a few babies who were very small, whose bodies hadn't been received into the research center in the same way as the others. No hospital of origin listed. Vague parent history. And it was clear they had been tampered with—inside the womb. Someone was already trying to fix the problem by disabling the damaged gene, but it hadn't worked, and they needed her expertise. After that, they wouldn't let her out of the building."

Emma has a sudden thought and her whole body goes cold. "You don't think . . ." She stops, not daring to vocalize it.

Nick's gaze is deeply sympathetic. "Rachel speculates on it, too," he says.

"On what?" Geraldine asks impatiently.

"Whether those small babies belong to missing teenagers," Emma says with a new surge of desperation. She jumps up. "They're inducing them early, to see if their experiments are working—they won't wait until they're full term. Oh God, I have to get Lainey back, fast." She glares around the room at them, wanting them to do something, anything, to speed up finding her daughter.

"According to what Rachel says on here," Nick says, waving the small flash drive, "Walcott didn't want to announce anything to begin with, until they were more certain of a cure, but then she suddenly changed her mind. Rachel said she seemed rattled by the news of the premature babies they'd analyzed, and didn't seem to be thinking clearly. Rach wanted to ensure her research was safe, so she went to a lot of trouble to get me this. Thank God for RGN, as we could pass it from hand to hand between trusted people, although there's still an incredible risk. There's a video of her on here and she's obviously frightened, says she hadn't been allowed out of the NBCC for a fortnight. I tried to get a message to her, gave her a safe address where we could meet, but she never turned up. I would have thought she'd be too valuable to the new government for them to harm her, but who knows."

"So, Mary Walcott was killed because she knew too much?" Emma asks.

"Perhaps she realized there was some sort of covert research plan, perhaps an effort to use the situation for personal gain or a power grab. I think her speech was going to blow the whistle somehow, make it impossible to continue. But the whole thing is bigger than even she could have imagined, and malign forces had other ideas."

"And this is all spearheaded by Whittaker and Hallston," Geraldine chips in. "But why on earth would they put a chemical in the water, knowing it couldn't be targeted and therefore might affect everyone, unless they knew already that they could fix it? Otherwise it's kamikaze. They might only succeed in wiping out the entire population."

"Perhaps it worked in their favor to delay announcing a cure," Emma suggests, her voice low and her eyes dark. "That way they keep everyone terrified for a while, and make them compliant. If they've gone this far, there's probably no depths they wouldn't stoop to."

The group goes quiet.

"I might have another answer to that," Nick says eventually. "Maybe Hallston and Whittaker thought they knew how to fix it, but something's gone wrong. From what Meena's told me, it sounds like this man Hallston has a history of botched experiments."

"Ah," Geraldine says. "You think they overestimated their capabilities, hit a snag . . . and now they need a group of teenagers to experiment on, and your sister to perfect the cure?"

Nick nods at the group. "Yes, but there's no way they could have got this far alone. They'll have ample support from other powerful players who believe that the end goal justifies the means and see entire swathes of the population as expendable. I think it's time for us to make a move—we know too much, and we're all in danger. I can't go home now."

Meena nods. "Sereena and I can be ready quickly."

"I think we should leave before daylight." Nick turns to Emma.

Her head swims. This is moving too fast. It's surreal and terrifying.

Nick senses her panic. "It's okay. Why don't you go home and pack some things. Get a few hours' rest if you can. I'll sleep in my car outside and keep an eye on anyone watching you."

"I know you're right," Emma says. "But I just have this image in my head of Lainey coming home and finding I'm not there . . ." She bites her lip hard to stem her emotions.

"You can't help Lainey while you're being stalked," Geraldine says gently. "You're better off going now."

The words reach her. Lainey's old life has well and truly gone, and so has Emma's. She needs to think strategically, not emotionally, and this is the only available course of action. It's time to take control and step outside of the box she hadn't known she was living in. "All right," she says. "I'm in."

SATURDAY, 3:32 a.m.

Lainey's insomnia is getting worse. Lights on. Off. On. Off again. *It's no good*, she thinks, turning them back on and casting around for something—anything—to distract her.

She should have eaten something, after all.

Then she hears a gentle knocking.

She freezes, heart thumping as she hears the click and beep of the key card at the door.

Dizzy with nerves and fatigue, she jumps out of bed to face her intruder. But it's only Jenny, in polka-dot black-and-white pajamas, her smile a little weary as she comes inside.

"You can't sleep," she says matter-of-factly.

"No," Lainey says. Then, "How did you know?"

"We monitor the room," Jenny admits, seeming uncomfortable. "I know it sounds intrusive, but we need to make sure you're safe and well at all times, so we just check in on you now and again. I promise there are no cameras in the bathrooms," she adds.

"I wondered if you were watching me," Lainey says cautiously, sitting down abruptly on the edge of the bed. Her head is no longer swimming. Cold clarity drips down her spine.

This place really is as bad as she fears.

Jenny's smile is tight. "I brought you a little something to help," she says, setting a plastic box down on the bedside table. When she turns around, Lainey sees she's holding a syringe.

"I don't need that," Lainey snaps. "I just need some food."

"I'm sorry, Lainey," Jenny soothes, like a patient mother reassuring her grizzling child, "but tonight you do. The kitchen is closed until morning, and we need to get you into a good sleeping pattern. Please, think about your baby. You'll be asleep in no time when I give you this, so lie back down."

Lainey doesn't move, but her body tenses, getting ready to protect itself, sending spikes of adrenaline to her muscles, tightening each sinew.

Jenny doesn't appear to notice. She pushes up Lainey's sleeve, running a wet cotton swab over her arm. "Okay, just relax now. Here we go."

No.

The word resounds in Lainey's head, as clear as if someone had shouted it in her ear. There's no time for thought. As the spike of the needle nears Lainey's arm, it's pure instinct that makes her grab Jenny's wrist, twist it, and redirect the syringe hard into Jenny's thigh.

3:39 a.m.

Drifting in and out of sleep, Emma dreams in fragments. Wooden dolls. Baby dolls. A newborn's cry. Maps that never end. A woman's haunted eyes.

Birds dropping from the sky.

3:39 a.m.

Jenny gasps as she stares at the syringe embedded in her leg. "What have you done?" she hisses in outrage, pulling the syringe free and raising her arm toward Lainey.

Lainey jumps up to ward her off, the heel of her hand shooting forward to protect herself. It meets Jenny's nose with a dull crack and Jenny staggers backward with a shriek, blood running over her face as she crumples to the floor.

Everything stops. Just for a moment. Just long enough for Lainey to take in the crazy scene. The bleeding woman on the floor. The open door.

This is a catastrophe.

It's also a chance.

Go.

In an instant she's all adrenaline, muscles on fire and her hand throbbing as she rushes across to tug at Jenny's watch while the older woman clutches her nose, her eyes streaming. By the time Jenny realizes and begins to push her away, the clasp is open, the watch already in Lainey's grasp. Lainey races for the door and pulls it closed, using her hands to balance the weight of it as it latches, to minimize the sound.

It's hushed and dark in the corridor, but she has no way of knowing how long that will last. She sprints down the dim passageway toward the lift, its doors standing open, the interior light beckoning her in. She slams the watch against the electronic pad and hits the buttons, repeatedly hammering the panel to get the doors closed and the lift moving. It takes only seconds to reach the ground floor, but her panic grows with every ragged breath, her heart racing, head spinning.

The doors open to one of the Jennies, standing less than a meter away with a fluffy pile of white towels in her hand. The woman looks up from checking her watch, her pleasant smile dropping into open-mouthed astonishment. Lainey lunges forward, pushing the woman backward hard. The woman staggers, the towels flying upward, unfolding as they drop. She lands with a thump and lets out a short scream. The reception area is dimly lit with soft side lamps, and Lainey hears more footsteps from the floors above as she races to the front doors, only meters away. Spotlights outside show a short stone staircase leading down to a gravel driveway, but when she slams the watch against the electronic pad, nothing happens.

Shit, shit, shit. She clocks the keypad, her heart pounding in her ears, syncopated with the banging of a door, a closer run of footsteps.

"Stop," the Jenny behind her cries, on her feet again now and pursuing Lainey who charges down the nearest corridor. The fire alarm starts to shriek in long, pulsating bursts that make Lainey momentarily put her hands over her ears, and she ducks into the nearest room.

It's the library. She turns back to see the other woman nearing the door, her face red and her hair disheveled.

"Stay away from me," Lainey shrieks with such venom the other woman holds up her hands and stops, as though Lainey is a dangerous animal caught roaming free in a zoo. Lainey glances frantically around, searching for weapons or anything else she might use.

"You don't want to do this, Lainey," the other woman says gently. "It won't end well for you. Just come with—"

Lainey darts forward and slams the heavy wooden door in the Jenny's face, cutting off the end of her sentence. There's a long wooden table by the wall, and Lainey drags it across, only seconds before the handle depresses. She pushes the table farther along and makes sure it's tight against the door, then backs away, watching the handle fly up and down, cheering inwardly when the door doesn't budge.

She races across to the huge sash window and tries to pull it open, but it's painted shut, dried glossy paint long settled into its cracks and crevices. She turns desperately back to the door, but she has zero chance of leaving that way. On the other side, more than one voice is calling her name now. She looks at Jenny's watch, still clutched in her hand. It won't help her anymore. She drops it and grabs a nearby wooden chair. Running at the window, she flings the chair at the wide, low glass pane with all her might, wielding it like a battering ram, the alarm providing cover for the noise. The glass cracks in a maze of divergent lines but doesn't break. She picks the chair up again and does the same thing, one, two more times before the whole thing shatters and cold air rushes in.

She sets the chair down and climbs onto it, stepping gingerly over the remaining shards still skewered into the window to balance on the outer ledge. It's only a short jump down into the rosebushes, but the thorns snare her as she lands, snagging and tearing at her clothes and skin. She dare not move as a car is racing down the gravel driveway, its headlights bouncing, throwing light around in jerky arcs. It brakes hard to stop in front of the house, sending hundreds of tiny stones spinning into the air. From her hidden vantage point, Lainey watches as three men jump out and hurry up the stone steps.

She may only have seconds. This is her chance. She rushes across the narrow gravel path that encircles the house, sprinting toward the thicket of trees. There isn't much moonlight, but she can see enough to make out the distant outline of the woods. At least there will be more places to hide up there while she figures out what to do next. She stumbles and staggers, her burning, throbbing feet further pierced by hidden stones. She's run perhaps a hundred meters when she becomes aware of more strobing lights behind her, and shouting, and she turns to see people with torches are running toward her. A fresh charge of fear gives her a new burst of speed, and soon all is distant and sludgy compared to the pounding and pulsing in her ears. Her lungs are burning, but she won't stop running until she reaches the tree line. The impressions of her footsteps in the dewy wet grass are horribly clear, and the three torchlights are already halfway up the hill and gaining fast. She rushes the last few meters toward the cover of the trees, grateful for the soft, damp cushion of recently fallen leaves, which temporarily soothes the ache in her feet. She inhales the earthy dampness as she aims for the high-walled perimeter of the grounds, winding between the tree trunks. Once she reaches the wall, she realizes it's at least twice her height and impossible to climb. She follows it, searching for a way past, and despairs when she finds no gate, no footholds, no ladder.

The longed-for cool air assails her in harsh slaps of wind that suck the breath from her lungs. The pajamas had been warm enough inside, but they're not meant for outside in late September, and her feet are icy. Already, she can't feel her toes. But this is nothing compared to the terror of going back into the house. If they catch her now, she'll likely be drugged and half asleep for days, if not weeks. She backs against a tree, listening, a cornered animal, breathing heavily, unable to make out any voices yet, but half expecting someone to grab her from behind. There's no choice except to keep going, even though she can see the ninety-degree turn of the wall already. If this is the extent of the grounds, and she follows it around, she'll end up back at the tree line within a few minutes, with nowhere left to run except toward the house.

"Spread out," calls a man's voice, alarmingly close. Flashlight beams begin to cut through a few of the trees not more than fifty feet away.

She scans the landscape, close to tears. And then she sees it. A sprawling oak tree with a tangle of branches skirting close to the wall, and one of them—an ancient bough—about four feet above her, leaning across it.

Climb.

"Lainey!" another voice calls. "Don't be scared. There's nowhere to go from here. Come out so we can talk."

She knows that voice.

The director is here, too.

A fresh rush of panic propels her over to the tree. She's an agile climber, having spent years checking birds' nests on walks near home, but now, as she climbs, the furrowed bark makes each step so agonizing for her wounded feet that she struggles not to cry out from the pain. She uses all the strength in her arms and legs to propel herself higher, as fast as she can. From her vantage point, she can see torchlight sweeping past the base of the tree.

She reaches the branch that abuts the wall and drops to straddle it, using her hands and the backs of her feet to shimmy along. It's only a few feet until she can finally see over to the other side. She scans the length of it, but as far as she can see there are no wires, no spikes. No cameras, either. Nothing to stop her.

No one had expected any of the girls to get this far, she thinks with a shudder.

A long, straight, tarmacked road runs parallel to the outer perimeter, free of cars at this time of night, but wide enough to suggest it could be a regular thoroughfare during the day. Her tread light, she scampers along the top of the wall until she can drop down onto a bench behind a bus stop. The sign doesn't tell her precisely where she is, but her heart lifts when she sees the three curved knives: the symbol of the county of Essex.

It means she's not too far from home.

She steps onto the road, checking left and right, trying to figure out which way to go. It's all too open, too exposed. Hopefully, they won't notice she's climbed the tree for a while and will continue searching the woods, but sooner or later that's bound to change. She needs to put distance between herself and Horcombe House as soon as possible.

She jogs straight across the road into the muddy, barren field on the other side, heading for the back fences of the housing estate that are visible a few hundred feet away. She can follow the fence line semicamouflaged in the darkness. It will feel much safer that way. Once there, she chooses to turn to the right and begins to jog along the periphery of the houses. Fatigue is overtaking her adrenaline now, and as she slows her panic rises. The ground is uneven and the pain in her feet intensifies with every step. The cold sears her eyes and assaults her body, the wind blasting her in cruel surges. Now and then her rustling movements set the local dogs barking, and each time she freezes, expecting an imminent attack as they scrabble at the wooden fencing. She can hear their frenzied panting, sense their desire to set upon her given the chance.

She has no idea how long she stumbles and staggers through the shadows, willing herself on without a clue as to where she's going, but eventually the fence line breaks and she is on a main road, with larger buildings on either side and a row of shops straight ahead. A short distance to her left is a brightly lit petrol station with two trucks and a car parked out front. She hides by the final piece of fencing, working out what she might do. She waits, letting the trucks and the first car go, not keen to approach any unaccompanied men. Finally, another car pulls up towing a shiny black horse trailer, and a middle-aged woman gets out wearing a padded green sleeveless jacket and jeans. Her bobbed hair is tucked behind her ears and graying at the temples. She looks cozy and sensible.

The woman finishes filling the car and scans her watch at the pay point on the pump. Lainey edges closer, standing out of sight of the main concourse, takes a gulp of courage, and calls out, "Excuse me! Excuse me!"

The woman peers warily across to the shadowy patch of bushes, as if hoping Lainey might be calling to someone else nearby.

"Please!" Lainey calls, her voice hoarse. Begging. It seems to convince the woman to venture closer, and Lainey steps a few paces farther out from the safety of the bushes.

"I've just run away from my boyfriend—he attacked me and I escaped," Lainey explains, hugging herself in the cold, scanning the area as though she's expecting him to reappear at any moment. "I need to get out of here fast—please, can you give me a lift?"

The woman stops, obviously alarmed. "You need to call the police, love."

"I tried that last time," Lainey says, shivering. "They didn't believe me, and he came after me. Please. I just need to get home. I'm . . . I'm pregnant."

The woman frowns. "Where do you live?"

"Whitehaven."

"I'm not going near there, I'm sorry."

"Okay." Lainey stifles a sob, stepping backward into the bushes, shaking with nerves and disappointment. She watches the woman hurry to her car, wondering how many times she'll have to do this and how long she can stay hidden.

Suddenly, the same car pulls up beside the bushes. The woman is leaning over, holding the passenger door open. "It's an hour out of my way, you know, and not much fun for the horse, but I can't just leave you here, can I? Hop in, then," she says. "Come on, love. Let's get you home."

"Thank you so much," Lainey replies, close to tears, climbing in and shuffling down in the seat so she can't be seen through the windows.

"You look a bit of a mess, my lovely. What's your name?" the woman asks, beginning to drive.

Lainey doesn't reply.

"It's okay. You don't have to tell me." The woman surveys the empty road then turns back to her. "You're really frightened, aren't you?" she asks gently.

Lainey nods. She'd thought she'd feel better as she got farther away, but she's only becoming more desperate. How long can she run for with no money? And if she's caught, what will happen to her when she's sent back?

The woman is still studying her. "You've nothing with you—not even your watch?" The question is curious rather than suspicious.

"I had to run—I didn't have a chance to put it on." In reality, she'd had nothing to grab, although she regrets leaving the little sonogram photograph. In the rush, she hadn't had time to snatch it, but now it's like she's left something of herself behind in that weird, horrible place. She doesn't want them having any part of her, ever again.

"Well, I'm Tessa," the woman says, cutting across her thoughts. "And that's Barnaby back there. I'm taking him to Chelmsford, returning him to his owner. He's been doing some rehab therapy with me."

"I work for a vet on Saturdays," Lainey murmurs.

"Do you now?" The woman smiles. "Another animal lover, then." Tessa begins to talk about caring for injured horses, and Lainey lets the words drift over her, appreciating the woman's efforts to help her feel comfortable. It's nice listening to someone talk about regular things. It gives her hope that other lives are still going on as normal; that not everyone's world has been turned upside down.

Her eyes keep closing as she tries to relax, and she drifts in and out of consciousness. Tessa stops talking and they drive farther into the night.

"Hello? What's this?" Tessa says suddenly, loud enough to make Lainey jump back to high alert.

A road sign flashes by telling them it's only twenty-four miles to Whitehaven, but as Lainey peers through the windscreen she sees a police car on the side of the road, lights still flashing. All the vehicles heading in the same direction are being pulled over, and there's a small line of trucks and cars. Instinctively, Lainey slides down in her seat until she's almost sitting on the floor, trembling convulsively. Could this be about her? Could they be searching for her so hard they'll set up checkpoints to find her? If so, there's no way she'll get home.

"Is this for you?" Tessa asks, gauging her reaction.

"Possibly," Lainey murmurs.

"You didn't run away from your boyfriend, did you?" Tessa persists, her tone neutral.

Lainey turns to her. "Have you heard of PreacherGirl?"

Tessa's brow furrows. "Yes, my daughter was telling me about that."

"I'm one of the girls she was singing about."

Tessa's eyes go wide a few seconds later, and Lainey knows she's worked it out. "You'll have to get out," she says, and Lainey recoils. Can she really know about PreacherGirl and hand Lainey over to them without a conscience? But then Tessa adds, "There's a door at the side of the horse trailer; it's latched but not locked. Slip in and get as low as you can. Barnaby is a sweet thing. He won't hurt you, not if you're gentle with him. Leave the rest to me." She pauses to edge forward in the line and stay close to the car in front, then hisses, "Go now, or you won't have a chance."

Lainey doesn't need to be told again. She opens the car door as quietly as she can, every noise feeling horribly loud. She keeps low, glad it's so dark here and there are no cars behind them. The large supermarket truck in front shields her from view as she runs to the horse trailer on tiptoes, her sore feet making her wince, and gently squeezes the latch of the side door.

There's rustling inside the box, and as she opens the door, the only thing she sees clearly are the whites of the horse's eyes. It looks as frightened as she feels. "Shh," she whispers, pulling the door closed just as the vehicle begins to slowly move forward. She slips in front of the horse, feeling its warm, dank breath on her face, praying it's as friendly as Tessa had said, and slides onto the floor beneath the hay feeder. Pulling the hay down in front of her, she huddles in the corner as the horse eyes her warily.

All she can do now is wait.

5:00 a.m.

A nightmare wakes Emma with a start, her galloping heartbeat thundering in her ears. As she comes to, the sound morphs into a hammering on her front door.

She jumps out of bed and sprints downstairs. Fergus is already there, growling, and Geraldine emerges from the lounge room bleary-eyed, having chosen to sleep on the sofa rather than take Lainey's empty bed.

"Don't open it," she hisses.

"Who is it?" Emma calls through the frosted glass.

"Police, ma'am."

"Could you show me your ID through the letterbox, please?"

A badge is poked through the narrow slot. She takes it and passes it to Geraldine, who shrugs. "Could be fake. How would we know?"

"If you don't let us in, we're legally entitled to force entry," the policeman calls.

It doesn't feel like there's much choice. Emma shuts Fergus in the lounge and opens the door, relieved she's not alone as she pulls her dressing gown tight around herself. Two men in gray suits stand on the front step.

"I'm Detective Stevens," the shorter of the two informs them, coming inside without being invited, his cheeks wobbling as he talks. His eyes are wide-set, and his wavy hair appears greasy at the roots and sticks out in bushy black tufts. "And this is Detective Omenuko." The tall, dark, sallow-faced man behind him nods. "We have reason to believe you may be harboring a person who has been detained under provision five of the Act for the Protection of Human Life." As he speaks, the taller man walks straight into the house and jogs upstairs.

"I have no idea what you're talking about." Emma glances from the policeman to Geraldine, trying to figure out what's going on. She hears the other man opening doors above them. "And you can't just . . . Don't you need a warrant?"

"Not if we think you're harboring a fugitive. This will only take a minute," the detective says, remaining by the door as though blocking their escape. "Please stay calm."

"Yes, relax, Emma, it's only a few basic human rights violations," Geraldine mutters. "Nothing alarming at all."

The man raises his eyebrows balefully. "If there's no one here, then you've nothing to worry about, have you?"

They all hover by the door while the second detective thoroughly investigates all the rooms in the house, checking behind furniture and opening cupboards.

"Can you unlock your back door for us, please?" he asks Emma, avoiding her eyes.

She follows him to the kitchen and does as he asks, holding on to Fergus to keep him calm. The man shines a torch around the garden and opens the shed, then pushes past her as though she's invisible. She hears him saying, "Nothing" to his colleague.

"Whom or what are you looking for, may we ask?" Geraldine queries in a particularly acerbic tone.

"If your daughter comes here or contacts you," the first man says to Emma, ignoring Geraldine, "you must call us straightaway. Here's my number." He hands her a card. "We'll be closely monitoring your movements. Do you understand?"

Emma is too stunned to speak. She nods.

The policeman suddenly says into his watch, "You can come in now, sir," and the two men head for the door.

"Who's coming?" Geraldine asks in confusion.

Emma doesn't have time to respond because the two men ahead of them move to either side of the door, revealing a tall, white-haired man in a dark-gray suit.

"Oh, Jesus," Geraldine says under her breath.

"Geraldine Fox, I presume?" Grant Whittaker offers her a curt nod. "It's good to meet you, but I'm afraid I have to ask you to wait here with these officers for a moment." He turns his eyes to Emma. "I need to speak to you alone."

5:05 a.m.

The smell of dung and hay is overpowering, and Lainey gags into her hand. It's hard to contain herself as the car inches forward, when everything inside her is telling her to move, to run. But she knows from the lights and engine noises that other cars have pulled up behind them now. Her only hope of concealment is staying still.

Eventually, there's a longer pause, voices close by, and a car door slams.

"The horse is skittish and prone to kicking," the woman says, sounding irritated. Lainey can hear that she's leading the officer down the opposite side of the horse trailer, keeping him away from the side door.

"Be careful." Tessa's voice is ahead of Lainey now, coming through the small gap above the rear doors. "Don't shine that light in his eyes, please, or he'll go nuts."

Lainey doesn't breathe. She's a statue, frozen with her knees pulled up to her chest and her head pressed into her thighs, making herself as small as possible. The horse shifts from foot to foot.

The trailer shakes and drops a little, as if the policeman has found a foothold, and then a beam of light flashes into the box over the top of the opening. The horse whinnies. Immediately, the light disappears.

"He's tired and grumpy," Tessa says. "Just like me," she adds with a snort of laughter. "I'm doing his owner such a favor delivering him. Especially at this hour. Normally, I make people come to my place."

Lainey's shoulders release a little. Tessa appears to be a pro at this.

"All right, then," the policeman says, his tone friendly. "Thanks for stopping. You can go."

Moments later, the trailer begins to move. Lainey hangs on to the bottom of the hay feeder as best she can to stop rolling around as the horse shifts from foot to foot, its eyes never leaving her. She wishes she could leap up and hug it, but instead mouths a silent thank-you as they speed through the night without stopping.

Lainey hopes Tessa is still heading to Whitehaven. It's hard to trust, to rely on the kindness of a stranger and not try to escape again from here. But what would she do: leap out and hitch another lift? Besides, her feet sting and ache and are streaked with blood, and she's bone tired. She has to believe that Tessa will keep her word.

She leans her head against the rattling metal and closes her eyes.

5:10 a.m.

Once the door is closed behind them, Whittaker surveys the small lounge with apparent distaste. Emma waits.

"Your daughter is keeping everyone busy this morning," he says, turning his steely eyes to hers.

"Is she?"

"You haven't heard from her?"

"No."

Whittaker smiles balefully. "I wonder if you'd tell me if you had."

She doesn't move a muscle, giving him nothing.

"I'd forgotten that Geraldine Fox is your mother," he says. "I heard the story a long time ago—that she left you behind."

Emma's aware of the dig. "It didn't look like you recognized me, either, at the hospital," she says.

"It wasn't the time for pleasantries. We were on a tight schedule."

"So why are you here now?"

He raises his eyebrows. "I'm doing you a courtesy. As a constituent of my hometown, whose child has grown up alongside my boy, I'm making you an offer." He interlinks his fingers in front of him. "And I sincerely hope you'll take it."

"What's the offer?"

"When we find Lainey," he continues calmly, "we will take you both to a secure location, where we can take care of Lainey for the remainder of her pregnancy. Since she obviously doesn't like being with her peers, she can stay with you, instead. In return, you will work for us and help us with all the women taking part in therapeutic trials."

Emma balks, realizing what he's suggesting. *I'm to buy Lainey her freedom by becoming complicit.*

"And by us, you mean . . . the government?"

"Of course."

"Are you in charge now, Grant?"

He laughs. "Are you after a scoop to share with your journalist friend? I suppose you want to know if I killed Mary, too?"

Emma's chest burns as it finally hits her. Despite the mounting evidence, the increasing markers of a terrible conspiracy, up to this point it had felt like something she might get out of or wake up from. But Whittaker's flat, robotic eyes are like tiny pins boring holes into every part of her. Of course, they have been watching her. Of course, they know everything. They've just been biding their time until they were forced to play their hand.

"*Did* you kill the prime minister?"

He lets out a low bark of laughter. "Well, let's just say, if Mary wasn't safe, with her vast security detail and her network of spies, then I doubt anyone is."

"I won't agree to anything until I've seen Lainey," she says.

Whittaker shrugs. "The police will wait outside, watching the house. We want you to gather your essential belongings, and Lainey's, ready to go. You have one hour."

"You seem very certain she'll head back here?"

"She's seventeen and pregnant, with no extended family nearby . . . I think the chances are high, but of course we're looking for her elsewhere as well."

"And if we don't want to come with you?"

"Then you'll be arrested, and Lainey will go straight to one of our more secure facilities for expectant mothers."

"Sounds like an offer I can't refuse, then," Emma says steadily.

He nods. "I'm glad you think so." He turns to go. "You are not to leave the house, Emma. When Lainey comes, we're arresting her—where we take her is up to you."

She understands completely. This vile man thinks he has complete control of her. "I'm sorry I didn't offer you a drink," she says as he puts his hand on the door handle. "But I've only got H2OBlue."

Whittaker turns around slowly, a cold smile pushing its way up against his thin, hollow cheeks. He holds her gaze for a long moment, as though that alone might break her.

She knows it's a huge risk to provoke him, but she has to know the truth. Emma straightens her back and waits, the pounding in her ears coupled with a breathless realization that she cannot unsay the words. Whatever she's started cannot be stopped. She's half expecting him to lunge at her, but he just growls through gritted teeth, "I don't know what you think you know, but I am too *busy* cleaning up everybody's *mess* to spend time discussing it with you."

She frowns. "You didn't start this?"

He scoffs and glances briefly at the ceiling. "Only a madman would do this."

"And your friend Hallston," she says evenly. "Is he a madman?"

This time Grant's face drops into shock. "How the hell do you know Hallston?" he asks, his shoulders slumping as he sways slightly, his hand squeezing the door handle, his knuckles white.

"A lot of people know about him," Emma says, trying to keep her voice steady. "His name is being whispered in large circles of influential people even as we speak. You should think about that when you decide how well you're going to treat me and my daughter."

For a brief moment, Grant's eyes betray a mix of incredulity and alarm. Then his brows crease, his eyes close, and when he opens them it's to glare at Emma with such vehemence that she inadvertently takes a small step back, closer to the wall.

"Get yourself ready," he snarls at her. "I'd have you arrested right now if we weren't waiting for your daughter. As soon as Lainey's here, the two of you will be leaving."

He storms into the corridor and yanks open the front door, the policemen hurrying behind him. As soon as the door slams closed, Geraldine rushes over and grabs Emma by the arms. "She's escaped," she says, bouncing up and down. "I knew she could do it! But why the hell did Grant Whittaker come here? No offense, but surely you're not that important to him?"

"I don't know," Emma says uneasily, "but perhaps Lainey's escape threatens the project, and he thinks his personal powers of persuasion will make sure we cooperate. He wants to bribe me—if I help deliver babies, they'll keep Lainey and me together when they find her. If not, I'll be arrested and God knows where she'll end up. But I mentioned H2OBlue and Hallston, and you should have seen his face."

"You did what?!" Geraldine is horrified. "Emma, you're insane. I'm surprised he hasn't set this place on fire already."

"They're watching me—and I have to be ready to go with them in an hour." Emma looks desperately at Geraldine. "And I can't go with Nick and Meena now, can I? Not when Lainey might be making her way home. I can't let her face these monsters on her own."

5:25 a.m.
The vehicle comes to a stop for a long time, and Lainey braces herself until

the side door opens a crack and Tessa appears, her face pale. "Are you okay in there? I'm sorry, I didn't dare pull over any sooner. We're on the back roads now, only twenty miles to Whitehaven. Do you want to sit up front again?"

Lainey begins to move forward toward the door, then stops. "Maybe not," she says. "They'll probably be hunting for me in town, too." She hesitates. "I don't think you should drop me at home." Her mind works frantically, circling endlessly through different ideas, but nothing seems safe. Her panic is mounting.

"So, where should I take you?" Tessa asks. "I'm sorry, love, but I can't be too long with the horse. And what about your mum and dad? They'll want to know you're safe."

Lainey stalls. There's nothing she wants more than to go home, but it's the first place the police will look for her.

The woman misreads her reluctance. "Do you have kind people to help you?"

Lainey turns to her. "Yes." The faces of those she loves swirl through her mind, and she sits up, a fresh idea reinvigorating her. "May I use your phone?"

"Of course." Tessa pulls it from her pocket and hands it over.

"Can I use your Messenger? I don't know numbers off by heart, but there's a friend on there who might help."

"Sure."

It takes two seconds to find Sereena and start a message. Lainey begins to type, then stops. She doesn't know this woman at all. She has no idea what she might do or whom she'll talk to once Lainey's gone. And the phones will be monitored.

She stalls, on the verge of giving up. This is impossible.

Then she remembers the stupid code they'd joked about at school the other day. She pulls up the drawing pad on Messenger and gets busy sketching a series of dots and lines. She's aware of Tessa watching curiously but angles the phone away so she can't see, feeling guilty when Tessa is going so far out of her way to help.

She presses Send, hoping it's clear enough. Sereena and Lainey have always had a sixth sense with each other, and she's never needed it more. *Please check your messages*, she prays, handing the phone back, knowing Sereena will respond to Messenger's notification—she always does, no matter what the time is. *And please know what I need you to do.*

"If you drop me off about a hundred feet past the gas station on Redhill Road, I can make my way from there," she tells Tessa. "Here," she says, tapping on the map, "I can show you."

They study the map together for a few moments, then Tessa nods. "Okay, hold on tight for another twenty minutes."

She closes the door, and Lainey settles uncomfortably, trying to ignore the aches in her legs and back from sitting on the hard floor. The horse's head moves toward her, and she reaches a hand up, letting its black nostrils blow warm air onto her fingers. Once they begin to move again, the horse turns away.

Lainey holds on tight, glad she has a plan. But the closer she gets to home, the more unbearable it is to think about getting caught.

5:40 a.m.

"We won't let this happen," Geraldine repeats as she follows Emma around the house. "I've sent word to Meena via a friend. We'll think of something."

"Either way," Emma says, feeling sick, "I need to pack." She goes to the window and pulls the curtain back a little, searching for Nick, wondering if he'd witnessed Grant's visit. He'd said he'd be out there, but it's impossible to tell if he's in one of the shadowy vehicles. She lingers, hoping for a sign, but nothing moves.

She turns around in despair. "Take my house key to Cathy. Hopefully, she can take care of stuff here. And beg her to take Fergus in." She pauses while Fergus sniffs at her heels, sensing something is happening. She can hardly look at him. "I'm trying to think of what else we'll need." She's already packed underwear, a spare T-shirt, a change of clothes for Lainey, toothbrushes and deodorant, and an old doppler machine she still has from when she'd attended home births. "I can't believe this is really happening."

"I know," Geraldine says, pushing the matryoshka dolls into the bag.

Emma frowns. "Seriously? They're not very practical."

"You can't leave family heirlooms behind! You'll thank me when they're worth a mint."

Emma raises her eyebrows but keeps the dolls anyway. Her breath catches as she checks the clock. Only twenty-five minutes until Grant's deadline. She pictures herself going down the path and getting into that unmarked car. Trusting them to drive her away and reunite her with Lainey. The thought is intolerable, but there's no other choice.

5:55 a.m.

"Thank you, you've been very kind," Lainey says as Tessa helps her out of the trailer.

"You're welcome," Tessa answers with a concerned smile. "Please be safe, okay?" She peers uncertainly around them, unable to see anything as it's still pitch black. "Are you sure you want me to drop you here, in the dark?"

There's only the long, empty road stretching away from them, and a ragged wire fence running next to the narrow pavement.

"It's okay. The town's just over the hill, and I know somewhere safe nearby. My friends will come for me."

"Well, if you're certain. I don't like leaving you in the middle of nowhere. It seems wrong."

"You've been great—thank you. Please don't worry—you need to get going with Barnaby," she gently reminds Tessa.

"All right, then, love. Good luck." Tessa squeezes Lainey's hand and walks back to the car.

Lainey hovers at the side of the road, not wanting to move until Tessa has driven away. The woman is obviously still in two minds as it takes her a while to get going, but once the vehicle and its horse trailer have become two distant dots of red brake lights, Lainey hurries toward the hidden gap in the fence.

6:00 a.m.
Sereena's heard from Lainey.

295

Emma stares in shock at Meena, who's turned up unannounced, handing her the note and hurrying inside. She's not even dressed properly, her hair unbrushed and her navy silk pajamas peeping out from underneath her long padded coat.

"What?" Emma hisses, grabbing Meena's arm, her heart in her mouth. "How?" She notices Meena is holding her watch. "You know they're outside. We've had police here already searching for Lainey. Grant Whittaker came here and tried to coerce me, to make sure we're both compliant when they find her."

"I know, I got Geraldine's message and I saw the police outside. Nick warned me too." Meena holds up the jammer and sets it on the table, gesturing for Emma and Geraldine to come closer. "Lainey sent a message, written in code—something the girls used to do at school, apparently."

Geraldine jumps up from the kitchen table, squeezing her fist in celebration, hissing, "Yes."

"It was two words: *Dylan* and *phoenix*. Does that make any sense to you?"

Emma frowns. "No."

"Sereena didn't know either. She called Dylan and woke him but didn't want to ask him on the phone. She went to see him and sent me confirmation that he knows. He knows where to go. Now, Emma, are you ready? Because as soon as I give the word, things are going to move fast. And"—Meena pauses and swallows hard—"you may not be able to come back here for quite some time. Lainey's probably seen way too much now for them to leave her alone."

The weight of Meena's stare settles into Emma's bones. "I know. That much was obvious from my chat with Grant." There's such an inevitability to this moment that it's a relief to finally reach it. "I'm ready," she says with conviction. "Just tell me what you want me to do." She looks desperately at Geraldine. "But what about you? Are you coming?"

"No," Geraldine says, "I'll stay here."

"Is that safe?"

"Let me worry about that," Geraldine replies. She turns to Meena. "We're almost out of time, aren't we?"

Meena nods. "Ready?"

"Okay," Emma says.

Meena types something into her watch. "All right, then. No going back now."

6:03 a.m.

It's like she's completing a strange circle of sorts, Lainey thinks, picking her way across the last of the long grass. Her progress has felt agonizingly slow, the pain in her feet excruciating. It's ironic to think that if she hadn't come here with Dylan the last time, she wouldn't be in this mess now.

Light is just beginning to wash away the darkness, but much of the landscape is still heavily shadowed. Every step forward is a leap of faith, with no way of knowing what might be hidden in the grass. She slowly succumbs to the cold again, unable to see the bridge until she's almost upon it. The large yellow eye of the phoenix warily watches her approach, its colors muted by the half-dawn, the rocks formless underneath it in the dim light. She walks toward its wings, spread wide and waiting, as though offering her protection.

Edging her way over the piles of rocks, she sits down inside the brick tunnel, her back against the damp, cold curve of it, and stares at the brickwork opposite, its tapestry of mildew and mold becoming more visible by the minute as sunlight creeps along the walls.

The narrow tracks still run through the tunnel, but the sleepers are now barely discernible, buried under the dirt. She sits near the rusted rails and contemplates the overcast dawn, the colorless sky. She's so cold. Sleepy too.

Once upon a time, trains had gone through here on the way to the old Whitehaven station. As fresh high-schoolers, they'd studied pictures of men in tweed jackets standing by a train emerging from the blackness, and then marched down here to find historical evidence and log it in their journals. Sereena had been in that class, and Dylan, too—though she'd hardly spoken to him back then. She and Sereena had picked daisies and dandelions and Mr. Gowan had told them off for splashing in puddles and getting their clothes wet.

It seems like another life now. A storybook memory.

Her mind is beginning to drift when there's an unexpected flurry of swift movements in her belly, like the flutter of tiny wings. A stirring.

"Was that you?" she asks, patting her stomach.

No response.

Lainey closes her eyes.

6:04 a.m.

Meena's tone becomes urgent. "Give Geraldine your watch, grab your bag, and I need to take Fergus."

"Why are you taking Fergus?"

"No time to explain now, Emma," Meena says. "Just trust me." She scoops up the surprised spaniel. "Stay behind the front door. Keep it unlocked. We'll get you, very shortly." And she's gone, hurrying away with a startled Fergus in her arms.

"Quickly, Emma, your watch," Geraldine hisses, and Emma fumbles with the clasp. Geraldine bundles her toward the front door, and they wait for what seems like an eternity. Emma is desperate to turn around and take one more look back at the house, but she knows it will only cause her more anguish.

"Someone will keep the home fires burning," Geraldine says, reading her thoughts. "I'll make sure."

"Thanks." Emma bites back tears. "If you speak to Cathy, tell her I'm sorry I didn't get a chance to say goodbye." She pushes the jammer into Geraldine's hand. "You'll need this. I hope there's a plan for you—I don't want to have to come and bail you out or mount a rescue."

"Don't worry, I'll be over the back fence before you can say 'dirty feminist'," Geraldine replies. Even now, she can make Emma smile.

"I don't know what we'd have done without you these past few days." Emma's voice cracks. "You've been wonderful."

Geraldine raises an eyebrow. "You sound . . . surprised."

Emma smiles. "I'm not really. You are Geraldine Fox, after all."

Geraldine laughs. "Not to you I'm not." She brushes Emma's cheek with the back of her fingers. "To you, I'm a little bit more, whether you like it or not."

The moment lasts only seconds before an almighty explosion sends them both diving for the floor. The front door bursts open, slamming against the wall, and Nick is yelling into her face. "Come on. NOW!" He pulls her up and half walks, half drags her down the path, and she only has moments to see the vehicle on fire opposite the house, the pall of smoke around it, the neighbors running into the road. Nick pushes her through the open rear door of a small white car, Meena at the wheel, and it's already moving as he leaps in beside her. Looking back, Emma sees Geraldine slip out of the front door, walking swiftly away down the road. *Go faster*, she implores her mother, scared someone will grab her, but moments later, Geraldine is out of sight.

6:05 a.m.

"Lainey! Lainey!"

Lainey opens her eyes. Sereena's face is inches from hers. There are hands on her shoulders, gently pulling her back to consciousness.

"God, Lainey, what the fuck's happened? No, don't tell me now, we have to get you somewhere safe." Sereena turns and says to someone behind her, "Come on, help me get her up."

As Sereena moves back, Lainey squints and sees Dylan. He doesn't speak, just stares, petrified.

"For fuck's sake, Dylan, let's go," Sereena snaps at him, trying to put Lainey's arm over her shoulder and pull her up. Lainey cries out in pain as soon as she tries to stand.

"Stop, Sereena! Look at her feet." Dylan moves to crouch beside her legs.

Lainey stares down at her feet. She can barely feel them. They are a grayish-blue color, streaked with dirt and blood.

"She can't walk like this." Dylan takes off his scarf and winds it gently around the bottom of her legs like a bandage.

"I walked quite a lot to get here, thank you very much!" Lainey objects, her voice croaky.

Sereena raises her eyebrows. "Well, if she's still snappy even in this state, then she'll be fine." She leans closer. "But I think we'll try to carry you anyway."

"Thanks for coming," Lainey says to them, her eyes stinging and blurry with fatigue and relief. "I was praying you'd see the message."

"'Course I saw it," Sereena says mock-indignantly, although Lainey can sense their worry in the way they move cautiously around her. "But you need to learn how to spell *phoenix* when you're writing in code."

Lainey tries to laugh, but then a sobering thought occurs to her. "You didn't wear your watches here, did you?"

"If you think we're that stupid," Serena answers, "you don't know me at all." She squats down in front of Lainey. "But we still need to move now, okay?"

Lainey nods, but she can hardly keep her eyes open, let alone stand. Her attention keeps wandering away from them.

"Sereena," she hears Dylan whisper. "She's delirious."

"Come on, then." Sereena sounds staunch and determined. "We just need to carry her up the hill. What about a chair lift? She can sit on our hands."

They move to either side of her and help her up, as Lainey clings tight with her arms around their shoulders. "Jeez, you're heavy, Lainey. We might have to do this in stages," Sereena huffs as they stagger away from the tunnel.

"Where are we going?" Lainey asks, her head dropping forward as she half passes out then comes around again seconds later, their movements jolting her.

"Mum has a plan," Sereena whispers. "She can get you somewhere safe. When we get to the top of the hill, a car will meet us. Come on."

They stagger and stumble up the slope, losing the chair lift grip so often, they end up almost dragging Lainey to the fence.

"Let me go first," Sereena says, and goes over the crest of the hill, out of sight.

For a moment it's just Lainey and Dylan, his arm around her, his warm breath on her neck. "I'm so sorry, Lainey," he says, his voice breaking. She can hear how much he's hurting. He stares into the distance, toward the place Sereena disappeared. "We'll have to paint that mural somewhere else, I reckon. Another time."

"Another time," she echoes.

300

Sereena reappears, hurrying back to them. "The car's coming. Come on."

"Let me know how you are, won't you," Dylan adds hastily. "If you can."

Lainey hobbles onto the road, supported by her friends on either side of her. The daylight means they are horribly exposed now, and she shudders, glancing wildly around them, her body instantly back in fight or flight as a car appears in the distance, headlights shimmering. They watch it draw closer, until it pulls up beside the trio and Sereena tugs Lainey forward.

"Hurry up," yells a voice from inside. "Get in."

Sereena helps Lainey onto the passenger seat. "Slide over, quickly."

"You're coming with me?" Lainey asks.

"Can't get rid of me that easily," Sereena says, slamming the door behind her. But now Lainey notices the fear in her friend's eyes. And she only has time for one last look at Dylan's ashen face, his arm raised in farewell as the car starts to move.

She puts her hands against the glass, and from nowhere, an enormous sob bubbles out of her. Sereena grabs her and holds her tight, and Lainey feels her friend shaking, too.

"It's all right, Lainey," a strong, steady voice says from the front as the car picks up speed. "My name's Kelli. I'm a friend of Meena's. You're both safe now."

You're safe now.

Lainey shivers, having heard that phrase so many times in the past forty-eight hours. But this woman knows Meena. And Sereena is here beside her. This time it might just be true.

6:10 a.m.

Inside the car, no one speaks. Emma is still absorbing the shock of their sudden escape. She clings tightly to Fergus, who had scrabbled over the central console from the front passenger seat as soon as he saw her, jumping onto Emma and licking her face.

"You didn't blow up those policemen, did you?" she asks eventually as the car races along a deserted suburban street.

"No," Nick says, "I primed another car in front of theirs. Hopefully, it distracted them for long enough. Besides, I made sure they had a flat tire." He turns to check out the back again. "There's no one following."

Emma stares at Nick. "Wasn't that a risky move, drawing so much attention?"

Nick shrugs. "We needed a diversion and it had to be fast. This is an old hire car, the plates are fake, and it's a watch-free zone. They can't track us while we're in here."

Meena's phone chimes, and her eyes move to it. "Oh, thank God, Kelli has Lainey and Sereena. They're on the move."

Emma grabs the seat rest in front of her, pulling herself forward, trying to see Meena's face. "Are they okay?"

"Yes, but there are no details. We'll be at the safe house in a couple of hours. They won't be far ahead of us."

Emma has been too lost in thoughts of Lainey to realize how much Meena has had a stake, but now she thinks of Meena's beautiful house and everything she's had to leave behind. "I'm so sorry, Meena."

Meena sighs. "Believe me, it's not your fault—I've been skating on thin ice for a while, investigating things I shouldn't. This new government will be after me soon enough, and Sereena's too feisty to stay out of trouble. We've all picked our side—we're the rebellion now."

Emma tries to take it all in and gives Fergus a grateful hug. "Thanks for getting Fergus out."

Meena snorts. "Lainey would kill us if we'd left Fergus! He was a useful decoy. It looked like I was collecting him from you so you could go with the police. Besides, we could do with a guard dog."

Emma smiles. "Well, don't expect too much. He'll bark, but he's more likely to lick and beg than he is to bite."

"Barking will do. And it'll be good for Lainey. I know she dotes on him."

They're leaving Whitehaven now, the rows of houses giving way to fields on either side. Emma gazes out the window as they speed along, not really seeing anything, aware of Nick sitting silently beside her. She turns to him. "So you're leaving town, too? Are you coming to the safe house with us?"

He turns and she sees how pale and tired he is. "I can't," he says. "Meena will drop me when we're far enough away from town and I'll make my own way back. I still need to find out what's happened to Rachel."

"I'm so sorry," Emma says, briefly touching his arm.

His tired green eyes meet hers. "I did some brief research on H2OBlue while I was holed up in the car outside your house."

She swallows, her throat suddenly dry. "And . . . ?"

"They used to issue regular press releases, but the last one was at the start of the year. No recent updates from the board of directors. Their AGM delayed. In other words, they've gone very quiet."

She closes her eyes briefly as she sighs. "I wish it were all over."

Nick looks away for a moment, then pulls a small object out of his pocket. "It's never been over. Last night, I compared an old photo of the board members with those on the Protec board. Four of the seven at H2OBlue were also at Protec, including Darius Hallston. This whole thing goes way back." He passes her the flash drive, his fingers lingering on hers as she takes it. "I've added everything I found on here. Keep it safe— and as soon as you can, share it with the world."

6:20 a.m.

"Lainey," Kelli says from the front. "We're up against time here. Can you talk me through what's happened, where you were, anything you remember? I'm sorry to ask you to relive it so soon, but time is precious if we're going to find the other girls."

"Isn't it dangerous to talk?"

"No. We're a watch-free vehicle." Kelly flashes her bare wrist. "We have friends in law enforcement who are on our side, but they need details if we're going to move on this. Do you have any idea where you were?"

Lainey swallows. "It was called Horcombe House."

"And how many other girls were there?"

"Twelve," Lainey says, "including Ellis," she adds, with a glance at Sereena. "We were well looked after, but there were lots of medical tests, and I think they were drugging us, too."

Sereena squeezes Lainey's hand as Kelli reaches for her phone. Lainey watches Kelli's fingers sliding over the screen as she drives, her attention shifting between that and the road.

Lainey's eyes are stinging. The headrest is uncomfortable, and she leans toward Sereena, drifting into a strange wakeful dream of shadowy figures chasing her and dogs snapping at her heels, until Sereena jerks forward, her voice high.

"Kelli? What's happening?"

Lainey's eyes snap open. Sereena is staring out of the front window at a police car, so close they're almost tailgating it. Lainey turns to see another marked car close behind them, too.

"Relax, Sereena," Kelli says steadily. "It's okay."

"What's going on?" Lainey stammers, her mind swimming with dreadful possibilities.

"It's okay," Kelli repeats. "They're on our side."

"What do you mean?" Lainey's voice is shrill in her ears. "Why are they here?" Even though there's nothing in her stomach, she's suddenly sweating and nauseous. "You're taking me back, aren't you . . . you're taking me back!"

"Lainey, the police—"

"The police took me there last time," Lainey yells, pulling at the door handle, which does nothing.

Kelli looks anxiously at her. "Please stay calm, Lainey. I'm sorry, but time is of the essence and I've called people I trust. More are waiting for us. But they need us to go to Horcombe with them right now if we have any hope of rescuing the others. If we delay, they'll disappear again."

There's a strange noise inside the car, a keening, wailing sound that Lainey doesn't realize is coming from her until Sereena puts an arm around her.

"Lainey," Kelli's voice is soft. "I'm sorry, but you're the only one who can ID this place. As soon as it's done, we'll go to the safe house."

"Kelli," Sereena sounds shocked and scared. "She's hurt. Her feet . . ."

"I know what we're asking of her," Kelli says in a low voice. "I wish there were another way."

Sereena sits forward. "Does my mum know about this?"

There's a pause. "No, she doesn't," Kelli says. "I'll explain when we reach the safe house and I think she'll understand. Sometimes you have to ask for forgiveness rather than permission."

Lainey frowns. She's heard that somewhere before, but she can't think because Sereena's voice is high-pitched now. "Kelli, this isn't right. You're kidnapping us. Let us out." She pulls repeatedly, desperately at the door handle, then bangs her fist on the window in panic.

"Sereena!" Kelli's abrupt shout stops Sereena in her tracks. The car veers toward a streetlight and Kelli hastily rights it. "Listen to me. Your mum thinks I've been working for her these past few years, but I was tasked to protect her."

"What? By who?"

"By Mary Walcott." Kelli sighs. "Your mum's a key figure in the Network and could make the difference in any trial. All this," she says, gesturing abstractly out the door to the fields beyond them, "it hasn't happened overnight. Walcott saw the creeping dangers long ago . . . she even knew what might happen to her. She was aware of her limitations as leader of the country; the different ways her hands were tied, the darker forces surrounding her, always watching from the shadows, biding their time."

"What's the Network?" Lainey frowns, staring out the window as the dawn turns to day, wondering if anyone is out there, watching.

"A group of people with influence who want to help," Kelli answers. "And who still believe in universal human rights. There are things the Network can do that the prime minister couldn't. Sometimes being a figurehead is a precarious type of power, but Walcott was smart. She saw the dangers and was aware she couldn't always play by the rules. She knew who her supporters were, and that her actions couldn't always align with her words if she wanted to protect people."

"So, she knew all about the Network, then?" Sereena asks.

"She didn't just know about it," Kelli says, her eyes fixed on the road. "She started it."

6:30 a.m.

Nick taps Meena's shoulder. "If you head down a side road now, I'll jump out."

Meena nods and turns down the next dirt track she sees, driving until they reach a small thicket of trees.

"I hope Rachel's okay," Emma says, watching as he pulls his bag onto his lap.

Nick grimaces as his tired eyes meet hers. "Me too. I can only hope they need her expertise too much to harm her."

Meena stops the car. "Here okay?"

"It's as good a place as any." Nick takes a deep breath. "Good luck to you both." His sad, soft gaze lingers on Emma. "Hopefully, I'll see you again soon." He gives her a brief, tense smile before he leaves, and they watch him jog toward the cover of the trees.

Meena swings into a three-point turn. "Right, then," she says. "Let's go find our girls."

Emma stares after Nick until there's only dark space between the tree trunks, then studies the USB clasped tightly in her fingers. She could sense Nick's hesitation when he'd passed it over. Whatever's on here, when they find a computer, they need to work fast.

7:20 a.m.

Two police cars line either side of the otherwise deserted country road. Lainey shudders as she sees the familiar high walls. They're back in the place of her nightmares.

She'd like to believe everyone's here to help, but it's hard to have faith. This could all be an elaborate ruse to get her back inside.

The police car in front of them pulls over, and Kelli parks behind it. A man and a woman get out.

"I'll just be a second. Stay here," Kelli says, jumping out of the car and meeting the others between the vehicles. They talk rapidly before the woman jogs over to Lainey's door and opens it, squatting down to speak to her.

"I'm Detective Jean Evans." Her expression is solemn. "How sure are you that this is the place?"

Lainey looks at the landscape around them and pictures herself running across the road and through the opposite field, along those high fences in the distance. "This is it," she says as Sereena squeezes her hand.

The woman nods briefly. "Don't worry, we're going first. We won't bring you in unless it's safe." She stands up and gives a hand signal to the other officer.

A four-wheel-drive police car revs up and races toward the black iron gates. Lainey flinches as the car crashes through and suddenly there are sirens all around them, as eight cars disappear in single file through the entranceway. Within seconds, all that remains on the road is Kelli's car and two marked police cars.

The sirens fade. Kelli gets back into the vehicle and shuts the door, and there's silence. A skin-crawling, spine-tingling, nerve-racking hush. A gap of time, a held breath. The kind of unsafe pause that might be broken by a sudden hand on a shoulder, or a face at the window.

Nothing and nobody moves.

Kelli's phone trills.

Lainey shudders.

"We can go in," Kelli says as she starts the engine, turns the car around, and drives toward the gates. The other police cars stay in position, their occupants hidden behind the glass.

As they go through the gates, the house appears ahead of them. Lainey checks behind them every few seconds, willing those gates to stay open.

The female detective waits on the steps to greet them, her lips pursed. Kelli gets out again and they exchange another brief word before she comes across to Lainey.

"What . . . what did you find?" Lainey asks.

The woman shakes her head. "Nothing. They've gone."

"What? What do you mean? There were at least twenty people in there when I left." Lainey falters. "There were, I swear," she says. "How . . . how could they disappear so soon?"

But even as she asks the question, Lainey begins to understand. Nothing had belonged to the girls. The medical equipment was portable. The director had used a laptop. The rest of it was all hotel fittings and furnishings. So, it wouldn't take too long to pack up and ship out. A few hours, maybe. A few cars.

She feels herself shrinking, as though her body is gliding down a tunnel, away from them all. She puts her head in her hands and tries to breathe as Sereena strokes her back. "What . . . what if I've caused all the other girls more trouble," Lainey cries. "They were obviously sedated somehow, but aside from that they were treated pretty well. What if I've made it worse for them?"

"Do you really think they were happy here?" Kelli asks firmly.

Lainey relents. "No."

Detective Evans leans forward. "We all believe you, Lainey. We knew they'd move fast." She hesitates. "Do you think you can come in and show us what happened here?" she asks. "You don't have to. If it's too much, we'll take footage of all the rooms."

"I want to help," Lainey insists, her fear overcome by flares of anger. Surely, they can't disappear just like that. Surely, they cannot win.

"Your feet," Sereena says, touching Lainey's arm, and the detective visibly winces.

"I'll get someone to see to those first," she says, hurrying away.

Another policewoman comes to carefully clean and bandage Lainey's wounds. Each shard of pain only increases Lainey's anger and urgency. If she had the means, she'd head inside and take a hammer to the whole place.

Kelli stands close, watching her intently. When the policewoman is finished, she crouches next to her. "Lainey, you can't blame yourself for this, okay. Whatever this is, it's much bigger than you and not one bit of it is your fault. Don't underestimate what you did today—you defied so many odds to get out of here. Thanks to you, we now have more information than ever before. We're in a war we don't fully understand, and it might last a while yet . . . but *you*," she says, looking intensely at Lainey, "you won a battle here today. All by yourself. And that matters. Everyone is proud of you, and it gives us courage, and hope. And now we're better equipped for what comes next, because of you."

Lainey nods gratefully, trying to absorb the words, but still struggling to push away the guilt. When she's ready, Sereena and Kelli stay on either side of her, supporting her, as she hobbles through the house. She points out the director's office—with an empty table and a pair of dead birds beneath glass. They find the dining room and the stags' heads staring sightlessly at one another across the long table, polished and bare. There's broken glass on the library floor, and she explains how she escaped and ran. They go up the stairs—even with the pain in her feet, Lainey can't bear the idea of the elevator—until they find her bedroom, bed rumpled, on the second floor. There's a small needle discarded on the carpet. She explains what it is. Detective Evans tells her their forensic team will take care of it, that they'll get DNA from it and identify Jenny.

Finally, they reach the top floor and find the emptiest room of all. No medical table. No equipment. Just a large cubic space with thick curtains at the windows. It's here that for a moment Lainey fears she's lost her mind, because how could they move all this out so fast?

"They examined me here . . ." she says desperately, praying she won't see the first flickers of suspicion. But in their eyes is only sadness and sympathy.

"They'll have had an exit strategy," the detective says. "This isn't an amateur operation, Lainey. The fact that you escaped at all is amazing."

After this Lainey's legs feel weak and she has to hold on to the wall. They help her back down the stairs and out to the car. "You were incredible, Lainey," Kelli says. "Let's go."

Sereena seems dumbstruck as they close the doors and buckle themselves in. The car begins to move, and Lainey glances up at the slope of hill toward the thicket of trees in the distance, remembering her escape, when a flash of light catches her eye.

She stares at the pool house. Sees the briefest glimpse of a pale, frightened face, one hand aloft.

"Stop!" she calls, adrenaline charging through her. "I need to get out."

Kelli pulls over and hurries around to her side, opening the door. "Are you feeling sick?" she asks, but Lainey is pushing past her, racing up the hill, numb to the pain in her feet, feeling nothing except conviction. Behind her, voices shout her name.

As she reaches the pool house, she sees the glint of a narrow broken window up close. She pushes hard against the doors, calling and calling. At first they don't budge, but then there are noises and the doors finally open. Two pale, pajama-clad girls with rounded bellies fall into her arms, sending her staggering backward.

There are footsteps close behind them. "Jesus," someone says, and there are crackles in radios. More voices. People gently prising them apart. A cry from Sereena of "Ellis!" and another sob, and then there are just two of them clasping each other tightly.

"You're safe now," Lainey tells Bianca, holding her upright and staring into her stricken eyes, seeing a mirror of everything she feels.

PART IV

delivery

BREAKING NEWS:
LOCAL JOURNALIST FOUND DEAD

The body of local journalist Jason Langford was pulled from the Blackwell River overnight. Langford had been reported missing by his father only an hour before his body was discovered, and his family were seen rushing to the riverside. Langford was well known and liked in Whitehaven for his friendly reporting style and his interest in local and national affairs, and many locals were in shock upon hearing the news.

Langford's colleague, who wished to remain anonymous, said the reporter had been struggling with the strain of writing about the Intrapartum X babies in recent months. On announcing the death, Superintendent Ian Fullerton said that there were no suspicious circumstances and no further details would be given. Langford's distressed family also released a statement asking for privacy to grieve. A Facebook page set up in Langford's name is asking that donations be sent to either the NBCC or the suicide-prevention charity OneLife.

10.

9:30 a.m.

T he dappled-stone cottage is lit by a cold, watery sun in the midst of a labyrinth of winding country roads. There are no other cars around.

"Didn't you think they'd get here first?" Emma asks nervously.

Meena checks her watch. "They can't be far behind."

Emma gets out slowly and glances up at the windows. Fergus follows and sniffs intently at the grassy tufts that edge the driveway.

A shadow passes behind a curtain and Emma startles. "Is someone here?"

"Yes, about that," Meena says, locking the car and heading for the front porch. "Let me introduce you."

As she talks, she opens the door and Emma sees movement on the upstairs landing. Fergus barks and places himself protectively before Emma, even though they both know he's a small, furry pushover. There are footsteps on the stairs, then a young girl of about Lainey's age appears, with olive skin, shoulder-length black hair, and a tiny diamond nose stud. "Hello," she says cautiously, her piercing brown eyes taking them in.

"Emma," Meena says, "this is Alyssa. You'll know her as PreacherGirl."

Emma gapes as she looks from one to the other.

"I really am famous, then." Alyssa smiles, but Emma sees that it's an effort.

Emma turns to Meena. "You've had her here all this time?"

"Yes," Meena says, giving Alyssa a reassuring but sad smile. "It was a necessity, I'm afraid."

Alyssa stands back to let them in. "Kelli messaged me—said I'm to expect lots of company. I'm really happy to see you—it's been hard on my own."

Emma follows Meena inside. The cottage is a series of small, tidy rooms with wooden floors and woolen pile rugs. It smells of pinecones and furniture polish. Fergus charges up the narrow staircase and down again, racing into the kitchen and back, overwhelmed by everything new to explore.

"I'll get you both some water," Alyssa says, disappearing into the kitchen and returning with full glasses. She hands them over and they all sit at a gleaming oak dining table.

"Alyssa's been here for three weeks," Meena explains. She turns to Alyssa. "You tell her. Start from the beginning."

"Okay, then." Alyssa studies her fingernails for a moment, composing her thoughts. "My parents knew something strange was happening at the NBCC," she explains. "Dad's a lawyer and Mum's in the police force, both working in Chelmsford. They were hearing rumors about the work going on: people disappearing, or too frightened to talk. I hadn't taken much notice until Jess disappeared. I was really upset about that. She's my best friend, and I was the only one who knew she was pregnant." She pauses to check they're following the story, then continues. "After that, I began listening closely to Mum and Dad's conversations. Mum was bringing home reports of missing girls, and Dad was helping her look into them. They're good people, my parents, but they were scared. They were finding out more and more, but just sitting on the information. I was getting so stressed just watching while they did nothing, so I began researching, too. I could see from online profiles that the girls they were talking about had all gone quiet. Meanwhile, there was still no word on Jess."

She gulps, her eyes pale and weary. "When I made up that song and put it online it was done out of anger and frustration. I didn't want the girls to be forgotten. I uploaded it without telling anyone, then went to bed. When I woke up it already had a hundred thousand hits. By the end of the day, it was almost up to a million."

She stops and inhales deeply before continuing. "I began to freak out. I realized what a huge thing it was turning into, and knew I had to tell Mum and Dad. They were furious with me, but I could tell they were more frightened than anything. Mum asked Kelli to hide me until things calmed down, and it all happened so fast after that. I came here, and then they disappeared. We don't know if they hid themselves, or if they've been taken by someone."

Emma's heart goes out to her, all too aware of the pain of not knowing. "I'm so sorry."

"Thanks." Alyssa massages her temples. "It's been a nightmare. I had no idea what I was getting us into, and I wish I hadn't done it."

"But if you hadn't," Meena reminds her gently, "perhaps even more people would be disappearing unnoticed."

Emma frowns. "So, you've been living here on your own these past weeks?"

Alyssa nods. "Kelli comes to see me when she can, but it's been tough."

"Well, I'm glad we're here to keep you company." Emma turns to Meena. "Although, shouldn't they be here by now?"

They share a worried glance. "Let's not panic yet." Meena holds up the USB. "We should distract ourselves usefully, and check out Rachel's files."

She gets out her laptop and switches it on, as the others take seats on either side of her. Her home page contains a scrolling news feed, and Emma senses Meena's posture suddenly stiffen. She follows her gaze.

Local journalist found dead.

"*No*," she whispers, as Meena puts a hand on her back.

10:45 a.m.
"We're here, girls."

No one has spoken much on the journey. The girls had spent some time with the police, while Kelli spoke to the detectives and got permission to take all of them to the safe house. Once in the car, Sereena sat up front with Kelli, leaving Lainey with Ellis and Bianca in the back. Ellis had tried to answer Kelli's questions, and asked if it was really true that Mary Walcott had been killed. When Kelli confirmed it, Bianca became upset and agitated, so they'd stopped talking. After that, the silence in the car had become weighty with so much left unsaid. No one seemed to want to break it.

Lainey surveys the double-story cottage warily—the bright-red door, the lace curtains on the downstairs windows—and wishes they were somewhere else. Somewhere familiar. But then Kelli opens the passenger door, ready to help her from the car, Sereena takes her arm, and Lainey breathes in the sweet, still air and relaxes a little. It feels different here.

The door opens as they move toward it, and Emma rushes outside, sprinting toward Lainey, with Meena close behind. Lainey is crushed inside her mother's hug, feeling Emma shaking and sobbing with relief. Lainey leans in, soaking up the familiar comfort. Then she feels scrabbling at her ankles. "Oh, Fergus," she says, crying with happiness, "you came too! Hey, buddy!" And she squats to fuss over him, while Fergus bounces up and down.

Emma steps back, scanning Lainey with concern, taking in the bruises, the strange, torn clothes, the hay and grit in her hair. Then she spots the dirty bandages around Lainey's bruised and swollen feet. "What happened here?" She bends over to look.

"I smashed a window. Climbed a tree. Ran a few miles barefoot, and hid in a horse trailer . . ." Lainey smiles weakly.

"You did?" Emma says in astonishment. "Okay, I want to hear all this, but let's get you inside so I can clean and dress your feet." She notices the other girls with Meena and Sereena, and Lainey watches as her mother's eyes flit across their swollen bellies. "What . . . ?" She turns to Lainey. "Did you all escape together?"

"We went back to the house," Kelli says, "with police backup, to try to get the other girls. But we only found Ellis and . . ."

"You did what?" Meena and Emma ask, almost in unison. Emma stares at Lainey. "You went back?"

316

Before Lainey can answer, Kelli steps in. "This is going to take a while to explain," she says. "Let's get inside and then we can talk."

11:00 a.m.

Emma can't take her eyes off Lainey as they crowd into the small lounge. It's her daughter, of course it is, and yet she can see already that Lainey is changed. There's no undoing this experience, even with comfort and time. Whatever Lainey's been through, it will be with her forever. All they can do now is help her live with it and find ways for her to respond with strength rather than despair.

Alyssa and Meena have taken Bianca upstairs to lie down. The girl is obviously distressed, and Emma had popped in hoping to examine her and the baby, but Bianca had curled up and pushed her away. She'll try again in a little while when Bianca's calmer, but just the sight of her fearfulness had brought Emma close to tears.

Alyssa had been upset too—relieved to hear news of Jess, but disappointed she hadn't been able to escape with the others. "It's so hard on her," Meena had said before following the two girls upstairs. "These kids, they blame themselves for everything. They can't see how much they're caught up in other people's games."

"We'll help them," Emma had whispered back, looking at the other girls sitting close together on the sofa. "And they'll help each other."

"Tell us what happened after Lainey left," Kelli says to Ellis as she sits sandwiched between Sereena and Lainey.

Ellis's eyes are wide. "It was total chaos in the house, everyone yelling at us to get up and get out. They told us to leave everything and go to the front steps, and we stood there freezing while the staff panicked and argued. They were waiting for vehicles and running around carrying things out of the house. They took the medical equipment away first in a white van, and then a car pulled up and some of the girls went in that one. The way they were treating us—I felt like cattle. Bianca's been having little breakdowns for weeks, getting more and more frightened, and I could see she was panicking, but some of the girls seemed to be in a trance, just doing what they were told without a word, and standing as still as statues the rest of the time. I wanted to plan with Jess and Britta, but they both went in the first car. And there was just a moment when everyone was so busy with moving equipment and rushing around that we were left alone, and the lights at the front of the house kept going off if there was no movement for a bit, so while it was dark I just grabbed Bianca's hand and asked her if she trusted me. When she said yes, I pulled her away from the steps and then we just ran. I knew they didn't lock the pool house, and I'd scoped the place out weeks ago while we swam. I'd decided that if I could push the heavy wooden towel box, I could wedge it between the doors and the lip of the pool. We got a head start in the panic and made it to the pool house, but I could hear people shouting and running up the hill and it seemed to take ages to push the box into place." Her voice cracks and she takes a few gulps of air before continuing. "We were so bloody frightened, but it worked. They were yelling and swearing at us, but those windows are high and narrow so they couldn't climb in. They smashed the windows with bricks and threw burning rags through them, but we used the pool water to put them out. Then it suddenly went quiet—they must have decided to leave—but I swear we didn't stop shaking until Lainey arrived."

Lainey listens, one hand over her mouth. *I did this*, she thinks.

As though reading her mind, Emma touches her daughter's arm. "None of this is your fault."

"Your mum's right," Ellis says to Lainey. "I'd almost given up. I was so scared, and I didn't know how to fight back. If it wasn't for you, I'd still be there. So thank you."

Lainey and Ellis hold one another's gaze for a moment, then Lainey nods. She turns to Kelli. "What now? How do we get the others back?"

As she asks the question, Meena and Alyssa appear in the doorway.

"Bianca's asleep," Meena announces. "I think we should take turns sitting with her so she's not alone when she wakes up."

Ellis stands. "I'll go and lie down with her. I'm exhausted," she says, making her way across the room.

"What about you, Lainey?" Meena asks. "There's a bedroom ready upstairs for you."

"And I can sit with you," Emma jumps in.

"Not yet," Lainey says. "I want to know what the plan is now. How do we get the other girls back?"

"Well," Meena says slowly, "before that, there are some things we need to tell you."

11:15 a.m.

The women explain slowly. Meena does most of the talking, with Kelli and Emma adding support. They go through everything they'd found in Rachel's files, the false reporting from the NBCC, the hypotheses about the water and Nick's discoveries, and what they know about Grant Whittaker and Darius Hallston, and how many people support them. They talk in gentle tones about the very worst of human nature.

The truth, as it comes, is terrible. Lainey absorbs it with a chill deep in her bones, her arms wrapped around her stomach, and an ache in her heart. So she hadn't imagined the darkness she'd felt as she'd sat in Hallston's office back in Horcombe House. The man was pure evil.

But there is hope, too.

"Rachel thinks she knows how to fix the problems the babies are having," Meena explains. "In a nutshell, so far they've been trying to disable a faulty gene, but Rachel's sure they need to insert more genetic material. It's much more difficult, but she thinks she's figured it out. Her work could end the whole nightmare, and we've got it all here. We can share it with the world."

Lainey listens intently as her mother sits beside her, and her best friend holds her hand.

11:35 a.m.

Emma studies the girls' faces as Meena talks, and watches the light flicker in their eyes. Innocence fades. Anger flashes. The truth settles over them like ash from a fire.

"Rachel didn't want us to wait to get this information out," Emma tells them as Meena takes a sip of tea. "And we owe it to Jason. We need to spread it widely, and we need to do it fast, before we get shut down."

"Hang on," Lainey interrupts. "What about the other girls? They're still missing. What if some harm comes to them if we release all this?"

"I understand your concern," Kelli says. "But what will happen to them if we don't?"

The girls fall silent. Emma watches, her heart hurting for her daughter. Lainey bows her head and a tear drops onto her lap, but then she sniffs and nods. "Okay, then. There's no choice."

"Right." Meena sets down her cup. "Let's put everything together, all of my research and Kelli's research, Jason's notes, the scientific data that Rachel's provided, and the information from Alyssa, Lainey, Ellis, and Bianca."

Her gaze falls on Kelli, who is leaning against the wall, listening. She responds with a fierce, determined smile.

"Hang on, how do we release everything?" Sereena asks. "We need to get people's attention and make sure this doesn't just disappear."

"Whittaker and Hallston aren't the only ones with powerful friends." Kelli steps forward. "The RGN network will spread this fast once they receive it, and our sympathetic politicians, judges, police chiefs, and corporate leaders will finally have what they need to oppose this new secretive government. And as for getting the public's attention . . ." She glances across at Alyssa.

Alyssa nods. "I think it's time PreacherGirl made her comeback, don't you?"

6:30 p.m.

Lainey watches Kelli, Meena, and Alyssa as they sit at the table with a laptop open, speaking in low tones as Kelli types. Sereena sits close by, observing intently.

Emma comes into the room, having been up to check on Bianca and Ellis. "They're both sleeping now," she says. "As soon as they wake up, I'll see if they'll let me take a closer look at them."

Suddenly, Alyssa flings herself back in her chair. "It's done," she announces. "We're live."

They all rush to the computer. The footage they've hastily strung together begins with four large white words on an empty black background. "A message from PreacherGirl." Designed purely for shock value, it hovers for a few seconds then goes into a brief, outrageous story—of missing girls and polluted water, damaged genes, and censored scientists. It leads to a grand finale: a corrupt cohort of wealthy businessmen, their names annotated onto their pictures from the university Conservative club, Protec, and H2OBlue, alongside the horror of a secret eugenics plot inflicted on an exhausted population. The final series of images shows Grant Whittaker's affiliations with all of them across the past twenty-five years.

The views counter clicks over to one. Then six. Then thirty-five. Within a minute, it's in three figures. Within two minutes, it's in the thousands.

"We did it," Kelli says numbly, watching the screen. "And it's been securely emailed to every government and RGN contact we have."

No one replies.

Tiredness crashes over Lainey. "I think I need to lie down," she says, leaving the room without waiting for a response and making her way upstairs. She falls onto the bed and sobs until she's wrung out from emotion. Despite the courage of this little group, she can't stop picturing events at Horcombe House and the empty rooms this morning. They'd moved a whole household in a few hours. How can a few ordinary people ever fight back against those with so much more power, more control, more resources? More of everything. Soon enough, those rich, corrupt men will rally somehow, and then what will happen to all the people she cares about?

A short time later, there are noises from the stairs and Fergus bounds into the room, jumping up to greet her with his tail wagging.

Emma follows him in. "It's happening," she bursts out, her face flushed, her voice breathless. "As soon as the views for PreacherGirl's new post began to rack up, people began sharing pictures and videos of themselves praising PreacherGirl, demanding they hear from Grant Whittaker about the missing girls and the latest science from the NBCC." There's a fiery glint to Emma's eyes. "Crowds are gathering outside the H2OBlue headquarters. And there's a new hashtag—#smashyourwatch—with footage of people destroying them. They're furious, and they believe us, Lainey." She sits down abruptly on the bed, staring toward the window. "Geraldine told me that when change came, it would happen fast. Looks like she could be right."

Lainey sits up, revitalized by her mother's words. "That's amazing."

She pauses, then adds, "You know, Geraldine often seems to have good instincts about things."

Emma laughs. "Maybe. Let's never tell her that, though. We might never hear the end of it." She pauses, sobering. "I hope she's okay, and she's watching all this."

"Me too," Lainey says. "But if anyone can take care of themselves, it's her."

"True."

They fall into companionable silence, which is punctuated by a few whoops and cheers downstairs. "Sounds like things are still going well," Emma says after a while, smiling, but her expression changes to concern as her gaze falls on Lainey. "It's been a crazy day. You should try to rest now."

Lainey shudders. "All those needles they gave me, Mum. I don't even know what they were. What if . . . ?" She touches her belly. "I'm not sure how I feel about this, but I don't want them to have done her any harm."

Emma startles. "Her?"

"They told me it's a girl."

"Did they now?" Emma strokes Lainey's arm. "Well, I don't think you gave them much time to do any damage. The girls were mentioning amniocentesis earlier on, but after seeing Rachel's recordings we're wondering if that was the gene-editing treatment." Emma catches sight of Lainey's fraught expression and puts a hand on her shoulder. "Try not to worry, we'll keep a close eye on them. As for you, I brought an old Doppler. We could listen to the heartbeat, if you like?"

Lainey thinks of the sonogram picture. The baby reaching out.

"Okay." She takes her mother's hand and closes her eyes. "Thanks, Mum."

"All right, then." Emma gently squeezes her fingers. "I'll go and get it." She disappears for a few minutes and returns with her backpack. She pulls things out onto Lainey's bed until she retrieves the little machine.

Lainey notices the matryoshka dolls. "Why on earth did you pack those?" She finds herself genuinely amused for the first time in days.

Emma rolls her eyes. "I know! Your grandmother thought they'd be worth something—she insisted."

"Well, I don't know if we should sell these—they're a family heirloom," Lainey says, beginning to take them apart. She hasn't looked at them for years; can feel herself becoming a child again as she watches the smaller dolls appear, each one emerging from inside another. She sets them side by side, but as she reaches the smallest, she finds a piece of paper wrapped around it. "What's this?"

Emma frowns. "I don't know."

Lainey opens it to see a series of numbers and a few words in scrawly handwriting.

Bank codes. Take whatever you need. It's my offshore account :)

Emma reads the piece of paper and holds it to her heart. "It turns out your grandmother is a bit of a legend, after all."

With a rush of gratitude, Lainey thinks of Geraldine. Sereena. Meena. Cathy. And her mum. They'd all ensured that, no matter what happened and however it felt, Lainey would never be alone. A surge of strength flashes through her, and she smiles at Emma. She can't give in to her fears, not with these women around her. They'd beaten the odds to make it this far, and they're not finished yet.

The dolls lie in a neat row beside them. "Right," Emma says, "are you ready?"

"Okay." Lainey lifts up her shirt, exposing the small, rounded mound of her tummy.

Emma squeezes Lainey's hand and then switches on the little machine and holds the Doppler wand to Lainey's stomach. They both wait while she adjusts it, searching for the right spot.

"There she is," Emma says with a smile. "That's a clear, strong heartbeat, Lainey."

Lainey listens. To galloping hooves. A clarion call. The thrum of generations.

Becoming three small words, repeating.

I
am
here

.

acknowledgments

As always, when it comes to writing acknowledgments, I am amazed at just how many people have contributed to making this book happen. This novel has been written over a number of years as part of my PhD studies, and I'm truly grateful for everyone who has helped me along the way.

To my agent Tara Wynne: you've been in my corner for over twelve years now! Thank you for your steadfast belief in me, and for championing my work in so many ways.

To Anne Fonteneau, Hannah Ohlmann, Jeffrey Yamaguchi, Ciera Cox, and all the team at Blackstone: thank you for your expertise and commitment, particularly throughout the challenges of COVID. Hopefully, one day I can thank you in person!

To Natasha Lester: every time, you know how to make my books better, and I love sharing early drafts with you. Thank you for taking time out of your busy schedule to provide advice and support, and for your wonderful friendship over this past decade or so.

To Dervla McTiernan: I have learned so much from you over the past few years! Thank you for every bit of encouragement, for our brilliant chats, and for reading drafts and making time for me. I will always remember your enthusiasm as we dined out and I explained *The Hush* to you back when it was still in my head—thanks for "getting it" from the start!

A huge thanks goes to Liz Byrski and Helen Merrick for their early support of my PhD idea: you both set me on my way and I'm grateful for your belief in me. And to David Whish-Wilson and Christina Lee: you have been wonderful. I have been fairly fragile at times over the past few years as life threw various curveballs at me, and your consistent encouragement and sage advice—not to mention your willingness to let me go at my own pace—meant that I finally got it done!

My gratitude also goes to Roberta Ivers, Cassandra di Bello, and Anna O'Grady: you have each pushed my work along to greater heights over the past few years, and I truly appreciate your efforts.

To my family and friends: thank you for being my most vociferous supporters, even though I have to miss quite a lot of events and socializing to get the work done. A particular thanks to Jacqueline Keelan-Wake for your friendship and enthusiasm for my books, and for your practical help in finding me child-free work hours! Likewise, Pippa Kidman and Collette Doherty, you do so much for my girls while I'm working, and I really appreciate it. And to Eva Peak, Niamh and Patrick Keelan-Wake, Avalon Kidman and Annywn Kidman, you are the kindest friends my girls could wish for and they're lucky to have you.

A special mention and thanks to Marina Hansen, who has come to help me launch every single one of my books over the past eleven years. What a gorgeous friend you are. And Fiona Thorp: you are always first in the queue to support me, and our catchups might be way too infrequent but they are always the best. To Punita and Aneya Mandalia, thanks for getting my book in the school library and for lending your surname to one of my characters!

Thank you to my cousin Sylvia Sanders for being an early reader and providing great feedback! And to my sisters, Tanya, Christine, and Mary: you're all brilliant, thank you for being in my corner. And all my love and thanks to Raymond Agombar and the Foster family for your continuing support. Thanks also to the team at Mindarie Chiropractic Centre—particularly Conor, Magda, Claire, and Donna—and Farida from TCM

Acupuncture, for looking after my neck and back during this painful time, even though I keep undoing your fine work!

Matt, you are a damn fine editor and I owe you more than one line in this story. I am grateful every day for your love and care. The books wouldn't happen without you.

Hannah and Isabelle: I love you both very much, and you helped to inspire this story. Watching the pressures on you and your friends from an early age has made me all the more determined to champion women and women's writing. Don't believe the lies that separate you from the world and your fellow women. You don't have to be anything other than who you are.

Over the past ten years I've been lucky enough to get to know a lot of writers and booksellers around Australia. Often our paths only cross sporadically, but I always find these individuals and communities are unfailingly generous with their time and support. If you're one of these people, thank you.

To every single reader: I literally couldn't do this job without you! Thank you for supporting me so I can keep writing. I always love hearing from you.

And finally, to my mother, Marian. Thank you seems such a small thing to say in the light of a lifetime of encouragement! You've been with me every step of the way, whether you're reading drafts and reporting back, or making notes on random research topics for me, or keeping your granddaughters busy and cooking my favorite food (which, let's face it, is usually cake!), or—and I know this pains you—missing out on our chatty phone calls so I can write. But we don't just love you for what you do for us. You're a knitting, quilting, gummy-drop-playing, book-loving, flake-cake-eating theologian who's trained umpteen RE teachers and loves travel and history and churches, and who can write Hebrew and speak French and sing so beautifully with the West Australia Symphony Orchestra that we burst with pride watching you. And so much more. It's no coincidence that I wrote a book about awesome mothers. Thanks for being you.